CW00591681

THE BEQUEST CHRONICLES

BOOK I

ROBERT FITZPATRICK

Grosvenor House
Publishing Limited

This book is published by
Grosvenor House Publishing Ltd
Link House
140 The Broadway, Tolworth, Surrey, KT6 7HT.
www.grosvenorhousepublishing.co.uk

A CIP record for this book
is available from the British Library

ISBN 978-1-80381-003-4
eBook ISBN 978-1-80381-086-7

PREFACE

This Chronicle began 35 years ago; it was written every evening, in my mind, on the 18.15 p.m from London Bridge Station to be told to my young daughter as her bedtime story...she never really grew out of hearing those tales. Finally, I have had the opportunity to write them down...and the stories are getting darker now!

THE BEAST OF GEVAUDAN

The Beast of Gévaudan is the historical name associated with a man-eating animal or animals which terrorized south-central France between 1764 and 1767. The attacks, which covered an area spanning 100 square kilometres, were said to have been committed by one or more beasts with formidable teeth and immense tails, according to contemporary eyewitnesses.
Most descriptions from the period identify the beast as a wolf, dog, or even a Werewolf.....

Descriptions of the time vary, but generally the Beast was said to look like a typical wolf, though it was allegedly as big as an elephant. It had a large, dog-like head with large straight ears, a wide chest, and a large mouth that exposed very large canine teeth. The Beast's fur was said to be russet in colour but its back was streaked with black.

Map of Old Aquitaine

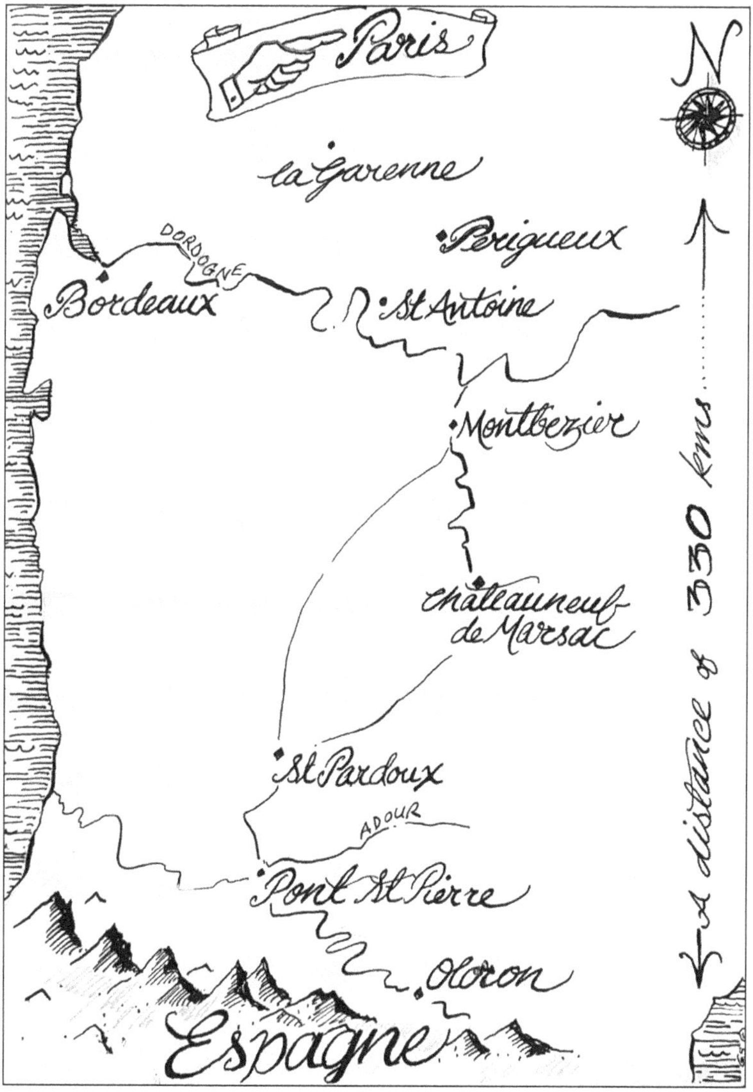

PROLOGUE

Napoleon had, at long last, been defeated. France was left to recover from the turmoil of his final years, but in the small town of La Garenne they had their own problems; mysterious deaths and sudden disappearances kept the rumours flying. When the Duc de Garenne died very suddenly, on hearing the news of a fatal shooting accident during a hunt, the shocked inhabitants speculated about who would take his place, his foppish son Louis-Phillipe, or his more down-to-earth daughter Catherine? A patrol of Gendarmes from the local barracks disappeared "off the face of the earth" according to their commanding officer. The arrival from Paris of a young officer, Roland Lebrun added fuel to the rumours. Had the earlier fatality been an *accident?*

The officer asked lots of questions and then suddenly left La Garenne, closely followed by Louis-Phillipe, then by Catherine and her cousin Amelie.

In rural France hunting was part of the culture and nothing was more highly regarded than a good hunting hound; Hugo Hound was considered the best in the whole of France. One day Hugo too went missing. Who could have realised that it was this hound who held the key to all the other events. What he knew and what he could do would change the lives of everyone involved. Roland Lebrun had been sent to find the missing patrol but finds himself obliged to protect the life of a hound and his strange traveling companions whilst himself being hunted by the son of the Duc de Garenne. He, Louis-Philippe, his sister, and their cousin are all plunged into a world of Werewolves and creatures capable of shape-changing; creatures with whom they have more in common than they can imagine.

CHAPTER 1

Soft moans occasionally pierced the gloomy silence. Huddled shapes lay on the bare floor or against the flaking walls of the once-comfortable room. In one corner, near a boarded window was a makeshift cubicle fashioned from splintered beams hung with military cloaks. On a pile of grubby blankets behind this temporary screen lay the body of a tall white-haired man wearing the soiled remnants of a French army officer's uniform, the breeches torn and bloody. A pair of mud-encrusted leather boots stood close to a pile of red-stained rags. Two other officers were standing beside the prone figure and both wore expressions of deep concern. Their unspoken thoughts were interrupted by a deafeningly loud boom which shook any remaining glass from the broken window frames…again and again came the sound and now the chamber was filled with anguished and fearful cries. The acrid smell of cordite filled the air and the older of the two men, André Lacoste, spoke quietly:

"M. le Duc, we must either move you or find a doctor who can treat your wound." The wounded man opened his eyes slowly.

"No, André, I beg you. We must try to find horses. I will be able to ride, I'm sure, and we must leave this place. The battle is lost, and we must make our escape."

The other officer, Colonel Lecaron, interrupted: "Sir, I will try, but many men are of the same mind. This farmhouse is becoming dangerous. The damned bombardment has started again." He turned to his companion and looking beyond the cubicle, he whispered: "What of all these other poor souls?"

These three men: the injured Duc Philippe de Garenne, Marshal of France, André Lacoste, the Duc's aide-de-camp and the third man,

Colonel Lecaron had been comrades in arms for a long time. Lucien Lecaron although much younger than the others, was a full Colonel and the Duc's second in command. André Lacoste had been manager of the Duc's estates in La Garenne but more importantly he was the Duc's closest friend.

****

These three comrades had accompanied Napoleon as part of his personal guard when he had gone into exile on the island of Elba. They had been at Napoleon's side when he made his final return to France. They had been close to the Emperor and they had spent many hours trying to dissuade the him from his last undertaking. They knew the outcome was inevitable, but they could not abandon him.

On the forced march Napoleon had made through France many veterans of his earlier campaigns had flocked to join the 'little corporal', an affectionate term bestowed on him by his own men because he lacked airs and graces. At first all went well. When the makeshift army approached Paris in March 1815 the King fled allowing Napoleon to enter the capital unopposed. For a while, life in the city almost returned to normal. During his stay, the Duc had taken the opportunity to visit his old friend, General Georges Destrier, Gendarmerie Commandant and rumoured by some to be the most powerful man in France – certainly the most feared. It was even said (at least in Paris) that kings, republics, and emperors might come and go but a Destrier always survived unscathed.

Destrier was interested in what his friend thought of Napoleon's plans, but the Duc could not bring himself to admit disloyalty to Bonaparte, even privately. The two old soldiers had met often and chatted about their homes, the campaigns Philippe had fought and family matters. The Duc's daughter Catherine and his niece Amélie were Destrier's goddaughters, and the General took a great interest in them. At their final meeting, as the two men stood to make their formal farewells, Destrier looked furtively around his office and towards the closed doors. Having assured himself that no-one could be listening he whispered to the Duc:

"I have had some very important news from La Garenne..." When Destrier had finished his tale, the Duc was silent for a moment and then asked: "And she is sure of this?" The General nodded: "Yes, my old friend, absolutely sure; she has seen this for herself – the first in many hundreds of years.

We have agreed that we must keep this secret. He must be kept safe…. Obviously, in view of…" Duc Philippe nodded wordlessly, and the two men shook hands, the final words of the General hanging in the air.

The three months during which the army remained in Paris had passed all too quickly. Napoleon's enemies were organising, and he decided he must strike before they were fully prepared. With his army of over 200,000 fighting men he began the march north towards the disaster that was Waterloo.

The French army, although outnumbered and ill equipped, fought bravely but suffered a massive defeat with many casualties. This time the three comrades knew there would be no more victories and the time for fighting was finally over. Time to go home. The dejected remnants of Napoleon's army had already begun straggling back home on foot through the countryside. However, during the final hours of the fighting, Duc Philippe had been wounded by a musket ball which remained lodged in his thigh and although his comrades had been able to staunch the blood and bind the wound using a makeshift splint, they knew that it was serious. They were also very much aware that medical treatment would be impossible to find in this terrible place and the Duc's best chance was to get home where he could rest and regain his strength.

Lecaron peered out at the awful scene in the outer room: men groaning, some whimpering in pain, others too still, too weak to cry out or perhaps already dead. He hid the sight from the Duc's eyes once more and looking at André meaningfully, left without a word. Outside an even more terrible sight met his eyes. What had once been a well-kept farmyard, then a field dressing station had become a graveyard. Row upon row of still figures were laid out on one side of the mud-churned courtyard, some shrouded, others with only a cloth to cover their faces…some with no faces at all. Near the rear wall was an even worse sight: piles of corpses had been left in the torrential rain, half-submerged in dense mud, their wounds attracting swarms of flies still buzzing despite the downpour. Trying not to look, his eye caught a slight movement in one of the piles; dear God, some of these men were not yet dead!

Horrified, he hurried towards the farm's outbuildings – he was a man on a mission. He must find some transport. Near the farmhouse stood a large barn, its roof damaged by a shell but with parts of the walls still standing. Lucien rushed inside in the forlorn hope that some animals had survived in there or had been overlooked. His luck was in that day for at the rear of the dilapidated building, munching placidly on some straw, were four horses all of whom seemed to be unharmed. Two even wore saddles.

Without further thought for their owners, Lucien grabbed the bridles of the two saddled horses and found bridles for the other two. Unchallenged, he led the animals back through the courtyard to the dilapidated door of the farmhouse and tethered the beasts to a splintered post at the foot of the sagging steps. They whickered nervously; their ears attuned to the hideous sounds of their kind dying nearby. Inside once more he forced himself to look neither left nor right and told André they should leave immediately.

Balanced on his one good leg and supported by his companions, Duc Philippe de Garenne limped from that place of horrors, men calling to them in desperation as they made their way outside. At the precise moment that the three came out into the persistent rain, the shelling began again in earnest and the farmhouse shook with the force of the explosions nearby. All at once, a single shell exploded close to the outer wall of the farmhouse which shook, teetered, and fell in upon the room they had just left, burying those inside forever.

"Oh, my poor France" said the Duc looking around him at the desolate scene. With some difficulty, his friends hoisted him onto the back of one of the saddled horses. André rode the other and Lucien rode bareback as he had often done on his parents' farm. With their kit stowed safely on the fourth horse, the group picked their way across the edges of the battlefield and away, turning their backs on the carnage and blocking their ears to the screams of dying men and horses.

No-one stopped them as they put some distance between themselves and the fields of Waterloo, but progress was necessarily slow because of the Duc's injury and the numbers of retreating soldiers struggling along the muddy roads. As they travelled, they met groups of civilians fleeing the carnage with heavily laden carts and mud-spattered bundles. Most of the soldiers they encountered were on foot, the majority without weapons, many without boots, trudging homewards. Some of the injured soldiers were being helped by their comrades but often the group came upon a man whose injuries had been too severe to continue and they too were forced to pass by. Never would they forget the things they saw.

CHAPTER 2

A day or so into their journey, they passed one of the rare carriages on the road, heavily curtained, transporting seriously wounded soldiers and as they passed by, Lucien caught a glimpse of a female face at the window. The carriage was being pulled by two farm horses obviously "borrowed." He thought how brave the occupants must have been. Perhaps they were the legendary 'vivandières'- women who had helped the army with water, food, ammunition and medical care. He thought it worthwhile to ask the young boy driving the mismatched team whether a place might be found in the carriage for the Duc to rest his leg, but the lad explained that regretfully the carriage was already overloaded. He was unsure the horses would be able to go much farther and, he told them, a young Gendarmerie officer had ridden ahead to try and find replacements. What neither the occupants of the carriage nor the three returning soldiers realised was how close they had come to a reunion that day.

Unknown to the Duc and his friends, whilst the soldiers had been fighting their last battle, his daughter Catherine, and her cousin Amélie had also been with the French army. Catherine had been entranced by the romantic stories of the vivandières and their heroism. She, like her father, had a powerful sense of duty and although she knew it would be dangerous she just had to go; her love of adventure overcame her fears – even fear of her father's wrath. However, in a lame attempt to protect her identity she had adopted the name of her cousin's family, the Giscards.

After the defeat, the two young ladies had been busy with the wounded but eventually Catherine realised they must leave the battlefield to try to reach home before her father. She so desperately hoped he and his companions had survived the carnage. The girls had lost their own transport in the confusion, along with many of their possessions, but had managed to 'acquire' a carriage and horses by sheer determination. Their journey had not been without incident both on the road and in Paris but at last they had reached La Garenne, luckily some weeks before the returning soldiers who had been forced to travel very slowly because of the Duc's painful injury. Whereas the girls had stayed only one night in the great city, the three soldiers had been delayed there for a week seeking treatment for the Duc's wound.

In many parts of France, the aristocratic houses had been looted and worse during the Revolution but the people of La Garenne had always respected the Duc who was liberal and generous. The contents of the great house had been left untouched whilst he and his estate manager were away. Even so it would take some time to restore even a semblance of order to the neglected interior, with its cobweb strewn bedchambers and dusty Great Hall.

Catherine's older half-brother Louis-Philippe had not felt compelled to join the army, preferring to remain mostly in Perigueux at the town house he had inherited from his mother. Thus, the great estate at La Garenne had been seriously neglected. Whenever her father had been away fighting, Catherine had spent her time at the home of her Aunt Marianne Giscard, her father's widowed sister. She and her cousin Amélie were less than one year apart in age. Home at La Garenne once more Catherine was aware that she must now set about preparing the great house as best she could for her father's return. This she did whilst her brother occasionally checked on progress – that was as far as his involvement went.

Sunlight was glinting on the black slate roofs of the round towers which stood at each corner of the great Château. That same sun warmed the back of the three comrades as they rode, muddy and exhausted into the courtyard after several weeks on the road. The old soldier still rode with great difficulty although the ball had been removed from his thigh. André Lacoste helped him down from his horse and he stood stiffly gazing at his home. He saw many signs of neglect, crumbling stones, cracked lintels, weeds growing through the cobbles of the courtyard, even some slates missing from the roof. The darkened windows of the great towers stared back at him with empty eyes and it seemed that only the stables and kennel block had been maintained in his absence. He knew then that leaving the care of the family home to his son Louis-Philippe had been a mistake. His son had never been interested in the estate, only in its revenue and hunting and gambling.

Hearing horses in the courtyard, Catherine, dressed now as a perfect lady, ran out to greet the men. No-one would ever suspect from her demure appearance where she had been.

"Oh Papa, you're safe! You're home."

"My dear daughter" he replied, hugging her, "at last I am home ...how you have grown. You are a young lady now, not the young girl I left behind."

"Yes, father. I am so glad to have you back safe and well and to have some pleasant company here again. I shall go this very minute and arrange a meal and beds for you all– If we have any linen without holes." Having courteously greeted her father's companions she ran off to the kitchens to find their elderly housekeeper and tell her the news.

The Duc and his companions took their mounts to the stables where a lone stable boy took over and gave the tired animals a much-needed meal. As Lucien left he turned to watch the lad. He seemed oddly familiar-Lucien had seen him recently, yet it would not come to him although he wracked his brains. The three men climbed the imposing stone staircase and went into the Château through the high carved double doors, rarely opened it seemed judging by the grooves they made in the dust of the main hall. The Duc was taken aback to see just how much his family home had fallen into disrepair.

"Let us share a good meal together" said the Duc and the other two men were delighted to agree. After so long without knowing where their next meal would be coming from, the food seemed at least to them, the best they had ever eaten. Once full, the three veterans sat reminiscing in front of the huge fireplace in the Great Hall, gazing into the flickering flames. Catherine joined them but sat in silence watching her father. The Duc's injury still hurt him more than he would admit but having the musket ball removed by an army surgeon in the field had been more frightening than the pain of leaving it there for a while. The doctor in Paris had eventually dug the ball out but had warned the Duc that some debris remained embedded in his flesh. Now the wound had almost healed but remained red and swollen. He eased it now by resting his leg on a footstool as he sat in the deep leather armchair Catherine had kept cleaned and polished in readiness for his return. She had seen this as an act of faith…he would come home.

"What will you do now, Lucien?" asked the Duc.

"I've seen enough fighting to last me a lifetime Sir; I want to work on the farm with my parents now, settle down, get married, have a family, be just like everyone else." The Duc smiled contentedly then stood up with difficulty.

"Gentlemen, now I must retire. We can at last lie down in real beds, even though they may not be made with the finest linens. Nevertheless, it will feel like sleeping on a cloud after these last few weeks! Tomorrow will be a busy day."

Next morning, the three friends toured the dilapidated estate buildings. The Duc was bitterly disappointed to see the evidence of his son's stewardship – or lack thereof –almost everywhere. The three men rode slowly giving the injured soldier time to rest. As they surveyed their surroundings, the Duc spoke: "We have a big job on our hands here André."

André nodded in agreement as the Duc continued: "Right, let's get down and look at the kennels, shall we?" The pack yelped with excitement at the approach of the three men. There were five or six small terriers, some glossy spaniels that had been raised as gun dogs and one very overweight bloodhound, Major. This dog was a favourite that the Duc kept only out of sentiment as his hunting days were now long gone. There was also a pack of magnificent chasse Hounds, a special breed which crossed bloodhound with lurcher. These dogs were mostly either white and brown or black and white with long silky coats, enormous fan-like tails and depressed long faces, their eyes permanently downcast. They were very lively animals and let out long Hound dog howls of excitement when the Duc approached. One Hound, however, stood out from the pack effortlessly. Although around nine months old he was already massive, his thick luxurious coat mottled with grey and white patches, a single black patch on his hind leg. He had long floppy silken ears and deep brown eyes and was gazing intently at the visitors. The Duc told his friends that this dog was known as Hugo Hound. It occurred separately to both Lucien and André to wonder how their companion could possibly know this after being away from home for so long. Surely the Hound had not been born when the Duc was last at La Garenne? However, from experience both men knew Duc Philippe was sometimes privy to information that he could not have known. His information was also invariably accurate.

He called to the Hound by name and Hugo obediently trotted towards him. When the kennel door was opened out he came, unprompted, and sat at the Duc's feet, his massive tail thudding enthusiastically on the ground and his great tongue lolling from his mouth – he almost wore a grin in fact.

You know, Lucien, this Hound has a lineage as long as my own" he laughed. Lucien approached the animal and stroked his glossy head. Unexpectedly for such a sizeable dog, Hugo reacted like any lap dog and immediately rolled over onto his back in an ecstasy of enjoyment. Obligingly, Lucien tickled the happy dog's belly.

At that moment, the Duc's son Louis-Philippe rode up to the group. He wore a fashionable city outfit made of the finest material, buckles of silver on his shoes and a lavishly plumed hat which he removed in a sweeping exaggerated bow which he made whilst remaining on horseback.

"Father, welcome home. You should have sent word. I was visiting Perigueux on, err, business; I find it just impossible to remain here for long because the Château is unfit for a person such as myself to live in." The Duc looked sharply at him. What business could his son have in Perigueux? Where had he found enough money for those fine clothes? Clearly not by working to keep the estate in order. Lucien too looked at Louis Philippe – how in heaven's name was this fop related to the brave old soldier?

Lucien knew that Louis-Philippe's mother had died when he was a child, the victim of a riding accident. She had been a keen horsewoman but had fallen from her mount in the forest and hit her head. The Duc had wed a second time but his bride, this time from Paris, had died in childbirth with Catherine.

"My son, I am glad that you have arrived at last; please explain to me, if you can, how it is that this Estate looks so run down and unkempt? I arranged enough funds for you to ensure the grounds and the house were maintained, did I not?"

Louis-Philippe was not looking at his father as this was said but was ostentatiously looking elsewhere. The Duc thought he was trying to formulate a believable reply or was perhaps embarrassed to be admonished in front of André and Lucien. Instead the young man demanded caustically:

"Have you spoken to my sister yet Father?"

"Yes, at least my daughter was here to greet me" replied the Duc gruffly and at this Louis-Philippe guffawed loudly.

"Perhaps you should ask her where she has been whilst you were away. She has been gallivanting about the country with our cousin dragging the family name through the mire." All at once the young man stopped short; he had noticed that Lucien was holding Hugo's collar. He nodded curtly to André and then spoke directly to Lucien with fury in his voice, ignoring his father: "What are doing? Put that dog back in the kennel immediately." The Duc watched his son's handsome face contort with fury. The young man's eyes protruded, and veins throbbed in his temples. He recalled what Destrier had told him in Paris and in that moment, he made up his mind:

"How dare you address a senior officer in the French Army in such a fashion. I am making him a gift of Hugo Hound as a token of my gratitude and of my esteem for the gallant service Colonel Lecaron has rendered to me and to France."

Despite his father's angry tone, the young man refused to be silenced. He knew, but without knowing why, that this Hound was very special, more special than his father could possibly know. Inexplicably, he felt linked to the animal by ties of ancestry, this dog's forebears had lived at the Château de Garenne for as long as the Château had existed. More importantly, how dare his father give away something that rightfully belonged to him? He was Louis-Philippe de Garenne, the future Duc. This animal was special…he knew it, what he had seen…He must keep him. Furiously he turned on his father: "That dog is mine, I have trained him, I have groomed him as the leader of my pack, and all my hunting friends agree he is going to be the best Hound in all of France - HE BELONGS TO ME!"

This irrational outburst embarrassed Lucien and André but confirmed to the Duc that he had made the right decision. Hugo was special and would be much safer with Lucien than at the Château. He shook his head almost pityingly at his son: "No, he is not yours. He belongs to the Château de Garenne. I, and only I, will decide what is to be done with him. He now belongs to Colonel Lecaron. Do not defy me."

Without another word, the tired old man turned his back firmly on his son and with great difficulty remounted his horse. The three companions rode off, accompanied by the Hound who trotted obediently behind the horses, his tail wagging enthusiastically. A very disgruntled Louis-Philippe was left standing alone, seething, and oblivious to his father's obvious pain.

CHAPTER 3

Once Lucien had departed for his own home accompanied by a very excited Hugo, the Duc asked Catherine to have lunch with him. He wished to speak to his daughter privately. As soon as she saw her father's face, she knew that she was in serious trouble.

"Sit, daughter" barked the Duc "your brother told me that I ought to ask you what you have been up to whilst I have been absent? He hinted that perhaps the estate might have been better kept if you had not gone off "gallivanting" with your cousin, Amélie… I know nothing of this. Were you perhaps visiting friends?"

Cursing her brother and his spiteful tongue, Catherine could not lie to her father:

"Well father, Amélie and I, well we, err, went on a journey…We… I decided that we must help France. I read of the vivandières who were coming together from all over the country to serve with the army; we heard terrible things about the lives of the poor soldiers and well, we decided we must volunteer."

In the silence that followed, the only sound was the crackling of the huge log fire and the gentle snuffling of the Hounds allowed to sleep nearby. Catherine waited with increasing trepidation for the explosion she knew was coming.

"My daughter? My daughter – and Amélie? Amongst the soldiers like common camp followers? I cannot believe it!" He had conveniently forgotten how keen he had been to train both girls in the use of firearms. The Duc's face became mottled with anger.

"I am shocked and ashamed of you. You cannot be a daughter of mine. What would your dear mother have said? What possessed you Catherine?" The old man was genuinely shocked and devastated by the news. He himself had seen what life was like for the women who had followed the army – the wives, nurses, vivandières and those other less dedicated ladies too. Even though he did have a sneaking admiration for their courage, he could still scarcely believe that his own daughter would put herself in such danger and that she had involved her cousin.

"Papa, please do not distress yourself so" begged Catherine, frightened less by her father's anger than by its effect on him. "Sit down and I will play the piano for us both, something soothing, and then I will explain everything to you, quietly."

"I don't want to hear the piano! Do not try to divert me, I want to know everything right now." Hearing his tone, all Catherine's carefully planned excuses fled like anxious butterflies. Finding herself unable to get out any words to staunch the flow of her father's anger, she stuttered "I…. really don't know what to say, papa, I... I" and she began to cry, loud wracking and genuine sobs. She felt hurt by his attitude and furious at what she saw as his hypocrisy, although she dared not say so. It was an indication of the strength of the Duc's anger that he was unmoved by her tears. He stood towering over her, still seething with anger, his distress now compounded by the nagging pain in his thigh.

"Well, if you do not know what to say, I do. Out…out of my sight, I cannot stand to look at you. Do you not know how fortunate you are Catherine? You have brought shame on me and this family. To think a daughter of the House of Garenne should … "In his anger, Duc Philippe could not permit himself to hear his inner voice. He knew, in his heart, that what his daughter had done was brave and admirable, not wicked, merely reckless. His anger had conquered all other considerations. He was tired, his injury always pained him, and his beloved family home was a wreck. It was all too much for him.

Catherine made a final attempt to pacify him "We only wanted, I wanted to comfort those poor wounded soldiers, men like you and André… I wanted to be a brave Frenchwoman." But she wasn't given the chance to continue.

"Out, out. Go and stay with your aunt until I can look at you once more…if that day ever comes!"

After her initial panic when she saw her father's reaction to the news of her 'little adventure' Catherine was beginning to regain her composure. After all, she was a young woman who had learned to cope with dreadful injuries, disease and often death. Some of the old Catherine was returning and when she remembered what she had seen, her father's fury was not nearly so daunting. In a calm and collected voice, still muffled a little by her tearful outburst, she spoke:

"Papa, I have tried to explain but if you do not wish to hear then I do not want to stay under the same roof as you." With that she stormed out of the dining room slamming the door behind her, the decanters on the long dining room buffet clinking violently. Catherine flounced past an astonished André in the cavernous hallway, and then stormed up the sweeping staircase slamming her bedroom door with such force that the ornate mirror standing on her tallboy teetered then crashed to the floor.

Ten minutes later Catherine struggled from her bedroom dragging an overstuffed valise from which poked various trapped items of clothing. At the top of the stairs she struggled to stand upright whilst holding the valise and André ran up the stairs two at a time to help.

"Mlle. Catherine, what has happened? I heard your father shouting and I have just met Louis-Philippe in the yard. He told me, with great relish, that you were in trouble. Just what have you done, eh?"

"Oh André, I was just trying to explain to my father why Amélie and I felt we must both go to help the French army, the wounded..."

"You did what? No wonder your father is furious Mlle. Catherine. What did he say?"

"I am banished, André" she wailed dramatically "He would not even let me explain. I don't know what my brother had already told him, but I wouldn't be surprised if he has tried to make it sound much worse than it was, just out of spite."

"Where will you go?" asked André, full of concern, and aware that of course Louis-Philippe would try to cast her actions in the worst possible light to his father – anything to prevent her touching a penny of what the young man considered "his" inheritance.

"My father has ordered me to go to stay with my Aunt Marianne" mumbled Catherine, her self-control beginning to crumble.

"Let me go and arrange for a pony and trap to take you, Mlle. Catherine" said André and left her sitting on the bottom stair, clutching her bulging valise. She looked up as her brother came into the great hall, allowing the heavy doors to bang shut behind him.

"Ah sister dear" he smiled "Off on your travels again?" but before she could retaliate he laughed and ran up the stairs past her, almost striking her with one of his well-polished boots. If looks could kill...Catherine thought as she stared at his retreating back. Could things get any worse?

Despite André's protests, Catherine obstinately insisted on driving herself to her aunt's country house, which would take half an hour or so. As she travelled, she sniffed back tears but more often she seethed with anger at the injustice of it all. When she eventually arrived, she was greeted by her cousin and her aunt. Immediately they both knew that something bad had happened. Her aunt was sympathetic but not very; she knew her brother would be angry with her too.

"I did tell you that you ought to tell your father straight away. I admit that I was proud of what you both did but at the same time I was at my wits' end worrying (even though I always knew you were safe)" she added quietly, as if to herself. Kate and Amélie exchanged puzzled glances at this. "I can imagine how he feels – he saw the dreadful slaughter and finding out now that you were in the thick of it…. come here and give me a hug, my dear. We both know his anger is born out of concern for you. We will find a way to sort this out. His anger will be short-lived, I'm sure. My dear, he's angry with you mostly for not telling him (and probably with me for letting you go). Leave this to me and I am sure I will think of a way to resolve it."

After a while Catherine managed to stop crying leaving her face puffy and crimson. She had red-rimmed eyes and a runny nose and even in her distress she could not help but wish she was able to cry like the heroines of her novels, discreetly and prettily. She sniffed at regular intervals and her aunt remarked that this was the first time she had seen her niece so genuinely distraught.

"I did in truth know that *perhaps* it wasn't a sensible thing to do" mumbled Catherine – "as was taking my daughter with you" interrupted her aunt. "But I did it with the best of intentions. Why can't my father see that? I wanted to serve my country. My father fought for France for many years and now he's angry at me for trying to do the same."

Kate moped moodily around her aunt's house and even Amélie's naturally enthusiastic nature failed to lift her gloom. After two weeks passed it seemed that both Catherine and her father were becoming more entrenched in their determination not to be reconciled. Louis-Philippe took great pleasure in his father's misery, but it was André and Marianne who bore the brunt of the emotionally charged atmosphere. Eventually, Madame Giscard could bear it no longer and sent for André.

"If the two of them can't get together to discuss the situation then we must do something. It's like living with a coiled spring" she confided to André. "She is impossible at the moment and although I love her as if she were my own daughter I can't take much more."

"Madame Giscard, I truly understand. I know Mlle. Catherine's tempers of old, but the Duc is adamant that she cannot come home yet. I am convinced that the reality is, of course, he is desperate for her to return but he won't give in. They are, if you will forgive me, both as stubborn as each other."

"I'm certain she does not feel truly at fault, André, but I think there may be some things she does feel sorry about, like not confessing as soon as her father returned home."

"The problem, Madame, is that her brother wastes no opportunity to impart any juicy items of gossip circulating about the *vivandières.* The longer this goes on the more the Duc's mind will be poisoned. Mlle. Catherine must speak to her father and soon. I do believe that he would prefer to know the whole truth from her, however unpalatable he might find it, but it should perhaps be accompanied by a measure of contrition."

"Well" said Madame Giscard "I have taken great pains to get both Catherine's and Amélie's versions of events separately and I am convinced that they are telling the truth. There is nothing at all sinister to be revealed. I understand Kate did meet a young man and I know from Amélie that she was very taken with him. However, I am certain that it was all very innocent and if I can convince her to tell her father everything, that should ease his concerns. As for contrition, well we can but try."

"Perhaps if she just apologised for deceiving him and for the upset she has caused? I believe that may well heal the rift between them."

"I value your advice my dear friend André. Thank you. I will travel to the Château tomorrow and bring those difficult young ladies with me."

CHAPTER 4

The Duc stood staring out of the window of his study, pretending to be engrossed in the view but inwardly composing himself. He had seen his sister's carriage sway up to the stone steps of the Château. He felt torn between renewed anger and relief. There was a brief commotion in the hall and Marianne knocked once and bustled in propelling the girls in front of her while André remained anxiously near the open door. There was a moment of complete silence, before she came around the desk and confronted her brother.

"Philippe, I have been forced to intervene because both you and your daughter are acting like children and frankly I have had enough. You should know better than to believe that your daughter would bring shame on the family name. Nor would she behave in such a way as to disgrace herself. Oh, and incidentally it wasn't *our* family's name she used, it was my husband's. Anyway, you should be proud…" and here the Duc let out an involuntary sound, a noise somewhere between a laugh and a cough. "Despite everything, I am very proud of what my Amélie did. Of course, I was concerned – but I envy their courage, don't you? In spite of the fact that" and here she turned to face her niece "I have received not one word of apology from you for the distress you caused *me*; you left in secret without a word of explanation. I have always treated you as my own child, Catherine, a mother to you all these years and yet I received… a letter! By then you two were well on your way. Now, here, in front of your father I demand an apology and I hope that this can be an end to the sorry affair."

The Duc remained silent. In truth, he had been completely caught out by his sister's anger, expecting her to plead her niece's cause.

He was unsure how to react now and, in the silence, Catherine stood with her head bowed, hands behind her back as she stuttered: "Papa, Aunt.... I am truly sorry for distressing you both. My only excuse is that I did it all for my country, but I realise the way in which I went about it was wrong, and err, ill judged."

"And foolish" added the Duc. "Yes" agreed Kate "It was - but I have done nothing to disgrace our families' names and I am only too willing to recount everything that happened, both the good and the bad although you will know better than I, father, just how bad things were.

I just want us all to be happy again." Catherine paused, having delivered her seemingly heartfelt, but in fact very well-rehearsed speech. Satisfied that she had done her best, she stood with eyes downcast as her father turned to look out of the window. He stood for some moments with his hands clasped behind him before turning to face the group once again, holding out his arms.

"Come here my darling girl, I forgive you and I am sure your aunt does too. However, I would like to hear your story. I regret losing my temper, because I am very proud that another member of our family – two members, in fact – were with me at the great battle (even though I didn't know)." Everyone in the room knew that at that moment he was thinking of his feckless son. "Now" he smiled. "I want to hear everything you mischievous young ladies have been up to."

André nodded discreetly and closed the door behind him but before leaving he caught the eye of the Duc's sister and they exchanged a look of admiration. How cleverly she had managed the whole thing he thought.

"Tell me everything. If my daughter should 'varnish' the truth a little I am sure Amélie that your open sweet face will betray it. Marianne perhaps you might like to hear it again? I have no doubt you have already asked many questions."

"Indeed brother. I can always compare versions can't I Catherine?"

"Oh papa, I swore I would tell only the truth and I will" cried Kate, smiling.

Kate and her cousin sat down facing the Duc, his sister sitting nearby. She told her father that she had read in old newspapers from Paris that women were serving in Napoleon's army. The papers had taken so long to reach their town that by the time she had managed to persuade her cousin to accompany her they had found the army readying itself for battle at Waterloo.

They had posted a letter for Madame Giscard but were long gone by the time she read it. (Kate did not feel it necessary here to mention that this was how she had 'arranged' it). She did not dwell too long on the things she and her cousin had witnessed for she knew the Duc had seen far worse and would not want to be reminded. She did detail their return from Waterloo, accomplished with a 'borrowed' carriage and some farm horses. A young officer, a Lieutenant Lebrun had escorted them as far as Paris, having found them stranded.

This officer had also helped find someone to take on the job of coachman, selecting a young drummer boy in the straggling line of returning soldiers. She explained that the same boy, Rene, was now working in the stables of the Château. The boy had stayed because he had no real family in the town he had come from. She also admitted that to her great disappointment, she had been left alone with just Amélie and young Rene in Paris when this Lebrun had seemingly abandoned them. During Kate's narrative, Amélie occasionally added a detail here and there. The Duc listened in silence, inwardly delighted that their behaviour had been exactly as he would have expected but still concerned that the girls had relied on a stranger for safety and had even spent a night in Paris almost alone.

Finally, the long tale was over and after a relaxed lunch, Marianne and Amélie left and Duc Philippe sat once more with Catherine by the fireside. He took the opportunity to ask about the officer who had accompanied the girls to Paris. Did she know anything about him other than his name? What was his regiment? She believed that her father was just satisfying himself that the officer was a suitable companion and failed to notice his growing agitation. When she explained that he was a lieutenant of the Gendarmerie Nationale, seconded to the Grande Armée, her father finally exploded:

"I will not allow some gendarme to behave in this way. He will not get away with abandoning my daughter. Clearly you have been upset by this and he will be called to account for his actions. When I do find him, he will answer to me and to your godfather. His career will be ruined, and he will be punished."

Kate was aghast; it was not at all what she wanted to hear. She recognised that her father's anger was rooted in fear for her safety and, to be honest, in some of her angrier moments she too had wanted to punish the officer for deserting her. However, the Duc's fury alarmed her. Her father was still a powerful man even under the restored monarchy through his noble lineage, lands, and property. Kate was also aware that her godfather was a very powerful man as Inspector General of Gendarmes, so she tried to calm her father by assuring him that the officer had behaved as a perfect gentleman always (sadly, she thought) and had done all he could. She hoped she had done enough to persuade her father.

****

Later that same day, Duc Philippe called André to his study. "I have an urgent letter for you to write. I would like you to arrange for it to be sent by courier to General Destrier in Paris. I need a favour of him. Oh! And can you try and locate a decent local artist? I have decided I would like to make an addition to a portrait in the Great Hall."

André wrote at the Duc's dictation and was quite shocked by the vehemence of the letter's contents. Poor young man, he thought.

In the weeks after father and daughter were reconciled, life at the Château began to return to normal. After lunch every day, Kate insisted on 'soothing' her father with a mercifully short piano recital, which he endured with more loyalty than enjoyment. He asked André if he could secure the services of a piano tuner but was assured that the piano was perfectly in tune although perhaps Mlle. Catherine was not. Worse still, when her cousin visited they performed duets – Kate playing the piano whilst Amélie tortured her violin into sounds reminiscent of a suffering cat.

"André, I love my daughter very much, but I love music too. She has many admirable qualities, she is a brave, beautiful, talented young woman who believes her gifts extend to music – they don't."

"Would you like me to see if the instrument might spontaneously combust in the courtyard, Sir?" responded his friend with a smile, aware that Mlle. Catherine played only because she thought it helped to calm her father's irascible outbursts; she hated the piano (much as Amélie had loathed her 6 years of violin lessons).

CHAPTER 5

M. Lafitte-Dupont became a frequent visitor to the Château. He was the bustling little Mayor of La Garenne, who was also the local Notary and handled all the legal affairs of the Duc. Kate noticed his visits would usually coincide with those of her aunt. The mayor, her aunt, the Duc and occasionally André too, would be closeted in the Duc's private study. Of course, she could not help speculating but the doors of the study remained firmly closed. She questioned her cousin closely, but Amélie knew nothing. She said, quite honestly, that her mother never told her anything. Meanwhile, her half-brother stayed away from home as much as possible, either off hunting with his friends all day or staying at his town house in Perigueux to gamble and drink unobserved. He therefore remained unaware of these meetings. One day Kate 'just happened' to be coming down the great staircase as the lawyer was taking his leave. When she caught her father's parting words she was immediately alerted to some secret from which she was being excluded:

"M. Lafitte-Dupont, I am well satisfied with the outcome of our discussions. I will be making an announcement tomorrow and I would be most obliged if you could attend upon me here tomorrow morning.

"But of course, Monsieur le Duc" replied the little round-cheeked man, clearly anxious to do his patron's bidding.

Kate, not wanting to be discovered eavesdropping, crept quietly back to the top of the staircase, and waited until the great door closed and her father had returned to his study. At dinner that evening her father addressed her and her brother, who was at home for once. He told them both he wished to see them together in his study the next day immediately after breakfast. Kate readily agreed, delighted to be about discover what was brewing. However, Louis-Philippe, unaware of the intrigue, decided to argue.

Sulkily he demanded: "For pity's sake Father, how can you be so thoughtless as to arrange a meeting at such an hour and at ridiculously short notice? I have a busy day ahead and will not be able to attend you at all tomorrow. Really too impossible."

His sister shuddered inwardly, expecting an outburst of anger from her father but the Duc remained composed. Smiling, he replied: "My son, if you do not wish to live in penury for the rest of your life then I strongly suggest that you make time to attend tomorrow." Despite the smile there was an icy menace in that voice which shook Kate. After this exchange, dinner continued in frosty silence and her attempts to lighten the mood failed dismally. As soon as Louis-Philippe had finished his meal he rose abruptly, announced that *as he apparently had no choice*, he would see them both the next day and stormed out of the dining room. As the glassware on the long mahogany sideboard tinkled musically from the force of the closing door, Kate looked across at her father who seemed, at least outwardly, quite calm.

"Papa, I am sure he didn't mean to upset you, he can be a little…." but her soothing words remained unsaid.

"Do not concern yourself on my behalf Catherine, sadly I understand exactly why my son acts as he does. Perhaps one day you too will know the reason. There is little that can be done about it, but still I will not give up on him." Inexplicably her father seemed almost angry with himself as he said this. Confused by her father's attitude Catherine offered to perform a new piece on the piano which she had just learned to play without sheet music. Her father managed to smother a huge sigh as he followed her to the salon.

The following morning, Kate and her brother breakfasted at the magnificent walnut dining table. Kate had dressed in a simple morning gown, a pale green silk confection with full sleeves in a flattering if dated style. She thought this would be appropriate to their meeting with the Duc, but Louis-Philippe had decided on a policy of flamboyant defiance and was wearing a lilac embroidered silk coat over creamy linen, his hair in a fashionable queue tied with an ornate silver trimmed lavender ribbon. His shoes, Kate noted, had been dyed to match the ensemble.

It was a fashion which would have been more appropriate at Court prior to the Revolution, but which was being revived amongst a small number of the younger surviving *aristos* who longed for a return to the "old ways".

Craftsmen had been found by André to repolish and mend the ancient table intended to seat at least 30 people. Such magnificence did not make for intimate dining. The occupants sat at opposite ends, glaring at one another, silently serving themselves from the old but brightly polished chafing dishes on the ornate sideboard. They usually avoided each other as much as possible but both were surprised to discover that their father had already taken his breakfast. It had been served privately to him in his study. Kate had lain awake for most of the night worrying about her father's obvious distress and unwisely decided to tackle her brother about his behaviour. Louis-Philippe was taken completely by surprise when his half-sister addressed him loudly:

"Louis-Philippe, papa is old and frail, still suffering great pain from his wound. Could you *please* try to act with more consideration? I am worried that he may not be with us for much longer and surely you could at least try to make the time left to him pleasant?" She smiled as she said this, hoping to revive some long-lost filial feelings in her half-brother. His response shocked her: "I would rather make his remaining years as short as possible – I would like to measure the time he has left in days.... even hours. The quicker I am rid of the old fool the better."

He stood to help himself from a steaming dish of kedgeree and thus failed to notice Kate's darkening expression. Unable to control her temper she burst out: "How dare you! How dare you speak like that of our father. After all that he has done for you? I cannot believe you can be so selfish and cruel."

"Done for me?" responded Louis-Philippe "Done for me?" His voice rose sharply as he walked the length of the table to stand towering over his sister: "He has allowed peasants to steal his land, land that should be my land; he allows those same peasants the right to hunt on land that will be *mine*, he gives away valuable animals from *my* kennels and he barely even treats me with civility. Today, for example, I was to have attended a very important hunt, at the personal invitation of the Duc de Perigueux. But no, no here I am stuck in this crumbling excuse for a house waiting for a summons from that old fool."

Just as Kate thought that her brother was about to lose all control, André slid quietly into the dining room and announced formally: "If it would please you Monsieur and Mademoiselle, the Duc de Garenne would like you to join him in his study." The tension in the room was palpable as the young girl stood whilst her brother hung back for a moment then walked slowly in her wake. André waited until Louis-Philippe, walking as slowly as he dared, joined his sister in the study then followed them inside and closed the doors, seating himself to one side of the Duc. On the desk beside the heavy bronze desk pieces, seals and ink pots stood a haphazard stack of documents some tied with faded pink tape, others creased and discoloured. Another pile lay on the left side of the desk; these looked even older. Kate was surprised to see that her Aunt Marianne and M. Lafitte-Dupont had already arrived. Her aunt was sitting by the study window while the Notary had a small table to himself.

He peered at the newcomers over his half-moon glasses, his large belly struggling to fit behind the miniature make-shift desk. A sheaf of papers also lay before him and he clutched an elderly quill pen aloft, hovering over an inkwell.

Instead of taking one of the two remaining chairs placed before the Duc's desk, Louis-Philippe remained standing and allowed his insolent gaze to rest in turn on each of the other people in the room. His face showed both disdain and confusion: "I understood that this was to be a private meeting, father. Why are my aunt, your estate manager and this… functionary here? I expected no outsiders."

For the second time in 24 hours, Kate braced herself for an explosion and for the second time her father remained calm. He told his son that there were no outsiders present, only friends. Everyone in the room was important to the matter in hand and he invited his son to sit. The young man threw himself into the remaining chair, sighing heavily as he did so.

CHAPTER 6

The Duc spoke carefully: "It is customary to wait until someone's death for their Will to be read. However, as my father explained to me, the Ducs de Garenne have only ever owned a very few personal possessions to bequeath to future generations and so…" Louis-Philippe leapt abruptly from his chair, unable to contain himself. "Sit down and you may learn something" his father growled "and so…as did my father and all the generations before him, I tell you both that I have no personal wealth or property to pass on to you. I will die almost penniless. Therefore, it is now my duty…" He got no further before his son was once again on his feet, his face a mask contorted with rage. He smashed his fist down onto his father's desk as the others watched anxiously.

"You damned old fool! I knew you were senile but not so senile as to have spent all our money. I demand you tell me now: where has it all gone?"

His father seemed completely unperturbed and spoke again ignoring the angry red face of his son thrusting into his own. "Please sit down and I will explain." Reluctantly Louis-Philippe took his seat, twitching angrily. "As I was saying, like all my ancestors, I will die penniless and it is now my duty to inform you both…."

"You cannot be penniless father, you own this Château, one of the oldest estates in all of France; you have at least managed to keep some of our lands, and we have the properties in Perigueux and some in Paris I believe. You never seem to want for money, nor does *she*" he glared at his sister "and you are happy to give away our finest hunting animals. Pray tell me, how can this be?" With an ugly sneer on his young face, Louis-Philippe stared at his father.

“I think I was about to say… in the presence of those most concerned by the Eleanor Bequest I now have to inform you of the terms of that Bequest - upon which this family has been built for many generations. You should both be familiar with some of Eleanor’s story?”

“God’s Oath, *get on with it!*” The young man’s outburst was this time silenced by a single look from Marianne.

“It is believed that Eleanor de Garenne inherited all the wealth of her father and her mother. This is the basis of the great Garenne fortune, yet no-one really knows its true origins. It was Eleanor who began the building of this great Château to defend this region of France against the English and to protect pilgrims on their way to Santiago de Compostella.” The Duc paused in his discourse for only a moment, but just enough for his son to mutter angrily once more. “Be silent” hissed his aunt, fiercely. This time Marianne’s vehemence shocked the young man into silence.

“We also know that Eleanor was married to one Guillaume de Rouen. From family documents, it seems she was still very young when she had a child called Hugo. No further details are recorded about her husband but in later documents she is described as ‘widow’. Despite her youth, she was in sole charge of the estate and it seems that to protect it and her son’s inheritance she drew up the Eleanor Bequest. There are no records to indicate she ever remarried. She devoted herself to La Garenne. I will now ask Mr. Lafitte-Dupont, whose family has served our family for generations, to explain further.” He nodded towards the Notary, ignoring his son’s expression. The little man began to shuffle papers until he found what he needed and adjusted his pince-nez:

“It has been an honour for our family, Notaries to the commune of La Garenne in the Department of the Dordogne; in previous times the province of Perigord….”

“Oh, for pity’s sake get on with it” hissed Louis-Philippe but the little lawyer went on unperturbed: “To…err…act for and on behalf of the Bequest of the Lady Eleanor de Garenne, hereafter known as The Bequest. The terms of The Bequest are that at the time of her demise, some 500 years ago, she left all her fortune and properties in trust to be applied as follows: firstly, for the completion of the construction and subsequent maintenance of the Château de Garenne and all its dependencies; secondly to provide an income for life to the person nominated as its Steward and to his or her immediate family solely at the discretion of that Steward, the residual annual revenue to be used to assist in any way possible all Pilgrims and *all* those who protect them and finally for the well-being of the residents of La Garenne.

The full terms are contained in these documents." The lawyer indicated the large bundle of dusty documents before him and selected one.

"Madame de Garenne specified that her only child Hugo would be the first Steward and that prior to his death he would nominate his successor." A few moments of shuffling kept the audience in suspense before he continued: "Hugo de Garenne did marry; one Marie de Monbezier and they had...let me see…four children. His choice of Steward was his first-born, a son named Philippe. Anyway, each nominated their successor, who must be of the house of Garenne. In addition, Eleanor made provision for two further Trustees to advise the Steward or to act on their behalf and to ensure that the decisions taken are at all times in accordance with the original aims of the Bequest."

"How does that affect me?" demanded Louis-Philippe now thoroughly bored by all this legal jargon. "I naturally assume that as Steward I shall have sole use of the estate and its benefits?" A deafening silence followed, broken by the calm voice of the lawyer: "Under the terms of the Bequest anyone raising an unsuccessful challenge to the actions of the Steward is automatically excluded from receiving any income from the Bequest. Over a period of 500 years the line of succession has remained unbroken."

The little man looked up from his papers and turned to the Duc, who then took over smoothly before there could be any further interruption:

"Thank you, M. Lafitte-Dupont. That was indeed a clear and concise explanation of a very complex document. I have already decided on my successor and advised my fellow Trustees - who are my sister Marianne and my good friend André Lacoste. This will be revealed only upon my death. My successor will also be Head of this House and will be..." He ignored an audible groan... "... responsible for the welfare of not just the immediate family, but also for the more widespread members of the family in whatever guise." No-one spoke for a moment since neither Louis-Philippe nor Catherine had been aware either of the details of the Bequest or of the identities of its Trustees. Both were equally puzzled by that last phrase 'in whatever guise'.

M.Lafitte-Dupont began to re-arrange his papers meticulously, straightening their edges before stowing them in the old leather case he always carried. The silence was at last broken by a loud clatter as Louis-Philippe stood up so sharply that his chair fell back onto the floor. He stood over his father, his face almost purple with fury:

"Just how much more humiliation do you intend to heap upon me? You dare to confide in a woman and a servant." He stopped briefly to look first at his aunt who glared back, and then at André who allowed himself a small smile. "You did not see fit to confide in me, your only son, and your only true heir. I am to become Steward of this family's wealth - make no mistake, father - I will tolerate no more of this nonsense about ancient secrets and agreements. When you are dead (and it cannot come soon enough for me) I shall inherit everything, do you hear? There is no court in this land that would uphold the ravings of a widow who lived 500 years ago. I will recover all the lands that have been stolen by the peasants too….and my Hound!" Louis-Philippe's face had become disturbingly congested and spittle flew from his lips.

The tirade was halted by M. Lafitte-Dupont, who coughed discreetly and spoke directly to the Duc's son: "On a point of law, Monsieur Louis-Philippe, the terms of the Bequest have been the subject of several legal challenges" he pointed to the pile of very old papers on the Duc's desk "and even petitions to the King himself. All, without exception, have failed. These terms have proved unbreakable."

The Duc stood to face his son who was clutching the edges of the desk as if for support. "I have, of course, given instructions that both of you will be entitled - for the rest of your lives- to a sizeable income from the Bequest, and in some ways, that might be better than being the Steward, something that carries some heavy obligations."

These words only served to fuel the young man's fury: "Sizeable income?" he screamed "Well I hope it's more than the pittance I receive now. What about my mother's fortune? I suppose you have thrown that away too?

I believe she brought a handsome dowry to you when you married – trust me, I will discover the truth of it!"

Until this moment, the Duc had remained admirably calm but now he drew himself erect despite his age and injury. His military bearing still commanded attention: "I fear you are mistaken my son. There has never been a single dowry in the whole history of the House of Garenne. M. Lafitte-Dupont can confirm that none has ever been sought or given."

The little lawyer nodded in agreement: "The town house in Perigueux, the one you spend all your time at? That was part of your mother's estate; it was bequeathed to her by her father and to you on her death, but its maintenance and all the staff costs have been met for many years by the House of Garenne. Do you think your long-suffering servants have worked for nothing?

M. Lafitte-Dupont has kindly looked after such matters in my absence. Perhaps, instead we should speak of the misappropriation of a considerable sum of money…by you. I left you in charge of the funds for the maintenance of this Château, your family home, yet nothing appears to have been done. If there is to be any 'discovery of truth' as you put it, it will be by me. As for the "pittance" you receive, your annual income almost equals that of the entire population of La Garenne, all 800 souls. Yet you persist in running up debts which are sent to *me*. André, would you oblige me with our accounts?"

The Duc sat down, and André passed him the ledger. The Duc leafed through the pages, pausing to read out extracts: "Tailor: 11,000 Francs; Shoemaker: 3870 Francs; an account for one Mlle. Clarine Latour, marked "Overdue" for 700 Francs." I also have here a vast number of IOUs for your gambling debts. These bills will be settled but they will be the last, do you understand? You must live within your means in future."

Louis-Philippe feigned disinterest, making an elaborate show of boredom by examining his buttons in detail. The Duc, finally pushed beyond endurance, roared: "*Get out of my sight...*now!"

Throughout these events, Kate had remained silent, sometimes surprised, sometimes horrified, but totally fascinated. She now rose and went to her father taking his hand: "Papa, please I beg you try to stay calm. Your heart…" She looked imploringly at her brother, but he gave her an impassive stare. "I am sure he meant nothing…" at which her brother laughed sharply, turned on his rather high heels and stalked out of the room slamming the door so hard that some of the papers on the desks fluttered to the ground.

The Duc caught his sister's eye then and she came to stand beside him muttering in his ear almost inaudibly. Kate tried to catch some of the conversation but could only make out one word: "*Renegade*".

The duke shook his head "No, no matter what I will not give up on him. *Whatever it takes.*" Whilst Kate was puzzled by this exchange her immediate concern now was to calm her father. Attempting to restore some measure of order, she led the group towards the Great Hall to take the Vin d'Honneur, the customary drink offered at the end of any meeting.

CHAPTER 7

Lucien Lecaron had been glad to see his family once again. His parents had once been tenant farmers but had been given their land by the Duc some years earlier. They had cared for it well but now they were growing old and had been forced to rely on Lucien's brother Raoul, who was neither soldier nor farmer. Raoul was lazy, surly and completely disinterested in work of any kind. His parents had begged him to do more on the farm. One day it would all belong to them both. But Raoul's reply was always the same, grudging and angry:

"Lucien has always been your favourite. Let him do it - I shall do my own share of the work but no more." The returning soldier had taken readily to farming once more and especially to caring for the livestock. This further alienated the two brothers since Lucien received praise and respect both from his parents and the townsfolk whilst Raoul was generally disliked even in the local bar where he spent most of his time. Lucien became a frequent visitor to the Château, as a guest of the Duc – Raoul had never been inside the gates – and this only added to his resentment. Consequently, Raoul chose to do even less, rising late and spending his time in the bar or with the chasse in the forest, for he was an enthusiastic drinker and a passionate if incompetent hunter. His pack of hunting Hounds were his only real interest.

Despite the failed harvest that year – the 'Year of no Summer' people had called it -Lucien's family farm prospered, and his reputation grew. This was in part due to his obvious connection to the Duc. Lucien now felt he needed a wife and his eye was caught by a local girl, the prettiest girl in La Garenne in fact, Marie

Lefebvre. What he did not know was that Raoul had, for several years, nursed hopes of marrying her himself. If his brother never returned from the Wars, one day the farm would be Raoul's alone. Unaware of this – for Raoul was always secretive and taciturn – Lucien set about courting Marie.

She was a well-built, creamy skinned young girl, with green eyes and hair which was her crowning glory, thick and reddish gold, but usually concealed by a cap which could barely contain its thick coils.

Of course, she was completely aware of her good looks which she used to advantage. Lucien was soon besotted by her, despite some unspoken misgivings of the Duc; she was quite a simple girl, looking for a good, kind and preferably handsome husband and Lucien was the perfect choice but Lucien, the Duc felt, could have found a better match. Marie had never even considered Raoul as a suitor. Her parents were delighted when the handsome young man came to ask for her hand, in the traditional way; they had known him since he had been a lad and readily agreed to their daughter's betrothal.

On his return to the farm that evening Lucien announced his betrothal and his parents threw their arms around his neck, delighted both for him and that now there would someone else to help them on the farm. Raoul however was not at all thrilled and stalked out of the farmhouse without a word. To add more salt to Raoul's imagined wounds, the Mayor, M. Lafitte-Dupont, declared that Lucien and Marie's wedding would be his last official duty. He was finally ready to retire. No-one was too surprised when, on the recommendation of the Duc, Lucien was asked to become the mayor's successor. Such an honour was usually reserved for professional men, but M. Lafitte-Dupont's only son lived in Paris and had expressed no interest in returning to the small town. Lucien's swift rise through the ranks of the army made him an ideal candidate. He was stunned and delighted at this news and happily accepted. Both Marie and his parents were also thrilled; his parents because they were very proud of their soldier son and Marie because she would soon be someone special in the town. Raoul remained silent and unsmiling....

To celebrate the betrothal a grand fete was held in the grounds of the Château and the whole town was invited to attend the event. Kate and Amélie were excited because this would be the first party to be held at the Château in many years.

Notably absent – 'on business' – was Louis-Philippe; equally absent was Raoul – no reason given. The day was warm and sunny, and barrels of ale and wine were lavishly provided. Everyone was very impressed with the new ale which the Duc had procured for the celebration. The huge oaken barrels were all marked "GB Brewery" - not a local brewer, people remarked.

An enormous barbecue pit had been dug from which issued delicious odours of roasting meat. Kate and Amélie decorated the tables with flowers and filled dishes with fruit and little cakes while the Duc, his sister and André distributed small bags of coins. The wine and beer flowed copiously and everyone there that day said it was the best fete they had ever attended. Lucien and Marie stood, surrounded by their friends and parents, while Duc Philippe stood smiling with André nearby. Both girls watched the happy couple wondering whether their own betrothals might ever happen.

Locked up in the kennels of the Château, the Hounds sensed excitement nearby and the sounds of noisy yapping came from them and drifted towards the party. Lucien, never parted from Hugo, took his Hound back to visit his old friends at the kennels and there was much sniffing and yapping with the pack. The great Hound really seemed to appreciate the visit and wagged his already enormous tail hard against his master's leg to tell him so.

The young man felt his life was almost perfect. He had survived so many battles and had returned an officer to make his parents proud. Now, he had good friends, he had a beautiful fiancée and next year the farm would do even better, and he would be Mayor. He would hunt with his Hugo, and they would all have plenty to eat. The sun was shining on Lucien Lecaron.

CHAPTER 8

On an unusually warm autumn day, some three months after the betrothal, Lucien and his brother along with the other men from the local chasse set off into the forest with some very excited Hounds. Raoul was very much aware that he was merely tolerated by the other huntsmen. This was yet another bitter pill for him as was the prowess of his brother's Hound, Hugo. For all Raoul's love of hunting he had only been able to assemble a ragged pack of mongrels and terriers.

It was one of the days of the year when the forests surrounding the Château were free for the use of the chasse and that day Louis-Philippe himself was to attend at his father's insistence (much to the dismay of the other huntsmen). The young nobleman had brought along his own pack of sleek Hounds who were all great friends of Hugo and their excitement at meeting him again was obvious. The men and dogs met on the edge of the woods chatting and laughing quietly so as not to disturb any game; the dogs anxious to be off and free for the day. The hunters carried a few ancient firearms, but mostly slingshots or roughly hewn stakes and walked forward in a long line, roughly three paces between each man, into the dense woodland, advancing into the darkening undergrowth. Louis-Philippe remained on horseback, slightly behind the line of men and on their flank but poised to take aim if game was flushed. He was not anxious to join in the banter of the 'peasants', which anyway would usually cease abruptly when he was nearby.

♠♠♠♠♠♠♠♠

No-one knew for certain what really happened that day.

At dusk, a sad procession approached the Lecaron farm. Four men carried a makeshift stretcher made from sacks tied to branches and on this lay the body of Lucien Lecaron, white-faced in death.

Raoul came forward to meet his parents and Marie at the steps of the farmhouse, the faithful Hugo at his side, whimpering softly. He told his parents without emotion that their son had been mortally wounded by a stray shot.

The dejected hunters left the body with Lucien's parents and Marie, both women incoherent with grief. The mourning men trooped back to the town to tell the gendarmerie and their neighbours of the awful tragedy. They discovered that Louis-Philippe had ridden ahead of them and was waiting with the Mayor, who was overcome with sorrow. The townspeople stood in the square and looked at each other in shock and disbelief and soon a group of men from the town accompanied by Lucien's father, set off to the Château. They were ushered into the Great Hall in silence but after a few respectful minutes elapsed during which the old soldier rose painfully to greet them, M. Lecaron came forward:

"Sir," he began, then faltered "I…I must…. must tell you that my beloved son Lucien died this day. A stray shot mortally wounded him. He lies now at the farm with his mother and his grieving fiancée."

"Lucien is dead? How?" The Duc advanced towards the old man to take him in his arms. Kate came to her father's side, shocked into silence, André standing white-faced beside her. He noticed Louis-Philippe at the back of the little group, his face impassive. The men from the town stood, hats in their hands, staring downwards. In the silence, the old Duc s paled and staggered back to grip an arm of his chair for support. For a moment he appeared to struggle to find words: "Sir, I err, would consider it an honour if you would allow your son to err be buried here, at the Château. I will ensure that his is a funeral fit for a hero. He was…." Suddenly Duc Philippe halted in mid-sentence and tried to take a step forward, his stricken face drawn and tense

He swayed as his injured leg buckled beneath him and he fell heavily onto the stone floor. The men from the town watched in horror, those at the back of the group craning to see what had happened. Louis-Philippe was nowhere to be seen. Kate knelt beside her father anxiously but only André heard the Duc's final whispered words: "No matter what it takes, remember."

Long moments passed before André stood up and announced:

"The Duc is dead!"

CHAPTER 9

On a bitterly cold day in October 1816 almost the entire population of La Garenne and the surrounding countryside were either crammed inside the courtyard of the Château or spilling out into the surrounding streets. They had all climbed the steep cobbles made slippery with rain to stand before the grand façade of the Château where an entire squadron of gendarmes were standing ramrod straight to await them. They were accompanied by their captain, the elegantly dressed Victor Falaise. He was a rare sight indeed, preferring to avoid all but his most essential duties to enjoy his favourite pastime, hunting. Today he wore his full-dress uniform, his boots polished and shining brightly in the dim light. A detachment from the French army stood shivering around the edge of the courtyard together with their drummers and buglers. In front of them waited a huddled group of local dignitaries and officials, many from Perigueux or even as far away as Bordeaux. In the background, the old Château seemed to be watching events through the blank eyes of its many windows while the bitter wind swept across the open courtyard and froze the faces of the waiting mourners.

For André Lacoste, this was the saddest day of his life. As a young man during the chaos of the Revolution, he had left his home near Lille, north of Paris, and had made his way across France in search of a peaceful corner where he could make a living. His parents had worked for the owners of a large estate who had fled abroad during the Terror and the young man had learned much about how estates should be managed as opposed to how they were often managed by the absentee, dissolute nobility. Eventually he had stumbled upon

La Garenne in the Aquitaine region of south western France. He had tentatively gone to the Château to seek any employment on offer. He did not hold out much hope as it seemed that this might be the sort of place he had come to despise, the family seat of a grand titled family. He had heard that they owned all the land as far as the eye could see from the top of the hill on which the great Château stood.

Nonetheless, unexpectedly he had found himself being ushered into the presence of the Duc himself. He had expected to meet some foppish aristocrat but instead found an old soldier who had served in the King's army but who had retired to his estate in disgust at the excesses of the monarch. The Duc now devoted himself to improving the lot of the many tenant farmers in and around La Garenne. He and André had talked for hours, devising plans for the tenant farmers so that the locals would be better able to fend for themselves, especially in bad years. The two unlikely allies had made great plans using new methods of agriculture to grow stronger crops and improve their harvests. Much to André's surprise, the Duc had proved surprisingly knowledgeable on such matters and they had become firm friends. However, when Napoleon Bonaparte had asked the Duc to help him, André volunteered to go with him. They had ridden out together accompanied by a young farm boy from La Garenne, Lucien Lecaron. This young soldier had by sheer bravery risen through the ranks during many battles and received a commission from the hands of Napoleon himself. Lecaron had become the youngest colonel in the Army. André had never married; Lucien had been like a son to him. Now André s life was empty.

The two coffins were borne by soldiers through the seldom-used main doors of the Château and down the stone steps. The unadorned wooden boxes were placed gently on gun carriages drawn by magnificent chestnut horses. Behind each carriage came one of the Château's fine hunters, saddles draped in black and each with a pair of highly polished riding boots placed facing to the rear in the brass stirrups. The cortege slowly travelled the short distance to the site of two freshly dug graves. Unusually, the Duc's sister Marianne headed the group of family mourners followed by his son, his daughter and Amélie. Louis-Philippe's face wore a carefully arranged blank expression, but his sister was unable to hold back her tears, which streamed down her face as she walked, supported by her cousin.

Next came the Lecaron family, Lucien's father and mother, Raoul and Marie. The old couple clung together as they walked, Lucien's mother bent and seeming even older than her years. Marie held Madame's arm protectively but Raoul, like Louis-Philippe, showed no emotion.

Behind the bereaved families walked the townsfolk with M. Lafitte-Dupont at their head. When the whole procession had reached the graveside, a military detail took the coffins from the carriages and placed them beside the freshly dug pits in the earth, stepping back one pace in unison, watched by a miserable Hugo Hound who had adopted a vigil earlier that day, between the two graves, his Hound face betraying loss and confusion.

As the two families gathered around, the local parish priest came forward for a brief service after which the soldiers took up the coffins and placed them in position to be lowered by heavy leather straps. The families retreated a few steps to allow the manoeuvring of the caskets, but the distraught dog would not be moved. A detachment of honour guards fired a volley of shots over the open graves and at the same time the gendarmes lowered the Duc's standard which hung on a pole beside the main entrance to the Château. Through all this the great Hound lay motionless, none of the noise seeming to touch him as he lay with his head on his massive front paws, his eyes closed.

When the town band struck up the first chords of the anthem of France, André retrieved the flag and presented it to Marianne who in turn gave it formally to Catherine - not to Louis-Philippe who had reached out to take it. Catherine clutched it to her as her tears fell while her half-brother scowled angrily. Madame Giscard stood motionless in the bitter wind watching the tearful faces of those around her; she also observed Louis-Philippe's detachment.

Once the coffins were finally lowered into the ground the families and the population of La Garenne stood waiting in silence. The only sound was the rhythmic thudding of the earth as it was shoveled onto the lids. Then at last it was over. As the mourners reached the steps of the Château keen to escape the biting cold, a single piercing howl of misery and pain rang out from the faithful Hound, who had finally understood.

oul, hoping to catch the eye of Marie, turned to catch instead, the eye of Louis-Philippe and for a split second their gazes met, Raoul's expression of fear meeting a gaze full of menace. The young man leaned close to Raoul's face and hissed threateningly: "Return that Hound to me!" Raoul recoiled and caught sight of Marie's shocked expression - she had overheard.

At a sign from Madame Giscard, M. Lafitte-Dupont announced that the Duc had wished everyone present to join the family in the Great Hall for a Vin d'Honneur. All the mourners slowly made their way slowly up the steps and into the Great Hall. Meanwhile Raoul put a rope around Hugo's neck and was attempting to drag him away from the fresh graves: the Hound was his at last. The only other person who did not attend the wake was Louis-Philippe who caught up with Raoul at the gates of the Château as the new owner struggled to drag Hugo along with him. Some of the mourners watched as an angry whispered exchange took place between the two. This ended when Raoul dragged the Hound down the hill as fast as he could whilst the nobleman stormed off towards the stables where his horse was waiting. The young man rode out at breakneck speed away from the Château.

In the Great Hall the guests were being served drinks and small pastries by the housekeeper and the stable boy Rene. Madame

Giscard had taken Kate aside as they entered and told her she must now behave as her position dictated. She was a Garenne and could not allow her great grief to show. Kate helped serve their guests whilst managing to control her tears. Mourners went to view more closely the paintings on the walls of the Hall – many of the locals had never been inside the Château before. One painting was especially of interest. It had recently been rehung and dominated one wall. It portrayed the old Duc on horseback in the foreground, against an arresting backdrop of the Battle of Villodrigo which had taken place during the Spanish Wars. There had been an interesting recent addition to the painting. In the foreground, two small figures had been added, two bareheaded young women, one with very dark hair, and the other with golden brown curls. They were tending the wounded and dying soldiers, oblivious to their surroundings. This had been the Duc's belated tribute to his beloved daughter.

As the last of the guests made their way across the now darkened courtyard, Louis-Philippe strode through them and up the steps of the Château, relieved to discover that he would not be forced to speak to anyone. His aunt informed him coldly that his presence was required in his father's study and reluctantly he went into what should now of course be his study.

At last, the Will! He was taken aback to see that his aunt had dared to take his father's seat behind the heavy ornate desk and that the old fool Lafitte-Dupont was also waiting. His half-sister and André Lacoste were seated facing Marianne and there was a tense atmosphere in the room as soon as he entered: "I believe you are occupying my chair, Aunt" drawled the young man. "Please be so good as to allow me my rightful place."

She barely glanced at him, raising her head briefly from the papers she was studying and casually pointed to a spare chair. "Sit down" she commanded and although her voice was quiet, the young man recognised its steel and abruptly sat beside Kate.

His aunt turned to M. Lafitte-Dupont indicating that he should commence proceedings. This time the little man had only a single sheet of paper before him rather than piles of dusty scrolls. However, he made great show of smoothing the single sheet before he read aloud.

"This will be brief. There is little left to say that was not said by his Grace the Duc. I can confirm that he achieved his aim of dying penniless…"

"Oh bravo" scoffed the Duc's son "Unbelievable……" but he stopped as Marianne gave him a look.

"Yes, indeed the remaining francs were spent in accordance with the Duc's last wishes on today's food and wine for the mourners. The sole task left is to read the Will nominating his successor as Steward of the Eleanor Bequest." The little man cleared his throat noisily and began to read, omitting the lengthy preamble for once:

"I have given great thought to this decision; the position is an onerous one. Not only is the Steward responsible for the future of the House of Garenne, but also for the whole populace and their wellbeing. The chosen person must put aside all personal feelings and do only what is right and proper. I am very sorry, my dearest daughter, that…."

Louis-Philippe jumped to his feet, interrupting the little Mayor. His father had finally seen sense. His face lit up with a malicious, triumphant smile but the Duc's sister gave a heavy sigh, raising her eyebrows. Her expression changed to one of withering scorn as she stared the young man back down into his chair as M. Lafitte-Dupont read on:

"I am sorry, my dearest daughter... that I should have to impose this burden on one so young, but I believe that you have the strength and determination to fulfil the task of Steward of the

Eleanor Bequest. I hereby nominate you, the Lady Catherine Marie Eleanor Mortaigne de Garenne, as my successor and head of the House of Garenne. This will take effect when you reach the age of twenty-one years or are married with the full approval of Madame Marianne Giscard, which ever event should come first. In the meantime, my sister and M. André Lacoste will remain as Trustees. My dear sister will be your legal guardian and acting head of the House of Garenne. I wish you all the happiness you deserve, my beloved daughter Catherine. To my only son, Louis-Philippe, I give to you only this advice: you receive and will continue to receive a substantial income from the Bequest. This will cease should you mount an unsuccessful legal challenge to my wishes. Be assured any such challenge will fail. Think long before acting, my son."

Ignoring his sister's pale face and the words of his father, the young man leapt, screaming, to his feet: "I will, I will challenge this nonsense and I will succeed!"

"As you wish, nephew" said his aunt mildly "I must then inform you that until a decision is made regarding your proposed challenge, nothing will change, you will still receive your income as before but as you may remember my brother forbad you to run up any more debts.

If you have any accounts sent to the Château, I will personally visit whoever has sent them, be they noblemen or tradesmen – or err women of your acquaintance – and explain that you lack sufficient funds. I am told that the conditions in a debtors' prison fall short of your expectations in every respect. Now you may leave."

Louis-Philippe strode angrily to the door which André held open for him, thus depriving him of the opportunity to slam it. Kate sat in silence trying to absorb all the events of the day. She looked at her aunt and whispered:

"What happens now?"

Madame Giscard left it to the lawyer to respond: "I feel confident that Louis-Philippe will challenge the Will and these matters can take many years to be resolved. However, I believe that in the meantime it is best to carry on as usual."

She nodded in agreement: "I fully expect that boy to act as if he is heir, but I hope that we can control his wilder excesses. However, Catherine we do have a more pressing problem at present, even though this is the day of my dear brother's funeral. I believe he would have wanted it. I will let André explain."

"The dreadful weather we have suffered has meant that this year's harvest is very poor, yet again. I fear that many will go hungry over the winter and worse still the people will eat next year's seed corn if there is nothing else. I know, Mlle. Catherine that your father was deeply concerned about this. He took seriously his obligations to La Garenne and its people. Grain and potatoes may be available but at prices none can afford. If we start to stockpile now we may be able to feed everyone through the winter. On your father's instructions, I have already drawn up a list of supplies needed, the merchants who have agreed to supply the estate and the prices they will charge."

Kate looked from André to her aunt and then at M. Lafitte-Dupont. So, this was her first taste of her new responsibilities.

"I know that officially this is not yet my decision to make but I feel certain that my papa would have said that whatever it takes, we must do it. We must not let our people suffer." At this her aunt nodded and the Mayor smiled: "Your father, Mlle. would be so proud of you. Very soon these decisions will be yours entirely."

Once Catherine and M. Lafitte-Dupont had left the room, André handed Marianne an envelope. He explained that immediately after the Duc's death, Louis-Philippe had instructed him to clear the Duc's desk without consulting either Catherine or herself. He had been reluctant to do this but in a drawer he had found a letter marked from the 'Bureau of General Destrier'. As he said this he looked sharply at Marianne, but she said nothing. The letter was almost a year old. Clearly, it had been read but replaced in the envelope. The General had not been able to attend her brother's funeral, although he had already sent his condolences. She opened the letter apprehensively then read its contents slowly and smiled at André:

"This concerns the officer Lebrun, now a Captain apparently. He was the gendarme who escorted Mlle. Catherine and my daughter on their journey from Waterloo. The General had written to reassure my brother that this Captain did not desert his daughter willingly; the General was responsible for sending the young man away urgently – to protect him. Apparently, Lebrun's father was a prominent Bonepartiste and the young man, having volunteered to fight with Napoleon, could well have been in danger after the defeat – clearly General Destrier had his own reasons for singling out this particular officer."

"Shall we tell Mlle. Catherine now?" asked André anxiously.

"No, I think not" his companion replied, after a moment's consideration. "She may well have forgotten him."

Marianne made no reference to the second part of the letter concerning Destrier's response to the Duc's assurances that 'he' was safe, for now.

SANCTUARY AND THE ARRIVAL OF A GUARD BEAR...

The eerie silence of early dusk was shattered by a thunderous pounding on the huge metal-studded door which was almost hidden in the shadows of the overhanging cliff. The door was flung open by a large grizzled bear whose bulk almost filled the height and breadth of the opening. He wore an old leather apron over a thick woolen waistcoat, a collarless striped flannel shirt.... and very elderly, misshapen carpet slippers. His metal rimmed spectacles were perched on the end of his long snout.

Standing before him on the threshold was an even larger animal, a giant Pyrenean bear. The new arrival wore heavy leather boots on his hind paws and stood taller than the door frame. His long muzzle was thickly crusted with dust and twigs and his huge yellow teeth gleamed in the failing light. He bent his enormous head downwards to bring his face level with that of the other:

"Sorry, sorry to be late; I got detained on the way here" the giant beast growled.

"Come in my dear Cousin. At last! You are welcome to Sanctuary Inn" replied Gilles Barbier, for that was the other's name. "Don't worry, old chap. What's 10 years between friends? We're just glad to see that you are safe – come on in and sit down. Your chair awaits. You can tell me all about it now you're here. The smaller bear grasped the outstretched paw of his giant companion. "Oh – and - err better wipe those muddy boots too. Don't want to upset the missus." The great animal, whose name was Ursian Legrand, followed Gilles inside:

"I see this place is still guarded by the Sentinels" Ursian growled.

"Oh, yes indeed but for how much longer?" replied Gilles "I have some news I believe will interest you. Our friend Athina has heard something of great importance. At last a Paladin has been found in the outside world!"

For the first time since he had left his own home, more than 10 years ago, the tired old animal felt he was finally safe... ....

CHAPTER 10

Over the next few months, Madame Giscard's judgement about her nephew proved correct: Louis-Philippe acted as though he was his father's successor in every respect, lord of all he surveyed. His arrogance was only reined in when his aunt made good her threat to visit one of his gambling cronies. At this he very reluctantly agreed that his recent debts should be deducted from his future allowance, but with very bad grace. Instead, he occupied himself in trying to arrange a marriage for his sister believing that if he could marry her off to one of his more malleable friends, he would then effectively gain control of the Eleanor Bequest himself in the very unlikely event that his secretly prepared petition to the King failed.

A further source of irritation was the title Duc de Garenne. During the Revolution titles had been abolished but the Duc had always kept his title at least locally. Napoleon had re-instated titles and he could once again legitimately be called the Duc de Garenne as a Marshal of the Grande Armée. When the monarchy had been restored, such titles were once again in the gift of the king. Many former aristocrats had petitioned successfully for their old titles. Louise-Philippe had pestered his father to make such a petition, but his father had refused on principle, preferring not to have his title sanctioned by the monarch. Although the young man would then have inherited the Napoleonic title himself, he had announced to the surprise of everyone that he would be known as simply "Monsieur" until 'the king himself confirmed the royal and rightful title of Duc de Garenne.' The sacrifice will be worthwhile, he thought to himself. 'Ah such were the trials and tribulations of being a "true aristocrat.'

In contrast, his sister was uncomfortable with her own title of "Ladyship" and would correct anyone who called her thus. She much preferred "Mademoiselle."

§§§§§§§§

The Mayor had remained uneasy about the death of Lucien Lecaron; no-one could say for certain who had fired the fatal shot. He had insisted that Captain Falaise of the local gendarmerie investigate the shooting incident. Everyone knew that accidents were quite common during the confusion of the Chasse and for that reason the Captain saw no need to carry out more than a cursory enquiry. He had been delighted with his posting to La Garenne, a corner of France where normally little happened to disturb his pursuit of pleasure and he could usually rely on the veteran Sergeant Brochard to do whatever had to be done. Thus, Falaise was free to hunt whilst avoiding involvement in any unsavoury work. The sergeant was an evil-tempered brute of a man, one glance from him could strike fear into the hearts of the bravest men. Knowing this, of course, he delighted in terrifying the populace, safe in the knowledge that no-one would dare to complain. As instructed, Sergeant Brochard arrived at the Lecaron farm to make enquiries but because he was sure it had been an accident he only asked Raoul a few disinterested questions.

"Nothing for us here lads" he called to his men but just as he turned to leave the farmyard his eyes fell upon the animal pen, and the soulful eyes of Hugo staring back at him knowingly almost as if the Hound recognised an enemy.

"Whose dog is that?" he bellowed.

"He belonged to my brother. The old Duc himself gave the Hound to Lucien and now, by right, he is mine" replied Raoul.

"A fine animal indeed, especially for these surroundings" said the sergeant eying the rather shabby shed in which Hugo was housed. "I would like to own a dog like that, in fact I think I shall own that dog. Make sure…. you will won't you…. that when you sell him – and I am sure you will soon want to sell him – you sell him to me and nobody else." The sergeant fixed Raoul with his most evil gaze and hissed: "I want him." Raoul's blood ran cold for a moment.

Lucien's parents had never really recovered from the bitter blow of his death. He had been their favourite and their hope for the farm. Barely a few months later they too died, broken-hearted and within two weeks of each other. Their funerals were sad affairs, attended only by a few of their neighbours, Raoul, Marie and André.

This now left Raoul sole heir to the farm and it took no time at all before he decided he ought to inherit Lucien's fiancée. He came calling at Marie's house with promises of how the farm could prosper if only she would return……as his wife. Marie was an uncomplicated girl and although she had truly loved Lucien, what else was there left for her now that he was gone? This was a chance for her to be mistress of what could be a profitable farm, and as she would one day inherit her own parent's house as an only child, their combined property would mean that they would be a family of some substance. After a very brief courtship, with Raoul always on his best behaviour in front of Marie's sceptical parents, they were married the following Spring. Many eyebrows were raised at the announcement and the townsfolk were more reluctant to celebrate than they had been to celebrate her earlier betrothal. Surprisingly, however, Louis Philippe decided to send not only his best wishes but a small bag of money. The guests were stunned by this unexpected generosity. Meanwhile, André felt he should attend the wedding as it was the family of his beloved friend Lucien, even though Raoul would never be the man his brother had been.

Marie wore the dress made for her wedding to Lucien, already a little small for her. She had begun to lose her figure; her rosy cheeks were fuller and her waist thicker. Raoul did not notice; she was the girl he had always wanted and more importantly to him, she was the girl Lucien would never have.

They had been married now for six months, few of which could be described as happy. Within a short time, Marie knew that she had made a terrible mistake. At first Raoul had tried to impress his new wife by working hard, tending to the fields and the livestock as his brother had done.

But that resolve was short-lived. For the second year in a row the summer had been unseasonably cool and damp and another poor harvest was expected.

He had very quickly become disillusioned that his efforts showed no signs of paying off, so he had begun once more to frequent the bar in the town square, spending the last of his meagre inheritance from his parents and leaving the unharvested crops to rot in the ground.

His wife was deeply unhappy and growing more and more concerned about how they would survive the winter. She brought up the subject frequently but whenever she did so, Raoul would reply that the grand folk up at the Château had provided food the previous winter and would therefore do the same this year. Marie questioned this for several reasons. The assistance given the previous year had been given in memory of the old Duc but now nobody seemed to know who was in charge. Many assumed that young Louis-Philippe would take over the reins but there were no signs of that happening. Raoul then tried to silence Marie by tell her that he had an ‘understanding’, always unspecified, that the young Duc would help them. She assumed that this was just bravado; she had seen the look of pure terror on her husband’s face when the nobleman had caught his eye at the funeral.

The women who now worked at the Château whispered that in fact it was the old Duc's sister who was really in charge. François Dupoire at the Town Hall told anyone who would listen (and everyone did) that the young Mlle. Catherine was a frequent visitor to M. Lafitte-Dupont but he, François, was sworn to secrecy about their meetings, which of course meant that he had no idea what was being discussed.

Like everyone in La Garenne, Marie followed all the gossip and like everyone else, she feared what would happen if Louis-Philippe did take control. However, rumours would not put food on the table and Marie was anxious that they should stand on their own two feet. She therefore focused on the one single thing that she believed could rescue them from their current plight, Raoul's most prized possession: Hugo Hound.

CHAPTER II

It was an evening in early October when the trees were already shedding their leaves and a cold wind swept through the ill-kempt farmyard. Raoul returned from yet another visit to the local inn only to be confronted by Marie, arms folded tightly, standing at the top of the rickety wooden steps of the farmhouse. Framed by the light of a single lantern she stood watching Raoul pick his way through the mud and the broken farm equipment. "I've got the solution to all our problems" she called to him: "Sell that Hound! There are plenty of folks who'll pay good money for him if he's as good as you say he is. Good hunting Hounds change hands for more money than we need for food all winter long."

Even though it was dusk Marie could see Raoul's face change: he looked sullen and angry. She knew that it was only Hugo's hunting prowess that made her husband acceptable to the other members of the chasse. His befuddled brain tried to grasp what his wife was proposing. "So where would I be eh? No special Hound, no hunting, no friends – and if I'm not part of the chasse what then? No share of the pot, no meat."

Marie shook her head: "You don't understand, you drunken fool! We would be able to buy meat at the market if we sell that Hound. Anyway, he may be special, but you brought home nothing at all last week." Raoul was silent for a moment before muttering: "Oh a fine time to bring it up, exactly one year to the day since my dear brother died and you're suggesting I sell his beloved Hugo." Marie wasn't fooled by this emotional outburst; she knew exactly what Raoul really thought about his late brother. For now, she held her tongue and went indoors -followed by her stumbling husband.

****

Hugo Hound was indeed a very special animal, much more than Raoul and Marie knew. Long ago he had discovered something quite amazing about himself: even when still only a puppy he was able assume the appearance of different breeds of dogs.

He found he could stand on his hind legs if he really concentrated but kept this talent to himself. His performances kept his kennel companions amused and amazed – his 'impersonations' were always popular, especially his version of a standoffish poodle.

Hugo always tried to take on the characteristics of the dogs he copied and so his poodle would step daintily over the rubble and mud of the pen tossing its ears haughtily. The special favourite of the pack was his marvellous mimicry of the old bloodhound Major who had shared his kennels at the Château. Hugo found that he could 'think' himself into the shape of the overweight, slobbery dog with mournful eyes and hang-dog expression. The other dogs would yip with pleasure to hear him moan in a gruff, depressed old voice 'I am soooo tireed…'

Such a dramatic change took the young Hound a little longer than his other, less complex transformations but frankly he rather enjoyed the low growl of approval from the other dogs in the pack that would always result. He had worked out for himself that all he had to do was to think very hard about what dog he wanted to become, and he could then assume that form. So far, he had never tried to be anything other than another dog although occasionally, when no-one was around he had experimented with walking on his hind legs. Only he realised that not only could he change his shape, but he could also think like his 'alter ego' at the same time as thinking like himself. As a bloodhound, he thought bloodhound thoughts – as well as his own. He did not allow this mystery to concern him too deeply; he kept this detail himself.

He often had very troubling dreams, dreams that made him howl and moan in his sleep much to the distress of the other dogs. His special friend was Mimi, a small white terrier with one black ear and inquisitive chocolate brown eyes. She was especially disturbed by his distress.

Hugo never revealed to the other dogs the details of his dreams but often he awoke conscious that he had been in some other place… somewhere dark and where eerie figures haunted the air around him. One particular memory stayed with him: in his dreams a lady would visit him.

She often came when he was very hungry. She had a pale, beautiful, unlined face which belied her silver white hair, which she wore long and straight. She confused the dog for she appeared clothed in a pale light with no real form. When she visited him she always brought him an extraordinary feeling of comfort and safety which took away his gnawing hunger. Sometimes he couldn't really see her, but he could sense her presence and she spoke to him in a soothing voice, patting his ears and reassuring him. As to what all this meant he had no idea, so he kept it all to himself. When he did let himself think about it, the thick fur at his neck prickled but not with fear…with anticipation.

That evening, he had been performing a very amusing greyhound routine after which, gradually, one by one, the members of the pack curled up in the corners of the pen and slept. Hugo eventually joined them although sleeping wasn't always easy for him; sometimes his vivid dreams also involved boars, bears, humans dressed in strange costumes, noises, fighting and... freedom.

Early next morning, with Raoul still feeling the effects of the previous night, the men of the chasse arrived and Raoul opened the pen, so his dogs could run free and mingle with the other hunting Hounds. One of the other hunters, Marcel spoke to Raoul:

"I hope your dog is on form today; I've heard there's a pack of wild boar been seen in the woods. If we can only shoot one, it will make a feast." M. Lafitte-Dupont had informed them that they had been given permission that day to hunt in the forests of the Château, but even better news was that the young Duc would not be accompanying them.

The hunters came to the densest part of the woods trying to stay downwind of where they thought the boars might be. The plan was to station some of men around the edges of the woodland with their primitive firearms and staves. The others would take the pack deeper into the woods, and the Hounds, led by Hugo, would find the prey followed by the terriers which would stampede the boars towards the waiting armed farmers.

Most of the prey would escape for no-one would stand and face a charging boar but if they could just shoot one…or two…

The plan was working; Hugo had soon picked up the scent. He got very excited, circling and whining whilst the other Hounds sniffed the ground excitedly, often confusing the scents in their enthusiasm. He sniffed the air and detected exactly where the boars were hidden but he advanced cautiously because a fully-grown boar could easily kill even a large Hound with the force of his charge. Hugo came into a clearing and stopped dead. A group of boars stood waiting anxiously, some of them very young. Clearly the females were trying to protect their young whilst the much larger males were arranged in a rough circle around them. Unable to stop himself, the Hound barked very loudly and hoped that the boars would decide to charge in the opposite direction. He was lucky - they decided on flight led by an enormous, snorting brute, his snout scarred from many fights and one of his huge tusks broken off at the tip. The whole troupe ran into the forest on the other side of the clearing and four of the boars crashed through the dense brush directly into Raoul's path. Although not the best of shots, Raoul managed to fire his gun into the group as they crashed past him. He knew that he had managed to injure the leader but had failed to stop the beast. The barking terriers followed, dodging and running through the undergrowth in pursuit of the terrified animals. The terriers could only sustain this frantic pace for short periods and as the noise of the fleeing boars could be heard in the distance, gradually the little dogs were forced to give up, panting and barking whilst they waited for their masters to catch up.

Always unpredictable, the boars had veered off in the opposite direction to the waiting hunters on the edge of the forest and the men knew they had lost their chance. "What should we do?" shouted one of the men. "They must be miles away by now." "But Raoul shot one, I know he did, so it may be slower than the rest." "Get Hugo. Send that Hound in after him" came the cries of the disappointed and angry men.

By this time, the rest of the pack had caught up; the excitable terriers ran in circles, barking in frustration whilst the Hounds tried once again to pick up the scent for the little dogs to follow.

"Find him, Hugo boy, go on" said Raoul and the other hunters shouted encouragement to the dog, urging him to do what he could do best. Off he went, sniffing the air for a moment then set off at a trot. He sensed that the wounded boar was close by, concealed by a coppice of trees on the other side of a small ridge.

The graceful Hound continued at a steady pace, trying to avoid making too much noise in the undergrowth. He knew that the other dogs were behind him; he could hear them crashing through the leaves and branches. Hugo was careful and liked to get as close as possible to his prey before giving his special cry to summon the terriers. He crept stealthily beyond the coppice and saw the wounded boar standing motionless in a shallow pool. Clearly, he had been hoping to disguise the scent of the blood from his wound in the water. The Hound approached the wounded animal who was making quiet snuffling, grunting noises to himself as he shuffled his feet in the muddy water. The distracted boar had failed to detect the Hound's advance and now stood holding up his back leg, the injury high on the animal's thigh. When the boar became aware of the Hound's presence he snarled and lowered his head as if to charge but this was only bravado. Hugo saw that it was the leader, distinguishable by his broken tusk. He also knew that the boar was doomed if the hunters caught up.

This was the moment when Hugo should have howled to bring the other dogs running. He saw in his mind's eye how the terriers would come charging in prepared to take on the wounded boar. Some of the terriers might be injured for it would be a bloody conflict, some might even be killed but they all knew what they were expected to do. It crossed his mind at that moment that his friend Mimi might be one of those victims. She was probably his only real friend.

All these thoughts made the Hound hesitate too long – the wounded animal snorted threateningly, as if preparing for a last desperate charge. Boars are naturally aggressive and in his pain this one would attack although he knew it was hopeless.

Undoubtedly, he was still a force to be reckoned with. The Hound knew he could be in serious trouble. Even if he howled now the few vital minutes it would take for the hunters or the terriers to come to his aid might be too long.

In that split-second Hugo had a flash of inspiration. He knew what he had to do – he could become a boar. If he could be another dog, he could be a boar too. No sooner had the thought come to him than his imagination took over and his appearance began to alter, the pressure of the moment seeming to speed the process. In just a few moments he was a boar, facing his former adversary. The old, injured leader stopped dead – was his injury playing tricks on his mind? He had heard the hunters in the forest coming for him, he had seen the famous Hound staring at him – Hugo's reputation had spread throughout the animal kingdom – and now a young handsome boar stood facing him in the clearing.

"What are you doing here? I don't know you. I told everyone to run and keep running. I knew I wouldn't make it, but I could hold off the hunters.... Go now. Save yourself." Hugo was stunned to realise that his prey was trying to help him; that he cared about his family enough to sacrifice himself for them and would even sacrifice himself for an animal he did not recognise but who was one of his kind.

"No" replied the Hound "I'm young and fit and I have a few tricks that they don't know about." He was aware that whilst he was Hugo the hunter, he was thinking like a boar, not a Hound, and moreover he was conscious that he had not only understood but answered the old warrior. "You...go that way, down into the forest again. They'll follow me, I'll bet."

The wounded beast hesitated a moment and then lowered his scarred snout, as if in a bow: "I am in your debt. If you do manage to get away, come and find me. I thank you once again.... Good luck."

Hugo watched his former quarry thread his way into the dense woodland limping badly. At the last minute, he felt his mind form the question 'Where will you be?' and to his surprise he seemed to hear in his mind the faint reply:

"Try to find Sanctuary."

"What, what is Sanctuary?" said Hugo, this time aloud.

"When you find it, you'll know. Trust me" ... came the faint response from beyond the trees.

The Hound now sensed that the terriers and the other dogs were very close. He remained in the guise of the young boar and as the pack grew closer, barking and anxious, he led them away beyond the ridge in the opposite direction to their original prey, as he had promised. When he felt he was far enough ahead of the yapping, excited pack he ran into a dense thicket of holly bushes which he knew would deter the dogs at least for a moment.

Hastily he changed his shape back and was once again Hugo, the Hound. He felt drained and very much aware of how much effort this latest transformation had been. Only a minute or two later, the pack arrived barking and sniffing agitatedly at the bushes where the Hound waited. They surrounded the holly bushes, and he assumed a look of confused agitation. "I was so certain he came up here." "Yes", said Mimi "I saw him too, just back there, I am sure I did. Why didn't you howl for us, Hugo?"

He had to think fast; he didn't want even his best friend to discover what he had done. "I don't understand it; he must have concealed his scent in the pool and gone into hiding. There were so many in there I got confused." He hated admitting he had failed, even though of course he hadn't. "I only picked up his scent when he made a break for it."

"Didn't see you run up there" said another Hound with what Hugo could have sworn was a slight smirk. "Oh, I went up on the other side of the hill, hoping to head him off. Raoul isn't going to be very happy."

CHAPTER 12

Taking advantage of his saviour's help, the wounded boar, who went by the name of Sangres Blacksnout, ran into the deepest darkest part of the forest as soon as Hugo had run the other way. His injury would heal if he was careful; the blood had almost stopped flowing but he was slow. He knew he had to rest before going on. The other boars would be safe as the hunters would follow no further now the light was fading. However, he was very much aware that he would never see his family again. They would keep running and assume he was dead, and this made him very sad. He was old now and understood that he would have been challenged more and more for his position in the troupe. A younger boar would now take over leadership so even if he did find them all again he knew he would be an outcast because his injury would make him slow.

After resting for the night, his leg, although very stiff, was feeling a little better. The shot had hit him in the hind leg but luckily the musket ball had passed straight through, leaving a clean wound. He would never again be the powerful adversary he had once been. The time had come, he decided – he must search for this mysterious Sanctuary. His father, the grizzled former leader had told him tales of this strange place many years ago. It had sounded like one of the many legends told when boars came together, a story of long ago and far away but Papa insisted that the tales were true; it was a place where all animals could never be tormented or hunted and lived together harmoniously. When he had asked where it was, the only answer had been a shrug:

"It is far to the south and when you need it, you will find it, my son." When Sangres had been injured his thoughts drifted back to his father's words and a powerful memory of the old legend.

Sangres looked around the dark forest and observed his old haunts for the last time; he would wait for nightfall and set off by the light of the Pole star. Instinct told him that if he walked in the opposite direction to this bright star, he would be going south.

In the dark he set off, limping awkwardly. He had been travelling for about an hour when he became aware that he was not alone. He found a small stream and waded along its shallow rocky bed in case his scent was attracting a bigger predator, very conscious that he was being followed. Surely it couldn't be those wretched pack dogs? He had gone over what had happened and could still make no sense of it at all. He was certain that he had seen the Hound watching him, certain too that he recognised it as Hugo the great hunter. Then all at once there had been a young boar watching him, an animal he didn't know but who had been prepared to aid his escape. Now he was being followed.......

He heard the wild flapping of wings breaking the silence of the night. Looking up into the trees, he saw a pure white owl perch on an overhanging branch. The owl's head was turned away from him, as though sleeping but the snowy head suddenly swivelled towards him, huge eyes glaring:

"Looking for something, are we? Sanctuary perhaps?" the bird asked in a slightly mocking tone.

Stunned by this talking owl and by the fact that the bird seemed to know his destination, Sangres stuttered: "Yes, I am – does it truly exist?" He forgot that he was answering a bird.

"Of course it does. Did you never listen to your father?" the owl replied in a sharp voice, laden with impatience.

"Well yes, but I thought it was just, you know an old fable."

"Not all old fables are untrue and when you reach Sanctuary you will discover the truth" replied the bird imperiously.

"How will I find it, err Mr. Owl, sir?" Sangres felt humbled by this bird, so much wiser than him if not stronger.

"I am Madame Athina, so it's Mistress Owl – For goodness' sake, old man. Your father told you Sanctuary will find you when you need it. Go on in the direction you are following but remember to look out for the shells – It will take several days, perhaps more, depending on how quickly your wound heals. You will know when you arrive."

'Old man'? Sangres was rather put out by what this bird had called him. He had been a patriarch and father of many sons, and she called him old man? Sadly, he realised that to her he probably was just another old boar. She was obviously someone special. She knew the legend of Sanctuary, she knew what his father had told him and strangest of all they could communicate with one another.

Whilst Sangres considered these events, the owl turned her snowy head to one side as if to dismiss him, flapped her wings once and was gone into the night. The old boar was finding his life turning upside down. He wasn't afraid exactly, more puzzled: these shells for example? Now what on earth was a 'shell' and why so important?

Living on foraged nuts (and truffles when he could find them), Sangres travelled by night and rested during the daylight just in case he encountered more hunters in the forests. The only other living things he saw on his travels, however, were great birds of prey always flying high above the trees. Of course, he was aware of the abundance of small woodland creatures going about their snuffling and shuffling business in the undergrowth. He was perhaps less aware that his arrival sounded an alarm throughout that same small animal kingdom and they were all hiding….and watching….as he passed, grunting on his way. He wondered whether the strange owl was still watching him from a distance.

He was not lonely for boars are self-reliant animals, but he sometimes missed the companionship of others of his kind.

In his travels the boar noticed that sometimes in a clearing or on the edge of woodland there lay a small pile of what he believed were those shells. He remembered he had been instructed to look out for them but wasn't exactly sure why.

Sangres of course had no knowledge of the sea and its creatures; he had lived his life in the dense ancient forests of inland France, but he sensed that these 'shells' had once been home to a creature of some sort. He did not trouble himself with thinking about where they came from, he left them alone. However, they did give him a strange comfort and make him feel safer - he must be on the right path.

He had already been travelling for several nights when near dawn he found himself approaching a wide, fast flowing river – one known to humankind as the Dordogne. He was tired from his night's exertions and decided that now was the time to rest up for the day, so he found a patch of dense undergrowth in which to conceal himself affording a good view of his surroundings. Before dozing off, he took a good look around to familiarise himself with the river which he must cross once darkness fell. The very first thing he saw horrified him. Floating down the fast-flowing river were huge branches, even tree trunks, carried along by the swift current. Some were almost wholly submerged and bobbed out of the water, their twigs and small branches showing briefly. This would make them even more dangerous. He knew if he collided with one of these he would be seriously injured if not worse. He would be forced to swim across the river in daylight which was against all his instincts. Years of keeping his troupe safe had taught him that travelling by night was safest, by day you were at risk from humankind, as he knew to his cost. There was nothing to be done however because the river would be far too dangerous to cross in the dark. He wondered if his injured leg would be strong enough to combat the fierceness of the current.

He saw that the other bank of the river was churned and muddy, quite steep and devoid of vegetation for cover. At the top of the bank the terrain looked more promising. There was a wide field of deep golden corn next to a newly ploughed field.

Beyond these fields lay what looked like a dense forest. The darkness of that forest beckoned to him; safety. 'Right' he thought, 'a bit of a rest and then I am going to make a dash for it'. As he dozed, however, he was interrupted by a sound that sent shivers down his knobby spine. Humankind voices! He tried to make himself as inconspicuous as possible down in the undergrowth and lay perfectly still.

The faint voices were coming from somewhere down near the riverbank and he risked peeking out from his hiding place. As a distant bell tolled he observed a couple of men who appeared to be floating on the river close to the bank on a kind of wooden contraption. He could see other men coming now to join them on this strange wooden platform which then crossed the choppy current to the far side of the river. Over the next few hours he watched amazed as this happened several times; even humans on horses or seated on carts drawn by oxen mounted the platform and crossed relatively easily. Once even a large conveyance drawn by four white horses crossed – Sangres was dumbstruck. What was going on? He would never understand humankind; why did they all need to cross this mighty river, what was on the other side which was so desirable?

He noticed too that the river crossing was used throughout the day and so his risk of being seen was much greater. He thought his best chance lay in the early morning, just after sunrise. Having made his mind up, Sangres ensured he could not be seen and settled down to doze, his empty boar stomach grumbling in disappointment. In the fading light he made out a pair of huge eagles, circling then swooping down almost as if they were taking a closer look at the place where he was hidden. He remained motionless and they rose high into the sky and flew into the setting sun. Sangres heard the faint sounds of human voices receding in the distance. He risked a look and saw that the wooden platform was now tied to a post on his side of the river. With nothing to keep his hunger at bay, at last he fell into a deep sleep.

At the first signs of dawn on the horizon the boar awoke to the sound of an owl hooting nearby. He cleared his rheumy eyes and peered out to see the snowy owl once more, standing on the ground in front of his hiding place. Athina had come back.

"If you're going to cross that river unobserved, you'd better start now. Don't worry about the trees, I'll warn you if any get too close, but hurry up, come on. I do so hate the sunlight."

Sangres rose and cautiously trotted towards the riverbank, tentatively placing one foot into the cold water but watching all the time for approaching logs or branches. "Oh, for heaven's sake, get a move on" squawked the owl. "I always thought boars were supposed to be fearless. I've seen braver dormice." Goaded by this insult, Sangres struck out into the river and true to her word, the owl warned him of any danger as his still powerful body pushed on through the violent currents. Soon he was on the other bank, shaking his thick fur to dry himself. "Now, off you go. You'll be safe from here to the forest" and before he could ask any questions, the owl flew off.

By the time Sangres heard the nearby church bell tolling six he had already made his way through the corn field and was halfway across the adjoining ploughed field, struggling to hoist himself up and over the deep furrows to reach the welcome cover of the trees. He caught sight of a pair of eagles each perched high in the two pine trees which flanked what appeared to be an overgrown path into the darkness. Sangres did wonder briefly if they were somehow connected to Madame Athina but this thought was put aside when he realised this forest would be a test of his courage – the gloomy darkness was not in the least welcoming and even with his sharp eyesight, he was finding difficulty in seeing his way. The rising sun still lay low in the sky and the thick canopy of the forest seemed to suck up what light there was. Sangres was feeling exhausted by his efforts so he decided, against his instincts, to take a rest until the sun rose high enough to see clearly. Pleased by his decisiveness, he once again concealed himself in some undergrowth and dozed off, falling this time into an uneasy, dream-troubled sleep.

As the sun rose higher, dusty shards of sunlight penetrated the trees around him. He caught sight again of those eagles, sitting on a high branch, watching him intently. Yes, he was being followed – hopefully by friends….

Although the sun must now be high above him in the sky, it was barely visible in this gloomy place. The thick trunks of the trees thinned out gradually, leaving him standing in a clearing with no cover, just a few piled rocks; there was little light from the sun yet this clearing 'shimmered' before him, as though fog and sun had combined to create a veil. Were his eyes playing tricks on him? Perhaps his wound had been worse than he feared, and he was becoming delirious. Shapes were forming before him and he sensed rather than saw the figures moving with no sound, dressed from head to toe in loose dark robes which hid their form and their faces. He was terrified although the shapes bore no weapons. They seemed to take no notice of him although they must have seen him. They continued instead to drift around the clearing, sometimes close to him. He could hear his own heart beating in his chest like thunder. Even wild boars can be afraid, he thought to himself, surprised as his hackles rose.

As he stood spellbound, a filmy figure would now and then detach itself from the group and come towards him only to disappear like a giant floating bubble, away into the thick air. The wounded boar knew that he was in the presence of something he could neither understand nor attack. Very slowly he moved through the clearing as if compelled by an unseen force. Glancing upwards he saw the eagles far above, watching., One of the birds made what could only be described as a bow with its beautiful wings and flew upwards and away into the distance. "I'm really on my own now" thought Sangres, "or at least I would be if I wasn't surrounded by these…. things."

Despite his misgivings, Sangres felt he must move on, even passing sometimes through the shifting shapes. Slowly he became aware that the shapes were in fact forming a sort of strange guard of honour on either side of him. He was aware of great warmth on his body which could only be emanating from them.

He allowed them to guide him, hoping that if he did so he might escape unscathed but too late he saw that at the end of the path was a towering cliff face. He was trapped! It had all been an elaborate ambush. He could backtrack but that meant re-crossing the eerie clearing; he could run left or right but he had no idea how far along the cliff face extended and anyway his damaged leg, although mending, was not in any condition to make a run for it. This was the end then; he must die here, trapped and alone. How very sad, he thought, and sat down heavily on his rump, ready for what must come next.

SANCTUARY –ARRIVALS

Well, well! Sangres Blacksnout is it? We expected you yesterday. Come with me and make yourself comfortable. We can make sure your wound is healing and give you some decent food and spring water."

The voice gave the boar such a fright that he leapt up, staggering a little on his painful leg but what he saw made him sit right back down again. If he could have rubbed his tired old eyes he would have. There before him stood a very large bear, taller than any of the human hunters from whom he had fled. This apparition wore oversized humankind clothes…and spectacles!

"Come on old chap. Oh, and don't worry about our friends here – they want to protect you." The huge beast waved towards the dark forest where vague glimmers of light still showed.

Slowly Sangres approached this giant beast peering up into its huge face. He had never encountered bear but was aware of such animals. However, he had certainly never seen anything this size - there would be no question of arguing with him. The old boar registered somewhere in the back of his struggling mind that apparently not only could he now speak "owl" but other tongues too!

The great bear led Sangres to the towering cliff face which to the boar had seemed an impenetrable barrier. Along the bottom edge of the cliff face were many outcrops and ledges. Underneath one of these the beast pushed at a large and ancient metal-studded door which he was certain had not been there just a moment before. Bemused, the old boar followed his host inside – everything was so surreal that the interior was, at this point, no more than mildly surprising.

"Brother, welcome to Sanctuary" growled the bear "I am called Gilles Barbier. Sit down, eat and tell me your story."

CHAPTER 13

Raoul arrived home late on Sunday night. After the disaster of the hunt he had gone straight to the bar; it had been a bad day for him and he needed to drown his sorrows before he received a tongue lashing from Marie and if he was lucky, a poor supper. He left his dogs outside, hungry and cold, to wait for him. The other hunters tried to commiserate but he was so surly and morose that they soon left him to drink by himself. By the time he reached home, Marie had worked herself up into a fury:

"Well? How are we going to eat this week?" she screamed.

Raoul raised his fist sharply to his wife, but she stood before him with her hands on her hips, daring him to strike her. She did not fear her husband; she despised him: "For heaven's sake sell that useless Hound Hugo. You know how the other men value him even though he never seems to bring us any luck. We are going to starve come winter." Marie lowered her voice, turning slightly away from Raoul: "Sell him or I shall tell what I know about your brother's death."

"And what exactly is that, my dear wife?" he sneered, ale lending him courage. Marie laughed unpleasantly. "Did you know that you talk in your sleep?" With this retort, she turned away, looking back once to add "Don't think I wouldn't."

Raoul watched his angry wife, with her flushed face and her grim expression. How she had changed since their marriage. The sweet-faced, smiling girl who had been betrothed to Lucien had disappeared; Marie's face had grown bloated and grey with cold and hunger and her once carefully brushed hair hung in greasy tendrils from beneath her grubby cap. Why had he married her anyway? She reminded him of his dead brother every day – and that was someone he would prefer to forget.

The dogs could hear the raised voices. They had not been fed and there was a general acceptance that they weren't going to be. Hugo, whose hearing was sharper than that of the other dogs, heard exactly what had passed between Raoul and Marie. He knew that Raoul was a cruel and unpleasant man and the Hound also knew upon whom his spite would fall – the dogs. They had all heard many arguments but the talk about his old master was something new. Hugo had loved his old master; every day they had gone for a long walk and Lucien had chatted to the Hound as though they were old friends. When they had both visited the Duc, the Hound had been praised and fed delicacies and generally made to feel very special. The Hound missed Lucien badly. He was aware now of what 'death' meant, and he knew that the humans he had loved most had disappeared from his dog life forever and that this was the life he must live until he too died. It was not a happy thought.

This realisation was a tipping point for Hugo; he knew in that moment that he must escape from Raoul soon and his mind was still pondering this when he eventually managed to fall into an exhausted sleep despite his empty belly. His strange dreams returned once again to haunt him but this time they seemed to make a little more sense – as if there was some important purpose to them. He woke very early, before sunrise, and began to plan his escape.

First things first; he needed to be able to open the gate of the pen. He had seen Raoul loosen the latch. Hugo had only his huge paws – to escape he would need a 'hand'. He went to the rear of the pen where it was darkest and thought very hard about being a human. It wasn't nearly as easy as thinking about becoming a different dog, or even a boar. Thinking back, he realised he had turned into a boar because he had been afraid. So, he needed a similarly intense emotion to make any really big changes. He thought about what Marie had said 'I'll tell the truth about your brother' and Hugo's blood ran cold. He began to understand at that moment just what it was like to feel human with all the anger, fear and worries they had. This powerful wave of emotion acted upon him and slowly he felt changes begin; he was taking on a human shape, a two-legs. The slow transformation left him standing upright, but still covered in his silky fur.

This did not concern him however as the only thing he needed was a working hand. He went towards the enclosure's latched door and put his adapted 'hand' through one of the many gaps in the planking. He made contact with the metal fastening and slowly lifted it and…the gate swung open with a noisy creak. He was free. Hugo was on the point of making his escape across the filthy farmyard when he looked back and saw the other sleeping dogs, amongst them his friend Mimi.

"If I leave her behind" he thought "she will be all alone in the pack and our master will make those dogs left behind suffer for my disappearance." He had always felt like Mimi's elder brother; she must be given the chance to escape with him. I need to make a proper plan, he thought as he closed the latch carefully and returned to the darkness at the back of the pen. With a great effort, he set his mind once more to dog thoughts and soon noticed his tail wagging again, his paws stretching painfully and his long claws extending. Exhausted, he put his head on his paws and slept deeply and, for once dreamlessly.

"Raaouul" said Marie, stretching out his name as she had once done when being affectionate, "I was thinking while you were asleep." Raoul was still barely awake and listened with half an ear in the darkness. "All the other men of the chasse are interested in Hugo. The Duc's son – and that sergeant from the gendarmerie - asked about him. So…stands to reason that there must be lots of other people who want him too. Advertise him for auction, Raoul.

Have that idiot at the Mayor's Office make a notice. He'll help you if only to find out what you are up to. If enough people are interested, then we can name our own price. Ha let that sergeant and *his Lordship* bid between them. Please, for me. Go and see François as soon as he opens up the office."

"As a matter of fact, after Hugo's pathetic performance yesterday that is exactly what I had decided to do" mumbled Raoul. Marie abandoned her wheedling tone immediately:

"Well do it then! Get down to the town hall" she hissed as they struggled into their grubby clothing. "Otherwise, I won't warn you again.... everyone will know about Lucien." Since Marie had shouted this at Raoul's retreating back, all the dogs heard it too.

When Marie finally opened the door of the pen and threw in a handful of meagre leftovers for the pack to scrabble over, Hugo slept on. Eventually one very hungry Hound struggled to wakefulness and immediately concentrated on his plan, realising that the effort required to 'be human' had exhausted him more than he had expected. That was something he would have to consider in his plan. Mimi had saved him a scrap of food and told him what she had heard whilst he had been sleeping. She asked anxiously:

"What does she mean? What auction? Err, actually what is an auction?"

"Don't worry" growled Hugo "I have a plan for us."

"Oh, a plan! What plan?" she yapped excitedly, but he would not be drawn.

"Well more of an idea of a plan" he muttered "but I think I know where we can go to be safe for ever.... well I say I *know* but I'm not sure where it actually is...but we will be safe. Trust me." The small terrier looked at Hugo, confused. She knew instinctively that her friend was not like other dogs, he was more than just her special friend, he was a very special Hound. She lay down again to consider what he had said: 'Trust me' -well she did of course but where could they hide even supposing they could escape? Later that morning she noticed that he was now leaning against the broken planking of the hut, with one Hound ear propped up against the wood and seemed to be listening very intently to the sounds of a chirping bird nearby.

"Don't tell me that you've started listening to the birds, Hugo."

"Well actually she came to talk to me. She just told me that the master has put up a notice announcing an auction – and the notice is to be posted in all the villages locally. I am to be sold to the highest bidder."

"Oh nooooo" howled Mimi, disturbing the other dogs.

"The bird also says she heard that tomorrow lots of the local landowners will be coming to look at me – although the price the master is expecting is very high. I am apparently much sought after." Hugo said this with a certain amount of dog pride although the news itself was not good. Mimi sat and thought for a moment: she was very puzzled by Hugo's behaviour.

Usually the birds strenuously ignored them, never helped them in the chasse and certainly never *chatted.* This was something entirely new and she wondered why her friend didn't think it odd too.

"Don't you think it's rather strange that out of the blue the birds have decided to speak to you?"

"Well, it was just one bird, and it's the first time ever – but very useful especially if they can let us know what is happening, eh?" He had decided for now not to divulge everything the bird had told him. Hugo smiled a dog smile at his friend's perplexed expression. "Don't worry about it now" he comforted her. His little friend was not a deep thinker, and she was happy to let him do all the worrying.

"Listen" he whispered, "This is what I am going to try to do but it has to be tonight.

****

François, the Mayor's clerk, general factotum and town busybody, had prepared a notice and arranged to pass on copies to the surrounding towns and villages. Raoul was expecting high bids for his Hound, and it had to be paid in gold. However, such was Hugo's fame as a magnificent hunting Hound, although not for Raoul, that his greedy master felt certain that someone would pay this huge sum. In fact, he was hoping to provoke a bidding war between the two chief protagonists. Such was Raoul's misjudgment of these two men!

Marie, for once, seemed happy and sang some old folk tune whilst she prepared his frugal lunch and Raoul whistled as he attempted to clear some debris in the yard, no more scrimping and struggling and once he was a rich man, he thought, he would be welcome at the chasse, even without Hugo. For once, he fed the dogs on more than scraps that night. 'Got to have him looking his best tomorrow' Raoul thought to himself. All the other dogs tucked in heartily to their unexpected bounty and having licked all the bowls clean, they quickly fell asleep. Hugo and Mimi however remained alert and watchful, waiting for Raoul and Marie to extinguish the lantern in the house. After the glow of the lamp disappeared, the dogs waited a while longer to ensure that the master and mistress were finally asleep.

The Hound then began his preparations by concentrating very hard on his master's anger and his mistress's discontent and slowly, very slowly his shape altered. The other little dog began to whine softly in fear as the transformation took place but quickly her distress turned to giggles as the change became almost complete.

"What's so funny?" whispered Hugo.

"I've never seen such a very hairy humankind" she replied, "you are still wearing your dog fur – hee *and your collar*."

"It's alright" said Hugo "I don't plan on ever doing this again – I hope – it does feel very strange – and actually quite itchy."

He crept quietly towards the door, put his newly formed ‘hand’ with its long dirty nails through the gap he had found and freed the latch once again. The door opened quietly this time and he held it open just enough to allow them both to escape, then Mimi said “No, don’t close it again; when the others wake up and find out the gate is open they will run away. Raoul will panic even more if all the dogs are missing and won’t know who to search for first.” She giggled happily at this thought.

“Inspired” whispered Hugo. “I was worried what would happen to our friends when Raoul found we had escaped; this way he will search for all the dogs and blame them all but none in particular”.

Hastily, they made their way across the muddy farmyard and off into the closest group of trees where he could transform himself back into a Hound undisturbed - for this was both exhausting and unpredictable. When his wet black nose and long wagging tail were back in place the two dogs set off together by moonlight along the road in the direction of the town, which lay to the south of the farm.

“Is this the right way?” asked Mimi “and if it is, where is it the way to?”

“Well, all I know is we must keep going south. We will be met, according to the bird.”

“Oh right.” Hugo had not previously shared this tidbit of information and it threw up so many questions for Mimi that she abandoned conversation and remained silent. In the square both dogs crept along, cautiously staying in the shadows. The other dogs in the town were sure to start barking if they sensed Hugo nearby. Nevertheless, he could not resist a quick peep at ‘his’ poster pasted on the notice board in the town square, clearly visible in the moonlight.

The Hound gazed at the poster, not understanding the words but somehow knowing that it was about him, Hugo of Lecaron Farm. Mimi stood waiting patiently for a moment then nudged him: "Come on, let's get going before we are spotted." They looked back one more time – both dogs knew they might never see their hometown again.

CHAPTER 14

At the first half-hearted sounds of the farmyard cockerel, the other dogs in the kennel at the Lecaron farm struggled out of their food-fueled sleep. They immediately realised that something was different – the gate was open. For them, this was too good an opportunity to miss - they raced out one by one through the open gate. Off they ran, some towards the small chicken coop and others into the fields, barking and yapping with delight. This was the happiest day of their lives and they gave no thought to the reason for the open door, nor to the absence of their companions.

“Wake up, wake up you idiot” screeched Marie “Can’t you hear? Those dogs are barking fit to wake the dead.... I think they are loose!”

“They can’t be” groaned Raoul, whose head was pounding after another night at the local bar. “I’m certain I latched the pen last night, I know I did.”

“Of course you bolted the door...with great holes in the sides of the pen! Just perfect for keeping a dog worth a fortune in gold. You are a total fool!”

Raoul rose hastily (and shakily) and lit the lantern in the gloomy cottage. Putting on his old boots and a shabby and worn cloak over his nightshirt he went out into the farmyard. Dogs were running everywhere. He saw that the door to the pen was now wide open and as the sun began its lethargic journey over the horizon he began rounding up his pack. Two of the smaller terriers had got into the chick coop – feathers were flying everywhere. The little dogs, each with a brown patch jauntily placed above one eye, looked chastened as they waddled back into their pen. It had been fun while it lasted.

It took Raoul until the sun was high in the sky to get all the dogs out of the surrounding fields or investigating various sniffing spots and back into their pen …all except two. He wasn't too concerned about losing Mimi; he considered her a poor hunter and rather fragile. If he never found her it was one less dog-mouth to fill but Hugo… Raoul was devastated. All his hopes lay with the Hound but as he stood, scratching his head worse was to come.

Just as he locked up the last dogs, literally bolting the 'stable door'…and belatedly piling some old planks against the wooden sides of the pen, a carriage drew to a halt near to the rickety wooden steps of the farmhouse. The large wheels had churned the thick mud which covered the farmyard. Raoul's already despondent mood deepened when he saw the crest on the door. The coachman leapt down from the box narrowly avoiding a pile of rotting manure and now, treading carefully, he opened the coach door. To Raoul's horror, out stepped Louis-Philippe. The young fop hesitated at the bottom step searching for a place to set down his shiny leather boot. Raoul glanced down – he knew those boots had cost more than he would earn in his lifetime. The door on the other side of the coach also opened and down stepped André Lacoste, his late brother's comrade. Lacoste was less fastidious than his master and strode around the horses to stand beside Louis-Philippe who waited impatiently for his man to announce their business. Raoul became conscious suddenly that he wore only a grubby flannel nightshirt, mud-caked old boots and his only cloak. Hastily he gathered the patched garment around him as André addressed him:

"M. Lecaron, the Duc's son has asked me to express his great disappointment in finding that you have advertised Hugo Hound for auction. He is sure you are aware that this dog was *loaned* to your late brother, *on the understanding* that the animal remained the property of the House of Garenne. Until now, the House of Garenne has permitted you to keep him." André looked uncomfortable whilst making this speech knowing the real truth of the matter. However, his master's frowning face spoke volumes. Raoul remained silent, quite literally dumbstruck with fear.

By this time, Marie had heard the commotion in the yard and had stepped out of the house. She stood twisting her apron nervously but listening intently to what was being said. She bowed subserviently to the young nobleman and more perfunctorily to his companion but when she heard André's words her face contorted with fury: "Ha, well no-one ever told us that - but anyway, it don't matter no more. This fool has lost him."

For the first time, Louis-Philippe deigned to speak: "Raoul Lecaron, I am very disappointed to hear that."

The young fop spoke in the educated drawl fashionable amongst his contemporaries, as if bored by his own words. "I really thought we had an understanding. Now may I suggest that you find Hugo and return him to me. I will – not that you deserve it – pay you a small sum for the inconvenience. We shall then put this difficult matter behind us, agreed?" Despite the light tone of his voice, both Marie and Raoul felt that this young man could be very dangerous if he chose. Louis-Philippe had inherited the bright blue eyes of the old Duc. In his father's face those eyes had twinkled with humour; now they sprayed fear and menace. Suddenly Raoul saw that there was something not quite human in the young man's face.

"Do not thwart me again, do you understand?"

Louis-Philippe turned abruptly and climbed awkwardly into the coach. André made a slight bow to Marie and to Raoul and joined his master. The coach swayed out of the yard at some speed, spraying muck and straw everywhere and leaving Marie and Raoul glaring at each other in the silence. Although still exhilarated, the dogs, sensing a change in the atmosphere, cringed silently in their pen. The stillness was shattered when Marie screamed in frustration, the scream ceasing abruptly when Raoul lifted a spade and advanced menacingly, but she stood her ground:

"Oh no, Raoul. Don't you dare touch me! I only married you because your brother was dead, and you would inherit the farm and a fat lot of good that has done me; you're a lazy, fat, idle…… I will tell all I know about that death, I will!"

"But I had nothing to do with my brother's death" whined Raoul running after her.

"Who is going to believe you? Beat me and I shall tell everyone how cruel you really are" hissed Marie, standing up to her full, if diminutive height.

"Will you never cease?" Raoul flung back at her in frustration as she ran sobbing back inside the farmhouse, leaving him staring out hopelessly across the fields. Eventually he went back inside where Marie was stirring something on the old iron stove.

"Well, woman, what do you suggest I do?"

"You could always offer a reward, husband" she replied, peevishly.

"Come now Marie, you know we have no money; how can we possibly pay a reward? Did you not hear the Duc's son say he would give me a *small* sum? It'll be nothing like the dog is worth, I'll wager."

"Think, think – you could even accuse the finder of being a thief and save yourself the trouble of finding a reward."

Raising her hands in despair at her husband's lack of cunning, Marie disappeared into their bedroom and returned with a bundle of her clothes.

"Whatever you decide to do I am going back to my parents' house right now" she spat. "There won't be enough to feed us both through the winter and I for one do not intend to starve. If you find Hugo, take the money from his lordship and then you can send for me." Marie stared at her husband expecting some response, but Raoul was beaten. He left her standing open-mouthed as he stalked off in the direction of the Mairie.

"That accursed dog! Now he's run away. Marie is driving me insane with her whining and if that wasn't enough, the Duc's son is now insisting it's his dog. Ah François! Why does the world treat me so ill?"

François hastily prepared a fresh notice, this time offering a reward for the return of Hugo Hound and immediately put one up on the town's noticeboard. He was just making some further copies when a troop of gendarmes rode into the square. They were returning from a three-day patrol of the surrounding countryside and were headed straight for the bar hoping for their first proper meal in days. Sergeant Brochard led them and he was just about to ride past when he stopped in front of the Town Hall and saw the two notices. François watched nervously. The two had forgotten that Raoul's auction notice was still prominently displayed now next to the reward notice. Of course, this immediately caught the eye of Brochard.

"Oh dear, gentlemen. If that Hound has been stolen or is missing then you should have let us know" said the sergeant menacingly, his dark eyes fixed on Raoul. "You! I told you to speak to me if you ever wanted to get rid of him. Why did you put up that auction notice eh?" Both François and Raoul looked at the ground, avoiding the sergeant's eye.

"Oh, oh Sergeant…It just happened last night" replied François "I believe Raoul was on his way to the Barracks, weren't you? As for the Auction Notice, well err" he finished lamely unsure what to say next. Raoul stood shuffling in uncomfortable silence.

The Gendarmerie was the very strong arm of the law in these parts and Sergeant Brochard was particularly feared for his fierce temper. Therefore, both men were caught unprepared when Brochard relaxed and broke into a wide, friendly smile.

"No matter friends why not give me the other notices and we can distribute them and organise a search. You'll soon have Hugo back. Then, Lecaron, I know you will give me first refusal, won't you?"

"Of course, Sergeant, of course." Raoul felt momentarily relieved - perhaps something was going to go right for him at last; then he remembered Louis-Philippe. What a nightmare it all was.

He returned to the farm after Marie's departure. She had taken not only her clothes, but half of the remaining food in the house, which had been packed onto their only cart pulled by the farm's only Donkey.

He smiled a wolfish smile as he looked in the direction she had taken: "Don't worry, wife" he crooned to himself "as soon as Hugo is back and sold I shall send for you – if hell freezes over."

Sergeant Brochard woke early the next morning. He had had a restless night's sleep but now he knew exactly what he had to do. He had been aware, even before he had seen the Notice, of just how much that dog was worth. He, like Louis-Philippe, felt drawn to this animal without knowing why. He walked over to his desk and with a little smile on his lips, picked up all the copies of the Lost Dog Notice and threw them into the stove, watching them briefly as they began to blacken and burn.

"Come on, wake up you lot. Work to do." The patrol mounted up and rode slowly out of the town. Brochard's second in command, Corporal Martin bravely enquired where they were going and was very surprised to be told that they were helping in the search for Hugo. "Shouldn't we tell the Captain what we are doing?" he queried.

"He won't even notice we've gone" replied Brochard smugly "He's gone off hunting again with his 'best friend' this morning, as usual."

The unfortunate patrolmen were forced to set off without breakfast, crossing the bridge at the far end of the town where they took the road south. The sergeant sensed that this was the direction the dog had taken. The odd connection which seemed to exist between him and the Hound drove him mad. He felt a compulsion to find the dog which went way beyond making some cash from him; he posed some unknown threat to the Sergeant, what was it?

CHAPTER 15

Hugo 'felt' the southerly direction he needed to take even when the sky was cloudy, or they were unable to see the stars. It seemed that this knowledge had been imprinted on his brain long ago. They walked at a steady pace until just before daybreak he stopped, looked around and said to Mimi: "I think we'll stop here.""Where is *here*? Are we…"?

"Well, no, I don't think this is it, but we should know more soon" said Hugo sounding far more confident than he felt. Something told him to stop and wait – he wasn't sure what – and so they sat down to rest. Looking ahead, he noticed a snowy white owl sitting on a fence post nearby. The owl appeared to be asleep with its head turned into its feathers. Not wishing to disturb it, the two dogs remained silent and thought about, perhaps, sleeping themselves. All at once, the head of the owl swivelled towards them and two large eyes fixed them with a stony stare:

"Well, you took your time. I need to leave here before the sun rises" the bird said impatiently.

Stunned into apologising, Hugo stuttered: "Err, sorry, we had to be sure that Raoul was asleep before we made our escape" forgetting that he was talking to a bird and the bird would surely not know Raoul. Mimi, meanwhile, looked first at him and then at the large owl, perplexed. Was her friend talking to this owl?

"Well, I suppose you have done your best" replied the owl ruffling its feathers in a rather peevish way. "Hugo Hound, we were expecting just you, but your little friend may prove useful." The large bird looked briefly at her and the little dog could have sworn that the impassive face softened for a moment. The Hound was too overwhelmed to wonder how the owl knew who he was and why it seemed to be expecting him. "Welcome to you both and welcome to the beginning of your great journey. I am known as Athina and I, along with some of my friends, will guide you. Just keep going south, you'll see the eagles overhead – they will show you the way. Just a word of warning Hugo, don't ever change into human form again until you have spoken to Gilles Barbier. We Paladins must be careful." The owl adopted an even fiercer expression as she said this and stared hard at both dogs. Several difficult questions had been raised by the bird. Only his kennel mates had ever seen his transformations, he was sure. Who were these Paladins? Who was Gilles Barbier?

"If you do need to, you may change into another dog shape, but always make sure humans don't see you doing it; you know Raoul has offered a reward for your return, don't you? If anyone were to discover that you can change shape, then… One last thing, further help is available to you - just look out for the shells along the way…." and with these cryptic words, the owl rose into the air and flew swiftly away. Both dogs exchanged confused looks: "OK. So, Hugo, what was all that about eh?" Mimi had stood watching the owl and the Hound obviously deep in conversation but had understood not a word. He decided to tell her the shortened version of the message rather than confuse her. He laughed: "Well she certainly knew an awful lot about us! I did appreciate her warning but honestly, I have no idea what it all meant."

"Warning? What about? What did she know? Who is she anyway?" Mimi's little black terrier nose twitched with impatience.

"Well she said her name is Athina and she knew about the reward offered for me. She knew about my shape changing abilities too and that I must never do it again until I have spoken to Gilles Barbier or I would be in danger. No idea who this Gilles Barbier is! She also told me we will be guided to where we are going and to look for 'shells' along the way. I think I know what they are, but I can't recall why I should know."

She nodded. She had only half-listened after she heard the word 'danger'. "Oh, and err, Hugo, one more thing: you always know things that I don't.... what exactly are "shells"? Is this one?" The little terrier nosed a pale shiny shape embedded in the nearby fencepost where the owl had perched.

"Ah" said Hugo "I guess so. That makes sense.... a shell is something that comes from the sea (don't ask, Mimi) so there must be a very good reason for finding one here, look I think the rounded end of the shell is pointing our way. Amazing." When they both looked up in the direction of the rising sun they saw that it was true.

"OK, I think" we have walked enough. Let's find a sheltered spot where we can rest." They both settled down in a thicket well away from the path they had been following and instantly fell into a deep sleep. Hugo was exhausted and awoke late, slightly disorientated, and looked around cautiously. Mimi was gone. Just as he was working out what to do she trotted back with a large bone in her small mouth. She laid it down carefully in front of Hugo and with a dog smirk told him: "I may not be as clever as you, but I can still scavenge." Both dogs ate greedily and refreshed by the sleep and the food they set off once again keeping to the path. "If you hear anything at all we must hide – I'm worried about what the owl told me. Ha! There was I thinking my shape changing was just a rather novel trick."

The meeting with the owl was on both their minds: "Don't fret, little friend. We'll just have to wait and see" said Hugo with more certainty than he felt at that moment. He had been thinking about his dreams again and although they no longer gave him a headache they were more vivid but now also comforting. He felt relieved without knowing why. "Look another 'shell thing'" yelped Mimi excitedly. She pointed with her snout towards another shiny object attached to an old signpost. High above the two dogs they saw a pair of magnificent eagles circling. They seemed to be following the animals' progress and this made them both feel safer. After a lunch of scraps again gathered by Mimi, they saw one of the eagles make an acrobatic twist in the sky and fly away in the way they had travelled.

"That's strange. We'll just keep going in this direction – look the other eagle is still with us. Better keep an eye on him just in case."

After about 10 minutes the first eagle re-joined its mate above them and they both flew off together in the direction of a stand of tall pine trees where they stayed, high in the sky. "Hm, looks like that's where they want us to go. There must be a reason for their behaviour" and both dogs set off at a trot towards the stand of tall trees. One of the eagles came down into the lower branches and sat a few feet above their heads. "Hallo Hugo…so this is Mimi, is it? Bad news I'm afraid. A band of men on horseback are coming along the road. You must remain hidden until they have passed by" whispered the eagle softly.

By this time, both dogs had begun to accept without question Hugo's ability to communicate with birds, but this majestic creature surprised them. The bird 'spoke' in a high, lyrical and slightly sing-song voice which was at odds with its imperious head and huge hooked beak. From this the dogs assumed it was probably a female eagle, although the glaring yellow rimmed eyes gave no hint of this!

"Thank you" replied Hugo "just back there I picked up a strange scent briefly, but the wind is in the wrong direction."

The other eagle then came down and perched beside its companion. Its voice was deeper and far gruffer: "I have been for a closer look. They are gendarmes, and they are searching for something. All of them seem to be keeping a sharp eye on the surrounding countryside. They've got four bloodhounds and have spread out on either side of the road too."

"I think that you may be their prey this time, Hugo. We'll leave you now but keep looking for us in the sky. When the coast is clear we will come back and tell you." The two giant birds swooped and rose high into the sky, disappearing over the treetops. Hugo and Mimi could now detect the vibration of horses' hooves on the path and their sharp hunting noses detected the scent of man. They took cover quickly and soon saw the troop of men, spread across the road, their bloodhounds sniffing and yowling, trying to pick up the scent. They knew bloodhounds were clever and Hugo was very worried that their scent would give them away. As they watched anxiously, Sergeant Brochard turned to his men:

"We've been riding for a whole day and these useless dogs haven't found anything – unless it was rabbits or rats."

"But they're trained to hunt humans not dogs and all these strange new scents are too much for them sir" replied Corporal Martin, "and anyway, Sergeant, how can we be sure we are on the right track?"

"Call it animal instinct. This is the way they went. We'll go on into St. Antoine and spend the night there. We can begin the search again tomorrow." The group reformed and slowly rode past the place where Mimi and Hugo were concealed, the bloodhounds baying and running in circles.

Hugo was certain their presence had been detected but the four Hounds seemed to have decided not to co-operate with their masters and passed by, ignoring the scent and deliberately not going too close to the hiding place. Both dogs stayed concealed for a while after the patrol had disappeared and then followed at a safe distance beside the roadway.

"We can wait until it gets dark and get past the place they're going to stay. It can't be far from here. Then we can be well away from them by daybreak."

"I've a better idea. We should stay behind them. We're hunters, not prey. It's what we were born to do. We'll follow them to wherever they're staying for the night, find some shelter then track them in the morning."

“That will only work if they go the way we want to go though, won’t it?”

“I think they’ll keep travelling south. That sergeant is a little too desperate to find me…there’s something in him that I can’t fathom.”

They did not have to travel much farther to get to the village of St. Antoine. Mimi followed the gendarmes on her own despite Hugo’s objections: “Look Hugo, nobody will notice me, they’re looking for a large, actually a very large Hound. I am a small terrier.” She hid in doorways and alleys until she saw the riders turn into a courtyard and dismount. Then she ran back to join her companion. Later, under cover of darkness, the two dogs found a derelict barn to hide in. Mimi ran off almost immediately returning triumphant with a huge meaty bone, obviously ‘scavenged’ from the local butcher’s shop.

“You’re really good at this, aren’t you?” said Hugo admiringly.“Always have been – some of the other dogs would hide bones for later but I always found them, and they never suspected” grinned his friend. “But Hugo, I swear I never, ever stole any of your bones.”

CHAPTER 16

Having arrived at the auberge in St. Antoine the gendarmes immediately demanded to be fed and made comfortable, kicking the other travellers out of the inn.

"We are on official business" barked Brochard at the owner's protests. "Food, drink and a good night's lodging for me and my men and send the bill to the Mayor of La Garenne...he'll pay... if he knows what's good for him!"

The inn stood at the intersection of 2 main roads. "I want two sentries on the crossroads at all times – 2 hours each – you and you first" ordered the sergeant, indicating the two newest recruits in his Company. "Then you two, then you and you" he pointed at his second in command and an old grizzled gendarme: "you can take the last watch. Stop any travelers and I will question them when I am ready. Of course, if you see any stray dogs, catch them and bring them in too."

The sergeant went into the dimly lit dining room where he noisily demanded food and wine. Despite drinking more wine than normal as it was at the mayor's expense he still slept uneasily. Something about the day had unsettled him. He should have been happy; if his plan succeeded he could become a rich man; he was certain of it. He could leave the service and return to his hometown in the south of France, live a comfortable life and have plenty to eat and drink. But was that really what he wanted? The dog was valuable but more than that, he felt an overwhelming desire to possess this animal, yet to make his fortune he must sell him. His conflicting thoughts lay heavy on his mind as he tossed and turned. It seemed only moments since he had lain down before there was a furious pounding on his door. "Can you come down sir?" A frightened junior gendarme pleaded. He stomped downstairs to the dining room and awaiting him were three men, two of whom he vaguely recognised. There was an upright middle-aged man with a military bearing. He had dark brown hair, pulled back to reveal greying temples. His companion was a younger, very finely attired gentleman. A third man sat hunched in a chair and was clearly a coachman, his cloak dusty and muddied and his hat crumpled and torn. He rested a crooked injured leg on a stool.

Four gendarmes were watching them uneasily. What's going on here?" boomed Brochard. "We arrested some travellers as instructed, sir but they insisted we wake you." The first of the men turned to the sergeant angrily. "I believe you are the sergeant of Gendarmes from La Garenne? Well you may perhaps recognise me. I am André Lacoste, the manager of the estate at the Château there. We were travelling home from business farther south late last night." The sergeant tried hard to interrupt but the older man was clearly furious and would not be silenced. "but when we reached the crossroads…these idiots -without any warning- jumped out in front of our horses making them bolt. Our coachman was thrown from the coach and is injured. Then and only with great difficulty did your men managed to halt the runaway horses. At which point, they accused us of trying to evade capture! We have been detained here, without explanation, for long enough."

The rapidly panicking Sergeant searched anxiously for words to defuse the situation, but André Lacoste then turned to his companion, who had remained facing towards the open door: "May I present M. Louis-Philippe, only son of the Duc de Garenne? Your *superior,* Captain Falaise is a great personal friend of Monsieur. Were you not present at the funeral of the late Duc? Do you recognise us now?" André thrust his angry face into Brochard's pale one.

Sergeant Brochard put his head in his hands – oh this wasn't going well.

“Well, what have you to say? Answer me sergeant. What exactly is your business here that you arrest innocent travellers and turn honest paying guests from this inn?”

Tackling peasants was one thing, dealing with the gentry was quite another: “Err, err” …. the sergeant began but one of the other gendarmes blurted out “We’re looking for Hugo Hound, Monsieur.” All the sergeant’s dreams seemed to shrivel and die before his eyes – how could he explain that he had mobilised the forces of the gendarmerie to find a missing…dog.

“Are you now?” drawled the aristocratic younger man, who until now had said nothing but looked on with disdain: “That seems a strange mission for this number of gendarmes. Well perhaps when you find the animal, you should bring him to me immediately and nothing more will be said of this matter.”

His companion looked at him in surprise. André had expected the young nobleman to fly into one of his uncontrollable rages – not make a deal with this idiot. The young man dismissed the gendarme with a wave of his hand while Lacoste recovered himself and stepped forward, his face up close to the sergeant’s own:

“You heard Sergeant. You have had a lucky escape. Might I suggest that you need to employ your time and that of your men more usefully in future. Now, we are going to take a room and after breakfast by the fire we will be leaving. I do not expect you to be here when we awake!”

“But….” Stuttered the sergeant knowing, as did his men, that breakfast had just flown out of the window and they would have to leave cold and hungry in the dark.

CHAPTER 17

Hugo and Mimi, who were lying awake in their hiding place, saw the patrol set off – heading south - just as Hugo had thought.

"Shall we follow them now?" asked the terrier.

"In a while, we don't need to be too close to them. I can follow that scent from miles away" laughed Hugo.

"Even I could track them. Don't humans ever lick themselves clean?" replied his friend, smirking.

"We have to get through the village remember, and they may have told people to look out for me. I know… I'll change into a terrier. Athina said that would be fine if necessary. No-one will be looking for two rather muddy terriers." So, some time later, two similarly coloured small dogs trotted casually past the inn, narrowly avoiding the wheels of a large coach with an ornate crest upon its door. The conveyance swung precariously out of the courtyard into their path and both passengers briefly noticed them but neither gave them a second glance. The coach headed north, and the two dogs trotted off in the opposite direction. Once out of sight, Hugo took a few moments to transform himself back into a Hound again.

"What was it like, Hugo, being a terrier?" asked Mimi excitedly.

"Well to be honest a bit close to the ground for my liking but all I needed to do was to keep thinking of chasing rabbits" the other dog laughed.

"Well I think you looked rather good as a terrier – but you have to do something about those ears."

Looking up they saw that more birds were flying overhead. It gave them a good feeling. Somehow, those birds were keeping them safe.

The dogs travelled along parallel to the roadway just to be safe and sometimes Hugo would stop – he could tell from the scents that they were getting too close to the gendarmes who halted every couple of hours. The two dogs, however, were anxious to keep going as long as they could to reach their unknown destination.

When forced to stop, Mimi would go off and amuse herself snuffling in the nearby woodland and trying to sniff out rabbits although she was no real threat. During one of these enforced rests the gruff eagle came down close to Hugo and perched on the lowest branch of a huge pine tree.

"Listen, Hugo, about these gendarmes. Athina thought they were out to collect the reward your owner has posted but she's concerned: there's something strange about the sergeant."

"I feel something too, but I can't tell what it is about him."

"Be careful! I need to know more of his background, but I sense from the way he's been behaving that he could be" …The eagle lowered his voice and inclined his head towards Hugo as if to share a secret: "a Renegade." The eagle looked at Hugo's puzzled expression and explained: "Athina can tell you all about them but for the moment you just need to know that he may be able to see through your disguises. Don't change shape again not even into another dog. Just stay well away from him."

The eagle departed leaving a very perplexed Hugo, his face still betraying his confusion when Mimi returned. She saw immediately that her friend was troubled. "You've been talking to those birds again, haven't you?" She spoke as if she was making fun of him but in truth she knew it was something serious. Hugo told his companion what the eagle had said, and her expression changed quickly. Now she was as confused as her friend. "I don't know what a Rengerade is. I thought he was just a human – they're all a bit strange, if you ask me."

Hugo replied, dog-smiling: "It's r-e-n-e-g-a-d-e, Mimi." "He looks human, but I wonder just what kind of human he is."

****

That night, the gendarmes pitched a makeshift camp. After what had happened at St. Antoine, the sergeant didn't dare stay at another inn. He just wanted to avoid any more problems. At each small village and hamlet that the troop passed through he asked the same question: "Have you seen a stray Hound? His master has disappeared and if we find this Hound it may help us." This of course was a lie but the only one he could think of to explain the presence of so many gendarmes seeking a dog. Everyone denied seeing anything – but that is often the automatic response to gendarmes.

"Are you sure you know what you're doing?" queried Corporal Martin. "We've been riding for two full days now and if the aristo from the inn says anything about this, you'll be finished in the Gendarmerie – and so will we."

Angrily Brochard replied: "This will make our fortune, man. I promise I will give you all a fair share of what I get – trust me."

Hm, thought Martin, the sergeant was usually right.... but this time?

"Listen, we must keep travelling south. That Hound will always go south until he gets to the mountains – now just follow orders." The Corporal went back to the other men with a worried look on his face.

"I think the sergeant is losing his mind. For now, we will have to do as he says but eventually we will have to return to La Garenne and what then?" The men muttered amongst themselves, unsure what to do but since most were afraid of Brochard and his foul temper, for now they agreed to go along with his plan and if questioned, they could always say that they were acting on orders.

Next day, Brochard called a halt on a ridge which overlooked the River Dordogne. The countryside had been changing as they travelled. They had now left behind the gentle rolling hills which surrounded La Garenne and had been crossing a high wooded plateau all day. Below them lay the river valley. There had been several attempts to build a permanent crossing at this point over the powerful river, but the spring floods regularly washed away any supports. The only way to cross for now was by means of a simple wooden ferry.

The sergeant ordered some of his troop to ride down into the valley and commandeer the ferry when it next came to their side of the river. "Make sure it stays on this side" he ordered. "We don't want the locals getting in our way." Next, he turned to Corporal Martin.

"Post lookouts on this ridge, I want a constant watch kept until nightfall to try to spot that Hound. I can feel in my bones that he is still on this side of the river, so either we catch the animal by the ferry or, if he tries to swim across, we will see him from up here."

The remaining gendarmes were assigned vantage points along the edge of the ridge and told to survey both banks and the surrounding countryside. Content with his plan and certain that from this vantage point his men would be sure to see the dog, Sergeant Brochard unrolled his own sleeping pack and slept. Tomorrow he knew he would capture Hugo Hound and he would be rich…

Hugo and Mimi too had reached the ridge overlooking the river and slept comfortably in a thicket, a short distance upstream of their pursuers. Mimi as usual had gone scavenging and came back with what turned out to be a veritable feast. A pair of owls took over night-watch duties for the dogs and safe in the knowledge that there was no immediate danger, both animals fell into a deep, twitching dog-sleep. Shortly before daybreak, they awoke to find Athina, perched nearby on a branch.

“Don’t you dogs ever wake at a reasonable hour?” she complained. “I’ve been watching and waiting for an age… I have to be off soon.”

The owl oozed disapproval but the dogs weren’t sure how to react. Meanwhile the owl re-arranged her feathers several times and then began speaking to Hugo ignoring Mimi pointedly: “Look down there at the river. We have been fortunate. It is foggy this morning. You should be able to get across the river just before sunrise under cover of the fog and a good distance further on before it lifts. Come on, get up, and get moving.”

“But, but” said Hugo still trying to focus after such a rude awakening “I thought it would be best to stay behind the gendarmes and that way we can keep an eye on what they’re up to?”

“That has worked until now but last evening the eagles told me that the men are also camped on this ridge and have taken control of the river crossing so you may be trapped. The only way to get across is in the fog. You will have to swim across, then make for the forest on the other side, at the top of the ridge. It lies to the east of the town of Monbezier. Stay sharp eyed and you should spot the shells along the way but go, go now. This river fog will not last above an hour and you have to put some distance between you and that sergeant.”

Without waiting for their reply, the owl flapped once and flew up over their heads and into the pre-dawn gloom.

“Well Hugo I take it we have our instructions?”

“Apparently, those gendarmes are controlling the ferry, so we have no choice. We must swim for it. Lucky we can both swim eh?”

“Err, yes but what about you using your unusual talents and turning into a small boat then I can ride across?” laughed Mimi as they set off down into the foggy valley, their sensitive noses reacting to the smells of the nearby river which they were still unable to see. Arriving at the riverbank they could hear muffled voices in the fog. Hugo could hear the ferryman angrily arguing that the gendarmes had to let him pick up his paying customers from the other side. They, in turn, were insisting that the ferry remain where it was until their sergeant arrived. The ferryman seemed unimpressed by this argument and became so incensed that the gendarmes threatened him with arrest, provoking an even greater tirade from the angry man as well as the waiting passengers.

Under cover of the commotion, the two dogs slipped into the water and Mimi stayed upstream of Hugo who was a strong swimmer, so she could lean her body against his and avoid being swept away by the fast current. The crossing was slow and very cold, the two dogs desperately trying to avoid being struck by half-submerged branches and other debris but eventually they collapsed on the other shore. They rested for some moments amongst some semi-submerged tree roots to catch their breath and orientate themselves. The little terrier was panting hard, her eyes closed, as she leaned against Hugo's broad back.

"Well done, little friend" said Hugo. "I never knew you were such a strong swimmer!"

"I'm very glad that's over" panted the little terrier. "I didn't know I could swim at all!" The current had taken them downstream from where they had started out, but such was the commotion on both sides of the river made by the angry shouts of the stranded passengers that no-one noticed two bedraggled dogs slip onto the bank, shake themselves vigorously and set off into the swirling mist.

CHAPTER 18

The mist was still too thick in the valley for them to be able to make out anything more than a hundred paces ahead, but Hugo decided they should take the road that snaked up the slope of the valley in the general direction of the forest before the mist finally rose. As the two damp animals trudged up the hill they could feel the gradual increase in temperature, a fact confirmed by the amount of steam rising from their sodden coats.

"Look Hugo, I'm all covered in fog" cried Mimi. She was still exhausted from her swim but when she had heard Hugo's plan she had decided to put her dog faith entirely in her friend. Learning to swim in a fast-flowing river had been quite an adventure for a small dog but one she was in no hurry to repeat. The sun was at last beginning to burn off the fog in the valley when one of the lookouts at the top of the ridge shouted that he had seen something.

"Sergeant, sergeant, something is moving up the road over there… look, yes I think it could be two dogs."

Brochard snatched up his spyglass and sure enough, two tiny specks were visible emerging from the mist on the opposite side of the river. By the size of the larger animal he was sure it was the Hound but now he appeared to have a companion. They were trotting along together, without a care in the world. The sergeant had enjoyed a wonderful night's sleep, dreaming of his good fortune to come. He had awoken certain that great things would happen to him that day and now seeing the two animals drove him into a frenzy:

"Mount up men, leave your kit. Get to the ferry now!"

The troop hurriedly did as they were ordered and rode down at a furious pace into the valley, thundering up to the landing where stood the other waiting gendarmes. They rode heavily onto the small craft and ordered the ferryman to take them to the other side immediately. He took one look and knew that it would be useless to argue. He called to the far bank to get the Donkeys ready. These animals were harnessed to a thick, muddy rope attached to a capstan.

They walked around this drawing the rope taut as the craft moved from the bank and the ferryman wielded a heavy pole that steered the vessel across the water. The anxious horses of the gendarmes whinnied and moved restlessly aboard the rather flimsy craft. Once safely across, the entire troop rode off at such a gallop that they almost capsized the vessel. The waiting passengers scattered in all directions, with much shouting and cursing. The men rode fast up the hill charging on towards the spot where the dogs had last been sighted. The pounding vibrations of hoof beats were soon picked up by Mimi and Hugo. "We need to get off the path now" growled Hugo, feeling the hooves approaching.

"Quickly Hugo, this way, this way – look a shell – and its pointing, yes to the forest. I can see the trees in the distance."

The two dogs swerved off the road and dashed into a cornfield in the general direction of the forest. Urged on by Brochard, the gendarmes spotted the dogs and the troopers charged onward to intercept the fugitives, riding into the still unharvested cornfield, their horses trampling the crops under their hooves. Hugo and Mimi were now running as fast their legs could carry them, literally running for their lives. On the far side of the cornfield was a newly ploughed field whose deep furrows made it difficult for a small dog to run in any direction but along the base of each depression; to change direction, they had to climb over the stiff mud walls of each furrow. Hugo could manage it, but his little friend was in trouble, her short legs struggling. Generally, chasse Hounds have great stamina and can run long distances; sprints are not for them. Terriers, on the other hand, can run very fast indeed but only for short distances. Thus, whilst Hugo was able to keep up a good pace, poor Mimi was finding things difficult, her breath coming in sharp rasping gasps as her tongue lolled out of her mouth. Neither animal was a match for a galloping horse, especially over this terrain.

As they ran, they heard a great commotion overhead. A vast flock of birds was circling and screaming noisily, swooping continually at the gendarmes. The birds were slowing the horsemen down, flying up in front of the horses, wings fully extended and attacking time and time again. Larger birds flew in with talons extended, swooping at the heads of the gendarmes and sometimes gripping their hats, even their hair.

The dogs were still some distance from the dense trees and safety when Hugo barked: "We're close but they are catching up fast – just look at the birds!"

"I can't.........I can't go any further, Hugo. They're not interested in me. You carry on and I will hide over there and catch up with you later." She collapsed, breathless, looking for any cover to hide herself. "I can't leave you behind, Mimi, not now" panted Hugo.

"You must..." and Mimi forced the decision by running off, keeping her short body below the height of the thick ridges of mud. Hugo heard one of the approaching gendarmes shouting:

"Look, there's one. That's the little white terrier!"

"Leave that one, that's not the one we need" cried Brochard and as Hugo heard this he took off in the direction of the gloomy forest. Dashing headlong into the trees, he soon found that the light from the morning sky was fading, the forest seeming to absorb any light and turn it to shadow. Briefly, he stopped to listen for hoof beats close by. He could still hear them but some distance behind him.

Like the old boar before him, Hugo soon noticed shadows were beginning to hem him in. The fur on his neck rose of its own accord and he slowed his pace, walking very carefully and placing each paw gingerly on the forest floor, uncomfortably aware that he was no longer alone. Close by, cobweb-fine shapes hovered at the edges the path taken by the frightened animal. The glistening shapes moved and changed as he watched, and his fear was such that suddenly he felt unable to move forward. He looked up and was briefly reassured to see his new friends, the eagles, dipping their wings to him. He was just able to make out their wheeling shapes between the tree tops high above him before the deep shade of the close-packed trees engulfed him. Then the birds too were no longer visible. He was (almost) alone. Hugo decided he must go on or… and set off, running haphazardly through the ever-darkening forest, the filmy shapes still pursuing him and occasionally crossing the path before him. Hugo had no idea whether or not they were friendly but having got this far he decided to take no chances and to run…run as fast as he could and see whether they followed him. He saw ahead of him that the trees were beginning to thin out…

A PALADIN ARRIVES AT SANCTUARY INN

"Doesn't anyone turn up on time these days?" boomed a voice which made Hugo jump. He advanced cautiously into the clearing to find, seated on an old log a...an enormous man dressed as...no, wait, not a man at all, a giant bear.

"Welcome to Sanctuary Inn. You must be Hugo. I am Gilles Barbier, innkeeper – come with me and have some food and drink. By the looks of you, you need a good rest. Then we must talk my lad."

Hugo dazedly followed the giant creature as he crossed the clearing towards a high cliff face where they passed under a dark overhang. The bear pushed on a stout iron-studded wooden door set deep into the limestone face and they entered a large flag stoned chamber which served as the main room of the inn. The interior itself was hewn from chalk and went a long way back, its depths obscured in darkness. The stunned dog looked around him and was amazed to see an impressive array of barrels stretching along one wall behind a polished wooden counter, supported by yet more huge barrels. This obviously served as a long bar, a bar at which stood... an even bigger version of his host... wearing knee-high leather boots. Had he been able, Hugo rubbed his eyes for this bear was quaffing from a pewter tankard dwarfed by a massive furry fist, its claws extended, elbow leaning on the bar. Beyond the bar, through a wide arch, Hugo could make out a dining area of sorts with an assortment of chairs and tables from various eras, some very high, some very low. However, most of the 'guests' were eating from the floor or mangers set into the walls. Farther back were many cubicles, strewn with straw and blankets. Was this where the guests slept, he thought? 'How curious! I seem to have found Sanctuary Inn...and Gilles Barbier.'

CHAPTER 19

Behind the long bar stood yet another oversized bear wearing a wide rather toothy smile, a lace trimmed cap and a rather smart wrap-over dress stretched across the broad expanse of her wide hips. Over her dark woollen dress 'she' was wearing a starched white pinafore. The smart appearance was marred only by a pair of large, ancient, loose slippers obviously made to accommodate her giant paws. Gilles Barbier went behind the bar and put his arm around her shoulders proprietarily: "May I present my wife, Madame Hortense Barbier?" and Hugo felt obliged to bow. The landlady was serving a bewildering but interesting array of customers. As Hugo and the innkeeper had entered the room the cacophonous conversation had abruptly ceased, and silence now fell on the bar and dining area save at the table occupied by four black bears. There was much loud guffawing and angry growling from this group. Hugo noticed that they were all staring intently at some small stones on the table. One suddenly slammed down a stone and stretched out an arm drawing all the other stones towards him. "Mine I think" he roared triumphantly, piling his winnings neatly in front of him.

"Ignore them, Hugo" said Gilles. "They are Fighting Bears. They're not allowed to fight at Sanctuary Inn, so this is how they manage to contain their natural aggression. Strange bunch!"

Several deer had run, panicking, into the stabling at the back of the inn and now some more normal sized animals gathered close to Madame Barbier. "What's he doing here?" demanded one of the animals, a grizzled wolf sitting with a group of other wolves, a deer and two comparatively small black and white bears, peacefully chewing leaves.

“He’s as entitled to enter Sanctuary as the rest of you” boomed the innkeeper.

“But he’s a hunting Hound. In fact, isn’t he err Hugo Hound?” Hugo was both proud and astonished that he was known so far from home. However, at the mention of the name Hugo, the atmosphere in the chamber subtly changed and a low murmuring began. From the general hubbub, one voice rose above the rest; that of a grizzled and scarred old boar who had been sitting in a dark corner.

He came forward and roared: “A Hound he may be, but he is also my friend.” The boar ambled over, snuffling quietly, to sniff Hugo. He greeted the Hound like an old friend and announced to the assembled company: “This Hound saved my life.” The boar then stood beside Hugo facing the assembled animals, his snout resting on Hugo’s cheek in affection. ‘My word’ thought Hugo ‘he has a broken tusk. He’s the boar I met in the forest.’ The boar addressed him in gruff but formal tones: “I am Sangres Blacksnout and I believe I am addressing Hugo Hound? I want to thank you once again for saving my life and I am glad that you too have found your way here.”

Slowly the atmosphere in the inn began to relax and the other animals began to speak quietly to each other, feeling secure now that Hugo had every right to be made welcome at Sanctuary. Some were even aware of just how important his arrival might be. Gradually, the timider animals drew nearer to Hugo, some investigating him with their noses and others just observing with interest. Amongst the last to come forward from the gloom at the rear of the Inn was a stunning white horse. The horse walked slowly towards the Hound, tossing her mane and snorting gently. Hugo thought there was something unusual about this handsome creature but was too tired to give it much thought.

“So, this is the Hound that looked like a boar, is it?” said Gilles to old Sangres Blacksnout, although he had already guessed at the truth when the boar had arrived a few days earlier. The other animals had doubted Sangres' story but here it was - a hunting Hound and a boar behaving as if they were the best of friends.

"Rest now Hugo, you have had a hard journey. My friend and I need to have a long chat to you when you have recovered your strength." Gilles Barbier indicated the huge black bear at the bar and Hugo looked warily up into the enormous face, with its gleaming yellow teeth bared in what might be a smile.

"I must find my friend Mimi, Sir" said Hugo. "I don't think she will find this place on her own. She would be too scared."

"That's very loyal lad, but don't worry now. Just you rest, and we will go out together and look for your friend later" soothed Madame Barbier and the Hound had to admit that he felt completely exhausted both by the chase and by his experiences in the dark woods outside the Inn.

Inside the Inn was pretty astonishing too, he thought. He followed Sangres to a place near the huge log fire and curled up, blissfully unaware of all the hushed conversations concerning him. In a few moments, he was fast asleep.

Mimi lay in a hollow depression made by the roots of a fallen tree. She was cold, hungry and very frightened. It was the first time in her short life that she could remember being completely alone, without either Hugo or companions in the kennels. She lay shivering, trying to think what to do. The gendarmes had pursued her friend as far as the edges of the forest, but they had not entered the darkness beyond. She had watched them skirting the edges, their horses whinnying apprehensively and their four bloodhounds refusing point blank to go any further. By the time she had regained her strength she knew that Hugo was long gone – which was just what she had wanted of course, but now…she wished he was here with her. He had gone into that eerie forest and to find him she knew that she must be brave and follow but instinctively she knew that it held unknown but powerful forces.

The little terrier forced herself to be calm and think: ‘perhaps if I go around the forest he might be on the other side’. The decision made, she crept from her hiding place and seeing no-one around she sniffed along the rutted edges of the thick clay where the field met the dense trees. Following the edge of the forest, she kept walking until she could walk no more but avoided entering the trees. As dusk approached, and the trees began to thin out a little, she came to a sudden halt. Before her rose a sheer grey cliff face where the forest ended. The cliff was too high for her to climb so she was forced further into the open. Although she had seen no-one all day, she had occasionally heard the gendarmes calling to one another. The sergeant and his men had had the same idea as the little dog. They too had investigated the edges of the forest but without entering its dark interior.

As the daylight began to wane, the men and their dogs gathered. Mimi had spotted an ideal place to hide, the base of an old tree whose twisted roots would easily conceal a small dog. She listened intently and hearing nothing she ran towards this new hiding place concealed by the uneven ground and the growing dark. She was hoping to avoid the men. She was mistaken.

The gendarmes were all gathered awaiting Brochard’s orders when he cried out: “Look, there’s that little white terrier! There can’t be two of them around here. It must be the one that was with Hugo Hound. It may lead us to him. Come on. Let’s follow it!”

“Charge…follow that dog” cried the sergeant and scared as they all were of the dark, forbidding trees they were more scared of their sergeant. Mimi panicked and ran skittering and skidding straight into the dense trees: she soon discovered that her fear of the forest was far less than that of being caught. She dashed headlong, tripping on low brambles and tearing around clumps of huge tree roots as she ran. Her instincts told her that she was no longer alone, but her fear was more of the approaching gendarmes on horseback. Her breath came in short, painful bursts and she was forced to stop and dive down into a clump of ferns, burrowing her little black nose deep into the damp earth to hide herself. Her heart thudded painfully in her chest and in her ears. Slowly she realised she could no longer hear the crashing of approaching hooves. In its place was a dense and absolute stillness. What had happened to her pursuers? Now all that she could hear was the terrified and eerie baying of the gendarmes' bloodhounds in the velvety silence.

****

The two dogs would never need to fear their pursuers again. Over several days, riderless horses were discovered in the surrounding area. Some mysteriously 'disappeared' to reappear working on the local farms and one even found its way back to the barracks at La Garenne…but no-one ever saw the men again, and the horses couldn't tell anyone what had happened. The bloodhounds too were nowhere to be found - but their fate was soon known to the two dogs. It was the ferryman who first made the connection between the stray horses and the patrol of gendarmes he had encountered. Before long, wildly exaggerated rumours abounded, a headless man had been seen riding through Monbezier; a wolf had devoured a child (always in the next village); a passenger on the regular stagecoach to Neufchatel had disappeared.

A local curé soon preached a sermon telling the townspeople all this was caused by their evildoing and to repent their sins by giving generously to the church. There had not been this much excitement locally since the old stories about the Beast of Gévaudan, some 50 years earlier.

Country people love nothing more than a mystery and amongst the local people living close to that unfrequented forest the rumours grew. The local newspapers revelled, as newspapers do, in reporting the incident with much sinister emphasis and the stories reached La Garenne soon after the lone horse arrived back. M. Lafitte-Dupont asked Captain Falaise what he knew but of course Falaise had no idea, nor had he any intention of finding out. Soon Louis-Philippe heard the rumours, but his first thought was 'Damnation! Now I will have to think of another way to find that Hound.' A few days later the young nobleman arranged a hunting trip with Falaise and his good friend Patrick Gounod, owner of the Dordogne Libre newspaper. M. Gounod asked the Captain what he thought of the disappearance and Falaise, his discretion blunted by several cups of wine, told him that he 'hadn't a clue' and that they had 'disappeared from the face of the earth'.

Next day the headline of the newspaper was "Official: Gendarmerie Patrol disappears from the Face of the Earth". It took no time at all for the Parisian newspapers to take up this fascinating tale with even more dramatic headlines and very shortly thereafter Falaise was prodded into action by a terse message from Inspector General Destrier at Headquarters in Paris ordering him to carry out a full investigation. His problem was that if he was being completely honest, he had no idea how to go about this, especially in a matter that was clearly important to his superiors.

Taking his few remaining men, Falaise had set off in pursuit of the "Lost Patrol" as it had been dubbed by the newspapers. However, when he arrived at the inn at St. Antoine it was not information he received but a very large bill, the one incurred by Brochard and his men. Moreover, so unpopular had Brochard made himself that anyone the patrol met was reluctant to provide any information whatsoever.

The ferryman, when questioned, had just shrugged and uttered an occasional reluctant "oui" or "non" but refused to expand on that! Disheartened, all Falaise knew in the end was that the missing men had crossed the river and their trail had disappeared. No-one in Monbezier could recall seeing any gendarmes. Lacking any further clues, Falaise returned to La Garenne, and prepared his scant report for Headquarters. This was basically an account of his problems with the innkeeper at St. Antoine and the locals' refusal to co-operate further – his conclusion? They had indeed vanished from the face of the earth.

CHAPTER 20

Whilst Hugo slept on, there was a loud pounding at the door of Sanctuary Inn. Gilles turned to his wife:

"We're not expecting any more visitors, are we?"

"I ….err…. think that might be the Sentinels knocking – better see what they want, Gilles" replied his wife, looking worried. Gilles cautiously opened the door and there on the threshold stood a small, shivering terrier, four anxious bloodhounds and behind them several very faintly shimmering but undefined shapes.

"What have we here?" Gilles asked kindly, bending down to see whether the terrier wore a collar. He opened the inn door wider and called to his wife: "My dear, can you come and take care of this little one? I need to speak to the Sentinels. There's been a bit of trouble with humans in the forest - but the Sentinels say they think they have dealt with them, thank goodness."

He disappeared, closing the door on the warmth of the inn but was gone only a short time, returning accompanied by the four bloodhounds. Madame Barbier had taken the small, shivering dog in her huge furry arms and laid her down gently near the fire close to the sleeping Hugo. Almost instantly she too fell into a deep sleep snuggled into the side of her friend. Gilles had taken pity on the bloodhounds and invited them to Sanctuary Inn. They could either spend their old age there or they could rest then decide what they would like to do. They too now lay almost comatose in a pile of legs and tails, full bellies rising gently as they slept.

When Hugo awoke, he was delighted to see Mimi, who slept on. He left her to dream twitchily but when she at last awoke, Hugo asked her how she had got there.

"Easy! First, I was chased by the men on horseback, then rescued by some nice err…things…then well the men on horseback sort of disappeared and I was at the door of this Inn, being welcomed by a huge err… bear in a pinafore.

Just a normal day really" laughed Mimi. Several times whilst on their journey Hugo had worried about whether it was fair to have brought her, but she seemed to be coping very well with everything in the circumstances.

She sensed his concern now and said: "I am really, honestly, having the time of my life, Hugo" and then abruptly, like a puppy, she fell into a deep sleep once more, dreaming of hunting, her nose wiggling as she snored softly.

Later, Gilles brought both dogs even more food which they scoffed appreciatively. Then the innkeeper motioned to Hugo to come and join him and his even bigger friend at the bar because they wished to speak with him. As Hugo approached, the huge beast who had been resting in an old and very deep leather chair introduced himself:

"Hugo Hound? I am pleased to meet you properly at last. I am Ursian le Grand of the Clan of the Guard Bears. Please call me 'Ursian'. We are all pleased that you have reached Sanctuary Inn. We have heard a great deal about you from Athina, but it is a pleasure to meet you in person at last. The eagles brought a message today that a meeting of the Grand Council was held last night to discuss what is to be done about you." Hugo sensed that this was important but had no real idea what or who the Grand Council was, nor why they would be discussing him. Ursian's voice boomed throughout the cave and the other 'residents' slowly made their way over to listen, except for a group of large lions who were fast asleep in front of the fire and the truculent Fighting Bears who continued with their game. Mimi hid behind the others keeping a wary eye on the sleeping lions but full of pride in her friend Hugo, obviously a very important Hound indeed.

"Gilles and I have been asked by the Grand Council to decide whether we can entrust you with a very, very important task." Hugo looked startled: 'what could I do that's so important' he thought to himself as the giant spoke after taking a long swig from his tankard: "Perhaps firstly you could tell us something about your life? Start from the very beginning if you can."

Hugo took a deep breath and began recounting everything he could remember that had happened in his short life. He was tempted to add that he was considered to be one of the finest chasse Hounds in all of France but after his earlier reception he thought better of that.

He began with his early life at the Château and included his strange dreams. Gilles and Ursian continually interrupted, prodding for more details, particularly about the old lady who had come to comfort him in his dreams. They seemed to know all about Louis-Philippe and Catherine. It struck Hugo that somehow both of his companions already knew much of his history. Ursian spent a long time questioning him as to how he felt when he changed shape, not so much when he was doing this to amuse his kennel companions but more when he had used his ability to fool Sangres and when he had escaped.

"Well, to be honest, I was a bit afraid for myself. Sangres, even injured, would have been a formidable opponent and the terriers were coming fast. I couldn't have lived with myself if Mimi had been injured…or worse." As Sangres bristled with pride at this backhanded compliment, a little voice could be heard from behind him: "Ohhh thank you Hugo" and Mimi peeped shyly around the vast back of the boar who now posed no threat.

Ursian stroked his long whiskery muzzle: “So, even though you were afraid you kept your wild boar shape until it was safe to change back?” Hugo nodded noticing that his companion was nodding his own great head in the direction of the innkeeper at his side. “Now let’s hear about your escape eh? Were you afraid then?”

“Well, I wasn’t in the same immediate danger then, not like when I was facing Sangres.” Again, the boar looked around at his admirers “but I didn’t know what was going to happen next. I overhead my master talking about me, saying I’d be going to Louis-Philippe or that awful Sergeant so yes, I was afraid but for my future.” He stopped, looking at his intent listeners “Why? Is there something wrong?”

Slowly, Ursian shook his head: “No, no Hugo, quite the opposite. Being able to control your shape when you are afraid or angry is really important, believe me I should know.”

Not really understanding, Hugo related his story and his journey to the Inn. Apart from the time it had been necessary for him to take on terrier form which drew several questions, they let him continue uninterrupted almost as if they knew most of it. When he had finished, Gilles went behind the bar and poured two tankards from the barrel marked “GB Ale” and clutching one each, Ursian and Gilles went outside into the clearing. When they returned, their tankards now empty, Hugo heard Gilles mutter “…If he can hold his shape when he’s….” but the rest of the conversation was lost as one of the lions lying by the fire (whose name, Hugo later discovered was Lucius) gave an uninhibited roar, followed by an even greater snore and rolled onto his back, his paws in the air.

Gilles sat once again on his stool whilst Ursian went behind the bar and refilled his tankard once more. “I expect you are wondering what this is all about, eh?” he growled at Hugo, who nodded slowly and answered: “Well, so many strange things have been happening of late. I was just a simple hunting Hound, albeit with an unusual ability but now I am being chased by armed policemen, while owls and eagles are interested in my welfare, calling me a Paladin instead of a Hound – I don't even know whether that's a good or a bad thing."

"Let me put your mind at rest, lad." rumbled Gilles gruffly peering at the Hound through his wire-rimmed spectacles: "It's a good thing, a very good thing, it explains why you can change shape as you do and why you are not just a simple Hound with a trick up your sleeve. To be a Paladin is special. All our guests here, save for Mlle. Mimi and our newly arrived bloodhounds, are Paladin except that none of them, at least now, can perform your transformations. They may look different but underneath we are all the same…we are all Paladin. Now settle back and we will try to explain as best we can. All the creatures here, all these different shapes and sizes, look at them."

Hugo did as he was bidden and took in the assembled company of bears, wild boars, some horses, lions, wolves and even a tiger plus many other forest animals, big and small. The strange white horse looked back at him and as she did so, he realised what was different: protruding from her forehead was a long, white, twisted horn!

"She's a unicorn" muttered Ursian "and even I don't know how that happened."

Gilles gave Hugo a few moments to take in what he was seeing and then spoke: "As I told you, underneath these shapes we are really all the same. We all shared the same ancestry long ago." Mimi had drawn closer to Hugo and appeared to be listening intently to what was being said – despite understanding not a word. Hugo realised he would have to explain everything to her – well as best he could!

Hugo looked again at the various 'residents. 'How can I have the same ancestry as this lot?' he mused 'look at them, well the wolves perhaps look a bit like dogs but horses? Especially that strange white one – and as for them' he cast an eye over the sleepy lions and tiger 'hah, overgrown cats they are and even lazier'. Gilles continued: "Our differences are really superficial; we have our animal ways but strip those away and you will find we are all pure Paladin. That's what we call ourselves just the same as the two legs call themselves 'human'."

"I could call them something else…" grumbled Ursian. "Pour another tankard" soothed Gilles.

"Good idea" grumbled Ursian but Hugo's eyes widened in astonishment as the already enormous animal seemed to grow before their eyes to such a size that he could reach beyond the bar and help himself easily. No-one mentioned it….so neither did Hugo, for now.

"Like I was saying, we call ourselves Paladin and although some may have forgotten that, those of us who live or have lived in the High Valley never forgot."

"The High Valley?" Hugo asked, perplexed.

"That is our ancestral homeland; It's where we all, everyone here, all truly belong and now, it may well be that many of us will be returning …that all depends on you."

Hugo looked concerned, a large dog frown developing on his wrinkly forehead. He said nothing as Gilles went on: "For the full story it is probably best you wait until you and Athina meet again. She is rather the expert. I can tell you that there was a time, very long ago, when all your ancestors were in the High Valley. They could all change their shapes. It wasn't until they left that they started to lose that ability…a question, Hugo?"

"Err yes, M. Gilles. Why did our ancestors leave?"

"There were some terrible things happening out in the world but perhaps it's best if Athina explains all that. I will tell you that they left to try and help humankind, it was indeed a noble cause." The innkeeper would not be drawn further on this. Instead he said "When your ancestors left the High Valley to help humankind they all expected to return when their task was complete, and most did; their descendants live there to this day. You, all of you, have cousins there. Some did decide not to return; they gradually lost their Paladin identity over time. They joined various tribes of their new animalkind or started clans of their own. They were content, but over time their animal side grew stronger and they lost their ability to change shape. These were given the name Poursuivants." Gilles paused to accept a full tankard and took a long swig giving Ursian his chance: "To those that did not wish to return, the Grand Council passed on the Promise of Sanctuary. This confirmed that for as long as there are Guard Bears there will be a place of sanctuary provided for the Poursuivants, a place they can come to when in danger."

"Yes, thank you, I was going to tell Hugo that. Although many hundreds of winters have passed since that Promise was first issued, it still holds good. That is why all of you are here today."

"It was a Bear Promise" grunted Ursian, barely audible over the mutterings of all the animals as they commented on why exactly they had come to Sanctuary.

"Of course, this place and the others like it weren't actually started for that reason. That's why the Sentinels are outside." At the mention of the Sentinels, Hugo's hackles rose of their own volition. He had been assured by Gilles and Ursian that these 'Sentinels' were entirely harmless to those seeking Sanctuary, but they still induced a cold fear in him. He hoped that later someone would explain exactly who they were or had been.

"Don't worry lad." Gilles placed an enormous paw on Hugo's head: "They mean no harm, they are here to protect us from humankind and a fine job they have done. Indeed, according to the stories told by residents of Monbezier they are still doing a fine job. Utter nonsense most of it is but it does keep people away from us.

You might meet Old Guillaume who wanders in the forest. It was he who warned the Grand Council that the Sentinels were declining in numbers here. It's happening at all the other Inns too. It won't happen overnight, and the younger ones have promised they will stay as long as they are able, but when they go…well the locals will eventually lose their fear of the forests and that will make it difficult to keep the Promise."

There was a low growl of disapproval which emanated from Ursian: "It's a Bear Promise."

"Yes, Cousin of course it is but I am trying to explain to Hugo what the problems are. To protect the Inns without the Sentinels would take all our clan and all the Fighting Bears as well - but eventually humankind would win. They would hunt us down as they have the wolves." Growls of discontent from the wolf pack greeted this statement. "Guillaume also says he has seen even more powerful weapons than the ones they use now. No, the Council is right – this has got to be done and you know it's right too. If we cannot protect our friends here, then we have got to get all our kind back to the High Valley." This last was directed to Ursian but then Gilles turned back to Hugo: "And this is where you come in, my young friend. The Council especially wants you back in the High Valley for your own safety. You are a true Paladin, the first in many a year. You could stay here and be safe but for how long? Anyway, what sort of life would that be for a fit young Hound like yourself? Look what fifteen winters have done to him."

Hugo looked at the largest of the lions stretched out comfortably in front of the vast roaring fire and thought to himself 'now that's exactly the life I am looking for' but said nothing and arranged his expression into one of disapproval.

"That's not the life for you Hugo, you have important things to do but until all danger is passed we must ensure that you are well protected."

"Mimi told me that the Patrol searching for me have all disappeared. I should be safe now."

"Them? They weren't a threat, more of a nuisance really. No, the real threat to you is from your old master, Louis-Philippe de Garenne. Athina is having him watched day and night. He discovered just how special you are when he saw you perform in the kennels. He realised what that meant - his Renegade side is becoming more and more dominant and he will seek to keep you under his control, eventually his hatred will overwhelm him for he can never be what you are: A Paladin. His Renegade side will compel him to kill you."

Hugo felt faint hearing this. That mention of Renegade again. Could it be true? He had felt something of a connection to this foppish young man, but never any affection.

"Don't worry Hugo, Athina knows his nature. He is lazy and a coward, so we will have plenty of warning when he comes for you. Trust me, you will be in safe hands all the time. So, how can you help us? All the Inns are now overflowing with those seeking sanctuary and more arrive every month. If we wait until the last of the Sentinels leave it will be too late. The Council wants to repeat the call to all Poursuivants to return to the High Valley long before that happens. We can get them to come to the Sanctuary Inns and escort them, but we desperately need to make more space at the Inns for the expected arrivals.

There was a time when humankind understood our ways. Just a few hundred years ago Guard Bears would have been able to lead the Poursuivants back home, avoiding the towns of course, but now… well take Ursian here" Gilles paused to take a breath and a quick swig from his neglected ale tankard. Ursian began removing one of his enormous knee length leather boots. Curious, the animals watched him and drew closer as he revealed his bare hind paws covered in angry blisters, scars and boils.

The animals gasped and drew back, embarrassed that he should have had to reveal himself like this. Ursian's eyes met those of Hugo, the old bear's eyes blazing with anger and hurt: "It was my own fault. I was captured whilst making my way to relieve old Gilles here. I trusted the son of an old friend and he betrayed me. Sold me to some fairground folk saying I was a shape changer."

"Be calm old friend" said Gilles trying to break the uneasy silence as Ursian slowly pulled on his giant boots with many grunts.

"Athina told me before I left the High Valley" Ursian spoke almost in a whisper which for him was a soft growl "that human attitudes had changed and that I must never ever use my 'special' abilities if I could be observed – which is how I spent ten years chained and forced to dance on hot coals for human entertainment." Ursian's eyes were now a fiery red and he was breathing heavily. The listening animals were stunned by this revelation and their eyes were cast down in shame for his suffering.

"Dear Cousin, you are safe now. More ale! Let the missus help you." Gilles' eyes met those of his wife who had entered the bar and she came forward to put a furry arm around the giant bear, leading him towards the beer barrels.

Ursian is right, Hugo. Remember that you must never ever be observed changing your shape. It is for your own safety."

"Yes, I see that now" said Hugo "Athina did tell me that but at the time I had no idea why."

"Athina told us that humankind had passed down amongst themselves legends of shape changers doing good then disappearing again – but now those legends have been distorted. We have been portrayed as monsters or demons, forces of darkness and evil. We are no longer safe. We were asked last night whether we thought that you could lead at least some of the Poursuivants, a pioneer group, back to the High Valley. We think you can do it." Hugo's face betrayed his shock and he was momentarily unable to respond. He watched the very comfortable Lucius roll once more onto his side, still sleeping. Feeling envious, the Hound said: "Of course, of course, I will do whatever you need me to do."

"Well lad, you've made up your mind pretty quickly!" Gilles smiled broadly, removing his wire-rimmed glasses. "Rest now and then we will try to come up with a plan. You will have Ursian here for company of course. The last ten years have taken their toll on his temperament and now he needs to refresh himself for a while back in the High Valley." Ursian, hearing this let out a low rumbling growl and Gilles looked at him sharply. "You know that I only speak the truth. I thought we had resolved this when you gave your word to Athina as a Bear. The missus and I and can hang on here for a bit longer and you can come back when you are fully fit."

Gilles retained the stern expression on his face until his friend nodded sadly: "I feel that I am letting you down, Cousin but of course you are right. If I had managed to control my temper… and I know that when I do get back here I shall be dealing with humankind more. If I lose my temper again then the future of the Inn could be in danger. I will go with you, Hugo – I still remember the way home." Ursian executed a graceful bow to Hugo, remarkable for an animal of his size.

"Right Ursian, that's settled. Now I shall go outside and get one of the eagles to deliver our message to the Grand Council."

CHAPTER 21

Hugo was sitting outside Sanctuary Inn with Mimi, Ursian and Sangres. The air was fresh and invigorating but with a distinct feeling of autumn in the nearby woods. The trees surrounding the clearing were a riot of autumnal colours, reds, oranges and yellows mingling with the intense dark green of the pine trees deeper in the forest. It had been a couple of days since he had agreed to lead the other animals back to the High Valley and he was now having doubts about this whole business.

"What if I fail? You can't just move a motley crew of animals like these halfway across France without anyone noticing – try hiding a group of lions in any crowd!"

"Well actually you can" interrupted Ursian "I was moved around France as part of a carnival for ten long years…." he paused for a moment, his face creased with sadness. "People are a bit wary of show folk; just because they don't have "proper" houses people are suspicious. Visitors come just for the shows and leave the show folk to themselves."

Mimi, who had been sitting with Hugo asked what they were discussing and when she heard, she was unable to contain herself. "I love fairs!" She yipped excitedly. She was momentarily silenced by a stern look from the others. "But I do" she muttered. "I saw one going to La Garenne once and there were lions and tigers and an ephelant…and a Bear." Ursian growled at the little dog sharply.

"Your little friend seemed very excited" Ursian muttered. "You tell her, just tell her I spent 10 years as an 'exhibit'. Caged by day, dancing on hot coals at night. Eventually the fair came close enough for me to reach Sanctuary Inn." As he said this, he gently stroked her head to show he was not angry with her as she cowered in silence. Once Hugo had explained, Mimi sat quietly hoping no-one would notice her terrible embarrassment. Hugo addressed Ursian:

"Travelling as a carnival might just work but we would need wagons with cages, like fairground wagons...and another problem, fairs have humans and without humans we would definitely be noticed.

I know I can change my shape, so can you Ursian, but Madame Athina told me never to do it again, at least until I had talked to Gilles about it."

"That's good advice Hugo. He's an expert because he changes back and forth all the time. He's off selling his amazing ales far and wide amongst humankind" laughed the bear.

"In humankind form?" asked Hugo.

"Of course, otherwise he couldn't keep feeding all his guests. He's out and about just now but as soon as he returns to the Inn we can speak to him. Meanwhile, I think we need to talk to the other animals. A few may want to remain here or even try and seek the High Valley on their own, but we have to give them all a choice." Ursian called all the animals together and explained that Hugo was prepared to try to lead them from the Inn to the High Valley. The Hound was the perfect choice – he was a true Paladin able to adopt humankind form and less temperamental than Ursian on his own, less likely to fly into a rage if challenged by a human. As for those animals who preferred to stay at the Inn, Gilles would be quite happy to have them stay but if they did decide to go alone then Ursian needed to make them understand that it would be a difficult and dangerous undertaking. This was especially so for the boars, bears and wolves for they were the most hunted by humankind.

"And what about me?" said the Unika the unicorn after they had listened in silence. "I am clearly rather different."

"Oh, don't you worry, we can stick a hat on your head and you can pull a wagon – people will think you're a horse" growled Sangres to the amusement of the whole company.

"Friends don't decide straight away – think about it and let me have your decision tomorrow" said Ursian who then returned to sit outside the Inn, smoking a long-stemmed clay pipe and humming softly to himself.

Shortly before supper that evening Hugo went out into the forest. He had forged an unlikely friendship with some of the Sentinels and could sit and listen for hours to their tales, especially when they talked about the Paladins who had protected them. Although they had no form, Hugo was able to communicate with them just using his mind.

One of the Sentinels had even known Hugo's ancestors: "They would always escort the pilgrims from La Garenne all the way here and then accompany the returning pilgrims all the way back again. You, young Hugo, are just like some of them. They could change from dog to human in the blink of an eye."

Hugo saw Gilles returning with his horse and cart, laden with provisions for the Inn. "Hallo, Hugo, picking up a few tips from the Sentinels, are you? Come on back to the Inn now lad, I have lots more news from the town, especially concerning you."

After the evening meal, Gilles, Ursian, Sangres and Hugo (with Mimi keeping close on his heels) gathered together in the private quarters of Gilles and his wife at the back of the deep cave. Gilles told them all the news; there had been a tremendous fuss north of the river about the patrol of gendarmes that had disappeared. The good news was that everyone in Monbezier had told those who came asking questions that there had been no sightings of them anywhere. However, the other piece of news was much more worrying. "Rumour has it that the patrol was searching for a dog – one with a large reward being offered for its return." Gilles looked over at Hugo.

"Just as Athina told us. That's not good but I don't think it changes Hugo's task, although it means that others will now know how valuable Hugo is, but not why. We will need to be more careful. Give it a few weeks and all the fuss will die down; humans seem very fickle in their concerns, they soon forget. Anyway, we need a bit of time for the plan to come together." Ursian nodded sagely as he said this.

"Ah, the plan" asked Gilles "what have you been hatching whilst I've been away?"

"We're going to form a travelling menagerie." Ursian paused to see what effect this statement would have "but we will need quite a bit of assistance from you, Gilles. We've discussed this with the other animals and we think the only way of getting them all safely to the High Valley (especially the ones people will be afraid of or have never seen) would be to travel as a carnival. That way we could pass through towns and villages without too much comment. People expect a carnival to have performing animals…I should know!

There are always troupes of gypsies on the roads of France. What we will need are wagons, like fairground wagons, complete with bars. Then it will be more believable, don't you agree? I have discussed the 'bars' thing with Lucius and his friends and even he agrees, for once. Only one problem I can see."

"Ha, only one?" said Gilles, as Ursian continued undeterred: "We are going to need quite a few wagons, large wagons and specially designed too for the animals and for the provisions. So, not only do we need what humans use to buy things, but lots of it!"

"Hm, I can see sense in what you say, and it could be a good idea. Let me think on it." Gilles took some paper and an elaborate quill and inkwell over to a table and began to write, all the while mumbling and arguing with himself 'How many lions? Hm …per day of course…. wolves, a minimum of 8 lbs. per day, horses – how much hay?' and so on. Hugo observed Gilles as he made his calculations and realised that Gilles was holding his pen as if he was a human. Moreover, he was writing humankind words and numbers. Hugo was astonished, and it showed on his face. Ursian realised what it was that Hugo found so amazing.

"I can do that too. We can show you how to do it if you like?"

Gilles looked up from his writing: "I need to know how many animals will be going and because you will be travelling with wagons, the journey will be much slower – that means a lot of provisions. I must start brewing straight away and get back down into the town to order the wagons. My wonderful GB Ale will raise enough human money - I hope. Hortense! We have lots of work to do. Hugo, you have a lot to learn and not long to learn it."

The following morning Ursian took a roll call of all the animals to establish which ones wanted to go with Hugo. Of the remaining animals, almost all wanted to find safety, but several felt they could make it alone, including the unicorn. Hugo and Ursian went to see Gilles: "That's a whole lot of food. It will have to be dried food for the lions and tigers and wolves and dried fish for the bears – you'll have to get some scavenging done along the way for berries and fruit, plus hay for the horses and, I suppose, the wretched unicorn? The dogs and wolves will need food too. Luckily, some of these animals can forage for themselves.

We'll need a couple of fair-sized wagons for the supplies and at least another eight, oh dear eight, for the animals. Then, for that many we are going to need at least 18 horses. Luckily, we already have 12 and they are prepared to work on the journey, but we will still need to find more. I think we could use Unika?"

"Ah well. Unika has decided she can make it by herself. Hugo and I have both tried to explain that of all the animals, even the fiercest ones, she is the most likely to draw comment, but she is determined. You try, Gilles."

"Righto, I shall have to get that unicorn to face facts quickly but meanwhile we do have those six gendarmes' horses resting here; we could ask them. They might like to come along too. Tell you what, I will go and speak to them all now. May be a good idea to have some spares eh?"

"All sounds good to me." replied Ursian "Once you've convinced Unika to come with us, you can tell her she's going to be a carthorse."

"Ok, so now Hugo we need to start your training immediately. Shape-changing into another animal is quite easy once you know you are able to do it - but changing into a human is much more difficult and will be exhausting."

"Yes, I know. On the two occasions I have had to change, even a bit, I found it very strange and tiring."

"The trick of it is to concentrate hard on two important things at once – one animal, one human. That way you can change back more easily. You just need to bring the 'animal' thoughts back into your mind, concentrating very hard and back you come. Works best if the thoughts of your 'animal' side are very happy ones It's best not to stay 'human' for too long though, a couple of hours at most, or you might begin to lose touch with your real nature. You can do it, with a bit of practice. I don't doubt it."

The bear added: "I always think of the High Valley when I want to remember being my animal self. It's never far from my mind."

"I always think of the missus" said Gilles, bashfully.

"Hugo, you can try but stay here where we can keep an eye on you. First, get a happy animal thought in your mind and concentrate on that. Then, think about 'humanness', something good that happened to you. As soon as you feel you are changing concentrate on holding the happy animal thought in your mind, sort of at the back of your mind to make sure you can change back... OK got that?"

"Alright, I'll give it a try right now" replied Hugo, making himself comfortable on the rug and closing his eyes to concentrate. He chose Mimi's joy at the thought of seeing the carnival and he fixed her happiness in his mind. Then he allowed his dog shape to be gradually transformed. Hugo rose onto his rear paws and found that he was quite tall, but not as tall as Ursian who, when upright, stood nearly eight feet high. "Not bad", said Gilles "take this cloak and wrap it around you to disguise all that fur" and he handed Hugo a thick grey hooded cloak which Hugo recognised as similar those worn by the Sentinels of the forest; he suddenly remembered he had seen something like this in his dreams. "You know you make a passable human – ugly of course and very hairy" laughed Gilles. "Now focus…and bring yourself back slowly to the true Hound that you are." Hugo concentrated on Mimi's shrill bark of happiness and the transformation began to reverse itself. The Hound found it quite painful at first and his body felt stiff and beaten but at last he was on all four paws once again.

"How was that?" asked Ursian.

"Not bad, I feel quite sore and well, itchy but it was easier than the first time I tried it. Then I only wanted to make my paw a hand but even so I really felt that my animal-ness was going…."

"You are going to need lots and lots of practice my lad – try it two or three times a day. By the time I am ready to go into town again you should be sufficiently good at it to come with me – as a furry human. Now, I must get back to my brewing."

"Let me give you a hand; I need to get some practice in for when I come back to relieve you here" growled Ursian and the two friends went off in good spirits to join Gilles' wife in the giant cave behind the Inn.

Hugo practiced a couple of times each day until it no longer felt so strange and uncomfortable. He now looked down at his 'new' self when he had changed and noticed how his limbs elongated to accommodate his 'human' legs and his chest broadened – it was a very strange sensation indeed. He even plucked up enough courage to go into the back room and look at himself in the bright shiny surface of a huge copper log box beside the Inn's open fire. He couldn't judge his looks as he hadn't known what he looked like as a dog but to him at least he seemed much like any other human man – if a little hairier.

During the time that Hugo was perfecting his changing process, Gilles was absent from the Inn frequently. Ursian got on with the brewing work with Hortense so that they were well stocked. Each time that Gilles returned his wagon was laden with bags and boxes until the barn was stacked high with provisions. Three weeks had passed, full of activity, when it was announced that they would be going to town the next day. Next morning Gilles and Ursian loaded the cart with huge wooden barrels of beer. "Bring a cloak Hugo and come along. I will take you to Monbezier with me – but first of course some clothes, I think. We will wait until we are nearly out of the forest before you change your shape though; I don't want you being human for too long to begin with. It will be strange enough meeting your 'fellow humans' face to face for the first time."

Hugo had become used to Gilles being oversized and he was accustomed to seeing a bear wearing leather boots, and sometimes an apron but when Gilles re-appeared he had been totally transformed. Gilles was now completely in human form, a tall, bushy-haired but somewhat rotund figure, resplendent in red trousers, a striped waistcoat and a thick greatcoat. The Hound was taken aback. The innkeeper was truly humankind but at the same time Hugo could see that he was still Gilles, a bear – amazing! Ursian then appeared and he too had transformed himself, but not quite so successfully. He was wearing some of Gilles' old clothes which barely fitted him. The trousers reached only to just below his knees and there was a gap between his boot tops and the trouser ends. He wore a vast striped shirt, stretched to bursting over his wide chest with his massive arms protruding some distance beyond the ends of the sleeves. Even in his full transformation,

Ursian was even more hairy than Gilles and he was forced to walk hunched over to minimise his height. His face, though now human in most respects still bore the wicked gleaming smile of a hungry bear, there was no disguising that. Ursian flung a cloak over his ill-fitting garments: "I shall need to ask your missus to make me something a little less snug" he laughed. "It's best to wear the cloak anyway" replied Gilles. "People around here trust no-one and any strangers they do see are usually pilgrims so it's a good disguise and at least people won't be inclined to ask you about your business."

At that moment, Mimi wandered into the room and upon seeing the two animals in their 'man' outfits she began to quiver with fear and to whine desperately. Hugo saw her hiding behind one of the heavy wooden settles and realised that to her they were strangers, giant strangers. "It's OK, that's Gilles....and the giant in the short trousers, well that's Ursian. They can change their shapes, just like me. It's just that you haven't seen them fully changed before. This is them in their humankind forms. We'll be seeing them like this more often now." Both animals turned and gave passably courtly bows to the little dog who immediately began to yip excitedly, her way of laughing.

"Are you going to change as well, Hugo?"

"Yes, but I shan't do it until we are nearly out of the forest on the way to the town."

Gilles looked at Mimi: "Hugo, I think it would be better if the little lady stayed here; the humans are still looking for you because of the reward and t'is known now that she was with you."

"To tell you the truth Gilles, I use Mimi to assist me change my shape – she is my 'happy dog thought' – so it would be most useful to me if she could come along?" He looked pleadingly at his companions.

"I think he has a point there, old fellow I can't see much harm can come to her while we are delivering beer and buying provisions. She can hide under a sack on the cart if anyone comes near" added Ursian.

"Alright", said Gilles, reluctantly "but tell her to at least try not to be noticed" and he fixed Mimi with a stern eye. "She will, she will" laughed Hugo as the little dog yapped excitedly but immediately cast down her eyes under the combined gazes of Hugo, Gilles and Ursian.

CHAPTER 22

They set off with Gilles at the reins, Ursian at his side and the dogs running alongside excitedly. Some Sentinels joined them for a while, occasionally talking to Gilles in low voices so that even Hugo, with his acute hearing, was unable to hear clearly. Hugo and Mimi had become more accustomed to the Sentinels now and the constant fading and reappearing no longer scared them. One minute there would be a seemingly solid cloaked figure beside the cart and the next a gauzy haze floating in the air.

At the edge of the forest Hugo changed slowly into his human form. Mimi had not seen Hugo practicing and was amazed by how "human" he looked compared with his early attempt. "You look quite handsome, in a human sort of way" she said, giggling. "I thought I would try and concentrate even harder and instead of just being any human, I might try to look like my old master, Lucien. You are too young to remember him well, but he was a really good man – and handsome too." Hugo slipped on the trousers and jacket that Gilles had brought along. At first the Hound struggled to get his limbs into the legs of the trousers and his paws into the sleeves of the jacket. The buttons were a real challenge for him but eventually he was dressed. How strange it felt to have a coat over your own coat. He also had to wear a pair of old boots – most uncomfortable on feet accustomed to walking on bare ground – and the grey pilgrims' cloak, the hood covering his head and shading his face. "Now climb up here" said Gilles, motioning him to sit between them, a rather cramped seat.

As the horse and cart lumbered along the track into Monbezier, Mimi ran on ahead and straight into the town. She knew she could find her companions again easily using her acute sense of smell and because they were a little unusual. The streets were all arranged in a grid pattern, with many leading to the central square. It was market day and the town was filled with gaily coloured stalls piled high with fresh fruit and vegetables, bread, cheeses and colourful displays of kitchenware and fabrics. There was a long wagon with a drop-down flap on one side.

This flap displayed every sort of knife, from tiny bone handled tools to enormous scythes. She found the local butcher's stall very quickly and was tempted to try to steal some bones, which were in a basket on the ground. She was still considering the possibility when she looked up at a face she knew only too well. It was Raoul. Mimi watched Raoul go wandering among the stalls of the market distributing some crudely hand-written notices and got close enough to one stallholder as he read it aloud:

**"LARGE REWARD OFFERED
FOR THE RETURN OF HUGO HOUND."**

Mimi's blood ran cold. She scampered back the way she had come as fast as her little legs would allow her and found Hugo and the others just as they were coming into the market square. "Hugo, Hugo, stop, stop at once, go back…. Raoul is here - over there, look" and the little dog pointed with her small black nose.

"What is it?" asked Gilles as Mimi ran in circles round the hooves of the horses and then jumped onto the wagon.

"She says Raoul is here" groaned Hugo.

"I assume this Raoul is the man you escaped from?" asked Gilles. Hugo nodded, shocked. His mind raced, awash with both dog and human thoughts. Ursian turned to him: "It's a good thing little Mimi was along with us. At least now you know he is here and won't be too surprised if you meet him. The problem with young shape changers like you is that if you get a sudden shock it can sometimes bring on a spontaneous change without any warning – now that would be a problem!"

"You surely don't mean I should meet him face to face?" said a worried Hugo. Meanwhile the little terrier, very pleased with herself, was muttering "I knew I could be useful, I knew it." Ursian bent down to pat her muzzle and she bristled with pride and gazed adoringly at 'her' friendly giant.

"Hugo, sit here beside me and start looking for this Raoul character, will you? It's best you spot him before he notices us although he won't recognise you like that. Best to be safe though so keep your hood up."

Ursian growled menacingly: "Don't worry lad, I have a few scores to settle with these humans. I'll protect you."

"Enough of that cousin" muttered Gilles. "We are peaceable folk around here. Hugo, ask Mlle. Mimi to keep a look out and see if she can spot him again in the crowd. But be careful – he could well recognise her."

"Don't worry! I can run through the market under everyone's feet – no one can catch me" and off she went in search of Raoul. It wasn't too difficult; there were many human smells, but she could sniff out Raoul without any problem and soon she located him next to the baker's stall. Mimi moved in closer to hear what was being said. Raoul was asking the baker about Hugo. "You're asking after a dog, Monsieur? Most people around here are more interested in finding out what happened to the lost patrol. It was only just over the river here that they were last seen."

"Yes, yes but they too were looking for my dog."

"Ha! A likely story. It's more probable that they were looking for the gold." At the mention of gold, Raoul's greedy little eyes lit up. "Gold?"

"Yes, it's an old story – supposed to be worth a kings' ransom. It is said that it originally belonged to the Knights Templar. But….it will never be found. If it's buried in the forest, well no one goes in there – apart from Gilles the brewer. Now he's a funny one. Nice enough and the best brewer around here, lovely drop of beer…." the baker stopped talking for a moment to savour the memory "but, he can be a bit, well, odd. Oh look, there he is now, he comes in for his supplies on market day and sells his beer to buy what he needs although no-one can understand why he needs so much."

Raoul looked round and saw three figures perched on the driving seat of a big wagon, laden with beer barrels. He caught a sideways view of one of the men and rubbed his eyes. He looked once again: "But it can't be Lucien? My mind is playing tricks, surely?" Raoul was thinking aloud without realising that a small dog was listening closely to what he was saying. Mimi ran excitedly back to the wagon and relayed what she had heard.

"Ah, not the tales of missing gold again" said Gilles with a sigh "I've been hearing that one for hundreds of years; there has never been any truth in it, but every so often humans take it into their heads that it exists and try to get into the forest. The Sentinels make sure they don't stay though and that puts everyone else off that idea for a while."

Hugo, however, was less interested in the tales of treasure than the fact that Raoul had seen him and thought he was Lucien. He now regretted his decision to try to look like his late master.

"Don't worry, Hugo, it's a good test of your human disguise; he didn't see a dog, he saw a human, his dead brother."

"Yes, I know Gilles, but I am worried that if he gets too close I may panic and just change into a Hound again. What if he tries to speak to me?" Hugo's heart was pounding. He was beginning to panic at the thought.

"Keep calm, keep calm. Concentrate as hard as you can on your old master Lucien. Remember what we have been told – he was very special too. Obviously, you had a very strong connection to him and if Raoul is brave enough to ask me I can tell him that you are a friar, under a vow of silence.” The one thing which had been causing Hugo some difficulty was acquiring any semblance of a human voice. Both Gilles and Ursian had heavy, gruff voices, muffled by their ‘beards’ but Hugo’s new ‘voice’ tended to crack and sound more like a yelp. The others tried to reassure Hugo: “It happens to all of us the first few times. You’ll soon get the hang of it. Try not to talk very much at first. Come into the tavern with me. I have business in there and it will give us a chance to get out of sight for a while.” Gilles and Ursian, followed by Hugo entered the dark interior of the old tavern. “I think Mimi had better stay hidden. Your old master has had a shock today already. If he sees her too he might become too suspicious.”

The landlord was pleased to see Gilles and came towards the group with arms outstretched: “M. Gilles! Delighted as always to see you. I’m down to my last barrel of your delicious Ale. You know how the locals love it. Your usual?” He was already pouring a glass of foaming beer for Gilles. “Your friends?”

“Oh, this is my nephew Bruno” said Gilles, indicating Ursian. “I’m training him in the arts of brewing. This fellow here is a friar on his way to Compostella. He has taken a strict vow of silence, but that doesn’t include drinking.” Hugo nodded but said nothing. He was really pleased to be accepted by the innkeeper so maybe the plan would work.

Mimi looked around to make sure that neither her friends nor Raoul were watching as she left the wagon and positioned herself where she could watch the tavern entrance unnoticed. In a few minutes, the landlord and Ursian came out into the market square and began unloading the vast beer barrels emblazoned with the large initials ‘G-B-A’ and rolling them down into the cellar. The great bear could carry two at a time, one on each of his massive shoulders and the innkeeper was impressed by his enormous strength. “I could do with a chap like you to give me a hand in the cellar" he said. Ursian was at that moment occupied with worrying that his ill-fitting breeches would take the strain but then replied: "I thank you sir but - meaning no offence- I could never work in a tavern; my mother would not be at all pleased."

Mainly due to the massive Ursian's strength, the job was done in no time and the landlord paid Gilles for the ale. The group then said goodbye and wandered over to the butcher's red and white striped stall to buy supplies. "I've got your order back at my shop, M. Gilles. You must be feeding an army."

"No, no just my nephew Bruno here" indicated Gilles, with a laugh. The butcher's eyes rose slowly from Ursian's belt and up, up to his huge head.

"Ah yes I see what you mean."

"Bruno, can you bring round the cart to the back of the butcher's shop and when we have loaded it, we will need to go to the fishmongers as well." Gilles paid the butcher from his newly acquired purse of gold coins and made his way with Hugo to the fishmonger, then onto the vegetable seller, who had stored boxes of fruit and vegetables for him behind her stall. He turned to Hugo:

"Well that should keep you all in food for a while at least. The dried foods I ordered will not spoil. Although that may become a bit boring anything is better than starving. Now let's go to the livery stable. I need to see if we can get some more horses."

Once there, Gilles selected three strong looking horses and explained to them quietly that they had a long journey ahead of them but at the end of it they would live in a meadow, free for ever from pulling carts and being beaten. They whinnied in pleasure at the prospect and Gilles made a deal with the ostler for all three of them. Just as he was leaving the stables, he noticed a rather sad face watching him from a gloomy stall. "I heard you whispering to my stable companions, sir. Can you please take me too?" The sad voice came from a small grey Donkey with visible whip marks healing on his flanks. Gilles returned to the ostler: "What about that Donkey? How much do you want for him?"

"A very sad case indeed. He found his way to the town alone, and clearly he has been very badly treated. His face alone puts people off – he even depresses me! He is really of no use in that state, so why don't you just take him for nothing M. Gilles? You being such a good customer and all."

"Excellent" said Gilles and tied the Donkey to the provisions wagon. The Donkey tried his best to smile his thanks, but the smile was no more than an upturned grimace.

CHAPTER 23

Their final stop in the town was at the carpenter, M.Gaston Gerard, who came out smiling with pleasure to greet Gilles. "Ah Monsieur Gilles, I think I have exactly what you wanted." In the large yard at the rear stood all the gleaming, newly built wagons, freshly painted in bright colours, their wheels shiny with red paint. Two were completely enclosed with a door in the rear, whilst another seven wagons had cages bolted to their bases. All were inscribed:

"HUGO'S AMAZING TRAVELLING MENAGERIE"

in large blue lettering. They each bore brightly painted depictions of animals, stars and moons in a riot of colours. "They are magnificent, M. Gerard. The paintwork…the colours…. you are a genius!"

"Are they not exactly what you wanted, Monsieur? I have no idea why you would want them….and I am not a man to pry into anyone's business…."

"I am going into business with my nephew here" Gilles indicated Ursian "it's about time he made his way in the world. I can take some with me now, but I'll have to come back for the rest." They hitched the newly acquired horses to the new carts and Gilles picked the most docile of the animals to pull the cart to be driven by Hugo and whispered in the horse's ear "Easy now lad, he's never driven a cart before. Take it easy on him and there'll be some sugar for you at our place." At the livery stables they bought even more hay, packed into bales and set off for home at last.

As they were about to leave the town Ursian realised that little Mimi was not with them. He went back towards the entrance to the inn and she crept sheepishly from her hiding place when she saw his huge figure approaching. He immediately picked her up and tucked her under his arm, then without a word, placed her on the wagon. She explained she had been watching Raoul who was now inside the inn, she explained and begged to be allowed to stay behind in case he pursued them. Ursian was unhappy about this but the little dog was so desperate to help that reluctantly he and Gilles agreed.

The party set off, the bright wagons drawing many interested looks from the townsfolk who stared dumbfounded at the marvelously wrought illustrations. They drove slowly onwards towards the forest, the wagons piled high with hay and food. Along the way, as the horses chatted amongst themselves, the little Donkey trotted silently behind the provisions wagon, resigned and withdrawn.

Once the companions had emerged from the carpenter's barn with the first three of their new wagons Raoul quickly downed his tankard of GB Ale and went outside to get a good look at the painted sign on the sides of those which remained in the yard. As he watched the wagons leaving the square, his mind was in turmoil.

He was sure he had seen his dead brother and now his dead brother was driving one of these wagons - which bore the name HUGO! However, his mind soon wandered from these strange events to the tale of missing gold. There was a fortune in gold, the gold was in the forest, the brewer was heading into the forest so…it followed that if Raoul followed the brewer, he could lead him to the treasure. How else could a simple brewer afford all the goods he had bought today? He must have found it. 'I'll take that treasure from him then I shall be rich' thought the simple man, simple but stupid. Raoul followed the convoy of wagons at a safe distance and Mimi crept along well behind her old master, watching.

At the edge of the forest Gilles halted, dismounted and slowly changed back into his animal form. "You can get back to being a Hound now, Hugo. No-one can see you."

"What about Raoul? I am certain he is nearby. We know he is following us and I can smell him, I can……he's over there, in that direction" and Hugo indicated the nearby trees with his human nose.

"Don't worry about him. I think it will be a nice surprise for him to see this" and both Gilles and Ursian burst out laughing. Unconvinced, Hugo jumped down from the cart and removed his voluminous cloak.

"Well, it will be good to be back as a Hound again but who will drive the wagon?"

They heard a slow, deep voice: "Don't worry. I shall follow the others. I have extra rations waiting for me." It was the horse that drew Hugo's wagon. "This is so easy, and I really don't understand why humans insist on sitting with us."

Hugo concentrated hard on Mimi dancing around and happy as he transformed himself back into a Hound. This time, because he had been in human form so long he found it surprisingly painful, especially stretching his face into the long sensitive Hound's muzzle. "Ooooh, that's better" said the Hound as his 'human' garments fell away from his body. He stretched back and forth on his four long legs and shook himself delightedly.

Raoul had indeed hidden himself nearby watching events, still believing he was undetected. Now he literally could not believe his own eyes. He watched first Gilles the brewer transform himself into a very large bear, and then his dead brother became Hugo Hound. All sorts of mad thoughts were rushing through his head; the first was that the excellent GB Ale he had sampled must have magical properties, but his focus was on Hugo. He had found him and not only that, he was close to a huge treasure. Soon, Raoul Lecaron would be a very rich man.

CHAPTER 24

As the convoy of wagons entered the forest, Ursian got down from the wagon seat and he too changed back into his true form. "The horses will make their own way now" he growled "I believe I have business close by" and he allowed himself a great booming, echoing laugh. Mimi meanwhile had remained some way behind Raoul, who now stood at the edge of the dark forest where the convoy had disappeared, swallowed up by the gloom. Although Mimi had become accustomed to being 'shadowed' when she roamed around the forest on her own, she was still anxious to keep up with the little convoy. Quite often when she got a bit lost, she had had to ask the Sentinels to guide her back to the clearing. However, today she sensed that they would have more important business than guiding her. Her mind made up, she ran as fast as she was able past Raoul, barking wildly, and made for the point where she had last seen the wagons disappearing. As she expected, the moment that Raoul saw her small shape fly past him he recognised her as the other 'escapee', Hugo's companion, and he rushed headlong into the forest, determined to catch the little terrier. She would lead him to Hugo….and that gold….

Mimi ran and ran, straight into the waiting arms of Ursian and was scooped up and carried back towards Sanctuary Inn. When they arrived, the new wagons were standing outside the inn being admired by the motley group of animals, some walking around them sniffing, others peering inside with interest.

Gilles looked enquiringly at his friend who nodded. "It is done" growled Ursian and walked into the inn still cradling Mimi in his huge arms. The horses belonging to the Lost Patrol were grazing nearby. Gilles strolled over to talk to them and they immediately trotted up to him and greeted him like an old friend. “Good day, lads. I will need you to come back with me to Monbezier this afternoon and collect some more wagons just like these.” Gilles pointed to the waiting carts. At this the horses lowered themselves onto their front legs, as if bowing and said in unison “We will be ready.” Gilles thought that sometimes military training was a great help.

That same day, after a hearty lunch, Gilles rode back into the town, leading the fresh horses and collected the remaining wagons and then preparations began in earnest for the great journey with much good-natured grunting, squawking and growling. The animals that would be in the wagons with bars tried them out for comfort and size, whilst it had to be explained to those that would travel on paws or hoofs that when travelling through villages or towns they must be tethered to the rear of the supply wagons. The animals were happy with their boxes or enclosures, the food was stowed away, and the route discussed and rediscussed.

At last, all was ready, and the travellers bid farewell to those animals that had opted to remain at Sanctuary Inn. Some of them were awaiting news of their families, whilst others were afraid to risk the unknown, that place called High Valley. No pressure was applied by Gilles and Ursian. Each animal was encouraged to make up his or her own mind. The only animal on which any pressure was exerted was the unicorn. Determined to ‘go it alone’ it had been explained to her quite forcefully that as a creature long considered extinct – or unique, as she described herself – she would be in much greater danger travelling alone than with the Menagerie. This appeal to her uniqueness finally convinced her that she must travel with Hugo, but she was very unenthusiastic about being treated as a ‘mere horse’ for the duration of the journey. At the lastminute the leader of the wolves announced that his pack would not be making the journey. If this expedition was successful, then perhaps next time but the wolves would have to be inside wagons where prying human eyes could not see them. Memories of the cruelty of humankind were too bitter, he explained. Gilles nodded and told him that he understood, and they were welcome at the Inn for as long as they wished to remain.

The menagerie left the Inn and travelled through the forest shortly after first light. Hugo had not had an opportunity in the excitement to ask about Raoul and no-one had mentioned him so now as Mimi sat on the wagon with him and the caravan passed through the forest, he took the opportunity to find out. Mimi giggled as she told him: "I was outside, on the edge of the forest and close to Raoul but I got distracted – you know what I'm like Hugo, can't resist following a scent – then I realised I couldn't see the wagons anymore. I made a sudden break for it and ran past him as fast as my little legs could carry me.

I could hear his heavy feet pounding along after me. I looked back, and I could see him just a few paces behind me, then…I looked again…….and a huge paw scooped me up. It was Ursian, but I swear he must have been twice his normal size. Anyway, Raoul was right behind me and he and Ursian came face to face! Ha! I've never seen anyone look so scared; Raoul just stood there, frozen. No one moved a muscle, but I felt sooo safe….and then there was a sort of clanking noise and the Sentinels began to appear. I got scared and shut my eyes tight. I could feel that they weren't nearly as friendly as they are with us. They sort of formed a group around Raoul whose face was pure white. One of them spoke: "We will take care of this now, my friend" it said and when I plucked up my courage and looked again – Raoul had gone….and so had all the Sentinels. I could just make out a faint mist disappearing into the trees and that clanking sound moving away from me. That's all I know, Hugo."

Gilles, accompanied by Madame Barbier, walked with them until then they reached the point where the forest path met the main road south. Here, very formally, Ursian bowed to Madame Barbier and took the paw of his friend: "I thank you for your kindness which I will one day to be able to repay" and he made a very courtly bow. "As soon as I have escorted Hugo and the rest of the company to the High Valley, taken a short respite and seen my family once again, I shall return to relieve you at the inn. Your rest, my friend, is long overdue." Gilles bowed in return to his old friend: "Just take care and keep safe. Give my best wishes to all at the High Valley and tell them we are safe and well and looking forward to seeing them all again."

As Gilles spoke his eyes filled with tears, partly because he was again losing his old friend and partly at the memory of the High Valley. He hastily brushed a paw across his face and abruptly turned away for a moment and then turned back to stand with his wife watching the caravan pass by along the main highway. The final wagon was driven by Hugo, in his Hound form, sitting on his haunches with the reins loosely held in his right paw. Gilles had taught him this to convince casual passers-by if he wore his cloak. In fact, the horses were quite able to drive themselves but as Hugo could now use both his paws like human hands without having to transform himself completely he wanted to practice.

Sangres and Mimi were acting as lookouts ahead of the convoy and some way behind Hugo's wagon a magnificent tiger, called Meera padded along. She too had been an escapee from a carnival, but her captors had attempted to remove her front claws and so her gait was a little unsteady. She had asked to be allowed to walk when the caravan travelled outside of towns to practice walking once more but agreed to be caged at other times. Gilles and Madame Barbier waved a final farewell and then turned back into the forest.

CHAPTER 25

Captain Roland Lebrun sat on the veranda of his shabby office. The building stood at the edge of the barracks close to the sea and on the dusty outskirts of Ajaccio in Corsica. He was enjoying the afternoon sun and his well-worn boots rested on an old wooden table which served as his desk. This was piled high with papers and documents secured by large stones rescued from the beach. He was dressed in uniform breeches and a flowing white shirt – no-one stood on ceremony here. The afternoon was still drowsy with heat and he had just enjoyed a satisfying lunch brought in from the local tavern. He sat thinking of how much his life had changed over the last few years, the battles he had fought and the people – one special person – he had met. At least this was better than his last posting. He had arrived in Corsica little more than a year earlier fresh from a long sea voyage from the island of Réunion, far away in the middle of the Indian Ocean.

After Waterloo, his hasty dispatch to that far-flung outpost of France had been quite a shock, not least the uncomfortable hot, damp climate of the island itself. Although he had shared a common language with the islanders he had not even had time to adapt to the culture, so alien from his own Parisian upbringing. Less than six months after his arrival with his men, he had been ordered back to France, this time to Ajaccio. To his further astonishment, he had also been promoted to the rank of Captain, the papers having been signed by no less a personage than the fiercesome General Georges Destrier. Now, here he was, at least one step nearer to his home and he wondered: what next?

That morning he had received an urgent signal ordering him to return to Paris and report without delay to the General. Frankly he had believed that he had been forgotten on this quiet French island. He spent his time hunting smugglers on the coast and bandits in the mountains and although he regularly filed detailed reports to Headquarters, he suspected that when (or even if) these arrived they were promptly filed in a basement, unread. The summons came as a welcome diversion and he unfolded and reread the order several times as he stared at the calm sea...Paris again…

He thought back to his last time in that city. After Waterloo, he had made his way back accompanying a group of badly wounded soldiers tended by two young ladies. He rode while they had travelled in a closed carriage. He had discovered the conveyance up to its axles in thick, sucking mud. The horses were exhausted, and it appeared that the occupants had been abandoned by the driver. The two young ladies tending the wounded were obviously gentlewomen, sisters Kate and Amélie Giscard. He had seen them briefly amid the confusion of the battlefield, tending to the wounded and dying. They told him that they had gone to Waterloo to become 'vivandières', ladies who volunteered to nurse, feed and sometimes supply ammunition to the troops. They were only too glad to accept his offer to escort them. He had gone back through the straggling lines of men until he found a young lad in a tattered uniform. He was called Rene and had needed little persuading to take on the task of driving the carriage. Roland had then ridden into the surrounding countryside and eventually 'borrowed' two stout plough horses to pull the vehicle from the mud and back onto the road.

The ladies had come to rely on him. Despite their dark, practical clothing with warm hooded cloaks that hid their features, they were obviously quite young, and he was instantly drawn to one of them: Kate. She was not as conventionally beautiful as her sister Amélie but had fine dark eyes and abundant honey-brown hair, strands of which were occasionally revealed by her hood. Both were clearly unused to such rough travelling yet not at all squeamish at the horrible sights along the way. Kate's determination was matched only by her gentleness, especially with men who would never see their families again. Amélie also coped well with the horrors they encountered but seemed less able to cope with the many deaths she had witnessed.

As they journeyed they had told him they came from a small town in the southwest, called La Garenne. Intrigued, he had enquired whether it was the home of the Duc de Garenne, Marshal of France. He had served under the Duc as a junior officer in a gendarmerie cavalry regiment during the Spanish Campaign. Mlle. Kate had appeared somewhat flustered as she confirmed that she knew of the Duc's estate which was near her home but did not elaborate further.

When they all eventually reached Paris, the officer was already smitten enough with Kate to ask both girls if they would like to stay with his sister and her husband before making their way home. Both his parents were dead, but his sister had remained in the Lebrun townhouse near Montmartre. However, on the outskirts of the great city they had found total chaos: the remnants of the defeated army, many of whom were drunk, wandered aimlessly through the streets, many on crutches, or wearing blood-soaked bandages over parts of their bodies. Few had boots or complete uniforms – they were indeed a sorry sight, the once proud army of Napoleon. The turmoil of the war had rubbed off on the citizens of Paris too. They seemed dazed by their country's defeat and the streets were lawless and dirtier than he had ever seen them.

"Ladies, I'm afraid I must leave you, but I am worried about how safe you will be even in a closed carriage amongst this rabble." He rode beside the window of the mud-stained vehicle struggling to make its way along the overcrowded streets near the River Seine. "I am under orders to report to Faubourg St. Honore immediately I return to Paris and then I shall make my way to my family home. It's close by Montmartre near Rue des Capuchins" he told them.

"Could you perhaps meet me by the church in Rue des Capuchins in two hours and I can escort you there?"

"Thank you, thank you Lieutenant – we shall at least be safe there whilst we prepare for our onward journey. First, we must get these wounded men cared for at the army hospital. Our coachman can then take us across the city to Montmartre. You will, I am sure, be there before us."

They had parted near the River Seine and the coach swayed away towards the Hospital des Armées near the Louvre. Only after they had left did Roland think that perhaps he should have given them the full address of his family house, just in case.

At Headquarters there were hordes of returning gendarmes milling around, trying to find out what they should do. He had to wait a very long time and when at last he managed to tell someone who he was, he was surprised to be told to go immediately to see General Destrier himself, Inspector General of Gendarmes. Many things had changed whilst he had been away. Many new faces, disorder everywhere. He was even more shocked when Destrier personally ordered him to leave without delay to command a unit bound for Réunion in the Indian Ocean. He knew that the place was sometimes known as the Bourbon Isle but that was the extent of his knowledge. According to the General, the island was in turmoil, there had been bloodshed in the capital of St. Denis and force was needed to settle matters. Roland had begged to be allowed a day to visit his family in Paris (and meet Kate again) but his request had been refused abruptly. "We need re-enforcements there as soon as possible. Every moment your arrival is delayed means more bloodshed!" Destrier had replied handing over his orders. "You have a long sea voyage ahead of you. Go now, your men are in the courtyard already. There's a frigate waiting for you at La Rochelle."

A serving officer must follow orders…but he had never forgotten that journey back to Paris, nor his travelling companions. Now he was returning to Paris once more… He had hastily arranged a boat to get him to Nice the next day. From there he managed to argue himself into an inside seat in a rocking, uncomfortable coach bound for the capital. It was a long, bumpy journey stopping at inns of dubious quality and even more dubious food.

Upon his arrival at Headquarters, he was escorted immediately to the office of General Destrier, without even the opportunity to change his grubby, dust-encrusted tunic. He remembered the General from their last meeting. Stern and efficient, he had survived all the mayhem of the Revolution, then the war and all the political upheavals thereafter.

The Captain was aware that the name of Destrier had been associated with government or the law in France for generations. He was ushered into a high-ceilinged office where his Commander sat behind a magnificently ornate but cluttered desk. The young man stood uncertainly in front of the General who was dressed in an immaculate uniform and seemed absorbed by the papers he was studying: "Sit down man! Give me a moment…now" said the General without taking his eyes from the sheaf of papers on his desk. "Can you tell me what you know about the so called 'Lost Patrol'?"

The Captain was completely nonplussed: "Err, eh well not much at all Sir. Not much news reaches us in Corsica and then only very slowly."

"Good exactly what I was hoping you would say. You will bring a fresh eye to the matter. There are too many rumours flying around and far too much speculation; ghosts, supernatural beings! We must deal with facts, not fairy tales - and the only fact as far as I am concerned is that they are all deserters. When they are found – and they will be, mark my words – I will give them a fair trial and execute every one of them." The General's voice rose with each word and he roared these last words, his face contorted with anger.

Roland waited quietly until the General calmed down a little "I apologise. This matter has made me very angry; what a fuss over a dozen deserters! All the garrisons are talking about it. Do you know I have had men refuse to accept a posting based on such fairy stories? Military men! Questioning an order!" The General hit the desk with his fist and the papers under his hand skittered across the desktop, some fluttering onto the floor. He retrieved them into an untidy pile and then handed them over gruffly. "Here. I want you to read this file - although frankly there's not much in it that will be worth the effort. Then I want you to tell me what you make of it." Destrier sat back in his deep leather chair and fell silent. The interview was obviously at an end, so the young officer rose, saluted as best he could with his arms full, and left. In the outer office he sat down, placed his hat on the chair beside him and began to read.

According to the file, the 'Lost Patrol' had been based in a small town in Southwestern France called La Garenne – the name jumped out at him and his heart leapt – Kate had said she came from a town of that name and her home had been in the south west too. 'Maybe, just maybe it's the same place' he thought. 'Perhaps I shall meet her again'.

The report from the local commander, one Captain Vincent Falaise was skeletal. The patrol had left the town one morning, but no reason was detailed in the report; they had apparently spent the night at the Auberge St. Antoine further south, then there had been some sightings of them the following day travelling south again – but after a sighting near the River Dordogne they had indeed disappeared. In the words of Captain Falaise "vanished off the face of the earth." He read the brief service records of the 12 missing men, but only that of a Sergeant Brochard was of any real interest. According to his commander, the sergeant had been at La Garenne for 10 years with an apparently exemplary service record yet there was a note that all previous records for him had been either lost or misplaced. He did not exist, it seemed, before his final posting.

The garrison commander had noted on the file that the sergeant had overseen an investigation into the death of a Colonel Lecaron. That name was familiar too. Colonel Lecaron, Chevalier of the Légion d'Honneur, was a hero amongst his contemporaries. He had commanded a cavalry regiment in Spain and tales of his courage were widespread. Roland Lebrun had a special reason to be grateful to him. The Colonel had saved the life of his closest friend, an Ensign by the name of Jacques Belaudie.

Shuffling together the loose papers of the file, the officer told an aide that he would like to see the General. Ushered back into Destrier's office, Roland gave his opinion: "Well Sir the report is pretty useless, especially the conclusion. How can any sane man decide the patrol has "vanished off the face of the earth"? Either they crossed the river and went to ground in the south or they have gone down river by boat and managed to conceal themselves in the dock area of Bordeaux.

No-one there would ask questions. Whatever caused their disappearance, the whole thing should have been properly investigated."

"Exactly. There's obviously a simple explanation. That's why I sent for you, Captain. I know from your Corsican reports – ha-ha, I imagine you thought no-one read them eh? – you can track people down very successfully in even the most inhospitable terrain. I want you to find these men." The other man was silent, amazed firstly that his meticulous reports had found an audience and then stunned anew by the General's order to take on this special investigation.

"Oh, yes and while you are about it, I would also like you to re-open the file on Colonel Lecaron's death. Bad business, bad business! I am certain that no-one even tried to get to the bottom of it - barely mentioned in that file you have there. The investigation was cursory at best and handed over to Falaise's sergeant. I owe it to the memory of my great friend the Duc de Garenne."

The General stopped for a moment, lost in his own thoughts; the other man's mind was focusing on what had just been said: La Garenne, Duc de Garenne? This had to be Mlle. Kate's hometown.

"Your warrants and all the papers you need – including all the information I have on the death of Lecaron – will be ready and waiting for you by the end of today. Meanwhile perhaps you would like to take a day's rest after the long journey from Corsica and if there's anything else you think you will need, let me or my ADC, Captain Fauchard, know."

"Well Sir, I think there is one thing. if I am to jog a few memories perhaps a little money might be useful?"

"Of course, I shall arrange a special appropriation for that very purpose. I look forward to receiving your report. Good luck and don't let me down, Captain Lebrun!"

The commander smiled to himself after Roland left his office. 'There, that should ruffle some feathers in the south. I must tell my friends to look out for this young man'.

CHAPTER 26

Roland left the General's office in a daze. Why had the General chosen him, he wondered? He went to find some urgently-needed refreshment, then arranged a bed for the night at the local barracks, citing the General's office as an introduction – which worked like a charm. The following day all the files were waiting, and he discovered that the investigation into Colonel Lecaron's death was about as informative as the first file. He collected his warrants from Captain Fauchard, expressing surprise when he read just how wide a brief he had been given, a virtual carte blanche. Fauchard smiled "The General thought you might need some leeway, just in case something crops up."

He paid a brief visit to his sister and her husband and they caught up on each other's lives since they had last met. He could not resist asking whether two ladies had come to find him nearly two years before. His sister teased him mercilessly: "Oh France suffers a crushing defeat, but my little brother is more concerned about his lady friends? War is hard!" She stopped laughing when she saw her brother's hurt expression; clearly at least one of these ladies had meant a lot to him and so instead, she assured Roland that he had received no female visitors.

At daybreak, he requisitioned two horses from the stables at Headquarters, using the General's name to good effect once again. His mount was a good animal, spirited but well trained and the second horse he used to carry his pack. He would be able to use the relay horses at each barracks along the route. He also drew a new uniform from the quartermaster, complete with pistols and shot, a musket and a carbine. He loaded these onto the packhorse together with his small cache of possessions and stowed the files in a worn leather saddlebag. He left the city through the winding streets which led to the Porte d'Orleans. Travelling as fast as he could, with his warrant having an almost magical effect, he was able obtain a fresh mount each time he stopped, always the best that the stables could provide. At last he reached La Garenne.

It was early afternoon and three days since he had left Paris. He rode straight to the gates of the barracks and was rather surprised to find the place almost deserted; four disinterested troopers were sitting playing dice in the courtyard. They seemed reluctant to give the new officer any information but grudgingly took his packhorse to the stables. He kept his own mount with him for the moment and went back out into the square, where François was just unlocking the Town Hall.

"Sorry to disturb you Monsieur but I'm looking for Captain Falaise. His own men don't seem to know where he is."

François was quite taken aback….it was the first time he could remember anyone from the barracks being even remotely civil to him. Captain Falaise ignored him; that dreadful sergeant had been either sarcastic or threatening.

"Well Sir, I expect that he is at the Château; he spends quite a lot of time there. He likes to go hunting with M. de Garenne and his snooty friends; it's all he does seem interested in. Are you here to replace him? I'm so pleased that at last your lot in Paris have decided to do something about what goes on around here" gabbled François.

"Sorry to disappoint you, Monsieur but I'm not here to replace the Captain. I just have to tie up a few loose ends."

"Oh…err well there are quite a few of those too. Yes, been some funny goings on around here" muttered François in an anxious tone, unwilling now to specify what these might be and worried that his words might reach the ears of Captain Falaise.

"Well, I'd like to talk to you about all these goings on, but I'll come back if I may?" Roland was anxious to get the investigation under way. 'I will be stirring things up but, in my time, not yours' he thought. He would have dearly loved to ask whether the man knew of a Mlle. Kate Giscard, but François seemed rather too keen to share his knowledge for the young officer's liking. He would not be the person to ask about any private or personal matters! He decided that rather than wait until Captain Falaise returned he would confront him at the Château, using the element of surprise to best advantage. Having obtained directions, he bade farewell to a disappointed François and set off.

As he reached the ornate but rusting gates of the main entrance to the grand Château, a groom came out to greet him and take his horse. The young man looked strangely familiar, but he thought no more of it, focused on finding the missing Falaise.

He asked the groom if the Captain was at the Château, but the lad replied: "I am sorry Monsieur, he came here this morning, but he has gone hunting with M. de Garenne. They are not expected to return until early evening." Roland realized that the young groom was still looking at him expectantly, but he had no idea why.

At that moment, André Lacoste appeared at the gates. "Good day, Monsieur. May I help you?"

"I am seeking Captain Falaise, but I understand that he is not expected back until later. I was just about to ask this lad whether I could wait until they return. My name is Captain Lebrun of the Gendarmerie Nationale."

"Of course, Captain. We don't get many visitors these days. René, can you please take our visitor's horse to the stables and find some feed and then ask Madame Renard to provide some refreshment in the salon." The groom nodded and with a backward glance at the officer he went off leading the horse. The other man turned: "I am André Lacoste; I manage the estate." They shook hands and

M. Lacoste led the officer into the main house where Rene re-appeared carrying a tray of coffee and small pastries.

"Some cognac perhaps? René?" asked André. "Excuse us, Captain, we have few servants. That young lad is happier in the stables with the horses than serving in the house." The captain looked at the retreating figure of René, yes, he was familiar. The old soldier was intrigued by his visitor's name – could this be the officer about whom the Duc and General Destrier had written?

The Captain asked whether André had known Colonel Lecaron and the older man looked downcast: "Of course. I was aide-de-camp to the Duc and I watched Lucien's rise from drummer boy to Colonel. I was proud to call him my friend. Now, sadly, both Lucien and the Duc are buried here at the Château."

"In strictest confidence I should inform you that part of my mission here is to re-investigate the death of Colonel Lecaron."

The other nodded: "and the other part is to investigate the disappearance of the patrol of Gendarmes?" he raised an enquiring eyebrow. His guest nodded. "Oh, I can see that the good Captain is going to be delighted to see you" joked André with a wide grin.

"I take it that you don't have much time for Captain Falaise?"

"No, frankly he is worse than useless" then André added in a quieter tone "…much like his friends."

"So, M. Louis-Philippe is not like his famous father then?"

"No most definitely not. His sister, Mlle. Catherine, is much more like her father – she even went to Waterloo, you know and nursed the wounded. Her father was very proud of her." André stopped abruptly. He wondered if the Captain would respond to this broad hint. He thought about pointing out the Duc's portrait which now depicted Catherine and Amélie but remembered Madame Giscard's advice and decided against it for now, at least.

The mention of a young woman from this town going to nurse at Waterloo made the officer's heart leap. If the Duc's daughter had been at the battle then surely, she would be aware of other girls who had been there as well. Nonchalantly he remarked: "What a coincidence: when I was on the way back from Waterloo I met a couple of young ladies, sisters I believe, who had also been nursing at the battle. Their names were Kate and Amélie Giscard and they said they came from a town called La Garenne. I wonder if you know of them?"

André considered these words but betrayed nothing. "Kate Giscard, you say? Not a name I recognise. I don't know many young ladies of this area" he smiled "but I will ask the Duc's daughter, Mlle. Catherine if she is aware of anyone of that name." Lacoste had decided on caution. "She's visiting her aunt today, but I will ask her when she returns." This way, thought André, she can decide for herself whether she wants to see the Captain again.

Roland decided to change the subject: "So, M. Lacoste, do you have any idea about what might have happened to this so-called Lost Patrol?"

"I am guessing that the official report doesn't mention that the Duc's son and I were arrested by them?"

"What? Not a word. Where, when?"

"Ha, I thought not. I was travelling with M. Louis-Philippe south of here. He was keen to restock the cellars and we had been told about some half decent vineyards near Pomerol. We were returning very late and as we approached the village of St. Antoine we realised that something was wrong, there were people sheltering in barns as we passed, and sentries had been posted at the crossroads. They ran out in front of our coach and in the darkness, of course, our horses panicked and bolted, taking us with them. Our poor coachman was thrown from the coach and was lucky to escape death. Then these gendarmes had the effrontery to arrest us all for attempting to evade capture! As you can imagine, M. Louis-Philippe was furious. He is his father's son in only one way - he inherited the Duc's temper. The gendarmes were more scared of disturbing their sergeant than M. Louis-Philippe's anger, but before morning his temper had reached boiling point and when someone finally fetched Sergeant Brochard he had quite a shock."

"Strange that Falaise did not think it necessary to report that; the innkeeper must have told him."

"Oh, it gets stranger" the other man replied: "One of the gendarmes blurted out that they were searching for a dog. I thought the Duc's son would become apoplectic but no, instead he just listened quietly and told them to carry on but bring the animal to him!"

Roland's mouth fell open in surprise "Almost the whole garrison was out looking for a dog?"

"It wasn't just any dog; it was Hugo Hound. We breed hunting Hounds here and some of ours are the best in France with a long and prestigious pedigree. Hugo Hound was the finest. He was a gift from the Duc to Colonel Lecaron (very much against the wishes of his son I should add). In fact, I think Louis-Philippe might do anything to get that dog back; he is totally obsessed with hunting. Here's another odd thing: Louis-Philippe spotted a notice at the Town Hall. Hugo Hound was being auctioned by Raoul Lecaron, the Colonel's wastrel brother.

We had to go straight to the farm there and then. Waste of a journey, by then the Hound had 'disappeared'. Louis-Philippe was quite beside himself with rage."

'Were these all just coincidences? A missing patrol sent to find a dog - a dog so valuable that Louis-Philippe might do anything to possess it. That dog's previous owner, Lucien Lecaron, dying in an unexplained accident?' Roland's mind flicked over all these events anxiously.

"If I recall correctly from the report, this Raoul was with the hunt when Colonel Lecaron was shot?"

"Yes, that's true and he is less than half the man his brother was although most of the town's hunters were also there. Rumours continue to circulate but François Dupoire down at the Town Hall is the one to ask. He's the fount of all knowledge, true and false, in these parts."

"Ah yes, he told me where to find the Captain and gave me directions here. I thought him perhaps too ready to discuss the business of others."

"All I will say is that these rumours only started circulating after Raoul's wife left him. She walked out a few weeks back. Lives back at home now. Then Raoul himself disappeared, just walked away from the farm. He's a nasty bit of work, lazy, unpleasant, and a drunkard... not to be trusted."

At that moment they heard furious barking outside and went to investigate. The commotion signalled the return of the pack led by a stylishly dressed young man, obviously Louis-Philippe. He was accompanied by a slim, dark haired slightly older man with a pencil moustache. This man wore uniform breeches but a leather jerkin. 'The elusive Captain Falaise' thought Roland and walking out onto the steps of the Château, he stood and watched as the pack barked and circled around the riders. Captain Lebrun was fully aware that he owed Falaise a salute although the two men were of equal rank. However, Falaise was out of uniform and the newly arrived officer wanted to impose his authority straight away. He offered no salute but instead introduced himself, speaking to Captain Falaise while Louis-Philippe watched impatiently:

"I am Captain Roland Lebrun, attached to the Bureau in Faubourg St. Honore. I have been sent here to investigate the disappearance of the men of a patrol of Gendarmerie Nationale based at La Garenne.

I am also instructed by General Destrier…" he paused to allow his announcement to sink in and to observe the faces of the two men before him "to re-open the enquiry into the death of Colonel Lucien Lecaron, Chevalier of the Legion d'Honneur, late of the 27th Cavalry Regiment of the Grande Armée." He completed his announcement and waited. Captain Falaise blanched and hastily saluted the other gendarme, realising the importance of this man's position. Even he recognised the significance of the reference to 'Faubourg St. Honore'. A direct command from the General himself meant that this officer was someone about whom he should be worried.

Hastily Falaise dismounted and stood to attention. "Well….err of course I will give you all possible assistance in investigating the disappearance of my men although I myself carried out a thorough search and made a full report……" Falaise's voice faded as he finished this sentence, realising first that he was out of uniform on duty as it were, and that the other officer probably already knew of his half-hearted attempt at an investigation.

"Yes, I've seen that report. *It's* the reason I have been sent here."

"But Lecaron's death was an accident." Louis-Philippe decided to chime in, having dismounted gracefully. He stood attempting to look disinterested but drawled: "I can't see why there should be any fuss about the matter."

"Hm…yes well I've seen that report too. Although Brochard wrote it, you signed it Captain? The sergeant of course is no longer here to defend himself." Without waiting for a response, Roland announced: "I'm returning to the barracks to see that my horses are comfortable and then I shall probably find…." He paused deliberately "… myself a good meal. I seem to have been eating 'on the hoof' for days. Tomorrow, I shall begin my investigations in earnest - starting with your records…"

At that moment, Louis-Philippe broke into a charming smile: "Captain you must stay here of course, and we shall dine together

– Lacoste, please have a bed made up for our honoured guest - I am sure that we will have much to discuss. I have not been able to visit Paris for years."

Roland omitted to mention that he himself had only spent two nights in Paris in the last two years. He sensed a trap. If the old Duc had invited him then he was sure he would have been flattered and pleased to accept, but this young man seemed to have his own agenda.

"I thank you most sincerely, Sir, but with regret I have to decline your most generous offer. I must see to my horses and I wish to make a very early start tomorrow at the barracks."

Louis-Philippe looked like he might argue with this decision but restrained himself. Meanwhile Captain Falaise was torn between returning with the new arrival to keep an eye on him or taking up the offer of a decent meal and a soft bed at the Château. Reluctantly he made his choice: "I'll return with you immediately and brief you." he announced pompously.

CHAPTER 27

As the two gendarme officers rode off Louis-Philippe stood watching, a worried expression on his face. Meanwhile Falaise tried to engage his companion in conversation but the other officer seemed deep in his own thoughts. By the time they got back to the barracks Falaise was completely unnerved. They rode together into the stables. “Is the animal here that returned without a rider?” asked Roland.

“Oh well err I think only one returned, but not too good on detail - Brochard’s department usually. Rather a pity he’s not around to give me a hand now” laughed Falaise nervously.

“It’s because he isn’t around that *I am*. I think I’d like to inspect the barracks right now Captain. I want to see if there were any clues left behind” barked Lebrun, leaving the other standing uncertainly in the stables, open-mouthed. At the men’s’ quarters everything appeared well ordered and neatly arranged. He looked inside each missing man’s locker which stood beside their cots. Most of their kit was still neatly folded, their second pair of boots standing polished and awaiting their return.

Next, he had a look around Sergeant Brochard’s small room where the only real difference was the addition of a shabby desk. Again, the room was neat, the Sergeant’s possessions folded into an old chest. Nothing seemed out of place here…except …he noticed in the grate a sheaf of partially burned papers, their edges brown and crumbling. He lifted one piece from the fireplace and read the words: “Missing……Hugo……. Reward” from the fragment. So, it was true! Brochard had been interested in that dog – interested enough to prevent anyone else from seeing the reward notice, Roland realised.

Falaise was more anxious than ever to befriend the newcomer: "We can eat at the bar - won't be as grand as the meal you would have had at the Château but good homecooked food nonetheless." The two officers crossed the square and Captain Falaise went straight to what had to be his usual table. Lebrun however looked around. It was still early evening and no-one else was eating yet but a few men were drinking. "I think I'll have a drink at the bar first, never know what you'll hear" said Roland, with a wide grin.

The other man looked uncomfortable; obviously mixing with the locals wasn't something he normally did. Reluctantly Falaise walked over while the other drinkers regarded them nervously, but his companion smiled warmly.

"Good evening to you. We are just here for a quiet drink, not on official business. Even gendarmes relax occasionally." The men at the bar relaxed a little too, seemingly comfortable with the new officer. They soon returned to their conversations leaving Falaise and Lebrun to themselves.

"What can I get for you gentlemen?" asked the barman.

"Red wine please, the local of course" said Roland. Two well-filled glasses were brought. "Have these on me gentlemen."

"No, I insist on paying" Captain Lebrun smiled to soften his words. "Accepting anything as a gift is strictly against regulations." Captain Falaise flushed at these words as the bar owner looked at him pointedly. After they had finished their drink they sat down at a table in the window. Several more locals had now arrived, obviously intrigued by the sight of the stranger sitting with the haughty Falaise. The café owner discreetly informed them that he was very affable, had even insisted on paying for his own drinks. He had even stood to drink at the bar like the other men. The meal was, as promised, good simple country cooking prepared by the landlord's wife. Both men ate it with relish and in silence. When he had finished, Roland turned to his companion:

"So, what can you tell me about Raoul Lecaron's disappearance?" Falaise looked flustered. Clearly, he had no knowledge of what happened in La Garenne and couldn't imagine how his companion knew these things. He appeared distinctly uncomfortable and Lebrun decided to turn the screw a little more.

"Do you believe these rumours going around about him, most likely just malicious gossip, don't you think?" Captain Falaise was squirming as he stuttered: "Don't know what you mean. Never listen to gossip. I think it's time I got back, lots to do tomorrow" and with that he stood abruptly, looking awkward but his companion remained seated in his chair, clearly relaxed.

"No, no, you go on. I'll just stay here a while longer."

Although this was said pleasantly enough, Captain Falaise knew he was being dismissed and although relieved he was torn between escaping and staying to see what was said in his absence. Although Lebrun was considerably younger than him, the new Captain had the look of a battle-hardened veteran whereas Falaise had avoided war service with a little help from his friend Louis-Philippe.

Roland remained at the table drinking his wine until the landlord came over and asked if he would like anything else. "I'll have another one of these" he indicated his nearly empty glass "and bring over a drink for yourself. I would appreciate a quiet word." Over several more drinks he was able to discover that Brochard had a reputation as a bully, but he had always been careful to avoid the wrath of the Duc or his sister, a certain Madame Giscard. Captain Lebrun said nothing but noted that name. The rest of the patrol that had gone with Brochard were just ordinary lads, some locals, most from farther afield, nothing special about them.

"Any thoughts as to where they might have gone?" the officer probed gently.

"Well, it's most likely nonsense but before Raoul left town he was convinced that they had found his missing dog, the Hound called Hugo; most men around here would have given their right arm to own that dog. Anyway, he was convinced they had found the animal and sold it and split the money between them then scarpered. Don't see that meself. They could have just come back here and carried on as usual, wouldn't be the first gendarmes to line their own pockets, err, begging your pardon sir, didn't mean to…"

Roland put up his hand "Don't worry, this is all in confidence I assure you. Now this Raoul, you say he has left La Garenne? He'd be Colonel Lecaron's brother?"

"Yes, people say he's disappeared but course that's not true. I saw him heading off south with a sack over his shoulder. The only thing he left behind was his flaming bar bill."

"Please allow me to settle that" the Captain told the surprised landlord "*Lucien* Lecaron saved the life of my closest friend when we were in Spain, so that is the least I can do. What do you think of the rumours regarding Lucien Lecaron's death? Any truth in them or just gossip?"

Delighted that what he had thought was a bad debt was about to be settled the bar owner volunteered his opinions thick and fast.

"Well, who knows? Brochard questioned everyone and they all agreed that although Raoul had been behind the chasse, it can only have been a stray shot. Raoul couldn't hit a barn door if he was standing in front of it. The Duc's son himself assured Captain Falaise it was nothing more than a tragic accident. He saw it all, he said."

"Indeed, it was tragic" Roland agreed and stood to pay his own and Raoul's accounts. He said goodbye to the landlord and the men still at the bar and made his way back to the barracks where he was very surprised to find that Falaise had waited up for him.

"So, made any progress?"

"Yes - but I need to think about what I have heard and probe further. Oddly enough your friend's name came up in conversation, second time today. I discovered that he, André Lacoste and their coachman met the sergeant and his men down at St. Antoine. In fact, his men arrested them."

"Ah well actually, M. Louis-Philippe did mention it at the time. Found it quite amusing I believe, but there was nothing they could tell me, so I didn't bother to put that in my report" replied the Captain, rather anxiously.

"Ah I see! His name also came up in relation to a much more serious matter.... but that can wait for the moment. I will see you tomorrow for I am more than ready for bed. I have stowed my kit in Sergeant Brochard's old room, I trust that is acceptable?" "Of course, of course, I just hope you are sufficiently comfortable." Exhausted, he fell immediately into a deep sleep.

****

When Catherine returned to the Château later that evening she found André and asked about his day expecting a brief résumé of domestic events. In response, he told her: "I have managed to organise two local artisans to start on the window frames in the Great Hall, sold two of our horses – and - oh yes! We had a visitor. He's a captain in the gendarmerie sent here to investigate the missing men. He was very personable. He asked after a young lady by the name of Kate Giscard? Strange coincidence that. I wrote down his name."

He shuffled the papers on his desk. "I'm sure it's here, no, yes, here it is, a Captain ...I can't read my own handwriting. Yes, it's a Captain Roland Lebrun. Does that name mean anything?"

The young girl's face lit up immediately: "André, stop teasing me! Where is he staying?"

Next morning, the officer discovered that Captain Falaise had already left the barracks – hunting again? Obviously, he thought, this man must believe that La Garenne is not exciting enough for him – apart from the disappearance of thirteen of his men and a mysterious death! He decided to take breakfast in the bar before calling on François Dupoire at the Town Hall. The nosy little man was eager to oblige:

"Good morning Sir, I am so desperately busy – all this paperwork! Look at this, the owner of the inn down at St. Antoine has complained to the Mayor yet again that both Captain Falaise and Sergeant Brochard pledged the town would settle their bill. They had no authority to do that."

"Do you have the bills there?" he asked the little man.

"No, sorry Sir, I passed them back to Captain Falaise although I do have the accompanying rude note... Here you can see it's for a tidy sum too."

"I will be passing through St. Antoine very soon myself and I will speak to Captain Falaise. I am sure he will give me sufficient funds to settle the debts."

"Captain, that would take such a burden from me. The whole affair is bringing shame on this town." François looked mollified and Roland dropped his voice as if about to take François into his confidence: "I must tell you that I was less than honest with you yesterday. My assignment here is to re-open and fully investigate the disappearance of those gendarmes and to open up a possible new murder enquiry into the death of Colonel Lecaron."

François blanched…" So, the rumours I heard were true. It *was* murder?"

"Possibly, very possibly and I expect to identify the culprit or culprits very soon. First, however, I need you to tell me all you know." The little clerk puffed with importance in his new role as confidante and told the Captain at length and in great detail everything he could remember of the day Lucien had died and the day of the gendarmes' departure.

He shared the (apparently) widely held belief that Lucien's death had been no accident, that Raoul had killed his own brother.

Roland had achieved his aim, his reasons for being in La Garenne would soon be spread far and wide. "Thank you and now can you tell me where I might find Raoul Lecaron's wife?"

The little man gave his new hero detailed instructions on how to reach the house of Marie's parents. However, no sooner was the gendarme out of sight than François hastily locked his office and dashed over to the bar.

"That new Captain is investigating a murder. Lucien Lecaron's murder" he exclaimed breathlessly. "He told me, in confidence of course, that he intends to arrest the culprits very shortly."

"Did you say culprits?"

"Yes, yes he is certain there's more than one person involved. Don't tell a soul, will you?"

CHAPTER 28

On his way to Marie's family farm, the Captain decided to visit the doctor mentioned in the Lecaron dossier, Doctor Gabarre, who had examined the body of the Colonel. He was ushered into the doctor's treatment room with great civility – obviously, news of his arrival had travelled fast. After the customary pleasantries, he asked the doctor directly:

"Do you have any idea of the type of gun that killed the Colonel?"

The doctor looked dismayed and then shook his head. "No, I am sorry. I have never been a hunting man myself and to be honest, given the number of injuries, sometimes even fatalities I see every year I am glad I have never been a devotee." Roland nodded agreement. Injuries during the chasse season were common, especially after the hunters had enjoyed a long and wine-fuelled lunch.

"Perhaps you could describe M. Lecaron's injuries a little for me? I know that it was some time ago, but any clue would be helpful." The doctor went to a wooden cabinet and took out a well-used notebook. He turned the pages slowly until he found the page which related to Lucien's death. "Here" he said indicating a free-hand drawing in the book "There were actually two wounds. One was high up on his back, a few centimetres below the nape. The second was in the lower abdomen. Hm… yes, the wound to the back was the biggest but the second wound was most damaging, it bled a great deal internally."

Roland took a moment to digest this information before asking the doctor whether, in his opinion, Lecaron had been shot once or twice, once from behind and once from the front, or whether both wounds were the work of a single shot passing through the body. Doctor Gabarre took a few moments before responding: "In my opinion, it is more likely to have been a single shot; if the ball entered his stomach with nothing much to stop it, it would have ploughed straight through the lower body and out again. On the other hand, a shot through the back that high might exit there." He indicated a point on his diagram. "Sorry I can't be more helpful, but my feeling is just one shot."

"Thank you, doctor, this has been most enlightening. One further question: did you note any powder burns on Lecaron's clothing?"

"Powder burns? Why?" repeated the doctor quizzically. "I am not sure I understand the significance of your question."

"Let me explain: the closer the gun is to the body, the more concentrated the powder burns. That way we can often tell how close the victim was to their killer." Gabarre nodded at this: "Of course, of course. I see that but again I can't tell you much. I kept none of his clothing. Perhaps his mother did?"

"Oh well. Doctor, thank you again." The Captain had hoped to glean more from the doctor's notes. When he reached the farm of Marie's parents, the Lefevres, the door was opened by a tall spare man who glared suspiciously at him and demanded who he might be.

"Good day sir, I am Captain Lebrun of the Gendarmerie Nationale and I would like to speak with your daughter about the death of Lucien Lecaron."

"Come in Sir" M. Lefevre's attitude relaxed markedly. "She is upstairs. She thought it might have been Raoul coming back. Last time he came here he was so angry that I feared for her life. Those rumours...well I told her to hold her tongue, silly girl."

"Spreading rumours can be a dangerous business" agreed Roland.

"Indeed Sir, but the truth will out eventually" replied Marie's father, calling up the stairs to his daughter who came down slowly and nervously. She stood looking down, her pale puffy face almost hidden by her long hair.

"Madame, good day to you. I would like you to tell me everything that you know about your fiancé's death" he said gently, smiling at the girl in hopes of putting her at ease.

"Oh Sir, poor Lucien. I did love him. He was such a fine honest man. We were to be married that Spring and we were very happy." All this came from Marie in a rush then she began to sob quietly. Roland waited until she could speak again. "When he died, I was devastated, I was feverish and ill for weeks and foolishly I allowed that vile drunkard Raoul to comfort me. I was weak, I was lonely - and I married him. He told me it was what Lucien would have wanted, to have me living in the family home.

I knew he would never be as good a man as his brother, but I eventually gave in. I am deeply ashamed. I was tempted because one day I knew the whole farm would be ours. I am not proud of what I did Sir."

"I have been told, Madame that you may have said things in the town, things about the death of Lucien…. Do you truly believe Raoul could have been responsible?"

"No, no sir, I never said *that*. I never thought it was Raoul – he's not brave enough – but I think he may know more than he says. Even if he had got close enough to take a shot at his brother, he would have missed. I was told that Lucien was shot in the back and not even Raoul would do such an awful thing. I do know that Raoul saw him fall."

"How do you know that?"

"Raoul suffered something dreadful in his sleep, Sir. Nightmares and the like, raving sometimes he was. While I lived with him they got worse and worse. Sometimes he would get up and stamp around in the dark but still asleep."

"Ha, guilty conscience" put in Marie's father. "Well I can't arrest someone for having nightmares, Madame. Did he say anything at all? There might be some clue there."

"He often told me, when he was awake, how much he had despised his 'oh so clever' and 'oh so honourable' brother and when he was feeling really mean he would crow about how I was now his. But when he slept he cried out often: 'not me', 'I won't tell.... not me.... I won't tell' or 'please, no' I tell you he really frightened me."

"So, about all these rumours I've heard then?"

"I swear sir, all I ever said was that Lucien's death was no accident. I never accused anyone."

"So why do you think it is that all the townsfolk seem to think it was him?"

"Oh, Sir" she wailed, looking over Roland shoulders at her father "I was so angry on the day I left that I may have hinted to some of my friends that Raoul was hiding something. I truly believe he knows who did shoot his brother but was more frightened of them than of me."

"Well thank you Madame for being so honest with me. You have given me some valuable insights about the incident. Now one last question: do you know the whereabouts of any of the clothes Colonel Lecaron was wearing?

I know that might seem odd, but they could be very helpful..." before he could say another word Marie's father looked meaningfully at his daughter. There was a moment's complete silence and then Marie gulped out: "Sir, I have something to show you. All this time I have kept something of Lucien's and no-one knew. I only told my father yesterday that it is locked in my trunk in my room. Wait there a moment and I will fetch it."

Marie ran quickly upstairs and after a few moments returned clutching a parcel wrapped in thick paper and tied with string. She reverently opened the knots to reveal a well-worn leather jerkin and there on the back of the stained garment close to the collar was a gaping hole, ringed with blackened blood and powder marks.

"This was the jerkin he was wearing when he died, Sir. I have treasured it but if it is useful in helping you find his killer then please take it." Roland examined the garment closely. The hole in it was rather smaller than he would have expected from a musket ball. He turned to Marie:

"I would like to keep this for now but when my investigations are complete I will return it to you." Marie nodded her agreement and the Captain left clutching the jerkin.

At the barracks, the Captain went to his room and laid the jerkin flat on a table then took a greatcoat from the garderobe of the missing gendarmes. Out in the yard several old gendarmes watched with interest as he stretched the greatcoat out, hanging it from two iron pegs on the wall, its back facing him. He took aim with his musket and fired. Taking down the smoking garment he studied the hole his musket ball had made and compared it to that in the leather jerkin. As he had surmised, the hole in the jerkin could only have been made by something smaller than a musket ball. He then studied the powder burns and made a diagram of the measurements. He repeated this exercise using his pistol, again meticulously recording the hole size and powder burn marks together with the distance of the shot and the angle. After several attempts, the sizes of the holes in the jerkin and in the greatcoat were very close, the spread of powder burns almost identical. Roland believed in being thorough and repeated his experiment twice more, the greatcoat now resembling Swiss cheese but at last he was satisfied.

It had been a pistol shot that killed Colonel Lecaron and fired at very close range! Taking the jerkin and the greatcoat back into his room, he parcelled them together with his notes.

CHAPTER 29

That afternoon Roland idly watched the Town Hall until he saw François leave the building. The little clerk made directly for the bar in the square and assuming that the Mayor would be alone, the gendarme took this opportunity to see M. Lafitte-Dupont in private. The Mayor was seated in his 'inner sanctum' and the officer introduced himself briefly and explained his mission. M. Lafitte-Dupont listened intently to the Captain's story for he too had been suspicious about Colonel Lecaron's death. He was happy to take charge of the package which the gendarme had prepared and assured the officer that it would be locked away in his safe, to which only he had a key. The meticulous Mayor even gave Roland a signed receipt.

Well satisfied with his progress thus far, the Captain returned to the barracks and finished writing up his report adding that his 'evidence' now rested with the Mayor of La Garenne. Sealing the envelope with red wax, he addressed it for the personal attention of General Destrier. A courier would start it on its journey to Paris that afternoon. He then strode across the square to sit outside the bar with a well-deserved glass of wine in the late afternoon sunshine.

"Proper stir you've caused in the town, Sir" said the owner "everyone is talking about you, wondering what you're up to." Roland smiled to himself. His plan was working; he always believed that if you made a few gentle waves in a pond somebody would get wet. 'I think I'll make a few more waves when the good Captain returns' he thought wryly. However, when he went back to the barracks he discovered that a note had been pushed under the door of his room.

"I hear that you have been enquiring about me. I am sure we shall meet soon. KG."

What on earth? Could his Kate really be here, in La Garenne and if she was – well why had she written such a strange note to him? He read and reread the note and his spirits soared so that the even the reappearance of Captain Falaise could not dampen them.

"Good day's hunting then?" he enquired sarcastically.

"Oh rather! Excellent actually – and how are your enquiries progressing?"

"They have gone so well that I have decided there are grounds to instigate a fresh enquiry into the murder of Lucien Lecaron. I know there have been a lot of rumours in the town but there seems to be more substance to them than I expected."

"Murder?" whispered the Captain, looking genuinely shocked at this news. "I can't believe that. "Who would have wanted to murder him? It was a hunting accident pure and simple. Not the first either. Anyway, M. Louis-Philippe assured me that he had arrived upon the scene just after the *accident*."

"Another item missing from your report, Captain... It seems that M. Louis-Philippe's name is always omitted! I think I must pay him a formal visit tomorrow. Then I must be off to St. Antoine. That'll be my first stop on the way south – oh, I have a bill to settle there on your behalf." Captain Falaise blushed. "Of course, of course I shall ensure that you are furnished with sufficient funds for that and for your journey, Sir" he said hastily.

"I have written my initial report to Paris, Captain Falaise. I dispatched it this very afternoon. I have reported to General Destrier that in my opinion, Lucien Lecaron was murdered and that I shall investigate the matter in full on my return from my mission to find the Lost Patrol."

"But surely you should be arresting Raoul Lecaron then? If anyone is guilty of murder, it's got to be him."

“No, I think not. I believe he is guilty of something - but murder? I don’t think so, no. Anyway, I told you, he has left town.” Roland abruptly changed tack: “How many people around this area own a pistol?”

Falaise looked perplexed at this question: “What, erm what? Well none to my knowledge. There aren’t many people here who have enough money to buy such a thing. No, can’t think of a single person.” Roland smiled to himself – no, he thought, except someone up at the Château.

“Right, do you fancy a *last supper* at the bar?” Roland asked, not expecting the stricken expression that passed across the face of Captain Falaise. “Oh, and one thing more, Captain” his words stopped the flustered officer in his tracks. “I will need a good mount for my journey and I notice that you are riding a very fine hunter.”

“Ah, ah yes. My Marron. He is indeed a very fine horse. I could not be parted from him.”

Captain Lebrun gave Falaise a moment to think about his beautiful horse before continuing: “I assume that horse is your personal property? The reason I ask this is because in a brief study of the accounts I note a rather large payment to the account of the Château, marked *“Marron”*?”

Captain Falaise’s terrified expression spoke volumes. “Of course, of course, take Marron for your journey.” Turning on his heel, he left without looking again at Roland. “Now I have urgent business I must attend to immediately.”

Before going to the bar for his evening meal, Lebrun lingered in the shadows by the Town Hall. From here he had a good view of the barracks and as he suspected, the Captain soon came out leading his horse and began walking in the direction of the Château. “A few more tiny ripples…." He thought with a grin and walked, smiling, across the square.

"Your usual, Sir?" asked the landlord. "Yes, but I'll drink it over here, by the window." He kept a sharp eye on the comings and goings in the square and after an hour observed the Captain riding back into the barracks. A few moments later Falaise strolled into the bar. "Done all I needed to do. Have you ordered?" he asked. "No, not yet, I thought I would just wait for you." The meal was taken in strained silence; they returned early, and Roland retired immediately.

****

The next morning, now riding the sleek chestnut-coloured Marron, Lebrun went directly to the Château and was greeted at the gates by André Lacoste. "If it's Louis-Philippe you're after I am afraid he left at first light. Said something about urgent business! He will be back tomorrow, but I am to prepare for a journey and he was being very mysterious. His friend the Captain paid him a visit before supper yesterday and after that he was in a foul temper."

"I'll bet he was" replied Roland, with a huge grin on his face.

"Something tells me you might have had a hand in that" replied André, amused. "Oh, by the way any news of the Giscard sisters? I told Mademoiselle Catherine and I think she may know their identity."

"Well I did get an extremely odd note signed KG."

"I hope you have news soon, Captain" the older man replied nonchalantly.

"I leave for the south tomorrow. I am determined to find Sergeant Brochard and his merry band, but please let M. Louis-Philippe know, if you will, that during my investigations I have uncovered some *shocking* facts. On my return I wish to interview him, in the meantime would it be possible to direct me to where the fatality took place?" "Of course but I can do better than that, I'll take you there myself". The two rode off into a forest on the edges of the estate, where André pointed out the gully where the hunters had told him Lucien's corpse had lain. Roland dismounted and took careful note of his surroundings, even making a rough sketch of the area. They rode back to the Château where the officer took his leave. "Farewell Captain, good luck with your search, I am sure that our paths will meet again".

On the way down to the Barracks he stopped to collect a baguette and some cheese for his lunch. As he arrived in the square, his eye was caught by a slight figure clad in a dark cloak whose hood concealed the wearer's face completely. It was not an especially cool day, so this struck him as rather odd. There was something familiar about the figure standing watching the barracks from an alley beside the Town Hall. Years of experience had made him alert to possible danger and although he rode on into the stables, he slipped from his horse immediately and concealed himself near the gate to watch the watcher. No one else was in the square but the figure was now cautiously approaching the gateway. As the figure passed him by he stepped from the shadows and grasped an arm as he whispered: "Please don't be foolish; I do not like to be spied upon."

The figure spun around to face him: "Oh, and I thought you wanted to see me" came the reply, as the hood was thrown back, revealing a mass of golden-brown curls caught in an elaborate knot, above a pair of shining dark eyes.

"Kate? Kate?" He stammered weakly.

"Of course, it is – who on earth were you expecting?"

Roland released his hold at once and looked at her. She was exactly as he remembered. Her skin was lightly freckled and smooth, with a deepening natural blush on each cheek from embarrassment at his intense gaze.

“So, Mlle. Catherine de Garenne told you I was looking for you?”

“Oh, good grief! For an investigator, you are so slow…. I *am* Catherine de Garenne. Now can we go inside, I don’t usually hang around outside the barracks!” she laughed and firmly grasped his arm. Roland unlocked the office and ushered the lady inside. As Captain Falaise had left early without explanation they had the place to themselves, but he was not at all sure this was appropriate, especially with someone he had just discovered to be the daughter of a Duc no less.

“I can’t believe you didn’t guess” she said with a huge grin.

“I was expecting Mlle. Giscard, not the daughter of a Marshal of France.”

“When Amélie and I went to Waterloo, I had to adopt a different name. I knew my papa would be furious if he discovered what I had done. When he did find out he practically disowned me. I’ve never seen anyone so angry in all my life.” Kate grimaced at the memory. “I used my aunt’s married name, Amélie’s surname, Giscard. It’s quite an easy name for me to adopt. My aunt brought me up as her own child alongside Amélie when father was away; my own poor mother died soon after I was born.”

“So, Mlle. Amélie isn’t your sister then. She’s your cousin? There is a striking resemblance between you.”

“Yes, why? Did you prefer her looks?” she teased, as her companion blushed self-consciously.

They sat together in the office and reminisced about their long journey back to Paris and the hardships they had endured. Even so long after it was difficult to look back on that time with anything but sadness, so they moved on to discuss what had happened to them both since. Whilst she was delighted to meet him once again, she burned to know why he had abandoned them in Paris.

“I waited for you, but you never came for us. What really happened?”

Roland had been anxious to know how the girls had coped alone in Paris. She explained how she had been detained at the army hospital. Kate and her cousin had found that there was total chaos; hundreds of wounded soldiers were waiting in the grounds in makeshift shelters and only the very worst injuries were being treated – and then only if the desperately overworked doctors knew they would recover. She had eventually forced her way in to see the director and explained emphatically that the soldiers in her carriage had managed to survive the long journey, so she was not about to allow them to die waiting for treatment. When she made up her mind, few had the temerity to challenge Kate….and she had been determined that these men would survive.

However, all this had taken quite a long time and having ensured that 'her' wounded men were comfortable, the two ladies realised that it was at least 3 hours since they had parted from their protector. They and their coachman were unfamiliar with Paris, so it took them another hour to reach the Square of the Capuchins church at the foot of Montmartre. Kate had to admit that she had been very disappointed when Roland did not appear.

They had been alone with only René, their young coachman in an unfamiliar city where the streets would doubtless become more and more dangerous as night fell. Roland listened to this in horror; he had not allowed himself dwell on what had happened until now.

The cousins had decided to wait until dark in case he should appear. Why had they not thought to ask for his sister's address? It became obvious that they had apparently been abandoned so they decided to take refuge in the church overnight.

The girls sent the coachman with the horses to find shelter and food for himself and the animals; they would not be so lucky. Very early the next day René had returned, and they had started back to La Garenne. At first, she had felt that she might never forgive him for abandoning them in a war-torn city, but she could not be sure that something had not happened to him. Her pique at his disappearance had been tinged with fear for him and sorrow for herself that she might never meet him again.

Roland was visibly upset: "Oh Mlle. Kate, do you really believe I would do that? I reported to my Headquarters and was ordered to leave immediately…for Réunion! It was a direct order from General Destrier himself and there was no time even to send a message. How many times have I thought about how things might have been so different? We lost each other once but now, well circumstances have brought us back together."

Kate smiled then, feeling comforted by the knowledge that clearly this man had never forgotten her. Ever practical, she asked:

"So, why are you here anyway?"

"I am investigating the disappearance of the Lost Patrol. When I have discovered the truth of the matter, then I must find out what really happened to Colonel Lecaron. General Destrier was not happy with the reports received in Paris on either matter and now, neither am I."

"Did you know that Captain Falaise came to the Château last night? The Captain was very upset. I heard him tell Louis-Philippe that you had *commandeered his horse*? After he left, my brother was extremely agitated. I'm not sure why and then he went off first thing this morning. I know it's wrong to listen at doors but how else will I find out anything?" Kate laughed. "There is definitely something going on between those two."

Frowning suddenly, she pretended to be serious: "When I asked you why you were here I was hoping for a more flattering answer, you know."

At this the young man blushed again and stammered out "But… err…I didn't know you were here – or that you were you. It's all come as a bit of a shock really, one minute I was in Corsica chasing sheep stealers and pirates, wondering if I would ever see you again; then I'm sent to La Garenne and here you are."

"You're still chasing people. Am I not more…interesting prey?" He said nothing, surprised by her blatant flirtatiousness. "If you are going to pursue me, Captain you will need to be quick. My brother is very keen to marry me off to one of his idiot friends. He really doesn't understand me at all. When I marry, it will be to someone of my own choosing, not his…"and Kate muttered in a low voice "…and I already know who I will choose."

"Oh" demanded Roland. "So, you are already promised? May I ask to whom?"

"Well, he was a handsome young officer whom I met in the north. It was a while ago now of course. Sadly, we lost touch, but I hope one day we can be re-united." She attempted a demure, downcast look but could not quite manage it so settled for fluttering her eyelashes theatrically. Kate had had little practice in the art of flirtation; all she knew came from romantic novels.

"Oh" He looked down, momentarily dejected but when he looked at her smiling face it was clear she had been joking.

"How can men be so blind? It's you."

Kate returned to the Château rather late that evening. Together, she and Roland had spent the time reminiscing, much to the barely concealed interest of the few gendarmes at the barracks. Later, they had taken an evening meal in the bar unchaperoned, occupying Captain Falaise's favourite table by the window, in full view of any passers-by. Roland had insisted on accompanying her back to the Château, even going so far as to hold her arm. All eyes were on them...tongues were starting to wag already.

He told her that he must leave the next day but as soon as his business was done he would return. Her eyes filled with tears at this and when he left her at the gate, he allowed himself a single touch of her cheek. She floated up to the front doors of the Château… just in time to hear her brother berating André over some small detail of a journey he was planning. This was news to her and so she none too subtly made minor adjustments to the heavy brocade curtains which hung on either side of the main doors, listening all the time.

"I didn't want the coach, you fool. Two horses will suffice, and we will take a pack horse too. Oh, and why my finest garments? Do you think we are going to the theatre? We are going on a hunt, a long hunt."

"Yes, yes Sir, I will organise everything. When will we be leaving?"

"Once Falaise assures me that this damned fellow has set off. He's trying to find the Lost Patrol. He's a dangerous one, I've no doubt he'll find the Patrol though - and lead us to that Hound. If he returns I may find time to discuss Lecaron's death with him since he appears so keen" Louis-Philippe laughed to himself as he spoke – clearly, he did not expect to have to do so. Kate just managed to conceal herself to avoid being knocked over by Louis Philippe as he strode out of the study.

"Poor André, why do you let him speak to you like that?"

"Mlle. Catherine, I assure you it is a small inconvenience. Indeed, I view it as a positive benefit. For as long as I have known your brother he has barely acknowledged my existence and then only when he needs my help, so he is indiscreet in my presence. That helps me hear many things. In the months prior to his demise, your dear father discussed with me several times how his son might react on finding out he was not the chosen successor. The Duc made me privy to many of his intentions, so I now hope to be able to fulfil the promises I made to him." She considered this. She knew that her father had often used André as his confidante, his discretion had been absolute. Nevertheless, she had to ask him now: "André, if you do not wish to disclose anything I will understand, of course, but if those promises concern the House of Garenne perhaps you may wish to reveal them to me?"

The old soldier smiled, certain that the Duc would have approved: "I promised your father that I would do my best to protect Louis-Philippe from his own failings and I will always try to do that, but I also promised to protect you, Mlle. Catherine, until you are in safe hands – those were your father's exact words, not mine." He said no more, leaving the final words of his promise unsaid: …"no matter what it takes."

"I relieve you of your promise to look after me. I can certainly look out for myself and I will soon – I hope – be in very safe hands."

"Captain Lebrun?" asked her companion with a sly smile. Kate was aware that André knew more of this matter than he was admitting but unaware that a breathless René had just told him that the 'whole town was talking! Mlle. Catherine had been seen going into the barracks alone with the new young officer'.

"If that is the case then you may need my protection even more. I believe the Captain may be in great danger from your brother. I fear for your brother's sanity sometimes. He seems both obsessed and fearful of the man for some reason. I am very much afraid that on this hunt, the prey may be human." Kate frowned, not really understanding how two men who had barely met could be at each other's throats. However, she knew her father's great friend well enough to be sure his fears were not unfounded. What should she do?

The next morning Captain Falaise rode back up to the Château at a wild gallop and demanded to see Louis-Philippe immediately on 'important business'. André ushered the captain into the dining room where the young nobleman was enjoying a lavish breakfast.

"He left early this morning and will be heading for St. Antoine, on my horse. The man intends to pay Sergeant Brochard's bill too. Damn it, what business is it of his? Squandering money belonging to the gendarmerie. He has no right. He's taken not only my Marron but also little Greco - as a pack horse!" Louis-Philippe looked at Falaise with an expression which told the captain to tell his friend everything quickly: "But, but he's coming back here after he has found out what happened to the Patrol."

"Vincent, my friend, you really must not allow that upstart to concern you. It's unlikely there will ever be sight or sound of him again. If he does find Sergeant Brochard I know whom my money would be on."

After Falaise had left, Louis-Philippe shouted in the hallway for André: "We will leave at first light tomorrow; our prey has a good head start and doubtless he will be asking questions along the way, so it will be easy to follow his trail." André bowed, a worried frown creasing his brow. He completed the preparations and then went off to find Kate.

"Mlle., Captain Lebrun left La Garenne this morning, heading towards St. Antoine on the trail of the gendarmes. I think that the Auberge there will be his first overnight stop.

We leave tomorrow morning at first light and it is as I feared. Your brother referred to him as 'prey'. I believe your brother thinks he will lead him to Hugo Hound but there is more to it than that - who knows what?"

"Please don't worry André. I believe the Captain can take care of himself but..." Kate did not finish her sentence.

CHAPTER 30

Roland rode south and at each hamlet he passed through he asked after the patrol and the replies he received confirmed the patrol had indeed been searching for a dog. By the time he reached the auberge at St. Antoine it was the late afternoon. He dismounted in the yard, taking his pack into the inn along with his weapons. He immediately sought the innkeeper. He wanted to get him on his side straight away, so he announced himself as an emissary dispatched from Paris with instructions to pay the outstanding account of the gendarmes. He rendered the whole sum and apologized profusely for the delay in payment. He even gave the innkeeper an extra bag of coins to compensate for any inconvenience. The astonished and delighted man accepted the apologies –and money- with great enthusiasm. He had never really expected to recover the debt and was only too glad to give information in return.

The Captain told him “Please do not blame the good people of La Garenne for this ‘misunderstanding’. I know that you were told that the Mayor would settle this sum, but you should know that it was not he who refused to pay. Those renegade gendarmes are to blame.”

The owner was so happy that he immediately offered every assistance. He was willing to go through again - and in great detail - everything that had happened. He told Roland that to him the patrol did not seem equipped to make a long journey and he had overheard nothing to suggest they might be about to desert.

"I know one thing though: they were pursuing a dog! I've heard since that it was a very valuable Hound, with a very big reward, so probably they were hoping to collect it. The odd thing is that the sergeant who was in charge seemed very certain that the animal would be travelling due south – though I don't quite know why that would be – most dogs that escape try to get back home." The innkeeper's version of events concerning Louis-Philippe's arrest tallied with that which André had given.

Next morning, as he was leaving he noticed that high in the sky above him flew a pair of fine eagles. Whenever he stopped they would fly off, but as soon as he set off again they would re-appear. By nightfall he was some distance away from any habitation and made camp. It was something he was quite used to doing and he prepared a simple evening meal over an open fire. By the light of his lantern he managed to write up his report to date and allowed himself to think back over the events of the last few days. He wasn't sure if the death of Lucien Lecaron, the disappearance of the patrol, the elusive lost Hound and the strange behaviour of Louis-Philippe were all connected - and if so, how? There were too many coincidences. The young nobleman had been present at Lecaron's death, had also been one of the last people to see the lost patrol and seemed obsessed with this lost Hound. Why was this never mentioned in any reports? This was turning into quite a puzzle.

Roland allowed his mind to wander to more pleasant topics…he had found his beloved Kate…at long last. He was just beginning to nod off wrapped in his blanket when he heard rustling nearby in a dense thicket of trees. Force of habit made him draw his pistol quietly and creep slowly away from the light of the dying fire and his burning lantern.

"I can see you perfectly well you know, I see better in the dark than in the light. I am no threat. I want to help you." The officer looked around him. It was pitch dark…but his eyes soon adjusted to the darkness as he stared into the woods. Nothing.... nothing but a white owl perched on the branch of the tree nearest his campsite.

"Show yourself" he shouted brandishing his pistol. He used his most commanding voice in the hope that it would strike fear into the intruder.

"I *am* showing myself" came the voice "you're looking at me for heaven's sake! Captain Roland Lebrun, emissary of General Destrier." Roland realised it was the husky voice of a woman!

"I cannot see you; I can see nothing but an owl. Come closer and identify yourself."

"Oh please." There came an exasperated sigh: "I despair of humankind sometimes – I *am* an Owl. You come closer to *me.* For goodness sake. Sometimes I don't know why I bother!" The captain approached the branch where the owl was sitting; he was extremely confused.

His instincts told him he was entering a trap. How could it be the owl who spoke? He crept cautiously forward ensuring that he did not pass in front of the fire to present a clear target for a shot. He circled the massive old oak tree knowing that the sounds came from this direction – but there was no-one on the other side.

"Up here! Alright, perhaps if I tell you something that only you know, you might believe me. You have been followed by a pair of eagles ever since you left St. Antoine (before that but you probably weren't aware). Furthermore, I know that you were fooled by Catherine de Garenne, weren't you? You thought she was Kate Giscard .... she came to your barracks two days ago. Hm...very indiscreet! Now do you believe me?"

"How.... how can you know all these things?" he said, confused and not a little scared. It really was a talking owl. Worse, a sarcastic talking owl! A sarcastic talking owl he understood...was he going mad?

"Ah, we have spies everywhere – as many as there are birds in the sky. I shall fly down to the branch nearest you, so we can have a sensible conversation."

The magnificent snowy owl flew down and perched on a branch just above the gendarme's head. "Ah, that's better" said the bird. "I can see you and you can see me….so please lower that pistol eh?" Roland hadn't realised he was still brandishing his pistol and immediately laid it down on the ground but still near his feet.

"I can see why we gave up trying to talk to humans when even a Paladin has difficulty with a simple concept" said the owl in an exasperated voice.

"A Paladin?" he queried: "I don't understand – well in fact I don't understand anything about this conversation."

"You, you are a Paladin – how else could I talk to you? I should perhaps introduce myself: I am Madame Athina. You are searching for the Lost Patrol. I can tell you now that you will never find them. They really have vanished from the face of this earth. But you, young man must undertake a much more important task. It is your destiny to ensure that Hugo Hound reaches safety, nothing more and nothing less."

He listened in astonishment. "Me? My orders are to find the Lost Patrol and that I will do, or at least find out what happened to them. Frankly, I don't think Headquarters would be impressed that *according to an owl* they have disappeared for good" said Roland, somewhat sarcastically. "Then you tell me I have a mission to save a Hugo Hound? I don't think so. When I find the missing gendarmes, I shall then proceed to bring the murderer of Colonel Lucien Lecaron to justice."

"I know all about your orders, but you must understand that Hugo's safety is paramount" replied Athina sternly. "It is difficult for you to understand but the future of our species – and by that, I mean you and me, Captain Lebrun – may depend on the success of his mission. I cannot stress this enough; Hugo Hound must be protected at all costs. He is being hunted by Louis-Philippe de Garenne – as are you! Do not underestimate the danger that both Hugo and you are in – that man has killed once, and he will kill again if he sees his chance – you could well be his next victim." Did this owl really know what he himself suspected? Did she know who had killed Lucien Lecaron? The gendarme stared, dumbfounded. Athina stared back at him unblinking.

"Now listen carefully: you must cross the river Dordogne and then go directly to the small town above it, called Monbezier. Make sure that you are seen there. I suggest that you stay overnight at the coaching inn then leave next morning. Make sure that all and sundry have seen you setting off towards the south." Roland listened, powerless to interrupt. "Then, when you are out of sight of the town, turn to the east and go into the forest. You will be completely safe although perhaps a little uncomfortable." Athina chuckled at this which was a really odd sound when made by an owl. "There you will discover what really happened to the lost patrol and you will find out too just why Hugo is so important to us all. Now I must go… I wish you good luckkkk" and as she said these words the owl spread her wings and flew gracefully up into the night sky.

His head was spinning 'Pull yourself together man. You must have had a dream. You are a captain of the Gendarmerie Nationale, now act like one' he told himself. His training took over and by the light of his lantern, he set to writing down everything that the owl had told him, read it once again and then tried to get some sleep on the damp ground, the cold seeping slowly into his bones.

He awoke with a start, briefly unsure where he was and then rose quickly and blew upon the embers of his fire to make himself some warming coffee. He once again tried to make sense of what had happened during the night. He looked around his little encampment and could see footsteps going towards the tree where the owl had been perched. He was certain they were his footprints. He wondered if he had been sleepwalking, not something he had ever done before – but at least that would be a sort of logical explanation. He sat down and looked at his notes. Yes, they were in his own handwriting, firm and clear. Sleepwalking, possibly, but sleep *writing*? Usually when he awoke from a dream he could no longer recall any details, no matter how vivid the events but last night's events were crystal clear.

Unable to process these thoughts, he decided to go on with his quest to find the Lost Patrol. He gave himself a good talking-to: 'I was sent to do a job and I will do it' but at the back of his mind was the thought that an owl had known something sinister about Louis-Philippe. She knew what he had sensed. Roland slowly kicked dust over the embers of the fire and collected together his small 'kitchen' and blanket. Above him, he noticed, the pair of eagles were flying once more. He rode slowly on and made his next camp overlooking the wide river valley. He could see some small flat-bottomed boats tied up; they would be loaded with cargo to be carried towards the great city of Bordeaux, where the river became part of a vast estuary. 'Could that be the way the patrol went?' he thought to himself. He could also make out a small ferry struggling with the strong current. He noticed that another eagle had joined the pair, having flown in from the north, and it was now circling high above him.

As he watched, one of the original birds flew off in the direction from which the newcomer had arrived; were they carrying messages? What was he thinking? Then he remembered what the owl had told him and realised that he had noticed eagles flying above him since leaving St. Antoine!

Before going down to the ferry, he rode across the top of the plateau from which the Lost Patrol had watched Hugo and Mimi and quickly spotted some kit bags, discarded in the undergrowth. Roland examined the contents of these bags and found some ammunition, and a few unfinished letters to loved ones but most importantly the remains of the men's food which had been gnawed at by the creatures that lived in the undergrowth. Obviously, the men had left in great haste. Surely anyone planning to desert would have taken all their food with them? It confirmed what he had learned back in La Garenne. These were men who were intending to return, not flee, as the old gendarmes left at the barracks had told him.

He led his horses cautiously down the steep riverbank into the valley and went first to talk to the crews of the river boats. He was hoping that they might tell him that one of them had taken the patrol down river, or that perhaps they had commandeering a boat, but the rivermen knew nothing and shook their heads at his suggestion. He continued to question anyone he could find whilst he awaited the arrival of the wooden ferryboat, which was struggling with the power of the river. The vessel carried a wagon, complete with horses, and a few foot passengers too. It was propelled by a system of ropes attached to capstans and steered by the ferryman. The capstans were turned by a pair of Donkeys harnessed to the ropes who plodded on methodically until the ferry reached the bank. As soon as the other passengers had disembarked, Roland led his horses on board and paid the ferryman.

The man looked surprised:" I didn't think you lot ever bothered to pay for anything" he growled, half under his breath. "There's always an exception that proves the rule" replied Roland jovially. "You must have been one of the last people to have seen that lost patrol a couple of months ago?"

"Oh yes, I saw them; they commandeered the ferry here when there were good fare paying customers still waiting. Wouldn't let me set it upon the river until their high and mighty sergeant came down the hill."

"Would that be Sergeant Brochard?" Lebrun asked, interested in what the ferryman might know. "That's right, Brochard, that's what they called him tho' I'd call him a few other names."

"You wouldn't know where they were headed by any chance?" the gendarme asked hopefully, although he knew from the Falaise's report that the ferryman had not been at all forthcoming on this subject when asked previously. "Well, I would have told the officer who came asking before you if he had bothered to pay his fare. They didn't go to Monbezier, which surprised me. They went charging off up the hill then across the fields heading for the forest. Ha, they must have had a desperate reason to go into *that* forest and they wouldn't be the first never to be seen again."

Roland reached into his pouch and produced a handful of coins. He gave these to the ferryman, smiling. "Take this for your trouble." At last he had a real lead. Once he disembarked, he rode up the path in the direction of Monbezier. As he left the flood plain, the path became steeper and soon he was riding alongside a partially harvested cornfield, sharp stubble protruding from the dark soil except where a wide swathe had been trampled by horses' hooves. The path of the swathe led directly towards a ploughed field beyond which lay the dense forest. All this confirmed the ferryman's story, so the Captain followed the track on foot. When he reached the ploughed field, he dismounted and looked at the ground. Although some time had elapsed, he could still make out some hoof prints which led towards the dense trees.

He took stock of his situation. If the Patrol was in the forest, then as fugitives they would have posted lookouts. He was clearly visible in open ground and if he went closer he would be an easy target for any half-decent shot. He contemplated whether to find a place with a bit more cover to watch the forest or to go directly into Monbezier. He could ask questions there and was sure to get more results than the hapless Falaise. His thoughts were interrupted by a pair of large eagles descending at some speed towards him. One landed about ten paces in front of him, on the ploughed ground and stood, fixing him with a beady stare. The other flew directly towards his face and at the last moment swerved away to the right, where lay the road.

Stunned, he watched the great bird repeat this performance several times before reluctantly acknowledging that again he was taking orders from birds. He went back to where he had tethered Marron and remounted as the eagles climbed high above him, clearly satisfied with their work. 'Something else to exclude from my report' he thought, smiling to himself.

CHAPTER 31

The market town of Monbezier was a lively place surrounded by a defensive wall with high crumbling towers on three corners. The fourth tower had crumbled completely into the now empty moat below. Anyone coming in had to pass through one of the main gateways, so Roland was confident that if the men of the Lost Patrol were hiding in the forest they would have to come here for supplies and thus pass through a gateway. Someone *must* have seen them. He diligently made enquiries around the town and became perplexed that nobody could recall seeing anything, although everyone had heard of the patrol. Disappointed, he decided to take a room at the inn in the square and having put his saddlebag in his room, he donned his one set of civilian clothes and went down to make sure his horses were settled in at the adjoining stables.

The stable lad was patting Marron. “A fine horse, sir” said the lad. “I see from his saddle that you are a gendarme. Same as the markings on the saddles on the horses we found wandering near the town.”

“Really? Where were they found exactly?” the Captain asked, intrigued.

“Wandering, Sir, just wandering in the fields not far from the forest, they were. Bridles and saddles still on ‘em and very nervous they were too. I asked M. Barbier about it, but he told me not to worry about things as don’t concern me.” Roland sensed a good lead. “So, where can I find this M. Barbier then?”

“Well, he comes to town quite often Sir, but I don’t know where he actually lives. The guv’nor will know though. He buys M. Barbier’s ale. Gilles Barbier is a brewer and good ale it is. He calls it GB Ale –everyone around here drinks it and when supplies run low, trade suffers."

The officer returned to the inn and at the bar he ordered a tankard of this famous beer – and it was, as he had been told – very good ale indeed. "Do you brew this yourself?" he asked, knowing the answer.

"No, Sir, I get this from old Gilles Barbier, the best brewer in these parts. I just wish supplies were a bit more reliable. Sometimes we can go for weeks on end without any but then other times, like four weeks since, he sells me so much I can barely fit it all in my cellar – haha but I still shift it all. I take my hat off to him, whatever he does to it, no matter how long we keep it, that beer never, ever goes 'off'. The man's a genius, if you ask me, but he is a little…well… unusual."

This made Roland even more curious, but he tried not to show it. Feigning nonchalance, he asked where Gilles lived but was disappointed to learn no one had any clear idea. Rather embarrassed to admit this, the landlord explained "He always goes off in the direction of that forest, but I am not sure….no-one in their right mind would go through there, it's evil it is, and…. Well least said the better. But you won't find anyone in the town with a bad word to say about Gilles, we all need his trade. A few months ago he commissioned a great number of huge wagons, specially painted – though why he would need wagons with cages I do not know – from Gaston the carpenter and filled them with hay and food from the suppliers here."

Roland turned over in his mind his 'conversation' with that owl. The 'evil' forest, the strange happenings… how he should make sure he was seen in the town and leaving it too –and only then enter that forest. The gendarme stood lost in thought until he heard the innkeeper addressing a newcomer: "Ah Gaston, I was just telling this gentleman about those new wagons you built for Gilles Barbier."

"Oh yes, took me quite a while to finish 'em. Even had to take on extra men, what with the 'special' refinements he ordered, bars and things; a specialist had to be found cos the local smithy couldn't handle all the work. Then there was the paintwork on the sides too."

"Did he tell you what he needed 'em for Gaston?" asked the landlord, intrigued.

"Well, he told me he was setting up his nephew in rather a strange business – didn't know he had a nephew – but he had me paint "HUGO'S AMAZING TRAVELLING MENAGERIE" on the sides in red and gold and old Sandor gave me a hand with some fancy artwork too."

"I thought his nephew's name was Bruno, you know, that huge fellow who lifts the barrels on his own."

Roland's interest was piqued: "'*Hugo*'s Travelling Menagerie' did you say?"

The officer stayed listening to the local gossip in the bar for a while, hoping for other snippets he could glean. As the bar gradually emptied, however, he made his way to bed, looking forward at last to sleeping on a soft(ish) mattress for a change. He slept heavily but woke refreshed and in the cold light of day, he once again tried to draw together the threads of all that he had heard. Try as he might to ignore it, his thoughts kept coming back to the conversation with Athina. Logically, as the patrol was seen heading for this mysterious forest they were either still in there or had made their escape. Why would the men want to disappear anyway – they knew the penalty for desertion, at best a long prison sentence, at worst.... well it was the General's preference that their fate should be much worse.

'I must make a reconnaissance of this forest. If I can find enough clues in there to justify it, I can request a fresh patrol to help me' he thought and pleased that he had at last a plan to follow, he ate a hearty breakfast and left the inn. He rode through the town, bidding 'good day' to all and sundry. The dark forest stood to the east and therefore it made most sense to leave by the East Gate, but the words of the owl stuck in the back of his mind and he decided to use the South Gate and when far enough out of sight of the town, he would make his way across country and back towards the forest. 'Why?' he asked himself, 'am I taking advice from a bird brain?'

Attired in full uniform he reached the South Gate where he dismounted and carried out a full and pointless inspection of the huge wooden doors hung on their giant metal hinges. Satisfied that his inspection and his departure had attracted sufficient attention, he remounted and rode slowly through the gate past the straggling line of smallholdings and cottages which lay beyond the ancient walls and out into the countryside.

When he was well away from the town he steered his horse off the road and into some dense undergrowth where he dismounted and stealthily made his way back on foot to ensure that no-one else was around. He left Marron and Greco happily cropping fresh grass while he watched the road and then, confident that he was alone, he remounted and made his way back in the direction of the forest.

Even before he reached the dense trees, the normally placid Marron let him know that they were approaching something which posed a threat. He felt the horse's reluctance and leaned down to whisper words of encouragement into the horse's ears. For once, however, his gentle words had no effect at all. The animal had slowed and was lifting one hoof before the other with great reluctance. Proceeding this way, they travelled perhaps another 30 paces before Roland was forced to dismount and take Marron's reins to lead him forward, all the while patting his flank and whispering in his twitching ear, whilst the horse rolled his eyes in fear. The smaller animal, Greco seemed less troubled, but it took all the Captain's persuasive powers to stop Marron bolting. Gradually he gained control and Marron seemed to recover his confidence a little as they went deeper into the forest, his master walking by his side. Soon the man began to understand the horse's reluctance for he too now felt a deep chill and an even deeper apprehension; he felt that they were not alone and the dark trees on either side of the path pressed in around them.

At first, he could see nothing, it was just a 'feeling', a vague presence. He had no idea what it was that had spooked not only his horse but himself yet as he walked, his normally perfect eyesight seemed to be playing tricks on him. A filmy mist obscured the path, making it increasingly difficult to see the way ahead. Amid his escalating panic he thought wryly that this was his punishment for listening to an owl. He smiled grimly at this thought and just at that moment the mist cleared. Relieved he saw that the sun was again clearly visible over the treetops.

HUMANKIND COMES TO SANCTUARY INN

Temporarily blinded by his sudden emergence from the gloom, Roland followed a wide shaft of dusty yellow light which struck the woodland floor cutting a path through the thick leaves underfoot, as if leading the way. Without warning, he had entered a bright clearing, the dark and threatening forest retreating behind him. What lay before him on the other side of the clearing was a steep cliff which formed a seemingly impossible barrier. He looked up to the top of the cliff which was overhung with tree roots and thick bushes. Then his eyes fell upon what was in front of him in the clearing itself...this was something far more daunting.

On a gnarled old tree stump sat a vast hunched figure. Roland realised that it was not human. It was a bear! A huge bear...partially clad in human clothing. The bizarre vision was smoking a pipe! For this was Gilles' favourite log; it was here that he did his best thinking.

Roland gripped Marron's bridle tightly; the horse however seemed less concerned about this vision than it had the forest. Nevertheless, the gendarme readied himself to retreat.

"You must be Captain Roland Lebrun. Welcome to Sanctuary Inn" boomed the huge animal jovially.

Was he hallucinating? Was this some sort of spell? He didn't believe in magic - well he hadn't until he had met the talking owl. Not only did this apparition talk, but it knew his name. Marron stood rigid, his ears twitching slightly but before the Captain could reply, the bear continued:

"Athina will be along very soon, young man. She's bringing some other visitors, but she told me to make you welcome. I'm Gilles Barbier by the way, landlord of this Inn and yes, before you ask, I am a larger than life bear in breeches!" Gilles' loud guffaw was the signal for a huge wooden door to swing open in what had before been a solid wall.... how had he missed this? The vision standing in the doorway however was difficult to miss. He was looking at another bear, this time wearing a bonnet and a pinafore!

CHAPTER 32

"Fine host you are, Gilles Barbier, letting our first human guest since I don't know when stand around in the cold. Here, come in Sir, I apologise for my husband's lack of manners. In his defence, it is a very long time since we welcomed any humankind" cried Madame Barbier. At this, Gilles decided to reassert his authority: "You follow the missus, Captain and I'll take your horses to the stables, rub them down and introduce them to our other guests."

Neither Madame nor Gilles Barbier missed the look of shock on the gendarme's face at this announcement….'introduce the horses to other guests'? The Captain's sense of reality was so rocked by events so far that he mutely removed his pack and weapons from Greco's back and allowed Gilles to lead both horses away; moreover, he could hear Gilles chatting as they made their way to another mysterious opening in the cliff face. He followed Madame Barbier through the vast oak door set into the cliff. A few animals sat either in the bar or beside the blazing log fire. These were the animals that had chosen not to accompany Hugo and Ursian but there were also some new arrivals. Everyone inside the inn regarded him with interest but not alarm; they had been warned of his arrival but knew that although he was a humankind, he presented no threat. Roland, on the other hand, had not had the same assurances regarding the wolves and other predators seated around the fire.

"It's been very quiet since Hugo left" said his hostess "but I am reliably informed that more humankind will arrive soon, one of whom is very important. She is a Paladin just like yourself, Monsieur -It'll be just like old times!"

I wonder what on earth she means, he thought, well beyond wondering why he was questioning the words of a giant female bear in a pinafore. He was tempted to ask her just what the 'old times' had been like but decided on another line of questioning: "Excuse me err Madame, but I have one or two questions that really need answering. How did you know who I was, that I was going to come here, that I am a 'Paladin'– and just what is that?"

Madame Barbier turned to look at the officer with an amused twinkle in her eyes. "Well, that's easy. Athina told us you were coming, and who you are so it stands to reason you have to be a Paladin because if you weren't, well, we wouldn't be chatting now would we?" Her logic was unshakeable, at least to her.

"Anyway, the lady herself will be here later, and I am sure she will explain it all to you much better than me." Without further ado, Madame Barbier disappeared through a door at the back of the bar leaving the gendarme alone with his confused thoughts and his new and rather terrifying animal friends. He couldn't wait for a full explanation from a magical talking owl. Gilles soon re-appeared from the back of the cave which served as living accommodation for many of the animals. "Young Marron is quite settled. Fine horse that Captain, as is Greco. Marron asked me to apologise to you for the embarrassing fuss he made in the forest. I've explained it all to him and he says he will never let you down again. Now sit down, make yourself comfortable." Gilles indicated the giant armchair, which was usually Ursian's, its cracked and worn leather seat still showing the deep depression made by a large ursine rear-end. Roland sat gingerly on the sagging seat and tried not to fall back into its depths.

"Oh yes, that's Ursian's favourite chair, you know. I keep meaning to get it reupholstered, perhaps even re-built for his return. You should find it comfortable." The Captain peered out at Gilles over the huge arm of the chair and thought to himself that whoever this Ursian was, he must be gigantic.

“Athina tells me you have been ordered to investigate the gendarmes that disappeared and that you are most insistent that you will not rest until you find them?” Gilles raised his bushy eyebrows: “Well, I told her there’s only one way to satisfy your curiosity and that’s to meet the old Comte. Nothing happens in this forest that he doesn’t know all about. He will already know of your arrival. The Sentinels will have told him. I shall go straightaway and ask him if he will see you. Make yourself at home and if you fancy a drink, well I recommend a drop from that first barrel, it’s the last of our Special Celebration Ale. I hear I may need to brew some more soon too!” Gilles gave a knowing wink. “If you want some fresh air, you are perfectly safe outside. *They know all about you*”.

Roland’s expression betrayed his misgivings. “Don’t worry. The Sentinels are our protectors.” Gilles bowed and left the Inn, leaving his new friend to survey his new ‘companions’. Half a dozen wolves padded over and sniffed around him whilst two bears sat at the bar drinking quietly from their personal tankards. ‘Maybe those Sentinels aren’t so frightening after all’ he thought.

He rose and went outside, closing the Inn door and hoping he could find it again. Sitting down on Gilles’ strategically placed log he took a proper look around the clearing, especially at the towering cliff face. He could see that the cliff extended the width of the clearing but now he could make out other doors that he was certain hadn’t been there when he had first arrived. They clearly led to the stables where his horses were resting and above them there was a second row of cave entrances, this time without doors but high enough to be well-nigh inaccessible. He turned his attention to the trees standing at the edges of the clearing. The first few trees were easily visible but beyond that it seemed that only filmy darkness swam before his eyes. A swirling mist was moving…. towards him…figures were approaching.

CHAPTER 33

On the morning of Roland's departure, Kate had ridden over to see her cousin, anxious to enlist Amélie's help with her latest "excursion." Her aunt watched from her bedroom window as her niece rode towards the house and then round to the stables. Aunt Marianne re-read a letter which young René had delivered the previous evening, chuckling to herself at André's words. He described the reaction of the townsfolk to her niece's indiscreet behaviour. "Ha! You're not the first Garenne girl to get tongues wagging" she said aloud. Her face darkened, however, as she read the second part of the letter – the doings of her errant nephew.

She heard footsteps bounding up the staircase and a knock at the door of Amélie's bedchamber followed shortly by muffled sounds of the girls chattering which were punctuated by Amélie's unmistakable laugh. She waited some minutes before crossing the landing to her daughter's room. The giggling, which had become almost constant, stopped abruptly. She entered without waiting for an invitation and just caught some hasty movements, but they were both now sitting demurely on the bed, watching her. Before Kate could say a word, her aunt chided her: "So I don't even get a 'good morning' in my own house?" Her niece blushed at this rebuke and for her breach of good manners.

"Please forgive me dear aunt Marianne, but I was in such a hurry to see Amélie."

"Of course you were because you have so much to share with her, do you not? I presume you have told her you spent yesterday afternoon alone with a young man, dined in public together and then allowing him to accompany you back to the Château?"

Kate's face flamed but without waiting for a response her aunt went on: "I trust that this young man is as you remember him? In which case, I should like to meet him, if only to thank him for delivering my girls safely from the battlefield."

Surprised, Kate shook her head: "I am so sorry, but he has been ordered to find the Lost Patrol and he left La Garenne early this morning."

Before she could say more her aunt interrupted: "I see. This Lebrun abandons you once, leaving you heartbroken and when he finally reappears he then promptly disappears - like a thief in the night. Are you really sure this is the man for you?" Kate blushed more than ever as she recalled just how angry she herself had been.

"Yes, I know. What you say is true, but…he had good reason both times."

"Well, I hope you know what you are doing. Make sure your heart is not broken again, Kate!" With this parting shot, Marianne stalked out of Amélie's room, remembering to leave her own bedroom door very slightly ajar.

Listening intently, she was eventually rewarded by the creaking of Amélie's door being opened and she heard the girls attempting to creep down the stairs. She waited a few seconds then strode to the top of the stairs, her arms folded tightly: "So, young lady, not so much as a 'good day' and now you are sneaking out without even a farewell!" Both girls jumped guiltily: "Err no, I am just helping Amélie take some clothes and things downstairs." Kate indicated a small valise that she was carrying. "As soon as we had taken these few bits to the hall, I was going to return to say goodbye of course. I was also going to ask whether dear Amélie might keep me company while my brother and André are away. They leave tomorrow on some wine buying trip and I get so lonely in the Château all on my own." She smiled what she hoped was a winning and/or pathetic smile, but her aunt kept her stern expression:

"Is this by any chance a 'Kate's truth'? Why the valise? Surely Amélie has a wardrobe suitable for most eventualities already at the Château? I have a much better idea! Why don't you stay here whilst Louis-Philippe is away?" The dismayed silence which followed this suggestion confirmed her suspicions. "No? I thought as much." She let out a sigh of despair, rolling her eyes upwards:

"Girls, the last time you went off together you were away for over a month. I was distraught with worry but still I trusted you both not to come to any harm and how wrong I was! That time you ended up in the middle of a war. I cannot go through that again."

"Mama, please do not worry. The war is over and even Kate cannot start one on her own. I am sure if we do make a small journey, it will perfectly safe" Amélie wheedled.

"I can no longer physically restrain you girls, though I wish I could. I beg you not to leave before at least sending me word of your intentions – and this time I would prefer the truth. You're not planning to elope are you Catherine?" and she turned a sharp eye on her niece. Kate shook her head vigorously, shocked by this suggestion herself.

"So, what do you have in that valise?"

"Just some comfortable clothes for the err… journey" her daughter replied, hoping that her mother would not ask to see the contents. Supposedly unknown to Marianne, to travel safely the girls occasionally adopted men's clothing and these were in Amélie's valise. Much more likely to upset their Maman however, were the other travel essentials – a pistol, powder and ammunition, a small hunting knife and a long thin bladed dagger which could be concealed easily in a boot or in the folds of a cloak. Much to Amélie's relief, her mother did not pursue the matter but accompanied them both down the stairs into the hall where she made a final attempt to dissuade them: "Can the two of you not engage in ladylike pursuits for a change? I swore to your father that

I would always care for you Kate. Going around the country unchaperoned was definitely not what he had in mind."

In a last-ditch attempt to stop the girls, Marianne decided to try a different tactic, the threat of forced marriage: "Remember, daughter, Louis-Philippe has often told me that his good friend M. Despierre would very much like to pay court to you. He is rich, well-mannered and comes of a very good family. A very large inheritance will one day be his, together with a beautiful home. Perhaps I should accept his offer on your behalf?"

At the mention of M. Despierre, both girls' faces became sour and Amélie put out her tongue making a grimace of distaste.

"Amélie Giscard, that is not how a lady behaves" her mother chided, but luckily for Amélie, Marianne was laughing too, for she secretly agreed that although M. Despierre was all of the things she had described, he was also fat, dull and as misogynistic as her nephew.

They said their goodbyes to Madame Giscard who stood nervously watching them ride off to La Garenne. She hoped that they would keep their promises. They reached the Château by noon to discover that Louis-Philippe was out hunting. The two girls hurried upstairs where Kate questioned her cousin:

"Do we have everything for our journey?"

"Of course, with my small cache and yours that makes 3 pistols, 3 hunting knives and a dagger – should be enough" and both the girls laughed quietly. "So, now you have forgiven him what do you think will happen?" But even with her cousin Kate remained reticent. They spent all afternoon together giggling and laughing but eventually, Amélie had to know just what their newest adventure might involve. Both girls were very conscious of their promise to tell Marianne their plans, but Kate was not convinced that her aunt would approve if she knew the whole scheme. She made a moue of concern.

“Mmm… I’m not sure my aunt would agree if she knew the whole story. My brother leaves tomorrow to follow Roland. André told me that my brother believes he will lead him to Hugo Hound in his search for the Lost Patrol. Do you remember? The dog that disappeared at about the same time as the Patrol. My brother becomes almost irrational when that animal’s name is even mentioned - even though the dog belonged to the Lecarons. It also appears that the Patrol said that they too were hunting for this animal. Next thing we hear, they’ve all disappeared! I must warn him that he is being followed.”

Amélie frowned: “I really don’t see why we need to get involved, Kate. If he does come across this dog and leads your brother to it then that’s the end of the matter, surely? There must be something you’re not telling me. Amélie looked at her cousin quizzically: You are planning to elope, aren’t you?”

Kate looked quite taken aback: “No Amélie, I promise I am not, the thought hadn’t even crossed my mind until your Maman mentioned it – although it does sound terribly naughty – I would never do that. Alright, the truth? André believes my brother intends to kill Roland.”

It was Amélie’s turn to look shocked: “I know that we both think he’s well, a little unbalanced but even your father only wanted to have Lebrun horse-whipped.”

“No Amélie, it’s got nothing to do with what happened to us in Paris. Do you really think my half-brother cares enough about me for that? He only cares about himself. Roland suspects that my brother had something to do with the death of Colonel Lecaron... and that it wasn’t an accident.”

“But, but, if it was no accident ….” Amélie did not finish the sentence, but her cousin finished it for her.

“Yes…Amélie, it was murder, and I have to find him before my brother does and warn him of the danger he is in. At least André is going with Louis-Philippe and perhaps he can restrain him, but I cannot be sure." Amélie knew that if she did not agree to go, Kate would go alone.

"I really don't want to lie to mama, Kate."

The other girl looked down, shamefaced, and was forced to admit that she had been a little economical with the truth in the past but now it was so important. How dangerous could it be?

"Please, please come with me Amélie. I promise all we'll do is warn Roland."

"Alright, but what do I tell my poor mama? We need to convince her that we shall be in no danger, so no lies."

"Don't worry Amélie, I am going to tell her the truth, that we need to deliver an urgent message. I have already told her my brother is going on some sort of trip, so I don't need to mention that again, do I? Anyway, my brother wouldn't dare harm us. We aren't in any danger, are we? I'll even put it in writing that I will not elope. That should keep her happy, don't you think?"

Amélie sighed: "No sorry. That still sounds like a 'Kate's truth'. If we are not in danger, then why don't we tell her the whole story?"

"Because…whatever I tell her, she'll panic and if I told her that the message I am delivering is that my brother is planning to hunt Roland down and kill him or perhaps that the Captain believes my brother is a murderer? Let's stick to my version.

After all we are going to be perfectly safe – trust me." Kate could be very convincing when she had to be; Amélie could also be easily persuaded.

They spent the rest of the day making ready and enjoyed a delicious dinner, ruined because they were forced to share it with

Louis-Philippe, some of his hunting companions and the ever-present Captain Falaise. To her brother's dismay, she took the precaution of inviting André to join them at table and he managed to keep the conversation away from any topics that might cause argument. Kate and Amélie were pleased that her brother was, this evening, taciturn and withdrawn despite the loud behaviour of his companions. At last he retired to bed 'in anticipation of an early start' the following morning. Once the other young men had ridden off into the night, barely able to sit on their horses, André joined the girls by the great fire in the drawing room where he confided that he was becoming seriously concerned about her brother's grip on reality especially concerning the dog, Hugo. This trip was obsessing him to the exclusion of all else.

Kate and her cousin appeared for a very early breakfast dressed in their prettiest, most feminine morning gowns, hair groomed, to wave farewell to Louis-Philippe and André from the steps of the Château. The young nobleman barely spoke but just as the two men were about to ride off, he came back to address them.

"I don't trust you two here alone. Be sure you behave correctly and give me no cause for shame."

André assured the young nobleman that the girls had given him their word and sworn on the name of the old Duc, to behave impeccably whilst he was away but this only fuelled Louis-Philippe's temper:

"The name of my father? He is dead! I am the head of the family now, not him. You are my sister, you are my responsibility, indeed my burden. Lacoste here is a mere servant, someone who works for the estate. You do not swear anything to him or on the life of our father. It is to me, me that you should make your promises."

André was silent, but Kate could not hold her tongue, looking furious as she tried to keep her temper: "May I remind you that our father nominated me as his successor to be Steward of the Eleanor

Bequest and Head of the House of Garenne. Until I assume that title, it is Aunt Marianne as my guardian who holds that place. It is to her that I have pledged my obedience, not you. "Amélie struggled to keep a straight face. 'obedience? really?' she thought wryly. Her cousin hissed: "I do not intend to allow you to control my life or attempt to marry me off to some noodle-headed…."

She did not finish this sentence because her brother turned his horse and viciously dug his heels into its flanks. He thundered off down the wide roadway leading from the Château, with André and the packhorse in pursuit, eventually disappearing into the shadow of the trees lining the route. As soon as the two men were out of sight, the girls rushed up to their rooms and changed into their travelling outfits. Kate had arranged with René for horses to be saddled and waiting and they loaded a pack horse with their luggage. They both kept a pistol concealed in their clothes. The absence of the gendarmerie in the area had recently given rise to a spate of thefts and attacks upon travellers. Their last act was to dispatch the young groom with a note to Marianne, a note over which both girls had slaved to find sufficient ambiguous reassurances to satisfy her suspicious mind. Both were unaware that Marianne had her own source of information!

She read the letter but told the young groom there would be no reply. She would be replying to this via a very different messenger.

CHAPTER 34

The girls rode slowly at first because they knew that the two men were on the road in front of them. They guessed that the men planned to spend the night at the only inn, in St. Antoine. Kate knew that Roland was at least a day ahead. He would be going south following the trail to the places where the Lost Patrol were last seen. While he was taking his time asking questions, of course, her brother would be catching up.

Late in the day, they avoided the inn of St. Antoine and set up camp in a clearing in the woods nearby. They found a stream from which to draw water and bathe their faces at least and then built a fire using a small silver tinder box. The fire was only for warmth because a last-minute decision to avoid inns so as not to draw attention to themselves, meant they were ill-prepared for campfire cooking. They had brought along only some bread and cheese, some dried ham and water in leather flasks to wash it all down. It would be enough for supper and breakfast, but they would need to buy more food at the next village.

After finishing their depressing meal of bread, cheese and water, they settled down for the night. On their journey from Waterloo they had slept on the road but then they had had a carriage and company. This time they were in a dark forest, the silence broken only by the occasional unrecognisable call from the darkness. Neither could deny that they were afraid. Near the embers of the dying fire they wrapped themselves in their heavy travelling cloaks, first making sure that the horses were tied securely to a tree. They curled up together at the foot of a large oak trying to make themselves comfortable amongst its thick twisting roots. It was an uneasy night: the ground was cold and hard, the roots gnarly and stabbing. Amélie lay staring into the darkness, regretting now that she had agreed to this adventure without giving it a lot more thought. As she stared absently into the wall of trees surrounding them she became uneasy; the hairs on the back of her neck rose.

Alarmed, she whispered urgently in the darkness: "Kate, Kate, look! That owl over there. It's staring, really staring at us. It hasn't moved for ages and it's making me nervous." Both girls stood up, ready to make a run for it.

The white bird suddenly flew down and stood on the forest floor still staring quizzically at the girls and gradually they became aware of a terrifying chill surrounding them, but they could not look away from the mesmerising eyes of the owl. As they stood transfixed, the eyes of the bird seemed to grow larger and larger, almost drawing them in. Kate clasped Amélie, both girls too terrified to speak and as they stood, rooted to the spot, the air itself began swirl and ripple creating ever-growing circles of shimmering light. The girls clung together, now with their eyes tight shut against whatever terrifying sight might be before them. It was a shock when Kate heard a sharp voice:

"Catherine de Garenne, what exactly do you think you are doing?"

The voice was that of an angry governess, but as Kate registered this fact, she was also aware that the voice seemed to emanate from the owl. Overcoming her terror – for of course this could not be happening – she opened her eyes and demanded: "How do you know who I am? What business is it of yours what I am doing anyway?" Both girls remained standing, holding each other. Instead of answering her questions, the bird muttered to herself:

"Ah, I knew it. Just as headstrong as ever."

Amélie opened her eyes. What was happening? Her cousin was talking, and the terrifying white bird appeared to be squawking back. "Kate. You're scaring me, why are you talking to that bird? You asked it a question. Have you gone as mad as your brother?"

"It asked *me* a question Amélie. Did you not hear it? I swear that it really is talking to me."

"Kate, you are exhausted, your mind is playing tricks on you. There are no such things as talking owls. Now lie down, pull your hood over your face and try and get some rest. We have a long day ahead of us." Amélie pretended a calm she did not feel as she tried to convince her cousin who reluctantly did as she was told and lay down, turning her back on the owl.

They lay rigid waiting for the vision to disappear but instead the circles of bright light intensified suddenly and for a moment the dark forest was as brightly lit as day. Neither dared risk a look and then they both heard:

"Catherine de Garenne, how dare you turn your back on me."

Kate looked up. This time the bird sounded exactly like her old governess. Same voice…and same tone. She rose abruptly, ignoring Amélie's terrified expression and turned to look at where the bird had been…but in its place stood a slight but imperious figure.

"I can't have a proper conversation with you both, so I have been *forced* to make a few changes so that your cousin Amélie can understand me. I hope she realises how honoured she is!" The snowy white bird had transformed itself into a slim female form wearing a pale flowing gown, trimmed with small silver charms. The gown was of a design Kate had seen in ancient tapestries at the Château. The creature's hair was very long and silvery white. It lay loose and flowed down her back in a straight, glistening cascade secured by a barrette of elaborately fashioned white gold. This ornament kept the hair back from a pale, thin face, with an aquiline nose, colourless lips and skin that was almost translucent, but it was the eyes… The eyes were still those of an owl, but so dark and shadowed that the girls could not clearly see them. On her head the woman, for it was certainly a woman, wore a plain white gold circlet with an intricate device at its centre, set with stones that twinkled even in the darkness. She stood before them, waiting while her transformation became complete and stretched her thin, pale skinned hands out towards them. On one hand, both girls saw that she wore a delicately wrought but very heavy ring. This too was of white gold but set with an enormous cabochon blue stone, its milky surface glowing; the setting of this ring was very old-fashioned, almost medieval and seemed too heavy for her thin finger.

Kate grabbed Amélie's arm, but they were rooted to the spot, transfixed before the woman who had a moment ago been an owl.

"I am Madame Athina. I ask you once again...Catherine de Garenne what exactly are you up to? Explain yourself this minute." Kate was still too stunned to speak, and Amélie stood open mouthed. Eventually, Kate stammered out: "We …. we are worried about Roland Lebrun. We know that my brother means him harm and we have got to warn him."

The pale woman replied: "Catherine, I can assure you that Captain Lebrun has already been informed of your brother's intentions. Now, I want you both to listen to my instructions carefully. Stay out of sight until your brother and André Lacoste have gone on their way and return immediately to La Garenne. You are meddling in matters which do not concern you." Her fierce expression along with the basilisk eyes indicated the severity of her message and they nodded silently. The tone of Athina's voice struck a chord in Kate's memory, the voice was that of her old governess who had been determined to break her spirit. It was not going to happen this time! "If you think that I am going to take orders from a spectre, ...a witch or even a talking owl you really don't know me at all. I love him …" Kate had surprised herself into admitting this "and I will not let him disappear from my life again, no matter what you or anyone else says. I thank you for your concern and for alerting the Captain to the danger. However, do not expect me to run back home. I won't do it. I will deliver my message in person."

"You truly are your father's child; he would have been so proud of you, even if you are as stubborn as he was." The strange apparition's face briefly showed resignation. With a heavy sigh she said: Very well, I will assist you but only to keep you out of harm's way. I will return before daybreak and I expect you to be ready. We have a long way to travel tomorrow. Oh, and by the way I am a h-a-r-u-s-p-e-x, so much less rude than being called a witch, I think."

The girls watched silently as the vision shrank, imperceptibly transforming itself into a pure white owl once more. Flapping her wings, she flew off into the night sky. For a moment the girls stood clutching each other whilst they tried to gather their thoughts. Eventually, Kate asked: "That really happened, didn't it?"

"It really did." whispered Amélie. "What should we do?"

"Well, basically she said we are meddling in things which don't concern us but there's a difference between things we don't understand and things that don't concern us. I certainly don't understand what she is up to, but I do know that it concerns Roland and my brother – therefore it concerns me too. I don't believe she means us any harm. If she had she would have struck whilst we were too scared to move a muscle. Anyway, it's strange that she knew our names, oh, and she knows about Roland's rank too - she called him Captain. She even knew my father. She said I was stubborn like him! I was quite hurt when she said that. I am only stubborn when I know I am in the right." Amélie was relieved that her broad grin was hidden in the darkness.

"Well, she will be back in the morning, so she says and wants us ready to ride at daybreak so obviously she is coming with us." Amélie nodded her agreement and they lay down once more, too agitated and too cold now to sleep.

Before dawn, they gave up the unequal struggle, arose and stoked the embers of their fire whilst they waited in trepidation for the return of the creature that called herself Athina. True to her word, just before the sun rose, the white bird flew into the clearing, landing on the ground beside them and began her miraculous transformation. Not quite sure what to say, Kate greeted her with a 'Good morning Madame' only to be reprimanded abruptly. "If I am to assist you, the least I expect is that you co-operate with me. I requested that you be ready to travel but instead I find you sitting around, your horses unsaddled. Get a move on please if you don't want to encounter your brother."

Obediently the two cousins doused the fire then saddled their horses and made ready to leave. Athina announced that she would ride with them: "I'm as light as a feather" she assured them. Amélie mounted up, but Kate wasn't ready yet: "You said last night that you had warned Roland of my brother's interest in him. Can you please tell me how he was and where he is now?"

Athina huffed, unwilling to be questioned but relented: "He was well, if a little surprised by my arrival and he's about one day's ride ahead of us.

If he follows my explicit instructions, you may well meet up with him later tomorrow. *We* can take a shortcut but meanwhile, rest assured, he is in no danger – quite a remarkable young man." Finally satisfied, Kate mounted her horse, sitting astride in her men's' breeches. Athina joined her, rising ethereally from the ground but perching side-saddle behind her. They re-joined the main road going south and Athina reassured the girls that Louis-Philippe and André were still at their lodgings, so it was perfectly safe. By now, Kate and Amélie questioned neither her information nor her authority. They rode for a couple of leagues into a small village where Kate was instructed to purchase provisions for that day and breakfast for the following morning, including some local wine which the haruspex assured her was ‘of fine quality and would travel well’.

Shortly after leaving the village, Athina brought them to a halt. “We’ll take that track” she indicated “it’s quicker and safer.” She floated down to the ground and they followed the direction of her pointing finger. They could see nothing there but woods and dense undergrowth. Then Athina waved her hand imperiously and before them lay a well-trodden pathway where only trees had been a moment before. Their horses shied a little as if sensing something unusual, but they rode on, leaving the roadway and following the newly revealed route. Nevertheless, Kate felt she must voice her concerns:

“My brother considers himself an excellent hunter; won’t he be able to follow our trail? He’s bound to be curious when he sees this bridleway?” Athina responded gently for once: “Not at all. It’s a Bear Road and unless you know exactly where to find them you will never see one.”

“Ah yes, I see, of course it is” Kate replied, wondering if she should ask if they were likely to meet any bears! Towards nightfall the party stopped and made camp. The haruspex walked off towards some trees and then returned informing the girls that the two men were some considerable distance behind them, on the main road and that Roland had reached the small town of Monbezier that afternoon.

Athina joined them for their evening meal although she ate nothing at all but did enjoy the wine they had purchased earlier. She spoke little, and Kate was disinclined to ask questions, the answers to which might be more confusing. The girls barely spoke to each other either. This surreal journey had robbed them of chatter. After supper Athina sat slightly apart from the girls and underwent her mystical changes. Once more a snowy owl, she told Kate that this time they must be up and ready to travel on her return, then her white fluttering form disappeared. Kate relayed the instructions to

Amélie and once more the girls were alone. As they lay wrapped in their heavy cloaks on the damp forest floor they tried to make sense of these latest events. Amélie began: "Her knowledge of events seems reliable; she's obviously being kept informed of your brother's progress somehow. We will just have to trust her." They could think of no alternative and so agreed to continue taking their odd companion's sharply delivered advice until hopefully they met up with Roland. That way the girls could avoid thinking about where exactly she was leading them.

They woke well before dawn and breakfasted early and quickly, hoping to avoid incurring Athina's displeasure again. When she arrived, she found them sitting on their horses, ready to leave. They noticed the faintest hint of a smug expression on her face as she took up her place on Kate's horse and soon they found themselves in open countryside. Again, Athina had to sooth Kate's fears that her brother would catch up them. Louis-Philippe and André were not only far behind, but on a different path and soon she and the girls would be completely hidden from sight. This was not altogether good news. Kate noted that the surrounding countryside was becoming hillier and Athina pointed to a sheer cliff and motioned them towards this as she raised her ethereal arm and waved it sharply from right to left. As they approached the solid rock wall a narrow opening became visible.

"You'll need a lantern, just wait here" she whispered as she slipped down from the horse, returning a few moments later with a lantern which the girls lit. Guided by the dim light, they made their way still on horseback deeper and deeper, the cavern becoming a narrow passageway which the haruspex explained had once led to the home of bears. Kate nodded nervously. Amélie sensed, via her horse's rising hackles that they were in a dangerous place.

As they rode single-file along the passage they reached a wider section where, in the flickering lantern light, they could make out paintings on the walls, paintings of elephant-like creatures, oryx and tigers. "I don't think it was *only* bears that lived here" muttered Kate but Athina did not respond. They skirted a small underground lake with stalactites and stalagmites, glistening in the lantern light, some so old that they had grown almost to touch each other and form crusty glittering columns. Reaching a fork in the way, Athina indicated the left-hand passageway which slowly became even narrower, the flanks of the horses brushing the rock face. Just when an intense feeling of claustrophobia began to create panic not only in the horses but the girls too, they felt the air become fresher and a tiny chink of natural light appeared ahead. They emerged into the daylight half-way up a steep hill overlooking a river which Athina informed them was the Dordogne.

"I must take my leave of you for a while. Go down and take the ferry. On the other side, I want you to climb up the hill then take the path towards the forest. It's clearly marked by shells but if you miss it one of my messengers will find you. I'll meet you at the edge of the forest."

Kate and Amélie looked beyond the river to the dark forest which lay above the valley on the other side trying to make out the terrain. When they looked back…they were alone. They followed Athina's instructions and much to their relief they found the track marked with shells, glad that they would not have to meet one of the haruspex's 'messengers'. Whoever – or whatever - those messengers were, they would prefer to avoid them. At the edge of the forest they dismounted and peered warily into the trees. Their attention was caught by one particularly tall pine tree and as they watched they heard a rustling coming from the high branches. Their gaze followed the sound upwards and there, on one of the stoutest branches was perched none other than the snowy white owl, who immediately flew down towards them but whilst still shrouded in the gloom of the forest, she transformed herself into her 'alter ego', the pale, slightly luminous Athina. She told them that they would be best leading their horses from here and just as Kate was about to complain that she did not wish to walk, her mount bucked and tossed its head in fear, breaking free of the tether she had fixed to it and running forward into the forest. “Oh no! We shall never find him in there” cried Kate.

“Yes, yes we will but quickly take hold of the other reins. Walk slowly through the forest, keep together and we will come to no harm.”

‘Hm – what can she mean?’ However, they were used to doing as she bid them and they hastily took the remaining horses’ reins. These horses were now exhibiting signs of panic but still the girls could see nothing except gloomy pine trees. They were about 20 yards into the trees when they too realised the problem. The air shimmered with filmy shapes. Absolute silence lay heavy through the woods, no animal sounds, no bird cries, nothing…Just as they began to lose their nerve, the filmy, translucent shapes merged to form a sort of ‘guard of honour’ beside the path through the trees. Athina led them forward and they walked on until the trees thinned out and there in a clearing, waiting patiently for them, was Kate’s horse. She took its reins but was suddenly more interested in something else entirely.

CHAPTER 35

Roland Lebrun sat apprehensively watching the forest beyond the clearing, trying to make sense of what he was seeing. He could make out figures taking shape on the path, a path which it seemed was lined by glinting cobwebs. More Sentinels? No, these were no ghosts. He could make out a figure, not clearly visible, which seemed to hover above the ground and behind this vision two more substantial figures, leading horses and walking very slowly towards him. All at once, one of the figures detached itself and ran towards him calling:

"Roland, Roland, is it really you? Oh, you're safe, you're safe!"

The gendarme was struck dumb. He stood up preparing to rush back to the safety of the inn but in a heartbeat, he realized that the petite figure running towards him was none other than his Kate whom he had left, he thought, back at La Garenne, safe and sound. He stammered: "Kate?" just before she threw herself at him and locked her arms around him, almost knocking him from his feet. She hugged him very tightly and kept repeating: "You're safe, you're safe, thank God you're safe."

"Yes, yes I am safe – but what are you doing here? I thought you were back at La Garenne."

"I discovered that my brother intends to harm you!" Kate gabbled breathlessly then took a deep breath: "Actually I'm sure he wants to kill you…so Amélie and I came to warn you. That's why I'm here."

"I know he is following me but if I were to relate to you all that has happened you would think me mad. I got that information through the strangest of messengers" and at this he smiled wryly.

Their reunion was interrupted by a long drawn out sigh – "Strange? Strange? I don't think I am strange." The voice came from the third member of the little group, an oddly familiar female, who had arrived silently behind Amélie.

"My apologies, Madame, I meant no offence, but the messenger was a talking owl, a very opinionated owl in fact ...I was not referring to you Madame. I do not think I know you. Are you a friend of these ladies?" at which both Kate and Amélie collapsed laughing while the gendarme and the oddly-dressed female stared. The stern pale face wore an expression of extreme disapproval, which suddenly seemed very familiar to him.

"Permit me to introduce Madame Athina. She is a…." but the sentence remained unfinished. He looked from the girls to the pale lady in consternation. "No, no, it can't be. I have met Athina and Athina is a…she's an…."

"OWL" shouted Kate and Amélie together, still laughing, whilst the other female said nothing.

"So, you have met her" he gasped. "I couldn't believe an owl could talk and I could understand what was being said. She knew all about…so many things."

"Yes, yes my dearest. So presumably you and I can speak 'owl' – let me finish - Amélie couldn't understand her and so Athina has changed her form into that of a 'haruspex' (apparently that's much politer than witch) so that she can speak more easily with humans. So, you see, it's simple." Kate tossed her hair to express a confidence in the situation that she did not feel.

Athina permitted herself a small smile as Roland regarded her more closely. The third figure was clearly a female, although she appeared ageless. Today she was wearing an oddly pearlescent yet colourless robe with a long overtunic woven of thick woollen material in a deep and intense shade of blue. The garment had a thickly lined hood. Her long straight hair glistened unadorned.

There was something in her silent face that spoke volumes to him. She had the intense stare of a bird and the effortless superiority of the owl he knew as Athina. They bowed to each other and he turned back to the girls:

"I thought I was going mad."

Athina spoke up: "As fascinating as this conversation is, can we get back to the business in hand? Hugo Hound is in danger. As I told you, Captain, Hugo must be protected. I need to speak with Gilles as soon as possible."

Looking into Athina's eyes, Roland realised with a shock that although the three ladies were beside him, she was floating very slightly above the ground. Accepting that this was just another strange event in a strange day, he explained that Gilles had gone to look for the "Comte": "I imagine you already know Madame, that my mission is to find the Lost Patrol and then to find the murderer of Colonel Lecaron."

Athina drew herself up in front of them seeming all at once much taller and he realised that she could exude quite a lot of menace for such a slight figure. At full height, she barely reached his shoulder, but he found himself somehow looking up at her. "You really must stop worrying yourself with human concerns. Concentrate on what is really important – to us, and by us, I mean all of *us here*. Now let's go inside. I think you will find that M. Gilles has already returned. After lunch, young man, you can accompany him to visit the Comte. He can explain what happened to the Patrol. Then perhaps you will apply yourself to more important tasks?" Making it quite clear that the conversation was now over, she walked regally forward to the Inn door, leaving Roland, Kate and Amélie in her wake.

Whilst she spoke to Madame Barbier and was greeted with great enthusiasm by all the guests of the Inn, the Captain looked at Kate and Amélie: “Do either of you have any idea at all what is going on?”

“Not really” the girls replied. This was proving far more of an adventure than either had expected!

“Well M. Gilles has promised that once I have spoken to this Comte I will understand more – oh, that’s another thing, just wait until you meet the Barbiers. Before you go into the Inn, there’s a couple of things I think I might need to be explain. Firstly, the Barbiers are giant bears, although they wear clothes just like us, well perhaps not exactly like us. They would probably look out of place in the salons of Paris. All the other guests inside are animals, most of whom would be unlikely to share your table shall we say and …most amazing of all, I can speak to everyone here. My report to Headquarters is going to be really, err… interesting.”

Both girls looked at him, then at each other uncertainly. Since meeting Athina their lives had been turned upside down. First, they had suspended their own belief as they watched an owl transform into something akin to a human; they had encountered ghost-like creatures in the forest and now Roland, who had been their rock, the man they had relied upon to escape from Waterloo was talking about giant bears…wearing clothes. As they walked towards the large oak door of the Inn, Kate clinging tightly to his arm, she whispered in his ear: “Have you been sampling some of the woodland mushrooms? I hear some are very powerful and bring on hallucinations.”

When Roland pushed open the door he was surprised to see Gilles had indeed somehow returned unseen to the Inn: “I understand that Mlle. Giscard does not understand our tongue so me and the missus have done a quick change in her honour.”

Kate leaned over and whispered: “Giant bears?” Amélie was close enough to hear and sniggered. A blinding glance from Athina silenced both girls.

"Young ladies" muttered Athina in a voice laden with menace "M. and Mme. Barbier have paid Mlle. Amélie the deepest courtesy by appearing in human form, you will extend to them the courtesy of not laughing or sniggering. Your mother, Amélie, would be so ashamed of you both."

Both girls looked shamefaced and apologised to the Barbiers, all the time trying to avoid Athina's relentless gaze. Despite adopting human forms, it was easy to see now that this was unnatural to both large animals. Their clothing covered their fur and their faces were at once human and ursine but their feet…pure bear paws! Mme. Barbier had prepared an enormous feast served at the vast dining table, although she apologised for the fare, insisting that she could not remember how to cook food for humans. Gilles offered either wine or Giant Bear Ale to drink. Lunch stretched on well into the afternoon until finally Gilles coughed theatrically to get everyone's attention.

"M. Roland, before we go to meet the Comte let me explain something. You live in this human world, right?"

The three humans looked at each other, puzzled by such an obvious question but nodded in agreement all the same.

"So, this is the only world you know of, isn't it? What if I told you that there are many worlds all around you, it's just that you can't see into them. When I first came to the forest oh, must be 350 winters ago, the old Comte explained it like this to me: see that door there? You know it's there and you know that outside that door is a forest, but you can't see that – well that don't mean it ain't there, does it? Likewise you can't see those worlds, but they're out there alright" Gilles sat back, looking satisfied, convinced that he made his point well. "Now excuse me, I must quickly change" and he ducked down under the bar counter and disappeared. When he reappeared, the girls knew how wrong they had been. This time he was pure Pyrenean bear, although still dressed in some of his oversized human clothes, still wearing his spectacles perched on his huge brown snout. The girls' mouths fell open in shock. This time when he spoke, he spoke in bear tongue, a language that Amélie could not understand.

"The Comte is accustomed to seeing me like this; I mean no disrespect to our guest. Now M. Roland, let's get going eh?"

Kate recovered from her shock in time to grab him by the arm as he rose from the table. "If you are going, then so am I."

"Mlle. Catherine, I give you my solemn promise that no harm will befall M. Roland. The Sentinels only wish to help us."

Kate looked at the oversized bear, who towered over her and realised that arguing with him would be pointless. Instead she tried a winning smile, batting her eyelashes as she whispered. "Pleeaase."

Gilles looked down, shaking his head: "Normally the Comte will only agree to meet me, or the Missus and he is making an exception in seeing this young man.

But…I think that he would perhaps be happy to see you. Yes, I think it might please him." Gilles looked at Athina meaningfully as he said this.

Amélie, once she had grasped that her friends were going without her, wore an aggrieved expression as she watched them cross the clearing and disappear into the shadows of the trees. She had wanted to go, or more correctly had not wanted to be left with the occupants of the Inn. Athina came up behind her and put a hand on her shoulder. "They are perfectly safe, you know, Gilles made a Bear Promise that he would let no harm come to them. Believe me, that is the most solemn promise of all."

CHAPTER 36

Roland and Kate followed Gilles in silence, aware of the presences around them, which they now knew posed no threat, at least according to Gilles. Gradually, however, they became aware that something very strange was happening. At a distance, the gendarme had gained some idea of the geography and size of the forest they were now walking in. By his reckoning they had traversed its entire length several times over, yet the trees showed no signs of thinning out. Gilles strode on, confident of his way and seeming to know every branch and twig along their route until they reached a small clearing. There was a broken tree stump at its centre and Gilles sat himself down heavily: "He'll be here in a minute; he always like to have a good look at visitors before he shows himself." His companions managed to share the large flat tree stump, quite tired now and worried about what might be coming their way. Roland began to have misgivings about trusting both his own and Kate's safety to a giant bear and indeed all their fates to a feisty owl and an unknown Comte.

All at once Gilles stood up and motioned to them both to do likewise as ethereal shapes formed a shimmering tunnel through the surrounding forest. Gilles told them the Comte was on his way. How Gilles knew this they did not know but they too felt something and the hairs on the back of their necks rose unbidden. They could hear noises deep in the forest, rustling and clanking as if chains were being moved or dragged. Both peered in the direction of the noises and saw at first just a shape, advancing towards them.

As it drew closer both were astonished to see that the figure was dressed in full chain mail and armour with creaking metal foot coverings, gauntlets and a helmet reminiscent of those seen in old engravings in the galleries of Paris or in schoolbooks. No-one could have pretended not to hear this knight's arrival as his armour was so old each separate joint creaked with age and rust. The face of the knight was not visible but sharp blue eyes peered through the visor of the ancient helmet. He removed a gauntlet and raised a skeletal blue-veined hand in greeting.

When he reached Gilles, his stature was more noticeable, a slight figure in comparison to the bear and even compared to the humans. Gilles and the gendarme bowed whilst Kate stood open-mouthed for a second before executing a perfect curtsey. The bear then began to speak directly to the knight. Roland listened closely and detected that although they seemed to be speaking French, or it sounded like French, it was of a dialect he had never heard before. The style was oddly stilted, but he clearly heard both his and Catherine's name mentioned, in fact the ghostly figure repeated the names several times. As he spoke he directed his words to Gilles, but the piercing blue eyes beneath the visor remained fixed on Kate.

"Sirs, I apologise for interrupting, but what language are you both speaking?"

Gilles turned to him briefly to explain that they were speaking French but a French that had not been spoken since the time when the Comte had lived on the earth.

"Don't worry, I can translate for you, but I really think you may be able to pick it up if you listen carefully. After all, now you can understand animal tongues, so this should be easy, eh?" The Comte has just, by the way, congratulated you both on being the proud possessors of two equally famous names. I've asked him if he would explain what happened to the Patrol you seek."

All colour had drained from Kate's face as she clung anxiously to the young man's arm. He could feel her shaking and whispered words of comfort as best he could. The ghostly old knight began to speak again in the only language he had ever known, and Gilles translated after every few phrases when the knight paused, struggling for breath.

The knight indicated with his pale hand that they should turn around and look behind them which they did, both expecting to see only dense woodland and perhaps the wispy presence of a Sentinel or two but instead they were looking at a bustling street in a city which Roland immediately recognised as Paris, the city of his birth. They both saw the great cathedral of Notre Dame and could reach out and almost touch its thick stone walls, but Gilles whispered:

"Do not move." They stood silently taking in the familiar square … yes this was Paris, but not as he remembered it. For instance, on the horizon he could make out a great tower which appeared to be woven from iron. When had they built that? The streets were much busier than he remembered and although there were still horse-drawn vehicles, some of the vehicles, incredibly, were moving *without* the aid of a horse. Passengers were using a wheel to control the shiny black conveyances amid an atmosphere of thick smoke and noise. His eye caught movement on the bridge, a column of men marching forward in his direction: gendarmes, although their uniforms were very different from his own. The amazed Captain counted the men, twelve in all, including a corporal. This struck him as odd – wouldn't they have a sergeant with them? He wondered why, of all thoughts, this had come to him and just as his mind searched for an explanation, Gilles whispered:

"The Comte asks me to tell you that, as you can see, nothing terrible happened to your colleagues. They are not dead, they are not suffering but they are just no longer of this world. The Sentinels removed them to another one, similar but not identical, to your own.""Roland? What are we seeing?" whispered Kate, quivering and clinging to his arm but the gendarme was too shaken to respond. He was trying to absorb what he had been told. How could it be that the Patrol were neither dead nor alive?

"I counted only twelve men – I was told there were thirteen. Twelve troopers and their sergeant, Brochard. Could you please ask M. le Comte where he is?" The gendarme was trying to concentrate on things he could understand. He tried to pick out a sergeant's uniform amongst the throngs of people – but very gradually the vision was dissipating until all that remained was the familiar gloom of the dark trees. Meanwhile, Gilles and the old warrior continued a lengthy conversation in the old language. Gilles turned to his companions:

"The Comte wants to make you understand that the world you have just glimpsed is only one of many. The Comte holds the keys to some of these worlds. He is summoned by the Sentinels when there is a need to deal with a troublesome visitor or a Renegade and it is he who invites them to pass over peacefully into another world. None so far have resisted his invitation. As they are no longer of this world they can no longer do any harm.

This Sergeant Brochard...well" Gilles paused as he took a deep breath "this Brochard is a bit of a problem. It seems the Sentinels cannot account for him and this can only mean that unknown to them not only did he escape but is also a Renegade." Kate shivered involuntarily at the mention of the word 'renegade'. Roland asked: "So he did not go to this...other, this err other world with his men? Might he have still gone but alone?"

"That I cannot tell you, but it seems very unlikely - I must speak to Athina about it but it is the worst possible news." The humans were not able to grasp fully the significance of this clearly serious turn of events. They would need to ask Athina or Gilles later. Meanwhile, Roland realised that it was true, as Gilles had told them, the language being used was becoming easier for him to understand, first snippets and then whole sentences becoming clear the more he concentrated.

He heard his own name mentioned, but his attention was riveted when he heard repeated mention of 'Catherine de Garenne' and another name which meant nothing to him: Eleanor.The Comte ceased speaking and bowed first to Gilles and then to the young man, taking his hand briefly. It felt like a breeze had touched him, but he managed not to pull his hand away too abruptly. The old man then turned to Kate and having bowed as deeply as his aged bones and uncomfortable armour allowed, he came forward and clasped her in his frail arms for only a moment. Although she saw him reach out for her she felt only as if a cobweb had brushed her cheek. She was terrified but stood firm as the knight turned abruptly and retraced his creaking steps into the depths of the forest. As they watched his departing back he seemed to merge into the gloom until all that was left was the sound of creaking and clanking receding slowly into the distance.

They turned to retrace their steps, thinking of what the old Comte had shown them. Emerging from the oppressive gloom of the deepest part of the forest, Kate broke the silence to ask Gilles why the knight had seemed to be so interested in her. She summoned her courage to ask: "Was that who I think it is, err was? Guillaume, Comte de Rouen?" Gilles responded slowly:

"Yes, you are right, his is indeed a sad story. Apparently, there is a very strong family resemblance between you and the lady Eleanor de Garenne, your distant ancestor. They had been married for just one month when he left her to fight alongside his brother Knights. He never returned. He told me, Mlle. Catherine that you are just as beautiful as Eleanor and he hopes that you and M. Roland will both fulfil your destinies in a way which was denied to him and his Eleanor. Athina once told me that he left this world without ever knowing he was to be a father." The young couple both looked down sadly. That this old knight had 'lived' on in spirit for so many hundreds of years, still mourning the loss of his beloved Eleanor was something so inexpressibly sad that neither knew what to say.

Gilles strode on ahead in the direction of the Inn whilst the other two walked slowly behind him, both allowing their minds to wander over the meeting in the forest. Kate was still shaking and clung to the young officer as if her life depended on it.

As they reached the clearing outside the Inn, Roland turned to Kate: "Come and sit with me. We are safe here although I am sure the old knight meant us no harm; to be honest, he seemed besotted. He never took his eyes from your face."

"I noticed that too. Only when I heard him repeating the name Eleanor did I realise who he might be. She, Eleanor de Garenne, founded our line although her own antecedents are as obscure as those of Guillaume. There seem to be quite a lot of family secrets from around that time. Papa once told me that this Eleanor had her heart broken when she was only 17, cared for her only child alone and devoted her life to helping and protecting pilgrims. She is legendary in our family and I am proud to be her descendant. That talk of Renegades troubles me though. I have heard that word used before, about my brother. My aunt and my father were talking about him and I am certain that this was the word they used. I don't know what it really means but judging by the concerns of Gilles and the Comte it must be something bad. I do know my stepbrother has an evil streak in him but…" She was visibly distressed as she spoke, and Roland held her as close to him as he dared, all the while stroking her hair to soothe her. He was looking at her with a mixture of confusion and sympathy which she did not feel able to deal with at that moment: "Do not worry, my love, I will explain everything one day."

Seated outside in the fading light, Kate felt she must try to lighten the sombre mood their meeting with the knight had provoked. She and her cousin had read many books (before they were inevitably confiscated by her aunt) where the heroines indulged in harmless flirtation. She had always wanted to try this for herself. "Eleanor must have been a great beauty if the Comte has remembered her looks for 500 years" she began. She was mightily deflated when her 'suitor' ignored this obvious bait and responded with a grin instead. "It's more likely that after all that time the poor old chap's blind as a bat."

Roland's speed of reaction surprised them both when he warded off Kate's attempted slap. Frustrated, her nostrils flaring, she hissed "At least your reactions are sharper than your wit, Captain Lebrun. I can't see what might have attracted me to you in the first place." But, try as she might, she could not keep up the pretence of anger for too long and eventually collapsed laughing. "Forgiven?" he asked, and she nodded. "I admit it, even to me that line sounded like a quote from a cheap novel." Since Roland's reading matter was mostly confined to armament manuals and military orders, he had no idea what she meant. He looked slightly lost and she hugged him even tighter and was about to explain when the great oak door of the inn opened. Amélie looked out and said sharply: "If you two could drag yourself in here, we are waiting to discuss matters of great importance." She stood with her arms folded and a stern expression on her little face then turned on her heel, dramatically tossing her head and flounced inside. "That girl…sometimes I think she reads too many books" said Kate taking the Captain's hand. "We had better go and see what Grimface wants."

Kate and Roland followed Amélie into the Inn where Gilles, who had already changed back to his human(ish) form was deep in conversation with his wife and Athina. Conversation halted abruptly when the couple entered. Gilles motioned for them to sit: "I think we owe you some explanations before we ask for your help." Athina clearly disagreed and 'tutted' impatiently at this. "I am told that your General Destrier thinks you are as sharp as any bear, so you will have no problem grasping any of this." Roland was unsure how they might be privy to the Commander's opinions, or whether this was indeed a compliment.

Gilles began: "You are curious to know why you can understand us in our animal form eh? Why you've been called a 'Paladin'? We are all Paladin here, including you, Mlle. Amélie, although you are what we call a 'Poursuivant'." He hurried on to avoid questions. "You all know now that this is not the only world. Well, the Paladins didn't originate in this world. Athina knows that other world only too well."

CHAPTER 37

Gilles looked at Athina who rose slowly, and it seemed with some reluctance. She appeared to be floating above the floor of the cave as she began her story. Her pale colourless robe now began to glow in a gossamer-fine cloud of iridescent silver. Her audience listened intently.

"That world was a cruel place. I was born many hundreds of years ago. For reasons long lost in the mists of time, our Clans had been banished. Even the Elders - and they were very old indeed – did not know why. All that was known was that our captors had led us across the Wasteland and abandoned us at the foothills of a vast mountain range, leaving us to die. There was no need to guard us, there was nowhere we could escape to, except back across the Wasteland. The mountains were seemingly impregnable. We were trapped, foraging for what little food could be found in the hills. For many centuries, explorers had tried to find an escape route, a way through the mountains. If any *had* found a way, then they had not returned to tell of their discovery. Most had returned despairing of ever escaping from that dreadful place. My best friend Pellerin and I decided that we would become the next generation of seekers and we, of course, would succeed where so many before us had failed."

As Athina became more and more involved in telling her tale, the others noticed that her iridescent, pale robes shimmered and glowed with ripples of light and changing colour which reflected in her gleaming, hooded eyes but she seemed unaware of the radiating light: "We would disappear for days roaming the foothills of the great mountains but were always confronted by towering cliff faces or dead-end ravines and caves. Disheartened, we resolved that we would make one last effort and if we failed, we must live out our lives in that miserable place….and then finally, finally we found it…deep inside a cleft in the mountains. We heard a distant echoing voice …telling us we had reached *The Eternal Divide*. I was, I admit, afraid but Pellerin was more curious.

He called out to the voice asking where the others had gone, but we were shocked when the Voice responded: "Yes *Pellerin*, I was one of those first Explorers –, many years ago – We too knew nothing of what lay beyond the Eternal Divide but were eager to find an escape - instead we found another world!"

"We looked at one to the other; I was anxious (to my shame) to hurry on to this new world and then return a great hero." Kate and Amélie exchanged glances. They had never expected Athina might ever admit to anything like shame. She saw their expression but spoke again: "Pellerin, as always was wise. He warned me that crossing this barrier would mean we could never return to bring others the good news. Of course, he was right; it should be for all of us to find this new land together. To do otherwise would be selfish – and so we returned. We were naïve, I see that now." Again, Kate and Amélie exchanged glances of disbelief but were cowed by Athina's stern stare. "We explained what we had found, expecting to be congratulated, but instead we were met with total disbelief. The Elders told us 'You are too young to have made such a discovery' or 'I was once an Explorer and I never found this cave you speak of' or even worse 'You have deliberately made up all these lies'. I wanted to cry – yes Catherine de Garenne, this time you are justified in looking at your cousin in surprise. I was very young then, younger than you are now. The Chief Elder – as was his right – had the final word and addressed everyone: 'We have been trapped here for countless generations and likely to remain here until we all die out. The Oursi will go with you tomorrow, Athina and Pellerin, and *we* will cross this Eternal Divide. I ask you that if you choose not to go with us you must send a representative who can tell you how to find this cave, if you then choose to follow'. My parents had lived all their lives on the edge of the Wasteland; they had no energy for a new world…they refused to leave. They did agree to accompany me to bid me farewell but would go no further."

Athina's voice faded a little, her face usually so fierce, softening in the candlelight. Her robes all of sudden seemed to be losing their iridescent sheen. The girls waited anxiously for her to continue. "We left at dawn the next day, accompanied by the Chief Elder and the Oursi, some members of the Aiguilli - Pellerin's Clan- and merely a handful of the Strigi, to which I belong. In total, we numbered about 150. When we reached the entrance to the cave, the Chief Elder spoke directly to the Voice we had encountered in the cave.

He said that these people had decided to make the journey and asked if it would be possible to send messages back. The echoing Voice re-assured him; 'he' would carry those messages from the other side, *Elysium* he called it, as far as this point but no further.

Hearing this the Chief Elder told those who were not going further to return to the cave in three days and he would send them a message. Of course, we were all terrified. Who was this invisible being? How would those remaining behind know the messages were from their compatriots? Was it a trap? 'Why won't he show himself' they cried. It was then that the Voice, fainter and sounding so very sad, explained. He too had once been an Explorer who had attempted to return. In consequence, he had been trapped here, in this cave, for all time, forever formless and between worlds.

Last to leave were my parents: they begged me, even then, not to go…but I was determined to seek out a better life. Eventually they left, never looking back. I never saw them again."

Kate bowed her head and murmured “I am so sorry, Athina” but the older woman seemed to be lost in her story: “We walked forward into a swirling mist, this time Pellerin leading, the Chief Elder between him and myself, guiding his way. He bade his Clansmen follow and slowly, one by one, they did. We followed the sound of the Voice into a dense fog. It was at this moment that we began to realise – we could no longer really see each other…we sensed each other’s presence, we could hear the muttering of the other migrants close by, but…we had *become invisible*.

Pellerin reassured us though. He seemed to sense what I was thinking: “I think our bodies are gone now…but somehow I don’t feel afraid at all’. As we stumbled onwards we became aware that there were others –although not of our kind - around us, moving in many directions, never walking close enough to be seen. Slowly we began to make out a hazy shaft of light ahead.

The Elder called to his followers, whom he could no longer actually see: ‘the Ursi will follow my voice, walk straight ahead. Do not be afraid! The Aiguilli will follow the path to my left and Athina, you will lead the Strigi on the path to the right. We will all meet once again in this new Elysium, I am certain’. I sensed rather than saw my people taking the right-hand path, through the swirling mist now mingled with sunlight.

Suddenly, the Voice, sounding hollow and more distant, announced to us all: ‘Ahead lies Elysium. There each of you may choose your form. You can be whatever you want to be. However, once there you cannot return until it is your time.’ There was nothing for it but to go out into the sunlight ahead. The mists parted, and we found ourselves standing on a wide path cut into the mountainside and overlooking a vast fertile green valley. For most of us it was the first sight of green countryside for we were accustomed to the burning harshness of our desert wilderness. We had reached Elysium. Our group moved down the mountainside and heard and felt the Elder's Clansfolk nearby; then I heard Pellerin's happy laugh – my spirits lifted at once"

The girls noticed that once again, Athina seemed to glow, her gown even more radiant than before and her face like that of a young girl. Kate had to ask, she just had to: "Could you see each other again? What did you look like?"

"Patience, Catherine. Being without form was a wonderfully liberating feeling I remember – at first. We could communicate with each other and in the first excitement of seeing our new home it didn't somehow seem that important. However, slowly –and I am speaking of many, many of your years - the natural desire to see each other took over." Kate thought to herself privately that Athina never referred to her 'previous' form and she began to wonder just what that might have been. Were those previous forms not appropriate to their new lives?

Athina took up her tale once more: "Faced with the opportunity to assume any form, what should we choose? Need it be practical?

Would we grow food, keep animals or…well, now we no longer needed to struggle against our environment in this lush green valley, we could be anything.

We had no real experience of any life except struggling to survive so it was difficult. I made my decision on a whim. I watched creatures called 'birds' every day, so free and travelling great distances with ease. I determined that I would be a bird: of course, it had to be an owl, that wisest of all birds. Pellerin too chose to take the form of a bird, but for him an eagle, the bravest of all birds, without fear like he was himself. The Chief Elder chose to assume the form of a bear, the greatest of all creatures and most of the Ursi decided to emulate him. However, there were those who were not comfortable with this idea; they chose to take human form.

As you have already seen, we can adopt other forms too. You have all seen Gilles as a human. When we first adopted our new shapes, we also took on the persona of that creature and when we change we also adopt that new persona but always stay in touch with our original one. Do you understand me? I have human thoughts now, but I never lose my owl side and for that I am truly grateful. Being human is sometimes too great a burden, and thus it proved for many of those who chose to assume that form. The cares, worries and crushed hopes involved in being human were simply too great a burden for them, so much so that they became trapped. That is why I have always counselled against it although even those closest to me, my nearest and dearest, did not always take my advice." Athina bowed her head for a few moments, deep in thought. "However, as humankind they did retain their ability to communicate with the rest of us, as you still can." She looked now her listeners.

"Yes Catherine, you have a question?"

"Err yes I do. Athina, were messages ever passed back to that other world you had left?" she asked timidly.

"Yes indeed; I am sorry to say that no responses were received. It was a matter of the greatest sadness to us all." As she spoke, Athina's robes sagged around her slim form, their grey colour lifeless and drab. "We so wanted to share our good fortune with the others.

We waited in the High Valley (as we chose to call Elysium) for many years, hoping for a message from those left behind but eventually, we gave up hope.

Over time, those who had assumed a humankind existence became restless decided to leave the High Valley in search of a life in the outside world. They were all my friends and I was sad to see them leave. There were thirteen in all, and (their leader too was called Roland) decided to offer their services to Charlemagne, a most powerful king." Her listeners nodded in agreement; they had all learned about Charlemagne at school; he had lived more than 1000 years before! "You, Roland are descended from one of these men. They distinguished themselves in combat and were given the name Paladin in honour of their prowess and status. They were popular at court and I often visited them where I was treated as an honoured guest. Charlemagne invaded what is now north eastern Spain. The army returned to Aquitania for the winter and I expect you all know what happened? *The Chanson de Roland?"* The three listeners nodded for they all knew the long epic poem. The two girls could recite great chunks of it from memory, having been forced by their governess to learn it in the original Medieval French! Both girls shuddered briefly at the memory of the terrible story.

"Ronceval was the site of that final battle, t'was where every single Paladin perished; it's about a day away from the entrance to the High Valley over the mountains" continued Athina. "Their actions to protect the retreat of the army was the stuff of legend but what was never recorded was that Pellerin summoned the Guard Bears to their aid. Sadly, they were too late to save the knights but wreaked a terrible revenge on their attackers. In fact, it was I who wrote the Chanson de Roland, and I myself translated it into French and presented it to the King. In honour of these brave men, those who remained in the High Valley then adopted the name of 'Paladin'. However, after this we had little further contact with the world outside our High Valley for many hundreds of human years.

Pellerin was by now chief of his Clan and he would fly far and wide, but we turned out backs on your world - our world was Elysium. Then the eagles began to return with tales of terrible suffering out in the human world. We learned of Pilgrims, good humankind making their way to Compostella or to Jerusalem and many other places of worship to pray for their fellows. They were looking to do good, searching for a better life; we could all understand that." Her intent listeners once more nodded in agreement.

"The coastal route to Spain and Compostella should have been the easiest but was controlled by brigands who saw the pilgrims as easy prey. Because of this, many pilgrims chose a far more difficult route, across the Pyrenees. This path passed very close to our home but bandits frequently attacked. Even when safe from attack, the pilgrims still found themselves at the mercy of local merchants who overcharged for even the most basic essentials. Even the religious community were not above profiteering from these travellers. They provided hostelries where the pilgrims were often relieved of their remaining possessions and cash.

The Chief Elder at that time – he was great-grandfather of Gilles and his cousin, Ursian le Grand - called what became known as the First Grand Council. This was a meeting of the Clan chiefs. It sounds very impressive but at that time there were only three Clans. I was invited to speak at the Council and put the case for at least protecting the pilgrims." Athina's robes had subtly changed once more and were now violet, glowing softly with a metallic sheen. Only this and her tone of voice indicated how passionately she had spoken all those years ago. "We had to do something to help."

CHAPTER 38

Then, miraculously, there was news: members of the other Clans, driven by desperation and starvation from the Wasteland, began to arrive. Bereft of their forms they soon recovered they too were able to travel out, if they so wished, into your world."

From Athina's sombre expression, they guessed that her parents had not been amongst those who had arrived. "Those that came wanted to choose their new forms in time and bears proved very popular! One Clan in particular, more, err, irascible than most became the Fighting Bears, which soon had a sub-clan, the Northern Bears but there were eagles, Hounds, horses, lions, wolves, wild boars, tigers and some owls too. Not all chose wisely of course. Some, despite the exhortations of Pellerin and myself decided to take human form, even some very close to me. Many who took this path joined a chivalrous order of knights, the Knights Templar." Athina paused, her complexion, her very appearance becoming waxen and grey. "All the Clans helped in their own ways. One of Gilles' ancestors…"

"Old Hubert the Humorous" grunted Gilles.

"Indeed." Athina hesitated: "He founded the Sanctuary Inns where pilgrims could rest in safety protected by Guard Bears. The eagles and other birds flew over the pilgrim routes and could warn them of any danger wherever it lay. In time, tales began to circulate of men that could become lions, wolves, Hounds or boars, even tigers. The pilgrims loved us, and we were and still are very proud of our achievements.

The local merchants liked us too of course because we always traded with them just as Gilles has still does to this day. The religious orders were not so enthusiastic. We dealt honestly with travellers. For the priests anything which might change shape had to be a Demon. They preached against us but still the pilgrims flocked to us, demons or not. The travellers knew they would be safe in our care. Some of our number were caught, tortured and burnt as witches or warlocks (which is why I much prefer the name haruspex!) Some humans embarked on the senseless killing of eagles and hunted wolves almost to extinction. This was something we could never understand."

Athina paused to take some water and waited briefly to see if any more questions were to be asked before going on: "Over time, some of those who had remained outside the High Valley began to lose their powers to change shape. (Gilles and his wife go back regularly to retain that ability). It was therefore agreed that those ex-inhabitants of High Valley, whilst still of Paladin origin, would be distinguished by the title Poursuivants, like Amélie here. They and all their descendants would have the Promise of Sanctuary and it is buried deep in all their natures. If they are in danger, they can find Sanctuary in one of our Inns where they will be safe. We have fulfilled that Promise for hundreds of years - but times are changing."

Gilles took up the story: "Some of the things that the old Comte has told me about what is in store for your world could reduce the strongest bear to tears. Oh yes, times are definitely changing, even in our forests. You've most likely wondered about the Sentinels? Not all the guests went on to complete their pilgrimages. Some were too infirm and others, well I think that whatever they were seeking no longer seemed so important. Perhaps they found it here and when they died, they remained here, protecting us as we had protected them in life. Humans are too scared to enter the forest and if they do…" Gilles paused to allow what he had said to sink in. "The

Comte has been aware for some time that the oldest Sentinels feel it is time for them to move on to the next stage of their journey, to finally leave this world. So, there will come a time, perhaps sooner than we think, when humankind will have no need to fear the forests.

The Grand Council has been discussing how we can finally fulfil the Promise of Sanctuary. We *must* get all of our current guests to the safety of the High Valley and only then could issue the Call to Poursuivants to go to their nearest Sanctuary Inn, and then we assist them to reach the High Valley. Only a few hundred winters ago, it would have been so simple.

The guests would have been escorted by a few Guard Bears, travelling by night, hiding by day, but at that time most of my Clan were used to the ways of humans. Few now leave the High Valley and only the Innkeepers like me and Hortense and our relief hosts are used to humankind and its ways. Still, it might have been attempted but for the capture of Ursian le Grand. My cousin was betrayed! If he could be captured, what would happen to more inexperienced bears?" This made Gilles stop for a moment, his audience silently waiting for his next words.

"It was suggested by the Chieftain of the Fighting Bears that he send columns of his bears to escort the guests, prepared to fight their way back to the High Valley through any obstacles but even the Chief of the Wolves – and they have most reason to hate humankind – baulked at the thought of what carnage might ensue. We have been wracking our brains as to how to proceed." Gilles indicated the collection of beasts scattered around the cave "This lot have arrived even since Hugo and Ursian left."

The three listening humans nodded, imagining the commotion that would be caused by wild animals travelling across the countryside.

"But out of darkness...has come a little light." Gilles addressed Kate: "Pellerin was asked to contact your father, Mlle. in order to enlist his help and he had already come up with the outline of a plan, not so very different from the one which Ursian and Hugo have concocted, but then sadly…." Gilles left the sentence unfinished.

Kate looked stunned; she now realised that her father must have known about these strange beings but had never told her. Might this then explain his obscure reference to *'in whatever guise'* when he had set out the responsibilities of the Head of the House of Garenne? She had asked M. Lafitte-Dupont about this phrase at the time, but he had just told her that she would understand in due course.

"When Athina reported that Hugo Hound had escaped and was on his way here, all our spirits lifted! The Hounds of La Garenne have always been special; they are all Poursuivants, after all. Hugo, however, is a full Paladin, the first born in the outside world in hundreds of winters. Ursian and I questioned him closely when he arrived, and he is completely at ease around humans and knows their ways too. He can change into a very passable human too – he even fooled his old master Raoul! Had your father lived, he would have enlisted some human help and escorted the animals himself. It was his suggestion to impersonate a travelling menagerie which could travel the roads of France unhindered. He told us, although we already knew, that humans usually never see what is under their noses…but well, when he…Pellerin was unsure he could find any other humans to whom he could entrust the task, although he did have his eye on someone. Luckily Hugo and Ursian have proved to be the next best option, animals who can *pass* as humankind, even quite close up. That's why they are, as we speak, escorting the whole menagerie across Aquitaine, disguised as…a Menagerie!" Gilles chuckled.

"Your father was right though. It is all happening before the eyes of humankind and they can't see it. But if Hugo or Ursian drop their guard for even a moment they would be denounced as 'shape changers' or worse if some Renegade or other were to catch up with them. That would put Hugo in mortal danger."

"I don't mean to interrupt M. Gilles, but I assume by 'Renegade' you mean people like my brother, don't you?"

"Yes, indeed Mlle. I was trying to spare your feelings. But it is true that if your brother catches up with him, he will unquestionably try to kill Hugo Hound. If he cannot possess what he believes to be his then he must kill it. That is the way of Renegades".

Gilles nodded to Kate then turned his attention to Roland.

"And that, young man, is where you come in. It is you that Pellerin had his eye on. He believes that the Menagerie needs some human assistance and he's rarely wrong." Gilles looked pointedly at Athina as he said this.

"With the full agreement of General Destrier you have been selected for this task. I believe your orders give you a virtual free hand to - what's the exact wording? "to investigate all matters you deem to warrant your attention and at all times to assist and protect those in need of assistance"? Roland looked aghast. He himself had been astonished by the virtual 'carte blanche' he had received from the General who had dismissed his concerns with 'Just in case something comes up.'

He was more astonished now that these orders were being repeated to him verbatim by someone he knew to be a bear.

"Err, err that's correct" he stammered. "But before I engage in any other matters I must account for the members of the missing patrol."

Athina had been sitting quietly while Gilles spoke but now she appeared to tower above those seated around the table. She rose like a billowing, shimmering cloud to look down on her listeners, unable to restrain herself. "You now know about your beloved Lost

Patrol. What more detail do you need? Now is not the time for trivialities; it is the time to devote your much-vaunted abilities to helping us!"

"Madame Athina" began the Captain displaying an outward calm he did not feel. "Although I am now convinced that twelve of those men are no longer of this world, Sergeant Brochard is unaccounted for. Before I can agree to help I must know what has happened to him. M. Gilles was reluctant to enlighten me." He looked first at Gilles and then back at Athina but neither spoke, so he continued: "If I can find no more information on the missing sergeant then I believe that my business here is finished. I am satisfied that the rest of the patrol will never be found, and I will report this to Paris – it won't be the first less than accurate account they've received. As to the other 'triviality' as you call it, the death of Colonel Lecaron - well I left evidence in La Garenne and that should be enough to convict Kate's half-brother of murder." At this, Kate and Amélie looked deeply shocked but let him speak: "At first light, I intend to leave here, arrest Louis-Philippe then escort him to Perigueux. A few weeks in our "facilities" there will convince him to tell the truth, I am sure." He looked at Kate as he said this and placed a hand on hers: "So sorry, my dear, but it is my duty and I must see this thing through, even though he is of your family."

"I do understand. Whilst Papa was away I saw little of Louis-Philippe and now I have moved back to the Château I have avoided his company as much as possible. I despise him for his treatment of our father. I am ashamed to admit I feel nothing for him and if he is indeed guilty of murder then he must suffer the consequences."

The officer turned to Madame Barbier: "I thank you for your kind hospitality and insights into an err…different life, but I will be on my way in the morning."

He nodded to the Barbiers and pushed back his chair from the table, not looking at Athina or acknowledging her stern expression.

CHAPTER 39

The awkward silence was shattered when Mme. Barbier spoke in her slow, deep voice:

"Well, if no-one is prepared to speak up then I will. I am so frightened of what might happen next." She fixed her gaze on the Captain. "You see, this ain't the first time something like this has happened and I think you have a right to know. I could never live with myself if it all started again, and I hadn't tried to prevent it." She sat down abruptly, flustered and embarrassed at her own outburst.

Roland tried to coax her: "So? What happened last time?"

"Tis obvious, ain't it? The Beast, the Beast of Gévaudan. It'll happen again, I know it will" she sobbed into her apron quietly.

Those words struck like a thunderbolt. They all knew this name. It provided something of a link between the strange, scarcely believable other worlds they had glimpsed and the harsh reality of the normal world they had thought they lived in. The Beast of Gévaudan sounded like some mythical creature, but it was not; nor was it only a tale which existed just to frighten naughty children. This was a real Beast, often referred to as "La Bête Feroce" which less than 50 years before had terrorised the southern part of the Massif Central. This vast rugged area covered a large part of central and southern France. The beast had roamed far and wide. It had once attacked people less than two days' ride from La Garenne. During his training, the Captain had studied all the accounts of the techniques used to bring about an end to the Beast's two-year reign of terror, a reign which had left more than 100 dead, some eaten alive with nothing left but a pair of clogs. Those that had survived had horrific injuries and even more horrific stories to tell. Finally, the King had been forced to act. Dragoons had been dispatched with the King's personal hunters; a huge reward had been offered to whoever could prove they had killed the Beast. This was no fantasy creature.

"Madame Barbier, I can see why you would be afraid if there was another Beast but what evidence do you have? How does all this relate to my mission? That the original Beast lived so long was due to the incompetence of those sent to hunt it. I have seen drawings of the animal killed by a certain M. Jean Chastel and it was in fact nothing more than a rather large straggly wolf that had undoubtedly developed a taste for human flesh."

Gilles spoke: "T'is true, that M. Chastel did kill a wolf but that was not the Beast. It was Ursian le Grand who eventually slew the Beast, I know; I was there."

Humans and animals alike waited. Breaking the silence, Roland demanded: "This is the same Ursian that's travelling with Hugo Hound, I presume?" but Gilles only looked at Athina, who nodded briefly as he took up his tale once more: "Perhaps you should sit back down my friend." He spoke quietly.

"It all started more than 55 summers ago. A young man, Fabrice Cailloux and his young wife Yvette lived near here, down on the riverbank. Nice couple, always friendly when you met them. They had been wed about seven years, I suppose. Young Yvette was desperate to have children, but none ever survived long." Gilles looked briefly at his wife who had tears in her eyes at the story. "Eventually Yvette had a healthy child, a little boy, the apple of her eye. When the little one was almost a year old, Yvette's mother took very poorly, so she went to care for her. When she returned home she was told her little 'un had drowned in the river. Fabrice had taken him in a basket to the river's edge. He said he had been fishing and had left the basket too near the water. The wash from the ferry as it comes across the river – you've seen that river – tipped the basket and the baby drowned. Rumour was that Fabrice may have been 'otherwise occupied' at the time. Anyway, whatever did happen, the relationship between the couple deteriorated very quickly. Fabrice propped up the local bar while Yvette brooded. Their arguments could often be heard." His listeners were enthralled by his tale.

"Then one Sunday morning, the butcher and his wife M. and Mme. Chaumes noticed that their daughter's bed had not been slept in. They asked questions in the town and discovered she had last been seen with young Fabrice so old Chaumes got his whip down from the wall and rode to the riverbank to find him.

When he reached the little cottage, the doors were wide open – but no-one was there. Even if Fabrice had run off with Chaumes' daughter, where was his wife? By midday, half the town was searching the surrounding countryside and along the river. At nightfall…well they found Fabrice and the Chaumes girl too, behind the stables in the town, covered with straw. Both had been ferociously attacked, blood everywhere. No trace of Yvette was found."

Gilles paused in his gory tale for a moment to puff on his pipe, knowing his listeners would want more. It was Roland who asked: "But you know more don't you M. Gilles?"

"Yes, I do. Young Yvette knew that no-one from Monbezier or anywhere around here would come into 'our' forest and so she took refuge near here after the murders. She was reluctant to go right into the forest, so she remained at the edge, living as best she could in the undergrowth, like a wild thing. The Sentinels saw her but did not trouble her while she remained outside. However, one day a hunting party came too close to her hiding place and so, afraid of capture, she ran into the deepest part of the forest. You all know now that the Sentinels are our protectors, protecting us from those with evil in their hearts. Should they detect Renegade blood then the Comte is summoned to assist them. Yvette must have had some much-diluted Paladin blood along with the cursed Renegade blood; enough to resist the Sentinels anyway and before the Comte could be fetched, she escaped."

"A Renegade then? Like Brochard?"

"Yes, she was a Renegade although no one could have known that at the time. When she fled the Sentinels her fear was so great that she lost her human form completely." The listeners waited, fear and anticipation sharpening their appetites. Athina took up the story: "We can only imagine her desperation as she wandered formless on the earth. Yet her long hidden power had not entirely deserted her. Her ability to create a new shape developed over time – with a wolf-like body that humankind call "Werewolf" or "*Loup Garou.*" But she was no ordinary wolf. Her hatred and pain fuelled her metamorphosis."

Searching his memory, Gilles confirmed: "This beast was taller than a humankind on its hind legs with coarse, matted fur all over its body; on its underbelly, the mottled skin was scaled and flaking, thick and sickly pale.

A hard, bony ridge ran the length of its back coated in thick dark fur. If that was not terrifying enough, it had huge tusks and a long snout with yellow fangs, pointed and glistening with foam. Each huge paw had five dirty poisonous claws which it used to attack as well as hold down its prey. Now you see why we fear these creatures? Remember these creatures were once Paladins so along with the remnants of Paladin power was the desire to reach the High Valley like her ancestors and gain entry. She pillaged her way across the country but at the entrance to the High Valley, the Guard Bears fought her off and wounded her mortally, or so they believed. The following day they went to make sure, but nothing was found in the cave where she had taken refuge. That is normal for a *Loup Garou.* When they die, nothing remains of their bodies which are but a creation of their own twisted minds. When one is only injured their minds can heal them but at a heavy cost. The more severe the injury the more mental power is required to heal, and their minds can no longer control their form. There comes a time if they are injured very badly that their will to survive is overcome and their 'form' disappears entirely." Gilles stared into the distance. His paw gripping that of his wife.

Athina looked at her spellbound audience. "Although the Guard Bears were sure she was gone for good, they decided to descend into the Low Valley just to make sure. Again, there was no trace and after fruitless searching it was concluded that the awful beast was truly dead. Any injured *Loup Garou* who escapes makes their way back to their previous 'home' so Pellerin ordered his clan to keep a close eye on this area just in case but nothing, no trace. There this story should end but it does not.

You know, don't you, that wolves attacked around here until quite recently? In remote areas, in bad winters it sometimes happened, so when reports of women and children being killed or disappearing in the Gévaudan region began it was not surprising. We only became interested when these killings multiplied and despite numerous hunts and scores of wolves being killed, the slaughter went on and on.

The newspapers of the time delighted in vying for the most outrageous description of the killer to terrify their readership. Flying dragons were described – well I haven't seen one of those in this world. Two headed dogs were being seen too but in Paris there was one newspaper that obtained a drawing and an eye-witness account of the murderous wolf. This description reached the ears of Pellerin who realised that this might be a *Loup Garou*. He doubted that the humans would ever kill it alone. It was he who asked Ursian le Grand to come down from the High Valley to dispatch the Beast. Gilles here saw it all, so perhaps you would like to tell the story?"

Gilles nodded "Ursian arrived here accompanied by two hunting Hounds that he had obtained from your grandfather, Mlle. Catherine. They would have been ancestors of Hugo Hound. An eagle told us that the Beast had been seen about 60 leagues from here, near to Pebrac, so we set off. It's just under two bear days' journey from here so we carried the Hounds on our backs to keep them fresh. We ran the whole way, day and night but...when we got to Pebrac we were too late. The beast had struck again, killing a young mother. Ursian vowed then and there it would be the last attack. We released our trusty Hounds just as the sun began to set. This was new territory to us and without our eagles as guides we were really in the dark-if you'll pardon the pun. We had been awake for more than two days, but we were determined. Luckily, the eagles returned just after dawn the next day. The Beast had been spotted during the night by an owl and it was now heading to a town called Figeac. After all her terrible deeds, Yvette was trying to get to her old home, Monbezier. With the eagles' help we set off, the Hounds on our backs once more and, just as the sun was getting high in the sky, the dogs picked up a scent. She could not be far away. They eventually found her peering into a cottage window, obviously searching for her next victim. She spotted us and made a break for it. The dogs gave chase and trapped her in a barn. Ursian called them off for she could have killed them and then he went in after her. She fought hard but was no match for an angry Ursian. I expected him to dispatch her with a single blow but after seeing what she had done to her latest victims out of pure malice, my cousin was in no mood for a merciful end. He inflicted single wounds to her time after time but avoided her sharp teeth until she begged for an end to her misery. Only then did he deliver the fatal blow and she vanished from this world forever." Gilles stopped abruptly.

Athina sighed: "That is the true story of the death of the Beast of Gévaudan." The listeners had been holding their breath at the climax of this horrifying tale. Then Roland asked: "and I assume that you are concerned now that Brochard could become another such *Loup Garou*?"

Athina nodded. “Renegades have escaped before but have not had the mental strength to develop such a form, but it is possible. If Brochard does, then Hugo could be in mortal danger. Like all *Loup Garou*, he will head towards the High Valley, his ‘ancestral’ home shall we say? The thought of the Valley will be all consuming in his mind, but he will not gain entry. If he somehow survives his battle with the Guard Bears, then he will seek out Hugo and try to destroy him. That is the way of all *Loup Garou*.”

“But why this need to destroy Hugo?” asked Kate “I understand that he is a special Hound, but they have no other connection, do they?”

“*Loup Garou* want to destroy what they could not have or what they see as the cause of their despair – it is their nature. Just as poor Yvette felt compelled to kill mothers and children when robbed of her child, so Brochard wanted Hugo Hound and was thwarted so he will try to destroy him. Now can you see that there is even more reason to protect Hugo? Now will you help us?” Athina’s eyes which were usually imperious for once held an expression of pleading.

CHAPTER 40

Kate was torn between wanting to beg Roland to help – he was, after all, a Paladin - and her fear that she might never see him alive again. The gendarme finally spoke: "If I were to say it would be easy for me to return to Paris, easy to pretend that all this is none of my concern I would be lying. If something like the Beast of Gévaudan were to re-appear, I wouldn't be able to live with myself knowing that I might have been able to stop it. All our lives are inextricably linked now with what I have discovered, and Kate will, I know, want me to act. Yes, Madame Athina, I will give all the assistance I can to protect Hugo Hound. After all, if I make an honest report on events then I have no future in the Gendarmerie anyway." He laughed as he said this, then more seriously: "At least I shall be able to leave the service with my dignity – even if everyone thinks I have lost my mind!"

Then Kate spoke: "You are putting yourself in great danger because of events triggered by my half-brother. I cannot let you risk your life alone so… I am coming with you. I know him better than you do, and I can perhaps protect you from him."

Amélie had remained silent all the time but now she had to speak: "Kate, Mama would be horrified that you intend to go off alone with a young man. You will need a chaperone, so I am coming too…so I can tell my mama I was always there with both of you." While Amélie had been speaking, Athina had risen from her chair – risen some considerable distance off the ground in fact and positively towered over them all: "Stop this nonsense now. Captain Lebrun will have enough on his hands dealing with Louis-Philippe and Brochard without having to protect two silly, helpless girls."

Amélie braced herself for the explosion which would come for certain from her cousin, but the Captain spoke first. "Madame Athina, you owe these two young ladies an apology. The first time I set eyes on them they were stranded, drenched to the skin, all alone but determined to get wounded men to safety.

Those that they could not save they comforted in their last moments. You might call them 'silly' but there are many good men alive today through their efforts."

"I apologise Catherine, Amélie for my words. Your bravery is beyond question. I was only thinking of the great difficulties which may be ahead for the Captain. If you are with him he will only have added responsibilities."

"I accept your apology, as I am sure does Amélie" said Kate graciously as Amélie nodded slowly "but I was thinking of how best to help him. You are mistaken if you think he will have to protect us. Amélie, could you please pass me an apple? A small one please, they are so much tastier" she smiled sweetly at her cousin as she said this. Amélie took from the nearest fruit bowl a small red apple but instead of giving it to Kate, she stood back from the table and threw the apple as far as she could towards the back of the deep cave. All eyes followed its trajectory and as it reached the highest point a single shot rang out and the apple exploded into a thousand juicy pieces. Those animals caught unawares at the back of the cave began a cacophony of braying and barking at the sudden shot but amidst the noise Kate turned to Athina: "And Amélie is a far better shot than I. Papa believed that she was the best shot in the whole of Aquitaine, young or old, male or female. Helpless? In need of protection? I don't think so."

While Gilles and Madame Barbier calmed their other guests down, Athina asked: "Very well, but Catherine, I assume that you have considered your future position and all that it entails?"

"I am aware of my responsibilities, but I do not wish my half-brother to cause further problems if they can be avoided. My heart is telling me that I should go but my father's last instructions to me were that in matters which concern the House of Garenne, I must put aside all personal feelings. I have tried to put aside my affection for Roland, truly I have. I have asked myself would I behave similarly should anyone else be placed in danger because of my brother. The answer is 'yes', I would".

In full flow, the girl was not to be interrupted by anyone. "I am proud that I have Paladin blood running through my veins, but I really have no choice, do I? How many times did Eleanor de Garenne regret that she did not accompany her Guillaume?" Athina winced at the mention of the name Eleanor and Roland noticed that she quickly wiped away a gleaming tear from her eye.

Throughout her impassioned speech, Kate had remained calm even allowing herself a smile when she spoke publicly of her feelings for the Captain but now she stood up and placed both hands firmly on the table. Amélie thought how much she resembled her dead father with her eyes now blazing and a fierce expression on her flushed face: "Well I will not repeat her mistake; I will be by his side, come what may." Again, in the corner of Athina's eye a tear formed, hastily and surreptitiously removed.

It was the second time Kate had got the better of Athina, who now looked instead at Amélie: "and I assume that your mind is made up as well?" She raised a quizzical eyebrow and Amélie smiled sweetly and nodded. Athina made one last attempt to take control of this situation and turning to the officer she spoke quietly: "This of course your decision. I am sure that despite the girls' obvious enthusiasm to help, your greater experience must tell you that this is something best done alone?"

In his usual way, Roland took his time to consider his reply: "Madame, to summarise: my task is to escort a dog and a bear, both of whom can change shape, together with a full menagerie of other animals to somewhere in the Pyrenees, all the while protecting them from a slightly deranged nobleman who is apparently a Renegade. This is a man I believe has carried out one murder but now wants to kill me. Meanwhile there is the possibility that a ravening *Loup Garou*, may materialise?" He raised an eyebrow in enquiry. "Whilst I have experience of hunting murderers, as for the rest? I have as much experience as these two young ladies and I gratefully accept any offer of assistance…" The girls grinned but their expressions changed when he added: "On one important condition: that they will do exactly as I tell them, without argument. I must insist on total obedience."

With unusual meekness, Kate nodded her agreement but in a misguided attempt to lighten the seriousness of the moment Amélie giggled: "Well, it would depend on what you wanted me to do wouldn't it?"

"Amélie behave yourself!" Kate exclaimed. Athina erupted: "Well, what a fine chaperone you would make. I shall see your mother tonight and will inform her of your plans. Catherine, your intentions now mock what you have told your aunt. Travelling with this young man with only Amélie as chaperone is most certainly not something she will countenance. Nevertheless…I will try to convince her to agree (against my better judgement) …" The girls hugged each other excitedly until Athina finished "…when I tell her that I too will accompany you."

Kate managed to hide her chagrin, thanking the haruspex for her concern very graciously as Amélie watched in disbelief. Then Kate delivered her own 'parting shot': "Madame Athina, please assure my aunt that although our plans may have changed, I will remain faithful to my promise and I will not elope; when we marry, it will be at the Château de Garenne like all my ancestors."

Her glee at having bested Athina was short-lived when Kate realised that she had allowed her tongue to run away with her; back in La Garenne Kate and Roland had joked about marriage. She turned, blushing, towards Roland, her eyes pleading with him not to say a word. She failed to convince Athina however who tartly replied: "Oh, my dear, I had not realised that you were betrothed. When I last saw your aunt – your *guardian*- she did not mention it which surprises me greatly. We are such good friends. So, when exactly did the Captain propose?"

Kate's heart sank as Roland began to speak: "I have not made a formal proposal to Kate" Athina's eyes narrowed… "because I did not wish to take such an important step while engaged in this manhunt. Moreover, Kate was most insistent that I must first ask for permission from her guardian. I agreed to do this as soon as I returned to La Garenne." He knew that Athina was very skeptical but decided not to embroider the story any further. Kate squeezed his hand and having recovered her composure carried on where he had left off: "Of course, until my outburst just now, we were going to keep this a secret as Aunt Marianne must be the first to know. I did not even confide in Amélie."

This was all too true, and Amélie nodded her agreement, relieved for once not to have to lie on her cousin's behalf.

Athina knew when she was beaten. Once more she appeared to grow in brightness, lighting the whole inn and appearing to hover above them: "Let us return to the business in hand. Hugo is a young Hound, only just learning to control his ability to change shape. If humankind ever suspect that he is different, then I fear for him. The sooner you leave the better."

Roland took from his saddlebag some Army issue maps. These he spread on the table, one covering the area around Monbezier and the land to the south, the other showing the route south into the Pyrenees. He pointed out the forest, and the river hoping that

Gilles would recognize these from the map. Gilles had seen maps before, although never in such detail, but he quickly mastered the layout and after Roland had explained that the second map was a continuation of the first, Gilles identified the route which Ursian and Hugo would be taking. He could even point out the way towards the entrance to the High Valley, in a mountain pass. Roland smiled wryly when he saw where Ursian was pointing.

"What do you find amusing, Captain?" asked Athina tartly but he shook his head: "No, I smile only because it's an amazing coincidence. I know that route through the Pyrenees very well. I came that way when we retreated from Spain three years ago. I would have given my right arm then for somewhere safe to hide from those English."

Gilles explained that he may well have passed close to the Valley's entrance but without guidance would never have found the place for not everyone could see it. The gendarme looked again at the route. A little south of Monbezier the road forked into two separate highways. Gilles had traced Hugo's journey down on the right-hand route. He saw that the young officer was studying the other route and volunteered that this was the stagecoach road from Perigueux to Neufchatel de Marsac and all points south. It seemed that Gilles was reading the Captain's mind for he then said: "If Kate's brother and his companion were to take the coaching road that might well delay them a bit eh?"

Gilles then outlined his own quickly conceived plan: "Don't let outward appearances fool you, Captain; I may look like a jolly landlord but remember underneath I'm a bear, one of the Guard Bears, and we are very cunning."

Roland smiled warmly at his new friend: "If we could fool Louis-Philippe for even one day it would take him at least another two days to get back to the right road. The two routes are quite a distance apart. More than a day would be even better of course. I assume that they should now be in Monbezier?"

Athina confirmed that Kate's half-brother and André Lacoste had arrived at the town little more than an hour before. No-one bothered to ask how she knew. By now, this seemed quite normal.

"Right - they will know that I was there and left by the South Gate."

"Oh yes, they certainly will" replied Athina "I am reliably informed that your thorough gate inspection was worthy of the King's engineer!"

He was unsure if this was intended as a compliment: "I would prefer that Monbezier is the last positive sighting they have of me. When Louis-Philippe realises he is not on the right road I want my trail, and Hugo's too, to be very cold. From now on, we must travel 'incognito' everyone." He looked at Kate and Amélie directly when he said this. "I have some civilian clothes with me…" Athina interrupted him and looked meaningfully at Gilles: "Gilles, I can rely on you for transport for myself and the young ladies?" He nodded agreement. "In that case, there is nothing further to discuss and I have much to do tonight. I will be back at sunrise. Please try to rouse yourselves early."

Before their eyes, the pale, glowing figure of Athina shrank, her glow diminished slowly, and, in the blink of an eye, she was once more a snowy owl, perched on the back of her dining chair. Gilles went to the door of the inn and opened in the top half of the door an owl-sized trap door no-one had noticed before. This allowed her to fly gracefully out into the darkness.

Mme. Barbier suggested that another meal might be called for, but the three guests politely declined, full from lunchtime. Gilles however went behind his bar and poured three foaming tankards of Giant Bear Ale, offering one to Roland, the other to Madame

Barbier, and prepared an elegant carafe of white wine and two glasses for the girls.

However, before Roland could sample Gilles' legendary brew, Kate rose and took his hand. She led him to Ursian's giant chair – which was in fact more like a sofa – and sat him down. She then stood before him with her hands clasped behind her. Head bowed and looking very contrite she burst out: "I am so sorry for what happened earlier, and I thank you for making me appear less ridiculous in front of that…owl…than I deserve. No sooner had you defended me than I go and prove that she was right to call me silly. Please do not think that I was trying to trap you into marrying me." She stuttered a little: "I shall not hold you to any of those things you said. I wish to put this incident behind us and start afresh. Sometimes my tongue run away with me and…."

Before she could continue her obviously rehearsed speech the Captain stood up and put a gentle finger to her lips, saying: "Sshhh. What if I don't want to put it behind me? Sit down please" and he indicated the space beside him. "Remember at La Garenne? You said I should hurry up and ask you to marry me? Since then I have turned that conversation over and over in my mind. I should have spoken then. What I said to Athina, well I meant every word. If you agree, I will seek your aunt's permission as soon as we return then I will propose formally."

Kate sighed. "and…I will willingly accept."

Sitting comfortably, Kate was already imagining their life together. Roland meanwhile was methodically arranging his memory of events so far. "Did you notice" he asked, "that the very mention of the name 'Eleanor' upsets Athina?"

"No, I can't say I did. Too busy trying to convince her – and it worked too. Do you think perhaps that Eleanor might have been very important to her?"

"Kate, we have much more to find out about her. Her manner may be a little abrasive, but I believe she is trying to protect you and Amélie. If your aunt agrees to you coming with me, then we are going to see a great deal of Madame Athina. Don't make our task harder by challenging her authority, please." Kate had promised this man, her fiancé, that she would do as she was told – most of the time – and so she agreed: "Yes, I will hold my tongue, for you. But if she treats me as schoolgirl…she reminds me of our old governess"

Amélie's patience wore thin after an hour. She found them sitting together, Kate's head resting on Roland's shoulder, eyes closed. Amélie coughed discreetly at first and then loudly and Kate woke from her reverie to see Amélie standing with her arms folded.

"Cousin, can we not have a moment alone?" However, Amélie was not to be dismissed so easily. "I hope my Maman discovers what a poor chaperone Athina is. She leaves us alone at every opportunity but if I was in charge you two would be kept separate and you, cousin would be engaged in some sensible reading." She was beginning to sound more and more like Athina!

Roland smiled: "Amélie, remember you promised to be obedient too – now go away!"

Amélie frowned but left them alone, muttering darkly "I shall only allow them to get away with that once."

Eventually, Roland and Kate rejoined the others around the dining table. Mme. Barbier insisted that as they were all friends now, she should be called Hortense. She set about preparing a 'light' snack before sitting down with them. The Barbiers were good company, less reticent without Athina's presence. Soon Kate felt relaxed enough to ask the question which had been on her mind. "M. Gilles, I am a Paladin. I assume that this is through my father's line?" Gilles nodded. "So, my brother must have Paladin blood as well, yet he is a Renegade?" She raised her eyebrows. "Pellerin told me you would want to know. All Renegades are descended from those beings who took human form. Most became Poursuivants, like Amélie, while some like Kate and Roland retained the ability to talk to the animal Paladin and are considered *full Paladin.*

The majority of Poursuivants remained content in their lives, unaware of their Paladin blood. However, there are some, the Renegades, that know something is missing, aware of their loss. It is these beings that become bitter, uncomfortable in their own skins and every searching for something they can no longer have. This resentment breeds evil thoughts- and sometimes deeds". Kate nodded deep in thought.

CHAPTER 41

André and Louis-Philippe had crossed the river near Monbezier. André paid the ferryman and tethering his horses, sat down with the other passengers on the narrow wooden boards that served as seats. Louis-Philippe however declined to dismount, looking – or so he thought – terribly noble and grand. This noble appearance was severely damaged when the ferry struck out into the current and was buffeted this way and that. He was forced to cling desperately to the horse's neck as it panicked and bucked in fear. The young man struggled to maintain his balance until the horse reared up, almost unseating him and threatening the safety of the other passengers. There was a general outcry from those seated near the horse and cries of 'throw him off' and 'fool'. The young man was accustomed to fawning respect – even if it was seldom meant. His face coloured as rapidly as his dignity faded so as soon as the ferry reached the bank, Louis-Philippe kicked his sharp spurs into the horse's flanks to propel himself as far and fast as possible away from those who had witnessed his discomfiture. André, however, was in no rush to disembark from the ferry and proceeded at a far more leisurely pace, untying his mount and its companion, bidding farewell to the ferryman and apologising to the other passengers. He made his way up the hill towards Louis-Philippe who waited impatiently. As he rode he was struck by the intense darkness of the brooding forest on his left. His eye caught a fine pair of eagles circling above them both.

By the time André reached the top of the hill, the young nobleman was smouldering with rage. "About time too. We need to find some accommodation in this godforsaken place; I must get a good night's sleep" he shouted angrily and rode on ahead. They passed the edge of the forbidding forest, riding on until they reached the town of Monbezier. In the main square, André went into the inn, whose fading sign indicating that it was *Le Gr-nd Hôtel de Par-s.* The shabby interior lived up to this damaged sign. He asked politely for their best room and a room for himself, indicating Louis-Philippe who remained seated on his horse outside. The little inn however had but three rooms and only one of those was available.

Relieved that he would be able to sleep alone in the stables out of Louis-Philippe's way, André said he would make his own arrangements. The innkeeper, however, had other ideas.

"But Monsieur, this room I have, it is a huge room, enormous and might easily accommodate both you gentlemen and more. I regret that my other rooms are reserved for some *important* passengers on the stagecoach due this evening, otherwise…." Impatience had at last won over hauteur and overhearing this, the angry young man swept into the Hôtel , demanding to know which room he was to occupy. He snatched the key from the hand of the stunned innkeeper and stalked up the stairs without a backward glance. The Hôtel 's groom had already taken his minimal baggage and was climbing the stairs when Louis-Philippe pushed him aside roughly. "Out of my way, fool" he cried "and for heaven's sake get that bag to my room immediately."

"Ah" said the innkeeper softly to André "I see. Never fear sir, I shall make sure that you have a nice comfortable bed in our stables and a fine meal too." In an even softer tone he said: "I thought that the Revolution had rid my country of men like him."

The long-suffering André just smiled and exchanged a few pleasantries with the friendly innkeeper. He asked casually how business had been and found out that most of the trade at the *Gr-nd Hôtel de Par-s* came from the passengers on the regular stagecoach service between Perigueux and Neufchatel, for which the innkeeper was very grateful. The only passing trade recently had been themselves, and before them a young gendarme.

“Nice chap, on his way to track down that Lost Patrol from La Garenne. I said to him, I said ‘What can you hope to find now?’ But off he went, down south. I told him that the last sighting that I heard of was down at the ferry and since then, well no-one has seen hide nor hair of ‘em. Still, suppose he knows what he’s doing eh? Oh, and I heard that the way he inspected the South Gate of the town one would think the English were coming again.” André listened to this news and thought he would tell Louis-Philippe this snippet of information to at least give the impression of co-operation. Accordingly, before supper he casually mentioned his discovery to Louis-Philippe. However, he was amazed by the young man’s reaction. The young nobleman’s patrician face contorted with rage, and he snarled in a low, angry voice:

“You never ask about that damned Gendarme. From now on just listen. Let me do the thinking and the talking.”

André could have pointed out that he had asked no questions, the information had been willingly and enthusiastically given to him, but he felt it best to keep his own counsel.

The mail coach had, by this time, drawn up outside the inn and the passengers who had been cooped up all day in the dusty, swaying conveyance were raucous. Their spirits were further fuelled by copious quantities of Giant Bear Ale, the local brew. Louis-Philippe looked on at his fellow guests as if they were a different species and swiftly retreated to his room. He had not bothered to find out where André would be spending the night.

Next morning, the frosty atmosphere between the two men remained, entirely matching the temperature of the air outside. Icy blasts entered every time the door of the inn opened with the latest arrival. The grinding wheels of a heavy cart sounded outside on the frosty ground and suddenly, the heavy door flew open and there stood a giant of a man, wearing a capacious greatcoat, thick-soled leather boots and an extra-long knitted scarf which was wrapped several times around his large whiskery face. He strode into the bar where locals and passengers were having breakfast and was greeted with great warmth by the innkeeper and some of the regulars from the coach too.

"Why, Gilles. Hallo! You're an early bird. How are you? I didn't expect to see you so soon after the last delivery. The cellars are still mighty full although if we have a few more nights like last night then I will be running short sooner than I thought" cried the innkeeper. Gilles smiled, clasping the man's hand: "Well, if you need more ale, I can put you down for some. I must start a new brew as soon as I get back home. Today I have a huge order that I must deliver as soon as I can to Neufchatel de Marsac. They're clean out of ale down there after that Lost Patrol business. At least it's done someone some good eh?"

The innkeeper looked startled: "What business? What's that all about then?" Gilles looked around, confident that he now had a large audience for what he was about to share with them.

"Oh, didn't you hear? The Lost Patrol and their sergeant pitched up in Neufchatel about a week ago now, spending money like water they was, leastwise until the inn ran dry and they had a run in with the local gendarmes. Fled down south, they have; what d'ya think of that? I have been going to Neufchatel for years and it's normally a sleepy little place. Now it's become famous! First the townsfolk were terrorised by a huge dog, and then these deserters turn up. Funny old world!" Gilles knew his words were having the desired effect on two listeners in particular. He continued loudly: "Well, must be going. The Missus ain't too pleased with me just now. Doesn't seem to understand that there's no point in brewing if you don't sell the stuff. To do that, I must sample the product, don't I?"

Gilles looked pleadingly around at his listeners, who began to laugh with him as the innkeeper, grasping Gilles' meaning busied himself filling a large tankard: "My friend, can I tempt you to a small libation?"

“T’would be churlish to refuse” growled Gilles, at which the whole inn erupted in laughter as the innkeeper joined him in a large pewter tankard of GBA. “So, they’ve finally surfaced In Neufchatel de Marsac you say?” Although truth be told the man was not actually very sure where that was, since he had never been more than a 15-minute walk from his own town in his whole life.

“Indeed” said Gilles “but if I was them....”and he paused indicating that he had more to tell “if I was them, I would keep running, far and fast. Yesterday I met a young gendarme on the road and he was on his way to Neufchâtel. When he finds them...” and here Gilles made a show of drawing his index finger across his throat before continuing “I wouldn’t like to be in their shoes when not if, he catches up with them. He looked a very determined man indeed, mean and determined.”

“I know what you mean, Gilles, old friend” said the innkeeper, “he stayed here the other night, friendly enough but....” And looking knowingly at Gilles, he let the sentence hang.

Gilles downed his Great Bear Ale in two enormous gulps, rose and shaking himself (a very ‘bear’ habit he found it impossible to break) went towards the door. “Well must be off now, I’ll probably be back at the end of next week” and with a gust of cold air, the inn door closed on the huge man who strode out into the square and mounted his wagon.

Everyone in the bar began to talk at once, discussing this momentous news. The fame of the runaway gendarmes had spread widely in France and those about to board the coach were agog as they were going to that same Neufchatel. At the table, André and Louis-Philippe had listened in silence to Gilles’ story, attempting to look disinterested but absorbing every word. The young nobleman now looked angrily at André: “You see, Lacoste! Hunters watch, they wait and sniff the air and eventually pick up the scent and then, when they do, they go in for *the kill* ...we leave immediately.”

"Yes, sir, of course. Where are we going, sir?" he asked, knowing this would infuriate his master. "You fool" cried Louis-Philippe "to this Neufchatel de.... you find out."

"Err, of course sir but...how shall I find out?"

"Oh, for pity's sake, ask, man, ask and be quick about it."

André, satisfied that he had been sufficiently irritating for now, approached the innkeeper.

"I wonder if you could give me some information, my friend. We heard what was said earlier and now he" (André indicated the retreating back of Louis-Philippe) has a fancy to go to this Neufchatel de Marsac. Would you have perhaps a map of the area we might purchase?" André knew this was very unlikely indeed and just as he had surmised, the innkeeper looked at him blankly: "A map? You'll be wanting a written down map then? Ha, I am not sure anyone has one of those things. You either know where you are and where you're going, or you don't go! What would be the point of going to somewhere you don't know, or even knowing where it was?" The logic of this was not lost on André, and smiling to himself he enquired: "Can you perhaps tell me the route of the coach then, so that we may follow?"

"Oh yes, I know that" replied the now-confident innkeeper who recited, as if by rote: "'The regular stagecoach travels from Perigueux, via Montbezier, destination Neufchatel de Marsac' - at least the one that stops here does."

Undaunted, André asked: "Yes, so if you got on the stagecoach here in which direction would you be travelling to reach Neufchatel de Marsac?" He saw his question falling into the void of the innkeeper's blank expression. "Who would know do you think?" At this the innkeeper's kindly eyes lit up as if inspired. Pleased to help he replied: "The coach driver! Ah, oh dear there isn't another coach stopping here until Friday. I could check the timetable...yes, but I am certain it's not until Friday." As the poor man scrabbled around beneath the counter attempting to find the dusty timetable,

André made a mental note to avoid GB Ale ever again, because of its obvious long-term effects.

Eventually, the innkeeper proudly produced a crumpled and dog-eared document and announced: “There, told you, oh I can’t make this out. The coach that comes from Perigueux ….” Gently André prised the tattered document from the innkeeper’s grasp and quickly made a note of the villages that the coach passed through on its way to Neufchatel. Luckily this took only a few moments because Louis-Philippe came bounding down the stairs, dressed and ready to travel. He threw his key towards the bar, narrowly missing the innkeeper and began shouting: “I have been waiting in my room these ten minutes at least. No boy has come to take my luggage. What sort of establishment is this? A gentleman does not carry his own baggage. We must be on our way.”

An embarrassed André averted his eyes as the innkeeper grudgingly went upstairs to collect the single bag and paid more than the innkeeper demanded by way of apology. As his master strode into the square, the other man went to fetch their horses who like him had spent a good night in the warm stables. The innkeeper emerged with Louis-Philippe’s saddlebag and handed it to André who secured it to their pack animal whilst the young man strode back and forth snorting, much like his horse.

The two men eventually rode off through the small town to the South Gate, following the route taken by Roland and once they had left the houses behind, Louis-Philippe insisted that they ride at a gallop despite André’s protests that they had a long journey ahead and that it might be prudent to conserve the energy of their horses. This fell on deaf ears. The young man spurred on his poor horse by striking him hard in the flank with his boot and galloped forward. When André caught up with the Louis-Philippe had halted where the road forked, neither route having any obvious directions.

As soon as André was within earshot, Louis-Philippe cried: "Did you know there were two roads? Which am I supposed to take?" There was a crude, hand-made sign. The signpost was askew and almost obscured by vegetation. It was pointing to St Denis de Prés, the first stagecoach halt. André smiled to himself:

"My apologies Sir. In the absence of any map, we are following the coach route. The left-hand road is clearly the one we need though. Look, you can tell by the ruts in the road made by the constant passage of cartwheels."

They set off immediately in the direction of St. Denis de Près and in a short while, the cart driven by Gilles Barbier came into view in the distance. "Come on, come on. Catch him, quickly, quickly. He can give us directions" ordered the agitated young man.

"Sir, don't you wish to question this man yourself?"

"Don't be ridiculous. You cannot seriously expect me to speak to someone like that...that drayman? In any case, the drunken fool probably won't be much help, but you must go and see." André resignedly rode on in Gilles' direction, increasing his pace just enough to catch the cart but still slow enough annoy his master. Gilles slowed his two heavy horses with difficulty and turned to greet the well-dressed man on horseback who introduced himself politely, unaware that Gilles' speech at the inn had been specifically aimed at him and his master. Exasperated, Louis-Philippe seethed quietly in the background, André and Gilles exchanged pleasantries and only then did André ask about the route; Gilles gave painfully detailed instructions, managing to mention practically every tree and hedge on the way. Louis-Philippe finally galloped ahead and sat on his fine mount waiting impatiently for André to catch him up. Assured that they were on the right road, according to the drayman, and that by evening they should be at the village of St. Denis de Près the two men rode on. Apparently, there was a half-decent Inn there too.

Gilles had told André that they should then head on to Gourdon, but the journey would take them three full days. Louis-Philippe huffed: "In that case we'll do it in two. Let's get a move on." As they disappeared into the distance, Gilles turned his wagon off the road and drove down a dirt track towards a cottage, half hidden by the dense woodland. Standing outside the cottage was an old-fashioned but serviceable coach. The carpenter in Monbezier had told Gilles about this conveyance, which he never really expected to sell – and Gilles had borne this it in mind for just such an occasion. An old sign propped beside it said "AV" 'For Sale' and Gilles tied it to the back of his dray, first ensuring its wheels were in working order.

CHAPTER 42

Kate and Amélie rose before dawn. They dressed hurriedly and went out into the bar area where Roland was already waiting. There they watched Madame Barbier absentmindedly open the small latched section in the upper panel of the great oak door; in a moment, the snowy owl flew out of the darkness and into the room. It was clear that the bear and the owl could communicate without words. The beautiful bird perched briefly on the bar and then hopped to the floor where she began the process of transforming herself into the shining graceful shape they recognized.

Athina was in a very business-like mood: "Has M. Gilles left already? I would like the transportation for our journey as soon as possible." Madame Barbier assured her that he had left before first light: "Young ladies, Mme. Giscard has agreed you may assist in this venture. Obviously, she only agreed because I assured her I would be chaperoning you. As Captain Lebrun suggested, you must travel incognito. I think this is a good plan – now Amélie you will be Mlle. Jeanne Blanc, and you Catherine will be her sister Simone. You are two young ladies making a journey to visit your aunt and I am your governess. To remind you of your roles, Madame Giscard has suggested that I adopt the name Dubois." Both girls paled at the memory of their former governess Madame Dubois. Athina then appeared to have a sudden afterthought:

"Oh, M. Roland" – now she was on first name terms with the gendarme – "I have informed Madame Giscard of your intention to ask for Catherine's hand in marriage. I even tried to impress her with your credentials." Athina paused dramatically… "and clearly I must have done a good job for she has somewhat surprisingly asked me to give you a message." She paused portentously "She has said that you *may* propose to Mlle. Catherine de Garenne."

Unthinking, Kate threw her arms around Athina who froze, motionless at this onslaught of affection. The happy girl nevertheless hugged her tightly for a moment before Athina escaped her embrace: "Girls, we must be ready as soon as Gilles returns. Have breakfast now and pack. Captain, I am sure you have many preparations to make."

The horses had been fed and watered and after a quick breakfast, he spent time cleaning and preparing his pistols, musket and carbine. He then did the same to Kate and Amélie's weapons – just in case. He assured himself that they were all in full working order then placed his army maps on the table, committing to memory every detail of their intended route after which he tried to do the same with the route that he hoped Louis-Philippe would take. He did some rough calculations of how far they would be able to travel each day, unsure of what transport Gilles would procure. He did the same for his pursuers, who were on horseback and jotted in his notebook the estimated distances between himself and the two men for any given day.

By now Kate, who had expected a proposal of marriage on the spot was trying not to show her impatience, pique in fact. She leaned on his shoulder, feigning interest in his calculations and occasionally asked for clarification of the figures he noted down. "Well" he explained painstakingly "If we can trust the eagles to tell us when Louis-Philippe eventually realizes he's been duped, we will know how long it will take him to get back on the road we are taking."

"Of course – that's important to know, isn't it? Once you have finished your calculations, isn't there something really important that you still need to do?" she wheedled.

"Oh yes. I expect M. Gilles will need a hand when he gets back so I shall need to see to the horses for the journey, pack the saddlebags…."

"Something even more important…? A question…?" broke in Kate exasperated. Roland looked distracted then reached across the table and picked up the carbine he had checked: "Yes I do have a question. The pistols you and Amélie have brought are good quality but short range. I thought that you would be better protected with one of these carbines – who do you think would make best use of it?"

"**Me** at this moment but …well for your own safety Captain Lebrun, probably Amélie …" Amélie leapt up from her chair seizing the carbine and looking at it lovingly. "It's a Schneider!

Wow, I never thought I would get my hands on one of these. I am told that it's possible to reload this even whilst riding…Amazing!"

The Captain shook his head, laughing: "Well Mlle. Amélie, that's the theory – much more difficult in practice." Kate listened to this exchange, scowling.

At that moment, a clatter of wheels was heard outside. Gilles was back at the Sanctuary Inn once more. The group went out as soon as they heard the jingling of the heavy harnesses and were very surprised to see what he had brought them. It was well-used but still serviceable coach. This vehicle had obviously seen much better days and perhaps it was best not to speculate on the fate of its previous owners. The interior was padded and upholstered in faded green woven damask but the door panels which had once borne a crest had been roughly repainted to obscure any detail, the paint was chipped and worn. Athina gave it a close inspection and declared herself well pleased with Gilles' purchase. He had also acquired a uniform at the livery stables in Monbezier but was unsure whether it would be a good fit.

"Captain, there's only one way to find out. Try it on and if it isn't a good fit then we can alter it, can't we?" Gilles threw a brown paper parcel down from the front of the cart and the gendarme deftly caught it and hurried into the inn to change. In less than ten minutes he reappeared wearing a slightly worn livery made for a shorter but wider man complete with a large tricorn hat. He looked slightly embarrassed.

"Err, I am not absolutely sure that the *beaumonde* of Paris would want me as their coachman. However, for the locals I am sure it will be fine" he laughed. Kate was mortified for him having to wear such a shabby outfit. "He looks ridiculous" she cried. Athina quickly pointed out, however: "He looks like the groom of a family who has fallen on hard times. That's perfect for our purposes and works well with this old coach. It would attract too much attention if he is wearing his uniform, we are all going to need to do a little playacting on our journey so that we will not be conspicuous. The carriage ensures that we can travel with him without attracting comment."

She looked sharply at the girls: "Remember, you are going to *pretend* to be demure, shy and obedient sisters, devoted to their very strict governess, me. I think I can play my role very well – don't you agree?"

Athina's superhuman hearing caught Amélie's muttered comments but she ignored them. Instead she said: "I have no doubt you will both be able to play your parts well too. Off you go now, we need to be on the road." Both girls winced at the convincingly governess-like tone of voice. Whilst Gilles was making the heavy horses more comfortable and removing their bridles, Athina asked how his mission had gone. He assured her that the two gentlemen were now on travelling on completely the wrong road.

Athina then took Roland firmly by the arm: "Do you not have unfinished business? Surely these surroundings are suitable for the question you have for Mlle. Catherine?" He blushed but nodded his agreement. Then he waited until the two young women emerged with their valises. "Kate, may I speak with you privately?" He led her towards Gilles' favourite log and sat her down gently, unaware that on that very spot, hundreds of years before, Guillaume, Comte de Rouen had proposed to his Eleanor.

Sinking none too gracefully onto one knee, the shabbily dressed 'coachman' asked the question which Kate had been waiting for: "Mademoiselle Catherine de Garenne, would you do me the honour of becoming my wife?"

Kate flung her arms around his neck and Athina almost smiled at the romantic moment, then coughed discreetly and spoke up loudly: "Well thank goodness we have that out of the way. Now to business."

They set off using Marron to pull the coach, with Amélie' s mount beside him. Gilles had explained to Marron what an important role he would be playing. Catherine's horse and the two packhorses were tied to the rear. Greco wore a blanket to hide the tattoo on his rump identifying him as a Gendarmerie pony.

Gilles led the animals through the dark forest. He had found blinkers so that they might not be spooked by the ghostly presences who watched silently as the convoy passed by. By now, they all understood that there was no danger, but the horses' instincts were to shy away from what they did not understand.

The gendarme sat on the driver's box with Athina and the two young ladies seated demurely inside. He wore a blanket across his knees, as coachmen did, but beneath this he had concealed both musket and pistols, whilst both girls had their valises with them – valises carrying a small armoury. As they came to the edge of the forest, Gilles checked that none of the horses had been frightened by the Sentinels. Marron, in conversation with Gilles at the Inn, had promised that he had now conquered his great fear of the forest dwellers, and had managed to remain outwardly very calm, but was still inwardly terrified. Gilles gently stroked his muzzle and neck, whispering quietly to the horse until the animal assured him he felt better. Gilles, more than most, understood what courage it took for a horse of Marron's sensitivity to cope with the presences in the forest.

When they reached the main highway they all said goodbye to Gilles, thanking him for his hospitality. Humming, the huge figure turned back into the forest, pleased with what had been accomplished so far. Travelling south, the carriage soon reached the fork in the road which André and Louis-Philippe had found. They took the right-hand road which would lead eventually to St. Pardoux. They encountered few other travellers apart from the odd farmer on horseback, or drivers of lumbering carts travelling to and from market. Happily, the journey remained uneventful but several times a day Athina would insist that Roland stop so that she could meet with one of the circling eagles. They brought news of Louis-Philippe's progress or of the whereabouts of Hugo and Ursian. At first, neither could make any sense of the conversations but gradually they became 'attuned' to the words between Athina and her bird companions. They noticed that although each bird used the same 'language' each one had a different intonation or 'accent', rather like regional speakers in France. They all marvelled at the speed with which information reached them. If only the French Army could have made use of such a network of spies thought Roland, then the course of history could have been very different.

CHAPTER 43

Hugo and Ursian's wagons trundled on their way and whenever the convoy came close to a village or a small town all the wild animals would board the wagons and look through the bars rather pathetically. Mimi always ran on ahead, in front of the wagons, as if clearing the way for the strange menagerie. Everywhere children and adults alike lined the streets for such a show was a rare treat. Ursian would then climb down from his wagon and put leads on three of the lions (having explained to them quietly what he was doing) and then parade them for all the world as if he was taking his dogs for a walk. People were astonished to see this giant wandering casually through the streets with wild animals perfectly under his control. If he asked them to 'SIT' they obeyed and if he asked them to 'ROLL OVER' they would do that too.

Many folks had never seen lions or indeed most of the other animals in the menagerie and so those who were brave enough to speak to this giant of a man asked him about them. Putting aside his hatred of humans, Ursian tried to put them at their ease by replying: "They are all quite tame, believe me, but this is only a small part of our wonderful show. We're going to our winter quarters south of here and we are travelling to join my uncle and the rest of the show. I expect we'll be back up this way soon and then we will have giraffes and camels and elephants …. even performing seals!" This explanation seemed to satisfy most people who couldn't wait for their return, despite many still being in the dark about camels, giraffes and seals. The wagons could then roll on unhindered towards the next village.

Hugo grew confident in his ability to change back and forth from Hound to human and sometimes he took turns at leading the convoy and even walked around with the lions. Mimi and Sangres had become firm, if unlikely, friends and curled up together to sleep at night, Mimi snuggling into Sangres' warm, round belly.

Feeding time for the animals was quite a sight, best done away from prying eyes. At first Hugo and Ursian had allowed all the animals to leave their cages to eat at the same time. Whilst they had all stayed at Sanctuary Inn, meals had been served to everyone together, and in an orderly way. However, away from the restraints of the Inn and the watchful eye of Gilles and his wife, feeding time had quickly descended into a free for all with the strongest of the animals dominating the proceedings. There was never much aggression but the strongest came off best just by dint of their size and power. The lions ate their own food but then started to play with everyone else's. The tight-knit clique of Fighting Bears who had agreed to come along usually kept to themselves, conducting endless gambling games, arguing and growling at each other without any real anger. However, at feeding time they felt they had to flex their muscles, especially in the presence of the lions and so the whole thing descended into chaos. Food was being thrown around and trampled on; some had even hit Hugo on the muzzle! Even Sangres would start pushing and shoving – and he claimed that he was a vegetarian. On the third day, with all the animals in the wagons, the procession passed through a small village and came to a halt on its outskirts. The animals, knowing it was feeding time, began to get restless and anxious to be set free.... but Hugo didn't unlock the cages and wagons. Instead, he had them drawn up into a semi-circle in a clearing by the roadside so that he could address all the animals together.

"You can't be trusted to behave like civilised animals" he announced gravely "so, I can only allow you to eat one species at a time.... you eat your food and go back to your wagons. Only then will the next wagon eat."

“Says who?” growled Lucius, the self-proclaimed leader of the lions.

“Says me” boomed Ursian in reply and Hugo realised that what he had heard from his little friend was somehow true. The bear could appear twice his size. He towered over the other animals casting a giant shadow. Lucius reluctantly shrank back cowering but unwilling to let the lions in ‘his’ pride see his fear. Even Mimi, who counted Ursian as her friend, quaked and hid behind Hugo.

“I think that’s settled then” said Hugo, amused. “First, I want the horses, M. L’Ane, (the Donkey) and oh you too Unika to come forward and eat. Then it will be the turn of the smaller animals and then Meera - you’ve done an excellent job today. Sangres, you’re next and Mimi too – I know at least you two won’t fight and then we can see who has been best behaved amongst the rest of you.” There was a noisy outbreak of growls from the Fighting Bears and general braying, but no-one had the temerity to argue and risk not getting fed. Hugo and Ursian went to one of the provisions wagons and sorted out the night’s foodstuffs and then began liberating the animals in rotation. Order restored!

After a few days of the new eating rules, Hugo announced that he was very pleased to see that the animals had at least learned some manners and could now go back to communal eating; in truth, it had taken much too long species by species as the browsers took an age to finish theirs. The chastened animals, embarrassed by their behaviour, managed to restrain themselves although the bears and lions still presented the most difficulty. They wanted they their own food *and* everyone else’s. However, Ursian found that by standing guard between them and with the administration of a few judicious cuffs from Ursian, they settled into an uneasy neutrality.

Each evening Hugo and his companions would settle down by lamplight and work out the route they would take the following day. They used an ancient map provided by Gilles which was supplemented by Ursian's recollection. He could remember some of the names of the places he had passed through and each day they still found some shells so at least Hugo knew that they were going in the right direction.

Once the feeding problems had been sorted out, the caravan made steady progress, usually about 15 miles a day, and Ursian thought it would take about a month to complete their journey, but that was dependent on the weather being favourable – which it wasn't. On very rainy days they would try to stay on firm ground as the roads were muddy, rough and unpaved. The wagons would often get bogged down, especially the heavy supply wagons. Ursian and Sangres would have to push and pull the wagons out of the mire, the huge bear using stout leather straps over his sturdy shoulders whilst Sangres would get behind the rear axle of the wagon and push. With their enormous strength, together they would usually get the wagons moving eventually – although they were usually covered in thick sprays of mud. Luckily, both animals were both lovers of the odd mud bath. During a particularly heavy downpour the caravan halted in the main square of the small town of St. Pardoux. Hugo and Ursian sat morosely under a canvas canopy attached to one of the wagons, while the heavy rain dripped down from the sagging structure, the holes in the canvas making it difficult for them to stay dry. Mimi crouched under the wagon but the unfortunate occupants of all the wagons were becoming cold, soaked and miserable. Ursian turned dejectedly to Hugo:

"You know, it's on days like this that I pity humans. If I was in my proper bear shape I wouldn't even notice this rain, it would just run off my lovely thick fur."

"I know", replied Hugo "we Hounds can shake ourselves dry at the end of a downpour – I used to enjoy that, especially if I chose to do it when my human master Raoul was nearby. He'd get soaked and curse us."

Slowly, the rain eased and to get dry they decided to light a fire and warm themselves and some of the smaller animals. They struggled to get the fire going using some damp sticks but then an officious little man, his long coat struggling to reach around his large round belly, emerged from an imposing building across the square. They saw that over the door of the stone building were the words 'Hôtel de Ville'.

The man crossed the square carefully for the cobbles were slippery with rain and he was wearing rather elaborate buckled shoes which he clearly wanted to protect. To Hugo and Ursian he resembled nothing more than a pig wearing shoes and a coat. They laughed as they watched him come towards them but stood to greet him courteously.

"NO FIRES IN THE SQUARE" said the little man, staring pointedly at them and dispensing with any politeness. "What is your business here?"

Ursian sat back down and in a low, gravelly voice he answered the man: "We are only staying until the rain stops and the road is dry then we will be on our way, *Sir*."

"The rain *has* almost stopped so you can be off now and put out that fire immediately."

Hugo had remained standing during this exchange but now Ursian also stood up, drawing himself up to his full, rather daunting height. He towered over the man and as he turned once more to face him, he opened his large mouth showing his sharp teeth, for once allowing himself the luxury of sounding much more bear than man. Without understanding why, the man was gripped by terror and turned on his dainty heels, retreating cautiously back across the square, pausing just once to look back at the damp group. Ursian sat down again with Hugo. "For a sou I would have broken him in two. I used to be able to deal with humans but now, after what they did to me well…. I have to really control myself when I am around them."

"I quite understand" replied Hugo. "He was very rude, wasn't he? Anyway, to save any further problems I will do the talking from now on and I'll only call on you if it's really necessary." They grinned at each other, understanding each other so well. They continued to tend their small fire thinking the matter now settled but the little man returned, this time with an officer of the gendarmerie at his side.

"I told you, No Fires in the square".

This time Hugo stood and left Ursian hunched over their small fire. "I am very sorry, Sir, but I can't see any notices forbidding a poor wet traveller from lighting a fire to try and get dry" said the Hound, in a gruff but conciliatory tone. The gendarme turned to the pompous little man at his side.

"Well, M. Duclos, he does have a point there. You really can't expect people to obey laws unless you post a notice." The gendarme was clearly no friend of the little mayor. Then he looked closely at Hugo, once and then again and his face changed.

"Do I know you? Your face is very familiar…."

Hugo's blood ran cold - could this man see through his 'disguise'? Did he see a Hound? Then the officer asked: "Are you by chance related to Colonel Lucien Lecaron – you resemble him so closely that at first, I thought it was the Colonel himself, back from the dead."

Hugo relaxed, remembering whom he had chosen to emulate in his human form: "Ah, yes, I am his cousin, Monsieur; I too lived in La Garenne. It was a terrible tragedy, his accident. Tell me how you knew my err cousin, Monsieur."

"That man saved my life and the lives of my men too. I was with the army in Spain when my patrol got cut off from our regiment and that demon Wellington launched an attack on us. We all thought we were finished when Major, as he was then, Lecaron broke from the line with just handful of men and charged into the British. Then he got us some horses and we managed to escape. He wasn't even in our regiment…. the bravest man I have ever met, his men would have followed him to hell and back, they trusted him that much." Hugo's heart swelled with pride when he heard these words about his late master. "I am very honoured to have met someone who served with …Lucien" said Hugo, meaning every word he said.

The mayor had fidgeted impatiently during this exchange. Now, more than a little miffed at being ignored for so long, he pushed himself forward between them, determined to be heard: "Captain, I want you to order this rabble to leave immediately. I want them out of the square right now and if they don't go I want you to arrest them all."

"I can't see any grounds for doing that, Mr. Mayor, we've had carnivals here before and we have never had any trouble" replied the Captain, exchanging a look with Hugo.

"That's all very well but I have made a new byelaw since the last time some of these itinerant rabble came to St. Pardoux. *No Fairs in the Town Square*."

"Ah I see" said the gendarme, hugely enjoying himself now. "So, it's no *fairs* not no *fires t*hen?"

The little mayor reddened to his eyebrows and his face swelled: "No, no fairs, no fires…nothing, nothing I tell you, without my express permission."

Hugo piped up immediately "But Monsieur, we're not a fair, we are a menagerie."

"I think he has you there, Duclos" said the gendarme deliberately not using the little man's full title. "Unless your new law includes menageries as well as fairs, oh and fires, there's nothing I can legally do. We can only uphold the law as it is written – when it is written of course." The Captain was grinning openly now.

"It's market day tomorrow and no-one will come if they can't get into the square. We hold a Charter and must by law hold a market every Friday rain or shine. You must support me and uphold the law" the mayor finished smugly; certain he was on firm ground here.

"Indeed so, Duclos" replied the captain "but I still can't see a problem. Nothing going on here will prevent the market taking place as usual. You can't make these poor folks move now, not in this dreadful rain. Make them travel in the dark? That would be too dangerous and if they were to leave in the morning, they would block the roads out of the town. That would prevent the market traders getting *in*, wouldn't it? It's a small market at this time of the year and can fit easily into the other side of the square anyway, the few stalls that set up in this weather. Now, if the menagerie agreed to stay another day, and leave on Saturday I am certain they would attract more people to see the wild animals - so there would be a busier market. There, perfect solution."

The captain turned to Ursian and Hugo: "Gentlemen, does that suit your plans? I can feel it in my blood that the weather will be perfect for you to travel on Saturday." The officer turned on his heel leaving the mayor standing with his mouth agape and the two friends smiling. After a short pause, the little man trotted after the gendarme, still speechless.

The time that the group spent in St. Pardoux was a huge success, which disappointed the officious little mayor no end. Ursian had marched around the town the next morning shouting at the top of his powerful lungs. "Come and see Hugo's Amazing Travelling Menagerie. We have…you won't believe it…the only unicorn in captivity!"

Unika was both delighted and angered by this announcement in equal measure. She was very proud to be the star attraction of the Menagerie but at the same time insisted on correcting Ursian every time, telling him that she was the *only* unicorn. Because of the unexpected announcement and because St. Pardoux had been starved of entertainment since their new mayor had been appointed, the people flocked into the square all that day and late into the evening, staring in amazement at the big cats and other animals, and especially the preening Unika. Hugo took up regular collections rather than making a charge as he felt that this was a better way to raise money and at the end of the day he and Ursian, after counting the bags of coins they had received, were delighted to discover that they had made enough to buy supplies for the foreseeable future and had even made a healthy profit. The local businessmen were delighted: the order placed by Hugo was one of the largest for many a day.

Hugo told Ursian that the best way to stay on the right side of the townspeople and the mayor – and those who had come into the town for the market too - was to give their remaining profit, very publicly, to the Home for the Poor on the outskirts of St. Pardoux. When Hugo announced to the assembled crowd that this was what they intended to do a huge wave of applause rang out across the square and the Mayor, who had come along to see what was happening, was forced to publicly thank them, despite hating every minute of it.

As they packed away for the night and the animals settled down in their cages, Ursian and Hugo sat together before their fire. "Is there no end to your talents, Hugo? Now it turns out you are a successful businessman too. We have enough to keep us going for the rest of the journey and news will spread of our charitable donation. People will be keen to let us stay in their villages and towns. I just hope the wrong people don't get to hear about it."

"I just wanted to ensure our welcome as we travel. We don't want to come up against another Mayor like M. Duclos eh?" Hugo laughed and they both settled down for the night, wrapped in their heavy cloaks.

The next morning all the animals were awake early and once all were fed and watered the unlikely procession rumbled out of the town square, just as the first people were coming to buy their bread. Everyone they met clapped them on their way and many insisted on shaking hands with Hugo and thanking him. Some commented privately that he had rather 'odd' hands, like well, like paws. All the animals both in and out of the cages were proud of their success but no-one was as proud as little Mimi. 'Her' Hugo was a great Hound and a successful businessman (err whatever that was). Even Ursian admired him. Her little terrier heart was bursting with happiness and pride.

CHAPTER 44

Most of the small towns on the road to St. Pardoux had an inn but Roland knew that once Kate's brother realised he had been duped he would be seeking lodgings on the same route. Therefore, to avoid leaving a trail, he tried to find lodgings at farmhouses – places Kate assured him her brother would find beneath his dignity. That way he hoped to preserve their anonymity.

Rural lodgings were easily found and Kate and Amélie played their parts, that of dutiful sisters, to perfection, helping the farmers' wives setting tables and generally trying to be useful. Despite the Revolution, the farmers' wives were usually deeply impressed by these gentlewomen treating them as equals. In fact, Athina was often complimented on the behaviour of her 'charges', to which she would reply: "I've always been a believer in strict discipline. I am afraid that when I was appointed their governess a few months ago they were so unruly as to be considered beyond control – but not now." However, she did glow with pride when the girls were praised.

However, one night the group found themselves without lodgings. As it grew dark, they realised they were approaching a small town, but Roland was very reluctant to stay there. He decided instead that they must spend the night in the coach instead. He pulled the vehicle a little distance off the road and explained that they should eat and then make themselves as comfortable as they could. Kate saw this as a golden opportunity to spend some unchaperoned time with Roland, so she was none too pleased when Athina informed her that she and her 'sister' would be spending the night inside the carriage, with Athina; the 'coachman' would be sleeping outside.

When they had eaten their meagre evening meal – cold of course - both girls retired with Athina. Kate waited in the darkness of the carriage, her head resting lightly on the window with Amélie leaning on her shoulder. Through half-closed eyes, she saw that as soon as Athina believed both girls were asleep she left very quietly. She stood for a moment gazing into the dark night sky before slowly becoming an owl once more and flew off into the night. 'Fine chaperone you make' thought Kate as she lay very still to make sure that Athina had really gone. When she was sure, Kate quietly opened the door trying to avoid disturbing Amélie: "And where do you think you are going? Sneaking off to meet Prince Charming?" whispered Amélie, sitting bolt upright.

"Be quiet I just have to go outside to…." hissed Kate.

"To see Roland" finished Amélie. "Sorry cousin but I can't let you do that. I promised Athina that I would act as chaperone and I will not break my promise to her, nor to my mother."

"Amélie, please" Kate whispered but Amélie was not to be moved. Sighing a deep, aggrieved sigh Kate finally gave up: "Alright, you win but I think you are enjoying this, aren't you?"

"Well, actually yes I am, and someone around here has to act like a grown up…young lady" giggled Amélie, managing with great difficulty not to burst into a loud laugh.

****

After four days on the road there were noticeably more carts and men on horseback travelling than previously. Athina informed them that they were all coming from St. Pardoux's weekly market. The mention of this town reminded Roland that despite Athina's views to the contrary, he was still a serving officer in the Gendarmerie. He was aware that in that town was a good-sized garrison and he resolved to file a report to Paris from there. At least General Destrier would know that he was alive and well, although how he could explain away events, he had not the slightest idea. He drove towards the old Gate, taking more notice of the gendarmes stationed there than they did of him. The guards took only a cursory glance inside the coach and waved them on. A winding cobbled thoroughfare led into a large, tree lined square. There was a board festooned with public notices, but Roland paid them little heed; he was more interested in finding discreet lodgings for his charges. On one side of the square was the old Town Hall or Hôtel de Ville standing next to the Gendarmerie. On the opposite side was a medieval building, with aged wooden beams and a weathered sign proudly proclaiming itself to be "*Le Grand Hôtel d'Aquitania.*" 'One to avoid' he thought.

Further down on the same side of the street however was a slightly shabbier establishment, more suited to their needs. The sign indicated that this was the *Auberge des Ē-oil-s*. He steered the carriage around the square and into the stable yard which was at the rear and out of sight of any prying eyes.

Roland insisted on caring for Marron himself, so he fed and watered the magnificent animal, rubbing down his coat and putting a warm blanket on his glossy back. Having ensured that the ladies and animals were being cared for, he made his way across the square to the barracks, clutching his orders from General Destrier.

Walking confidently past the sentries outside in the yard he pushed open the heavy double doors marked 'General Office'. At the high desk before him sat an elderly corporal who did not look up as the doors opened, his face buried in a ledger. Roland waited patiently until he could wait no longer and rapped lightly on the desk, coughing politely to attract the man's attention. Forced to look up, the corporal slowly peered over his bottle thick glasses. His hand indicated three sad looking wooden chairs: "Sit down and wait. I'll get around to you when I can." He went back to his ledger so what happened next came as quite a shock. Roland banged on the high desk so hard that the papers jumped up and scattered onto the floor.

At the same time, he put his orders right up to the corporal's face. The unfortunate man struggled to keep his glasses in place and gather his papers as the angry Captain hissed: "***I am*** attached to Gendarmerie Headquarters in Paris, and I am the ***personal emissary*** of Inspector General George Destrier. You will stand to attention when you address me, and you will summon your commanding officer. NOW!" Frustration had brought on a sudden need to shout.

The corporal attempted a salute whilst dismounting from his high stool; he staggered across the room towards the door marked 'Commandant' and knocked anxiously. The poor man all but fell inside the room and Roland could hear raised voices from within. Although he tried very hard to retain his stern manner, the Captain felt an acute need to smile. He heard 'but he's here, sir, he's here now, in the office and he's really angry' followed by a deep rumbling reply: "Right man, pull yourself together. What's his name?"

Roland heard the stuttering corporal trying to explain that he had not managed to catch the name. Suddenly the door was flung back and there stood the Commandant, the corporal trying to hide behind him. The officer was hastily buttoning his tunic as his eyes met Roland's own and the two officers stared at each other. Roland knew him very well, his old friend Jacques Belaudie!

"Good God, what in the name of Heaven are you doing here Jacques? The last time I saw you was on the retreat from Spain in '14."

Belaudie came forward with arms outstretched and the two men grasped each other in surprise and joy, the Commandant privately wondering why his old comrade was not in uniform.

"I could ask you the same thing, Lebrun. I heard you were posted to Corsica, you lucky dog, but this imbecile has just told me you are here on Destrier's business? You'll be here for the signal then?"

Roland said nothing, looking more assured than he felt – what signal? - but did not to interrupt his friend for the time being. Jacques went to the office strong box and with a key taken from a large key ring attached to his breeches, unlocked the old creaking lock. He removed first a sheaf of papers then took out a sealed envelope which he presented ceremoniously, his hands betraying a slight tremor.

"My friend, I would appreciate it greatly if you could assure the Inspector General that you received this with the seal intact. I can personally assure you that this envelope has never been opened." Beads of nervous perspiration stood on Belaudie's forehead. He took his friend's elbow and drew him into his own office, closing the door on the nosy corporal.

Belaudie sat for a moment, gathering himself: "About a week ago we had a signal from the General himself – something unknown in this backwoods garrison – commanding us to pass on a signal to his personal emissary immediately upon arrival. Unbelievably, the signal also said that if the message should *not* be passed on, or any attempt be made to decode it, then he would hold the entire garrison responsible. Well, you can imagine? Every day that the signal was not collected...well... and we didn't even know the emissary's identity or when he would show up. I am assuming you really are here on Destrier's business?" Jacques asked nervously.

Roland showed his friend his orders and could see him visibly relaxing when he recognised Destrier's seal. "Please use my office, my friend, I shall see to it that you are undisturbed." The Captain left, closing the door gently behind him. Alone, Roland took from his pocket the small dog-eared book given to him by Destrier, his Code Book. He leafed through the thin pages, looking at the symbols it contained, and then turned his attention to the wax seal on the envelope his friend had given him. He carefully removed this then slit open the envelope which contained only one sheet of thick paper. With the aid of the Code Book and quite a lot of patience he read the following:

"DESTROY AFTER READING.

REPORT RE PATROL UNDERSTOOD.

GOOD WORK. WILL DISCUSS WHEN NEXT MEET.

HUGO NOW TOP PRIORITY.

DO NOT FAIL. CONGRATULATIONS TO YOU AND KATE.

TELL GOD-DAUGHTER EXPECT WEDDING INVITATION"

The Captain sat and studied the message. What report? He tried to understand. How had Destrier known what was happening? Roland had so far sent no reports about anything since leaving La Garenne? He felt relieved that he would no longer have to write an embarrassing account of the bizarre events in the forest. The true fate of the Lost Patrol was so unbelievable that although he had gone over and over in his mind what he could write, even a hint of what had really happened would have disgraced him at best; at worst, had him committed. Discovering that Kate was his commander's goddaughter – well that was yet another surprise.

He decided to compose a non-committal response right away:

CONFIRM MESSAGE RECEIVED SEAL INTACT.

ALL UNDERSTOOD AND PROCEEDING AS INSTRUCTED.

CONFIRM WEDDING INVITATION. GOD-DAUGHTER WELL.

He went out into the main office where Belaudie was waiting alone and asked him to arrange the sending of his coded response. His friend watched while Roland went to the smoky wood burner, opened the door and placed the original message into the flames. They both watched until he was satisfied that the paper was reduced to ashes and turned back to Jacques, who still stood holding the folded message in his hand.

"Don't worry my friend, I have set the General's mind at rest that everything was in order."

Belaudie looked relieved: "I have only been here a few months and it's been hard enough to gain the confidence of these men. They've all been garrisoned here for years and are set in their ways. The threat posed to them by all this didn't make things any easier. Anyway, tell me how did you get here unnoticed? I have had men posted on all the ways in and out of St. Pardoux since last week waiting for our mysterious arrival and it turns out to be you."

Roland looked down at his rather scruffy garb and, imitating a thick Corsican accent, which made him almost unintelligible, said "Well, as you can see, I am a master of disguise" and burst out laughing. Belaudie examined his friend's ill-fitting dusty clothes and boots which had clearly belonged to someone before him. "Well, I don't know what a master spy is supposed to look like but…maybe that knife sticking out from the top of your boot is a clue?" The other man laughed ruefully. He had not thought to remove this and was slightly embarrassed that his friend had noticed. "Of course, all good spies have one" and both men clapped each other on the shoulder laughing together now. Then Roland became serious. He had decided that should they encounter Bouchard; they might well need more weapons to defeat such a creature.

"Actually, Jacques I do need your help. My orders allow me to requisition any supplies I feel I may need. So, I would like to raid your armoury for a few things, couple of carbines, couple of muskets, three pistols, yes that should suffice…and oh, of course powder, lead shot and if you have any, the special steel shot too. I'll take as much of that as you can spare. Oh and a couple of bayonets would be good too. I think that's about all for the moment." Belaudie looked dumbfounded.

"You'll be signing for that lot I trust? I don't want it held against me in case you are thinking of starting a small revolution. Who's going to use all this stuff?"

"Me of course, Jacques – I might want to start a small war, if you must know." The Captain followed his friend into the bowels of the barracks and selected the weapons he wanted, placing them in a large canvas bag which weighed him down. Belaudie silently speculated on the purpose of all these weapons but said nothing. Upstairs, he looked directly at his friend hoping Roland would be prepared to explain what this was all about but suspecting that wasn't going to happen. When the other man remained silent, Jacques Belaudie called for one of his lieutenants to arrange for a room at the barracks. This forced Roland to explain that he was staying in the town at the L'Etoile – albeit in the stables. He also explained he would not be there under his own name.

"Of course, my friend" Belaudie replied tapping the side of his nose sagely: "I completely understand" as if he dealt with secret agents daily. "At least join me for dinner then. I usually dine there at least once a week – the barracks kitchen is perhaps not what either of us are used to. Anyway, we can talk of old times if not new. My spies tell me that two rather attractive young ladies are staying at the inn." He laughed knowingly, and Roland's mind raced ahead, thinking how he should handle this situation. They had been through a lot together in Spain and had become firm friends, so he was very tempted to take up Jacques' offer, but he needed to keep up the pretence that he was just a groom. Dining publicly with the commandant of the garrison might not be a good way to do that. If Louis-Philippe should pass through St. Pardoux he must find no clues, no trace of them. Two ladies, with their governess had stayed the night at the inn, their only companion a nondescript coachman. The Captain believed that should Louis-Philippe pick up this snippet of information he was unlikely to make any connection to his sister and cousin.

"Forgive me Jacques, but for your safety as well as my own, I must refuse. I am worried enough about being seen coming here, let alone having dinner with an officer. You know how capricious Destrier can be?" In fact, this was a shot in the dark as Roland's knowledge of the General was confined to two brief meetings in Paris and the very strange signal he had just received. Jacques had never even seen the General, but his reputation was fearsome. Belaudie now felt foolish; suggesting dinner had clearly been a mistake.

"My apologies, my friend. Here was I looking forward to discussing old times and perhaps engaging two pretty ladies in conversation for a change and of course, I just wasn't thinking. Our worlds are far apart, I fear. Mine is now in this backwater garrison, and yours…well I can only guess at the importance of your mission."

"Oh Jacques, you cannot know how much I would like to sit and chat over old times and drink some wine. I hope that I can return soon and take you up on your offer but for the present I must remain inconspicuous". He was planning to retire early to get his party on the move as early as possible next day. With that in his mind, he took his leave of Belaudie, struggling to carry the large canvas bag of armaments, but refusing his friend's offer of help. He made his way across the square to the stables and caught sight of Kate's small, pale face watching him from the hôtel window but pretended he had not. Even before he had a chance to close the stable door Kate scurried in behind him leaving them both in the warm gloom. She put her arms around him and they held each other. She explained that she could only be a moment because although Athina was resting, Amélie was now taking her own chaperoning duties very seriously and wouldn't let Kate out of her sight.

She put her hand gently on his arm as he turned to face her.

“What is it, Roland?” she asked “When you walked across the square just now your face looked so anxious. I have never seen you frown like that before.”

“I am not so much worried as puzzled” replied Roland “I have just received a coded signal from my superior, General Destrier. I believe he is well known to you, is he not, or is that another of Catherine *Giscard’s* little secrets?” The young gendarme feigned a stern expression despite his twinkling eyes.

“I am sorry, dearest, I know that perhaps I should have told you before, but I didn’t know how. It is quite difficult to work into any conversation that one of the most feared men in France is my godfather, or that I call him Uncle Georges – even more difficult to disclose that he is in fact the sweetest, kindest man in the whole world. Everyone has completely the wrong idea about him and I cannot understand why.”

“Well, threatening to punish an entire garrison if his signal to me was not passed on would perhaps go some way to explain this, er misconception?” he smiled seeing Kate’s embarrassment.

“Oh, Roland no. There must have been a misunderstanding, I am sure.”

“Well, it appears he knows things that I have not told him, including the fact that we are to be married. He sends his congratulations, by the way, together with a demand for an invitation; naturally I took the liberty of extending one to him – I could hardly refuse, could I? Anyway, he knows all about the gendarmes I was sent to find. He has now ordered me to protect Hugo Hound! Now how on earth did he know about that?”

“Perhaps a little bird told him? Athina has been out every night, but how……oh, I must go. Amélie will be here looking for me as soon as she realises I am missing. Shall we at least dine together this evening? I think even Athina might allow that – although Amélie might not.”

"Absolutely not, my dear, eventually your brother will realise that he has been misled and come looking for clues. I want to leave nothing for him to discover. "

Kate looked disappointed but even she had to agree that this made a lot of sense. Then he added: "Anyway, my love, I believe you *will* have a gendarmerie captain to dine with this evening, but not me. I discovered to my surprise that an old comrade in arms, Jacques Belaudie oversees the garrison here and he mentioned he had heard of your arrival. He is a good man and we were very close during our time in Spain. I would give him my last sou – but I draw the line at my fiancée."

"Ha, abandoning me already eh?" chided Kate but at that very moment the stable door creaked open and there stood Amélie, hands on hips, her expression stern and challenging: "I think our Cinderella has been left alone with Prince Charming for long enough." Kate was quick to respond: "Well, cousin dear, if I am Cinderella, someone has to be an ugly sister." but when Kate saw the expression on Amélie's face she knew that her time was up. She said her goodbyes and took Amélie's arm to walk out of the stables, whispering softly in Amélie's ear: "Spoilsport."

CHAPTER 45

By the time Kate, Amélie and Athina came down for their evening meal, Captain Belaudie was already seated in the dining room, sitting alone at the best table. As soon as he saw them he stood up and made a very formal bow: "Ladies, please permit me to introduce myself. I am Captain Belaudie and I am dining alone this evening. I wonder if I might ask you all to join me." Although both girls knew that a friend of Roland's was commanding officer here they feigned surprise. Kate, in character, maintained her reticence; Amélie had no such scruples and responded eagerly. "Oh yes That would be lov……very nice" Her voice tailed off as she saw the expression on Athina's face. "Er…I am Mlle. Jeanne Blanc, this is my sister Simone. We are traveling to the home of our aunt. May I present Madame Dubois, our governess." As Amélie looked at Athina she noticed that there was indeed something reminiscent of their former governess…

Belaudie made great play of pulling out the chairs from the table, first for 'Madame Dubois' then for 'Simone' and finally for 'Jeanne' who had waited to sit beside him, much to Athina's displeasure. Jacques introduced himself properly as commander of the local garrison. Athina nodded curtly at his introduction but remained stonily silent.

Amélie enjoyed herself enormously, flirting outrageously with Jacques and pretending not to notice the frowns of disapproval from her 'governess'. Kate listened to the flow of conversation but contributed only occasionally, her mind occupied by other matters. The meal was nearly over when a corporal entered the dining room.

He stood at the door then very discreetly approached the table, nodded politely to the ladies and whispered in Jacques' ear. Belaudie hastily removed his napkin, stood, bowed to the ladies and prepared to leave. He apologised (particularly to Amélie, Athina noticed) and explained that urgent business meant he must return to the barracks immediately. He would return later if he could.

After he disappeared out into the square, Kate turned to her cousin and with mock seriousness said: "Amélie you are behaving disgracefully. Have you no self-respect?" and Kate mimicked her cousin, fluttering her eyelashes coquettishly and giggling. Amélie looked rather shamefaced but pleaded: "But Kate, he is the first eligible gentleman I have met in an age. Truly he is a vast improvement on all those young fops that your brother brings home." Although Kate agreed with her entirely, she was reluctant to pass up an opportunity to have some fun at Amélie's expense. Their banter was cut short however by Athina's abrupt announcement that she must leave immediately. To Amélie's disgust, this time she made Kate promise to ensure Amélie's good behaviour. "Of course, dearest Athina, I will make sure that her behaviour is everything that you would wish – I think I am going to enjoy this."

Athina rose and walked swiftly from the dining room and straight out into the night without a backward glance. The two girls sat at the table looking at each other questioningly but Amélie then saw her opportunity: "If, my dearest cousin, you should wish to spend some much-needed time with your beloved Roland I for one would say nothing." Kate looked at her cousin, feigning shock. She replied in an aggrieved tone: "How dare you ask me to break the solemn promise I have just made to Athina, Amélie Giscard! I shall do no such a thing." Obviously, Kate had been more convincing than she thought for Amélie groaned: "Oh well, it might have worked" and they both burst out laughing, their unseemly noisy behaviour turning heads in the dining room.

The girls had been sitting chatting for about five minutes when Jacques Belaudie returned, his face an angry mask. He explained that the pompous mayor, M. Claude Duclos, had come to the barracks insisting on speaking with him and had presented him with a whole list of new and, in Jacques' opinion, petty laws which he wished enforced with immediate effect. "The man is completely mad, each week he amuses himself by drawing up more and more laws and proclamations – I swear this town has more laws of its own than all those in the Napoleonic code." The mood lifted however when Belaudie discovered that the fourth member of their company, the frosty governess, had 'retired for the night' and although Kate remained she decided to allow Amélie the pleasure of a little flirtation.

That evening a good time was enjoyed by all although Amélie heavily over-imbibed. Gradually the dining room emptied of locals and travellers alike, leaving just Kate, Amélie and their new acquaintance seated in the window, whilst the maids began to clear the dining room. Eventually the Captain rose with some reluctance and formally took leave of both ladies, hoping that he might have the opportunity to see them again the following day. Kate cut short Amélie's heavy-handed attempt to detain him further. "We must retire now 'Jeanne'; if we are not in our room shortly I know that Madame will want to know where we are." This less than subtle hint to Amélie brought her to her senses and she bade Belaudie goodnight with a very sweet smile, tinged with mischief. She turned on the stairs to see him looking after her.

She gave him a tiny smile then followed Kate up to their room, still with a smile on her face. "Well, Kate, do not expect me to turn a blind eye to anything you want to get up to in future" and Kate in turn, assumed a beatific smile as she responded in a gentle voice: "But Amélie, dearest, I cannot imagine why you thought that I might want to spend time alone with Roland. That would never enter my head." Amélie's mouth fell open in a silent "Oh" – that rare occasion where words failed her, and the girls began giggling quietly. When Athina returned just after midnight she found her charges still awake and sitting on their bed, weeping with laughter but unable and unwilling to explain why.

“I suggest that you both get a good night’s sleep. This will undoubtedly be the last comfortable night for some time and we must be up really early tomorrow, we have far to travel” and with this announcement she left them to prepare themselves reluctantly for their last night in a real bed.

The sun had barely risen over St. Pardoux when Athina woke the girls and they went down to have some breakfast. Amélie had a sore head after the evening before and winced every time if as much as a glass clinked, but despite her protestations of being unwell, she received no sympathy from either Kate or Athina. Roland took his breakfast in the stables and then harnessed Kate and Amélie’s horses to the carriage and drove it round to the front of the hôtel with the three other horse tethered behind. Still playing the part of a groom, he went upstairs and collected the baggage and loaded up the carriage but before leaving he slipped into the barracks to bid farewell to his friend. Belaudie greeted him with sullen eyes and a nod of the head: “I may have imbibed a little too much last night” he groaned.

“Did you meet the ladies you told me about?” asked Roland.

“Yes, I certainly did” replied Jacques “but unfortunately they had their governess with them for most of the evening. So stern and watchful! She had a slightly witchlike presence, I thought. One of the ladies was, to me, a little standoffish but the other one, well I think she took a bit of a liking to me. I can tell you I really liked her, but I don’t suppose I shall see her again. They are travelling to stay with their aunt and leaving today. These were definitely extraordinary young ladies. They told me that they had been at Waterloo! What do you think of that? If it’s true, then it must have taken some courage. Anyway, I need to go and get some no, lots of coffee.”

Roland winced at the mention of Waterloo. "Jacques, can I have a word?" Speaking in a low conspiratorial tone Roland confided: "Look, Jacques, a lot depends on this. Can you please forget you met me and more importantly, you met those young ladies? Please make sure your men don't speak of it to anyone. I can't explain but I promise, one day…Trust me, General Destrier would not approve of any gossip."

His friend responded at once: "I understand my friend, or no actually I can't fathom any of it, but you can rest assured that whatever secrets you or they have, those secrets are safe with me."

CHAPTER 46

On Gilles' advice, Louis-Philippe and André followed the route of the Neufchatel coach. The young nobleman for once seemed to be in fine spirits. He prided himself that it was entirely through his efforts that they were following the trail of 'that policeman' as he referred to Roland. André on the other hand was more sceptical but did not express his doubts to his master. He had learned the hard way that information so easily obtained was unlikely to be very reliable. Nevertheless, it would keep his master out of mischief. Most of their days were spent riding in silence, André occupying himself studying the eagles who seemed to be their constant companions. He thought he had begun to detect a pattern in the birds' behaviour.

To begin with, he had ridden beside Louis-Philippe and noticed that no matter at what speed they travelled, a pair of large birds would remain directly overhead. When they stopped, so did their 'escort'. He then began lagging behind his master to observe - the pair flew over Louis-Philippe's head, not his. Once a day, just after noon, another pair of birds would appear and take over what André now thought of as watch duty. A larger, solitary eagle joined them a couple of times each day and would fly away after a few minutes, sometimes in the direction from whence it had come, other times ahead of them. All this intrigued him greatly.

After several days of observation, he was convinced that the birds' behaviour was not random. From his time in the Army, André knew of the usefulness of carrier pigeons, but this was something quite different. The pigeons acted on instinct but also hours of painstaking training. These great birds seemed to be working together as a team in what they were doing. As was his nature, when André did not immediately understand something, he mentally filed away every scrap of information, hoping that one day he might find an explanation.

The two men had failed to spend one comfortable night on the road from Monbezier. Each day they would pass several inns en route but in his obsessive desire to catch up with Roland, whom he believed was only at most one day ahead of them, Louis-Philippe would insist that they press on to the next village. Inevitably, by the time they got there if any lodgings had been available, they were taken. Usually, they would be invited to bed down in the stables where they might have been comfortable and warm, but the nobleman refused to suffer such indignity and would insist they follow the military example and make camp outside the town. This seemed to fill Louis-Philippe with a sense of pride and he lectured André constantly about this being the 'proper military life'. The older man just smiled, never betraying his inner thoughts. Louis-Philippe's sole experience of 'the military life' had been when his father had taken him, at 15, to Regimental Headquarters. André recalled that on the first night the young lad had really enjoyed himself. The food in the Officers' Mess had been excellent and the whole spirit of the evening was one of military camaraderie. However, the Duc's hopes that his son might have the makings of an officer had been dashed the following day. The regiment had gone on exercises and his son had begged to go too. He had been assigned to a crack platoon, as a favour to his famous father. These men were hardened veterans and knew that their lives were dependent upon each other in battle. Weak links were not tolerated, especially amongst the officers.

The men clearly resented this spoilt young man who attempted to give them orders and their contempt for him had been obvious. A young lieutenant had been obliged to step in and order the boy, Duc's son or no, to return to the command post. When

Louis-Philippe met his angry father, the boy had flown into a mad rage, demanding that the platoon and the young lieutenant be punished. Instead, the Duc, ashamed of his son's behaviour, had ordered him to return immediately to La Garenne. This escapade constituted the sum of Louis-Philippe's 'military experience'. Contemplating that incident, André realised with a heavy heart that he and the Duc's son were the only ones left now who knew about it; the Duc dead of shock and most of that platoon dead in the many bloody conflicts since. Even that young lieutenant who had dared to order Louis-Philippe to leave was gone too – Lucien Lecaron.

On the eve of what Louis-Philippe believed would be the end of their quest, he ordered André to collect supplies as they passed through the last small village before Neufchatel; this he did willingly whilst his master rode on ahead to select what he described as a "good defensive position." Despite Louis-Philippe's strict instructions to the contrary, André had made some discreet enquiries along the way, trying to ascertain for himself just how close they were to Roland Lebrun. On each occasion, he had been met with blank expressions. This trail was cold, and André was intrigued by the lack of information. He had no wish to assist his master, but his curiosity was aroused by the knowledge that someone who had left an obvious trail as far as Monbezier could disappear so easily. Recalling a fork in the road south of that town he laughed inwardly: 'you're good, Captain, very good'. André also thought of the letter which General Destrier had written to the Duc about this officer. His commanding officer had told the Duc that Captain Lebrun was 'highly recommended by a mutual friend'. 'Now I can see why' mused André, smiling.

Amongst the supplies which André had bought, at his master's insistence, were three additional boules, the crusty round loaves baked throughout France. Just outside the village he swiftly erected their two tents and started a fire, watched by his master who stalked up and down flapping his arms to keep warm. The young man grabbed the crusty, warm boules from André and secreted them all in his own tent. André watched this but said nothing for he had kept another one back for himself. As soon as Louis-Philippe had devoured the ham and cheese, he retired to get a proper night's rest before the most important day of my life' as he grandly announced: "Tomorrow will be the day when I, Louis-Philippe de Garenne, begin to reverse the misfortunes that have been heaped upon me." André winced. 'Oh dear' thought the older man, knowing that his master's good humour was unlikely to last much longer, and that the following day was unlikely to yield the expected results.

As the young man had consumed the lion's share of the wine he could soon be heard snoring loudly in his tent. Satisfied that he would not be disturbed, André delved deep into his saddle bag to find the military maps which he had secretly brought, contained in a leather case. By lantern light, he found the one he needed and spread it on the ground, retracing the route they had taken as far as the fork in the road outside Monbezier. Then he traced the alternative route which he now believed Roland had taken. By his rough calculation, it would take at least three days to reach the point where he thought the officer was by now and André was pleased that the Captain was safe for the present. He once again buried his map case deep within his saddle bag, extinguished the lantern and eventually drifted off to sleep in his tent, his mind still running over events so far.

André was awakened by the sound of loud gunfire - Louis-Philippe must have risen bright and early. Pulling on his jacket he dragged himself out of his tent to find the young man reloading his precious musket. André recognised this firearm for it was Louis-Philippe's pride and joy. It was a rifled musket based on a design the English had used to great effect in the recent wars, manufactured especially for him by one of the finest gunsmiths in France. This weapon had been the subject of a longstanding argument between the boy and his father, for the Duc had openly accused his son of stealing funds from the Château for its purchase. It was but one of many unresolved contentious issues at the time of the Duc's death.

Louis-Philippe stood facing a small tree, with the musket resting on a branch before him; he took aim and fired once again. André looked along the line of fire to see that the three boules of bread had been set up at varying distances from them. The first, an obvious hit, was about 40 paces away whilst the second was some 60 paces away with the remaining loaf some 100 paces distant. The young man had by this time reloaded once more and took aim. He sent crumbs flying from the edge of the farthest 'target' and his good-humour, André noted, was already beginning to dissipate.

"I ordered you to rise early! Instead, here I am, freezing in this icy wind, no fire, no coffee, no breakfast. Get a move on man!" André dutifully rekindled the fire from the previous night and began to prepare coffee, thinking that it was hardly his fault that there was no bread when his master called him once more. "Go and fetch those loaves. I want to admire my handiwork." The patient man collected the targets and, on his way, back to the encampment examined each of them. The boule which was closest had been hit very slightly left of its centre, the second slightly more to the left whilst the third was only damaged close to its edge. The nobleman, however, was delighted by his marksmanship: "Best shooting I've done in a while. I'll wager there isn't a man in the whole of France who could do better."

André nodded and smiled, which his master took for approval and admiration. Instead, André was in fact thinking 'any man perhaps – but I know of two young ladies who could do a whole lot better'. After a very meagre breakfast of leftovers supplemented with morsels of mutilated bread, the 'military man' began pacing once more, his hands clasped behind him as he strode around in 'Napoleonic' mode. "Lacoste, these are my orders. Today we ride to Neufchatel. You will go ahead into the town and reconnoitre.

I want to know what accommodation is available for a man such as myself – you must stay elsewhere. I think it better we separate. I will stay under an assumed name. No one must know it is *me*. This time, you may make discreet enquiries about those we seek".

"Absolutely, sir. I will carry out your orders. What should I actually ask?" This simple enquiry had the most shocking effect on the young nobleman. His face turned dark puce and spittle crept from the side of his mouth as he screamed at André: "Lacoste, just do what I tell you to do. I will do the thinking." André was truly shocked by the sudden change. The ranting had exhausted Louis-Philippe, it seemed. He sank onto a tree trunk panting and red faced – surely this was not the reaction of any normal man, thought André.

"Sir I apologise for questioning your orders" said André, trying to gently defuse the situation. Immediately mollified, Louis-Philippe looked up at André smugly, failing to catch the expression on his servant's face. As a gesture of goodwill, the young man even folded his own linens as they broke their camp.

By early afternoon, the busy town of Neufchatel was in sight. It nestled in a river valley with the main town standing on the riverbank nearest them. André was instructed to ride down alone, and he quickly located the most comfortable Hôtel in the town which stood in the main square. The Hôtel de France was quite an imposing building but dominating the square was a raised stone platform on which stood a rare relic of the Revolution – a guillotine, albeit now missing its murderous blade Across the bridge, on the edge of the town André found a simple, friendly inn then rode back to Louis-Philippe. The younger man was seated on a milestone, once more cleaning the musket he had used earlier.

"Sir, the finest establishment in the town is the Hôtel de France, in the Place de la Revolution, the main square of the town. However, you may wish to stay elsewhere as there is one aspect of the..."

André was interrupted: "This Hôtel de France is the best Hôtel?" enquired the young man, smoothly. "Yes sir, but…"

"In that case that is where I will stay" he announced. "What are you waiting for, man? You have work to do." André nodded but in a kind gesture he remembered to ask Louis-Philippe if he might need cash to settle his bills. André knew this would only flummox the nobleman. As expected, his master panicked at the very idea: "What, no of course not. They can send an account to the château." André knew the nobleman was so accustomed to charging everything to the Château he struggled even to identify the various notes and coins. Revelling in Louis-Philippe's discomfiture, André told him: "Sir, I fear that our credit does not extend this far south; even if it did, well you would be forced to reveal your true identity would you not?" This was said with great solicitude but with tongue firmly placed in cheek. André offered a small leather pouch to Louis-Philippe which the young man sullenly snatched from his grasp: "I assume you have furnished me with funds to cope with every eventuality?" the young man demanded.

"Of course, sir. Now I shall go and make my enquiries. How shall I contact you though? Shall I come to meet you after dark?"

"Right, right. Very well. Meet me at 6 p.m. outside my Hôtel."

"I shall be there sir but if I might suggest - if you are trying to remain incognito, would it perhaps be best to meet further from your Hôtel and out of sight?"

"Exactly what I was thinking. Err, right. Meet me in the nearest Cafe to my Hôtel ...err you must find the right one."

CHAPTER 47

André agreed and, shaking his head in despair, rode on and checked in to his own humbler lodgings overlooking the river. Having settled into his room and laid out his small cache of possessions, he strolled back over the bridge to enquire at both the Town Hall and the Gendarmerie Barracks about the reports of the sighting of the Lost Patrol. To do this he posed as a journalist, who had heard a rumour and of course used a false name: Philippe-Louis Garenne.

As André had already guessed there had been no sightings of the Patrol. Certain now that Captain Lebrun had successfully fooled his master, André retired to a Cafe on the shady side of the Place de la Revolution, almost opposite the entrance to the Hôtel de France. There he engaged the owner in conversation and quickly established that the story of a huge Hound terrorising the town was equally false. More customers drifted in and André took his drink and sat by the window where he could see across the square but keep an ear out for any snippets of information. Two things were certain: Roland Lebrun had been tipped off somehow that he was being followed and the old drayman had been part of it. André was also certain that somehow Mlle. Catherine had warned the Captain, but if so where was she now? Most likely with Mlle. Amélie! His train of thought was broken when he looked at the large ornate clock above the counter and saw that he only 5 minutes until his rendezvous. He waited anxiously for some movement at the Hôtel entrance.

The nobleman had also been doing some thinking on the short journey into town, but his thoughts were a mixture of fantasies about life after he had gained control of the Eleanor Bequest and

Hugo Hound. He planned visits to Paris where he would go hunting with the king and of course be appointed as a much-valued advisor at Court. Dark thoughts of revenge also surfaced aimed at all those he perceived as having slighted him. At present that *policeman* stood at the top of his list - he somehow sensed this man was his pre-ordained adversary.

The upstart knew too much – or thought he did. Catherine, his half-sister, was his enemy too. She had stolen "his" inheritance, charmed his father into giving her everything, along with his meddling aunt Marianne, who lived 'rent free' in one "his" houses and never gave him the deference which was his due.

He also harboured dark thoughts about that other Lecaron, Raoul, who only remained alive because killing two brothers might have looked suspicious, even to that idiot Falaise. As for that silly giggling cousin of his, Amélie, she was always trying to humiliate him in front of his friends by showing off how good a shot she was…his list was extensive indeed but when he was Duc Louis-Philippe, richest man in France…He had snapped out of his reverie as soon as he rode into the main square. He noticed that the previous name of the square written on an enamelled plaque, had been painted over but was still barely discernible: Place du Roi. The new name however gave him quite a jolt: "Place de la Revolution". However, this was nothing compared to the shock he felt when he saw the monstrous shape of the old guillotine left for all to see in the centre of the square. Albeit bladeless it still loomed darkly above him, enough to turn his face pale as he fingered his neck subconsciously. He tried hard to avert his eyes as he rode towards the Hôtel de France. Lacoste had been correct; it was an imposing building with a covered entrance where coach passengers could alight without being exposed to the elements. A groom eagerly leapt forward to take the reins of the young man's horse: "Will you be staying the night, Monsieur?" the young lad politely asked, eager to help in the hopes of a tip.

With his customary attitude to all who were not of his station, Louis Philippe looked at him blankly: “Of course. Why else would I be here?” he snapped. Clearly this gentleman was of some means and so a good tip was perhaps still in the offing: “Well sir, I will take your horse to our stables and bring your bags up to your room. May I have your name Sir?” Louis-Philippe’s mind was in such turmoil that he completely forgot himself in the moment: “It’s de Garenne of course” he hissed but the groom just took the reins from Louis-Philippe’s shaking hands and led the horse towards a side entrance, wide enough for coaches.

Louis-Philippe watched the young man go, leaving him standing at the door of the hôtel , unsure how to proceed. He had already betrayed his name and now he realised that despite staying at many hôtels in the past, André had always been there to smooth his path. Lacoste was the man for these trivialities. He pushed open the well-polished double doors of the establishment and lacking a little of his normal swagger, approached the reception desk. Behind the desk sat an old gentleman dressed in black who peered at the young man over his wire-framed spectacles. “May I help you, Monsieur?” he asked with the bored tone of someone who had asked this question countless times before. For once the young man restrained himself. Normally he regarded disinterest as insolence but to remain incognito he checked his temper.

“Your finest room?” he drawled. The Hôtel ier shook his head: “Sadly that room is taken but I can offer you our second finest room. Are you alone, sir? Most of our guests prefer to share – keeps the cost down don’t it?”

Now really regretting his decision to handle all this himself, he checked his impulse to shout very loudly and answered: “Yes, indeed, but I do not wish to share.” The Hôtel keeper nodded, said nothing but reached into a drawer in the desk and withdrew an official-looking form.“Err, what is this?” the young nobleman was looking at the paper nervously now.

“Well Sir, the local Gendarmerie insist that everyone who stays in the town completes one of these forms – if they can. I dunno why and it’s a lot of bother if they can’t write I can tell you. Then there’s the err ‘married couples’ who are very unwilling to fill ‘em in if you get my meaning. Course they usually give a false name hahaha. We often have more than one room occupied by couples called ‘Martin’”.

Louis-Philippe was still casting around desperately for a convincing false name to put down on the form when the groom returned with his bags: “Grandpa” he asked chirpily “What room shall I take Monsieur de Garenne’s bags to?”

“Room 2, Patrice if you would” said the innkeeper now looking a little suspiciously at the well-dressed young man. “Would you be, by any chance, related to the Duc de Garenne Monsieur?

My son served in the army under that man. True gentleman he always said despite the title.” As he said this the man actually spat “My son reckoned he’d have managed to keep his head on even around here. Ah those were the days, Sir, never been busier than then but of course, always made sure any aristos paid up front eh?” The old man cackled to himself. The young man paled as he thought of the abandoned guillotine in the square and he hastily tried to regain his composure: “Eh no, no. The name is actually Garenne, not de Garenne”

“That’s a shame, that is” replied the innkeeper “I am sure my son would have wanted to shake the hand of any member of the Duc’s family. Well Sir, if you follow Patrice up those stairs, your room is at the front on the right. Get a lovely view of the square too.” As he took the key from the old man, Louis-Philippe realised all at once that the ‘lovely view’ would be of the guillotine. It did not fill him with joy. He turned back to the desk and with studied nonchalance, asked whether a room was available at the rear of the Hôtel in case the room at the front was noisy.

“Well there is Sir, you’ll be needing Room 3 then, t’is cheaper but t’is more a dormitory than a room. All the male coach passengers share it. Gets a bit rowdy in there sometimes. Being cooped up all day in a dusty coach gives them a terrible thirst, it does. Sometimes I even have to call in the Gendarmes what with the singing and fighting and all. Gendarmes like it I think. Since old Madame in the square had her blade removed things have been very quiet here. Still, it’s your choice.”

“No, no, on second thoughts, I will take Room 2” said the young man hastily, snatching back the key and almost running up the stairs. Patrice had lingered on the landing, still hoping for a tip, but quickly realised that this wasn’t going to happen. He scurried back down to await a more profitable arrival.

Louis-Philippe immediately drew the thin curtain in his room to hide the view. He withdrew his gold pocket watch and saw that he had a little time before his rendezvous with André. He recalled what the innkeeper had said, that the Gendarmes were underemployed now, nothing to do but keep rowdy guests in check…he felt a deep sense of gloom descending on him when the clock in the square chimed six sonorous times he rose and went out into the darkened square to meet André outside the Cafe: “Right, Lacoste, tell me everything you have discovered” he said anxiously, already feeling pessimistic.

“I made numerous enquiries at the Mayor’s office and the Gendarmerie, as you instructed, I even used a false name.” (Well there was truth in that) “Brilliant thinking on your part Sir… but, well I am very much afraid that no-one can recall any troop of gendarmes, no reports of any large dogs terrorising the neighbourhood either.” As he spoke, André watched his master’s changing demeanour, the clenching and unclenching of fists but he was undeterred: “If I may say so Sir, I believe that your faith in the words of that old drayman in Monbezier might have been misplaced. He may even have been spinning you a yarn.”

"I blame you Lacoste for allowing me to put my faith in the ravings of a drunk. We need a plan…now." Although André could not see his master's face clearly, he knew that it would undoubtedly be reddening with anger, a vein throbbing ominously at the temple. Calmly André spoke with feigned deference: "Sir, I have followed your instructions closely, yet made no progress. Perhaps we are entirely on ......"

"Shut uppp" hissed Louis-Philippe, trying to whisper and scream at the same time. His voice had become almost falsetto as he struggled to control his temper. André knew that for now he had pushed his master as far as he could. On a different tack he politely enquired whether they should now try to purchase a map.

"Yes, yes find a map immediately. Bring it to me first thing tomorrow morning. Do not fail me again or you will wish that that infernal machine" he nodded at the guillotine "still worked." The younger man turned on his heel and strode back towards his hôtel .

André watched until he saw Louis-Philippe enter the building by the light of the portico lanterns then walked contentedly back to his own lodgings across the bridge. He thought he might ask the landlord if he knew if any maps of the surrounding area which were available. He was very surprised that the innkeeper possessed one. After much rummaging, the man triumphantly produced a much-folded map drawn on yellowing waxed paper. "This cost me 50 sou twenty years ago and what a waste of money it's been. It was drawn up by the old schoolmaster. He's been gone a few years now. Claimed he was 'well-travelled' he did. Later I found out he had only ever been as far as Monbezier in his whole life. Still a lot further than I've ever been – to be honest, I b'aint sure where Monbezier is. The only thing that's right on this map is the word FRANCE hahaha." André stopped him before he could continue.

"Well that is interesting. I asked only because I collect old maps. Doesn't matter whether they are accurate or not.". André would not have been surprised to see "here be dragons" on the scruffy line map. “Perhaps we can come to an arrangement – 50 sous you say? After 20 years, I think I can improve on that sum, reward you for the time you have looked after it, perhaps?” A price was quickly agreed, and André ordered dinner. Between the very substantial courses he examined the old map, comparing it mentally with his own, much more accurate version, still concealed in his saddlebag. In a silent toast, he raised his glass to the old schoolmaster’s incompetence. ‘Worst map I have ever set eyes on; may your soul rest in peace’.

First thing next morning, André presented himself at the Hôtel de France and asked the young groom to look after his horse whilst he went in search of his master. He soon saw Louis-Philippe in a far corner of the dining room, engrossed in a copy of the “Gazette du Sud-Ouest.” When he caught sight of André in the doorway, the young man waved him away anxiously. André did as he was bidden but walked only a few paces to the side of the main doors from where he overheard with some amusement the groom enquiring: “Will you be wanting your horse brought round from the stables, M. de Garenne?”

“It’s Garenne, Garenne you insolent fool. Not DE Garenne” and the young man strode past the groom, ignoring the question in his haste to reach André. “Did I not say I do not wish to be seen with you? You could give away our whole plan.”

“Our plan Sir? Of course! Inspired! Staying in a Hôtel under your own name when traveling incognito. The subtlety stuns me, it is beyond my…”

“Enough! Did you get…” he saw André was clutching a waxed package and snatched it from the older man’s hands. André felt obliged to add: “Sir, it is a very old map. The previous owner could not vouch for its accuracy.”

“Look Lacoste, let me deal with this.” Louis-Philippe then made his way back into the Hôtel but realising André had remained outside he forgot 'the plan' and ordered his servant to follow him. In a small drawing room, Louis-Philippe unfolded the map and laid it on a writing table.

Once more adopting a 'military pose' he circled the table, his hands clasped behind his back. He studied the faded lines on the old map intently. When he had finally found Neufchatel, indicated by the largest red dot, he traced the journey back to Monbezier. Triumphantly he turned to André: "Well the distances shown would seem to correspond with our journey so far…ergo, the map is indeed accurate. I'd wager those that said it might not be accurate had never even set foot outside this godforsaken place. See there" he indicated the fork in the road below Monbezier "that is where *you* lost the way." André looked at his master's pointing finger: "I fear so." Louis-Philippe glanced sharply at André, then decided the man meant every word.

Louis-Philippe fed on flattery and saw no irony in lecturing the seasoned military man with far greater experience than himself. "I think I know where he's headed" he stabbed the map with his finger "and that is where we are going." André looked closely at the map; Louis-Philippe was indicating the small town of Oloron Sainte Marie. This was a town with which André was acquainted from his military days, but he said nothing. "I suppose you are wondering why I know that's the place" continued the young man. "Instinct. All great generals possess it. Now, let's be off. We have a lot of time to make up."

Inwardly, Louis-Philippe was himself wondering why he felt so strongly drawn to this small town in the mountains. Why was he so certain it was the gendarme's destination? He traced the route he proposed to take, across country to St Pardoux, then onwards to the small town of Pont St. Pierre. "We will cross the River Adour there and then onwards towards Oloron. The map shows the distances as quite small" - but André knew better.

"One day to here" said Louis-Philippe confidently indicating St. Pardoux and I calculate that we should be at most two days behind that policeman. Then the hunt will begin in earnest."

"For Hugo Hound, Sir?" asked André innocently as his master's face took on a sly expression: "Yes, yes, of course. Settle my bill and let's get going." He threw the pouch of coins he had obtained earlier back to André who went to pay the account. He tried not to notice the expression of the old man at the desk, whose sneer showed just what he thought of André's master. Louis-Philippe was already mounted and anxious to leave. The men rode out of the square, towards the river. Crossing the square, the low autumn sun cast a long, well defined shadow of Madame *la Guillotine* across the horsemen, one of whom kept his eyes averted until they reached the bridge. As they set off in the direction St. Pardoux, André once again noticed that the eagles were following despite their new direction.

CHAPTER 48

As their carriage left St. Pardoux, Roland turned to Kate who had been permitted, for once to sit up front alongside him: "So, a little standoffish last night I hear?"

Kate tried to look disdainful: "Well, someone had to be. Honestly, Amélie had far too much wine and was making a complete fool of herself. I do not know what your friend must have thought of us."

"Well, my dear, to be honest he seems quite taken with your cousin and...." Before he could finish the sentence, she interrupted sharply: "Well of course he would be, the way she almost threw herself at him" her face the very picture of self-righteous indignation. Expressionless, Roland went on: "He remarked to me how brave he thought you both were, being at Waterloo. I assume that it was Amélie who told him? I had to order him never to speak of it. I just hope no-one overhead. I wouldn't want your brother to get wind of that."

Kate pulled her hat down and looked away, pretending to scrutinise some sheep in a field they were passing. Noticing the gesture, he gently asked: "It wasn't Amélie who mentioned it, was it?" Kate turned back to face him very slowly. She was blushing a bright red. "It was me. I was really indiscreet and now I've proved Athina right, again haven't I?" She hoped Athina had not heard this exchange. "I was honestly trying to change the topic of conversation at table; it was all getting mighty flirtatious and Amélie was actually reciting passages from one of her romantic novels! Please don't be cross with me – I promise I won't do anything so stupid again."

Roland smiled to himself at her embarrassment but assured her that he was not at all angry, but they were *trying* to travel incognito. For the rest of the morning, Kate was subdued, and the journey passed almost in silence. At lunchtime, the captain unwrapped some bread and cheese he had acquired in St. Pardoux, but Amélie flatly refused to eat.

She had been sprawled across one whole seat inside the carriage for most of the journey. In a pointed gesture, Kate offered her cousin a little wine, which Amélie declined, pale-faced. As they ate, Roland observed that there was much more commotion from the eagles overhead than usual. He had become used to seeing two but now there were four, sometimes five, and others were flying in and out, as if delivering messages

As he watched, one particularly magnificent bird joined the other four and flew in circles with them, before descending and slowly coming to rest on a fence post very close to the coach. The bird folded its enormous wings around its powerful body, fixing them with a beady eye. To the surprise of the others, Athina immediately rose and performed a graceful curtsey before the fine eagle, its eye and beak glinting in the noon sun as it watched proceedings imperiously.

Athina spoke: "My dearest Pellerin, I am delighted to see you. Allow me to present to you my travelling companions, Captain Roland Lebrun and Mlle. Catherine de Garenne." By the time she had said this, they had both risen and the gendarme bowed before the bird, although not sure why he felt compelled to do so. Kate then executed a dainty curtsey too, following Roland's lead. "I am afraid that our other travelling companion, Mlle. Amélie Giscard, daughter of Madame Marianne Giscard, is somewhat indisposed today." Athina nodded towards the carriage where Amélie had managed to drag herself to the window to see what was happening. She looked out at her companions, the large bird and the food, her eyes bleary and bloodshot, then nodded and returned to the comfort of her bench, falling back into a hazy sleep.

The eagle inclined its huge head at each of the three in turn and then addressed them in a clear, if croaky, voice. It seemed that Louis-Philippe had reached Neufchatel before realising he had been duped. However, this morning he and his companion had taken a new course which would eventually lead them to St. Pardoux. The gendarme remembered the calculations he had made back at Sanctuary Inn and he knew that it should take the two men slightly less than three days to reach St. Pardoux. "Meanwhile" continued Pellerin "Hugo and his party are, I am afraid, in great need of assistance. Although the weather is slowly improving, the River Adour is in flood trapping the caravan on this side of the river. They can still rely on their guise as a travelling menagerie for safety at present, but they will soon be facing twin threats."

"Brochard?" asked Athina anxiously.

"I fear that it could be. A *Loup Garou* has been sighted several days to the north. I think the time has come, Captain, for you to follow your General's orders and protect Hugo. Now if you would excuse me, I would like a few private words with Madame Athina." He flew gracefully about 50 paces off and settled once more, this time on a low branch whilst Athina seemed to glide towards where he perched. Roland and Kate watched as she nodded regularly at Pellerin's words but try as they might, they could not make out what was being said.

"I think I must be going mad" Roland whispered. "That eagle, his voice, even his expression seems strangely familiar."

"Mm, I know what you mean. Sometimes when Athina is being an owl I have the feeling I know her. That's so strange. I seem to, well, recognise her almost - but it's as though her present guise is hiding something deeper. Anyway, what do you think they are talking about?" As they watched, the great bird called Pellerin flapped his huge wings one single time and rose gracefully back up into the sky, slowly gaining height until he was almost invisible to the naked eye. Athina returned to them, her feet drifting in a misty cloud on the ground. "I think that the time has come for you to take your leave, Captain. If you ride hard you should reach Hugo and the others quite quickly; we will follow on and wait near the river to stop Louis-Philippe should he try to get up to mischief."

Roland led Kate a short distance away where they could speak for a moment in private, this time with Athina's blessing. She was very apprehensive about his departure, but he reminded her that this was what had been agreed at the Sanctuary Inn. "Yes, yes, I know" she sighed "but it didn't seem so real, or so immediate then. Now it's about to happen and I am afraid for you." He tried to reassure her but nothing he said seemed to calm her, so he tried a different approach.

"Kate, I am depending on you. You and Amélie must play your parts as you promised, don't you see? Once I have caught up with Hugo I need to keep as much distance between him and Louis-Philippe as possible. If you can slow your brother down in any way, so much the better.

I am certain that between the two of you, you can distract him – especially with Athina in tow. But, my dear, do not put yourself or Amélie in any danger."

"I won't do anything stupid; I promise you. I have learned my lesson, but before we say goodbye, please tell me you have forgiven me?" Kate stood with her hands clasped behind her back, shuffling her feet. "Please, Roland."

He smiled: "Of course, there is nothing to forgive. I wasn't angry with you. I was just worried." He stretched his arms out to her, but she was quicker. She threw her arms around his neck and hung on tightly, her feet leaving the ground. Eventually she let go and they walked back together to where Athina was waiting. Amélie had staggered out of the carriage, still very unsteady on her feet, but at Roland's next words she rallied considerably.

"Right, before I leave I have some gifts for you ladies." He reached under the coachman's seat where he had stowed the canvas bag. He distributed a carbine, a musket and a pistol to Kate and a musket and a pistol to Amélie, telling her she could keep the carbine he had already provided. Then he gave them a supply of powder and shot, explaining that the steel shot was only to be used if they encountered the *Loup Garou*. As Athina looked on, he presented each girl with a shiny bayonet, showing them how to attach the weapon to their carbines, rather than the unwieldy muskets.

Amélie came alive. She was torn between examining the musket – "Army issue, isn't it? Looks like the latest model too" – and fixing the bayonet to her carbine. He exchanged a look with Kate: "Has she always been like this?"

Kate rolled her eyes upwards: "Not always, I don't think she was this bad when she was…10. We did have rather an odd upbringing." She laughed then, her expression becoming serious once more. "When you said you had a gift for me Captain Lebrun, I had hoped that perhaps it would be some small memento of our betrothal, something to keep, a ring possibly, some 'token of affection' you know."

The Captain stroked his chin thoughtfully, "I'm sorry Kate. I was so busy trying to acquire weapons to protect you that visiting a goldsmith completely slipped my mind.

Anyway, it seems not only Amélie steals passages from novels" he smirked. She had been caught out.

It was time for Roland to go. They helped him load Marron and Greco with the remaining weapons and, hoping to avoid further distress, he quickly took his leave. With a single, lingering backward glance at Kate he rode off and was soon lost to sight on the road ahead. Watching his departure, the girls decided that now was the right time to get rid of their carriage. Firstly, it would be quicker on horseback and, of course, one of them driving a carriage would have been a very suspicious sight. Riders would draw less interest. Athina agreed reluctantly to ride the packhorse, and they re-distributed their bags onto their own mounts. Between them they pushed the old carriage into some undergrowth then rode on at a steady pace.

Roland made good time. Marron was anxious to prove his worth after his humiliation in the forest – he prided himself on showing no fear and that had not been his finest moment. The horse trotted confidently onwards so that when the gendarme decided to make camp, they had covered well over a third of their journey. Roland consulted his map by lantern-light and estimated that he would reach Hugo by midday the following day, so if his estimate was correct he would have the afternoon and at least two more days to get the caravan across the river and maybe another half a day and hopefully more to put some distance between them and Louis-Philippe. Just before dusk, he noticed one of the eagles that shadowed him swoop away from his companions and fly quickly north, presumably, he thought, to tell either Athina or Pellerin where he was. He smiled as he thought once more of his first meeting with the owl. Now he didn't even notice – talking to birds was commonplace, in fact he would not have been at all surprised to receive a visit from Athina that evening. However, none of the birds visited him and he awoke bright and early, refreshed by a good night's sleep and having eaten the remains of his food he set off once more.

CHAPTER 49

Hugo awoke bright and early and crawled out from under one of the wagons to survey the valley below. For the first time since they had left St. Pardoux it wasn't raining. The sun was just rising, casting a pink glow on the tops of some very high mountains in the far distance. The Hound was excited, finally things were looking up: perhaps today was the day they would get moving once more.

The journey south from St. Pardoux had been slow and laborious. The party were slowly climbing higher and higher and each day brought more bad weather. The road, such as it was, had turned into a quagmire that sucked at the wheels of the wagons. Even little Mimi, light-footed as she was, had difficulty negotiating her way and eventually gave up her quest for shells and hitched a lift on the wagon driven by Ursian. Some days they had only travelled a league between daybreak and nightfall. Ursian and Sangres had spent much of their time each day extricating the wagons from the mud and Hugo felt that even Ursian was beginning to lose heart.

There was a general sense of relief where they were told by a great eagle, 'Aiguillin' according to Ursian, that they should make camp and rest until the weather improved and they could cross the river. Hugo felt fairly confident that most of the animals could swim, but what of the wagons? According to the bird, the stone bridge which Ursian remembered well had unfortunately been blown up by the retreating French army a few years before and its wooden 'temporary' replacement had recently been washed away. Aiguillin guided them to a safe spot, an area of flat grassland halfway down a sloping bank, a place well known to Ursian. Hugo could hear rushing water below, but the mists hid the river itself. The slope had been a little too steep for the horses to control the wagons, so all the animals were released, on strict promises extracted by Ursian, to be on their best behaviour. Hugo then led them down whilst Ursian and Sangres applied themselves to the task of shifting the wagons.

Hugo was delighted to discover a sturdy stone hut with a strong door and he was able to use his paw/hand to open the latch. He discovered it was bone dry! The first wagon down was the supply wagon which was quickly surrounded by the lions and the Fighting Bears, who slowly circled it emitting low sounds. Hugo was concerned and rightly so, for large though he was, he was no match for any of these creatures should they choose to become angry, so he decided to try an appeal to their better natures: "Lucius, you promised Ursian that you would be on your best behaviour."

"Course I did, but that was a Lion promise, not a Bear Promise. It's them that you should be talkin' to" growled the lion.

Hugo turned to the largest of the Fighting Bears who leaned nonchalantly against the wagon: "You need to know, Hugo my old mate, its only Guard Bears who live up to their promises; we are Fighting Bears and Gilles says the only promise we ever kept was to have a fight!" All his friends chuckled and nudged each other at this, ignoring the poor Hound's expression of exasperation. However, he was saved from further problems by the arrival of the second wagon and with it, Ursian.

He was propping it up against his broad back, whilst Sangres was at its rear, broad leather straps around his powerful shoulders, his sharp hooves digging in hard to stop the wagon from descending out of control. As soon as they were on the level, Ursian took charge: "Right you lot" he addressed the Fighting Bears "for the rest of this journey you are *honorary* Guard Bears. You will be guarding the supplies with your lives. If as much as a morsel goes missing, you will have broken a Bear Promise and you will pay with your lives." As Ursian spoke these last words he grew in stature standing on his huge hind legs until he was looking down upon the other animals who cowered before him. "As for you" the suddenly monstrous beast continued, turning his fierce eyes to the lions "you pathetic, overgrown cats. If you want to raid our supplies then you will have to fight all of them and if any one of you survives, you will then answer to ME!" Ursian let forth a long low growl showing his huge yellowing teeth and neither group, Hugo knew, would be likely to question his authority. Just to be on the safe side however, Hugo and Ursian unloaded the contents of the supply wagon and placed everything in the little hut.

There was only a simple latch on the door, but no lion or Bear could operate it with their paws. Hugo thought to himself that all animals had to revert to their animal nature sometimes!

With nowhere to go, the animals mainly stayed in or under the wagons. Anywhere they could stay dry was desirable. A huge storm had blown up, massive streaks of lightning shooting across the black sky whilst thunder seemed to shake the very ground they were on and it reverberated around them. The animals were disturbed, despite knowing about storms and although Ursian and Hugo took over the small hut they made regular patrols to sooth their charges during the night. Next day, during a brief pause in the heavy rain, Ursian tried to show Hugo where the country town of Pont St. Pierre stood. "Probably should just call it St. Pierre 'cos there is no Pont" laughed Hugo. He also showed the Hound the place where they would try to ford the river to avoid the town and where, in the very far distance their goal lay, the High Valley, Elysium. Hugo saw his friend's dark brown, almost black eyes fill with tears and he could feel the strength of the bear's desire to get on the move, to go home. Ursian had described to him his ten long years in captivity; it had been his mistake to be captured and he, and he alone, must suffer the consequences and achieve his freedom. Now, so close to the place he loved, he felt even more strongly bound by his Bear Promise. "I do long for my home but no, Hugo" he said, as if he had read the other's mind "we started this together and will finish it together at the Gates of the High Valley."

The Hound forced his gaze from the mountains in the far distance as they changed colour from dusky pink to bright, sparkling white as the sun rose. He dragged his eyes instead downwards to the wild river below, which at last was visible. Ursian still seemed to be entranced by the sight of the mountains: "The Pyrenees" he grunted "just over there, that's where the Gates are."

"So, we're almost there? We've almost made it, haven't we?" Hugo's tail began to wag so excitedly that he was creating a breeze.

"No. Those mountains are so high that they look closer than they really are; they are more than two whole bear-days away and we have still got to cross that…" Ursian indicated the river below them. Before he had left La Garenne he had never seen a proper river in his whole dog life.

Since then, he had managed to swim across the Dordogne river, which was both wide and fast-flowing and he had crossed other smaller rivers by bridge, but he had never encountered anything like this. The fast flow had broken its banks in places and had formed small shallow lakes. The current ran slower nearer the banks, but the central flow was a raging torrent of muddy water, sometimes being pushed up into great waves where it smashed against the rocks underneath the surface. Protruding from the water there were four splintered wooden stanchions. The ropes attached to these were being pulled and tossed by the angry current. This was all that remained of the 'temporary' bridge. In the shallows on their side of the river was a rough wooden platform secured to a thick post sunk deep into the riverbank. Hugo saw that on this post was fixed a notice board. Hugo's mind brought back images of other words on notice boards: *For sale by Auction: Hugo Hound of Lecaron Farm*

Ursian sensed his friend's unease "That river runs close to the High Valley. It'll take a few days without any rain up there for the waters to return to normal; fortunately, it goes down as quickly as it rises but we cannot wait too long, Hugo. Tell you what, once we have fed the animals we'll go down there and read what's on that noticeboard. I think it's probably to tell the humans about when that 'thing'" he indicated the bobbing wooden platform "tries to cross!"

Hugo looked confused but then realisation dawned: "Is it a boat then?"

"Well, sort of" intoned a morose deep voice behind them "What else could it be?"

Hugo looked around sharply to find the Donkey behind him, peering down at the river. It was the first time that the animal had spoken since they had left Sanctuary Inn aside from an occasional 'thank you' at mealtimes. "I used to work on the one near the town where you found me. Round and round and round all day, first one way then the other. I could have told the humans there was a better way to do it but who listens to a beast of burden?" The Donkey's long sad face spoke a thousand words.

The Hound had a flash of inspiration. "Why don't you come down with us to the river M. L'Ane?"

Whilst the animals were enjoying their morning meal, the great eagle Aiguillin landed amongst them. He informed Ursian and Hugo that finally it had dawned on Louis-Philippe that he had been fooled. He was in a foul temper and he and André Lacoste was now heading towards St. Pardoux. There was still no immediate danger but Aiguillin had been sent by his father, Pellerin, to tell them they should cross the river as quickly as possible. Help was being sent to assist with both crossing the river and handling the Renegade. Ursian examined a sharp extended claw: "I need no help with Renegades" he growled.

"Lord Ursian, you know how my father prefers to deal with these matters. Would you excuse us for a moment Hugo, I need a private word with Ursian?" and the magnificent bird walked slowly away to a nearby bush.

The Hound nodded and wandered off to look down at the river as Aiguillin drew Ursian aside: "Lord Ursian, my father has called a Muster of all the Eagles." Ursian's head turned sharply, his dark glittering eyes boring into those of Aiguillin.

"So, it's true. There is a *Loup Garou* on the loose?"

"That is the extent of my knowledge Lord Ursian. Once we have had our Muster I will know more but for the moment he felt it better not to add to Hugo's burden."

"I agree" growled Ursian. "This 'help' we are to expect, is it… humankind?" He spat out these words bitterly. "Yes, but the Paladin line runs strong within him and my father is confident of his abilities. The Lady recommended him."

"Hmmph" was the only response. Aiguillin then called to Hugo and spoke formally to them both: "I must take my leave. I have a long journey to make. For a few days, it may be only the owls who will meet with you and keep you informed. Rest assured though Louis-Philippe cannot move an inch without us knowing."

Inclining his magnificent head so that his beak almost touched the ground, Aiguillin launched himself downwards towards the river then effortlessly wheeled and soared up into the bright sky until he disappeared to everyone save Ursian, who followed his progress towards the High Valley.

Hugo watched his departure then settled back down to studying the river, struggling to come up with a plan to cross in safety. Having summoned Donkey, the two companions made their careful way down. Hugo was curious to know what the eagle's message had been but Ursian remained vague: "Oh, he was just warning me that we would have 'humankind' assistance as if I hadn't already guessed that. Pellerin sometimes concerns himself in human affairs too much in my opinion."

When they reached the bottom of the hill they had to wade out through marshy grassland to reach the floating platform formed by wooden planks connected by stout ropes and cross-pieces to hold the structure together. Nearby on the slightly tilted notice board were two old notices, each headed "Commune of Pont St. Pierre." The one that was clearly the oldest was torn, smudged and yellowing with age. "Ursian read:

"Until the bridge known as Pont St. Pierre is rebuilt,
travellers may use the temporary structure known
as the Pont Neuf.
Crossing the Pont Neuf during times of bad weather
is at the travellers' own risk"

The Hound and his companion looked at the broken stanchions just visible above the flowing river, festooned with ropes and debris. "Well that's true enough. You'd have to be mad to risk crossing that" Hugo laughed nervously although he was more concerned than amused. He was trying to read the second notice when he saw that Donkey was aboard the platform and taking a great interest in the fierce flow running in the middle of the river. He seemed totally unfazed by it. Unsurprisingly, the second notice read:

"The Pont Neuf is closed for Repairs.
A ferry service is provided for travellers.
This can be used every day except Saturdays,
Sundays and Fête Days.
This service is available between the hours of
8.00 a.m. and 4.00 p.m.
but does not operate between 11.30 a.m. and 2.30 p.m.
This ferry will not operate in times of bad weather.
"ALL PASSENGERS TRAVEL AT THEIR OWN RISK"

A third Notice which had been nailed on a tree at the edge of the flooded bank read:

"Ferry Services suspended due to bad weather"

The animals began to laugh – humankind! Hugo shook his head then clambered onto the makeshift ferry. He sat down, depressed, at the front of the bobbing wooden platform wondering what to do next. 'It was all well and good Aiguillin and Pellerin advising us to cross the river' he thought 'but have they any idea what that actually involves?' He was aware that Ursian was nearby because every time the bear moved the ferry dipped from side to side.

"Why so glum, Hugo?" the bear asked, with a note almost of joy in his voice. Hugo just pointed his long muzzle at the centre of the river.

"You're overthinking the problem. My old papa used to tell me that when you have thought about a problem deeply and you can't see any solution, then go back to using brute – (well he really said bear) force. I've been talking to M. L'Ane here and that's exactly what we should be doing, so let's get started." Ursian's enthusiasm was contagious, and Hugo stood up, his tail gently wagging with optimism.

CHAPTER 50

Roland reached the top of the hill above the river by mid-afternoon. He had ridden hard all day, stopping only to pick up some supplies. Both Marron and Greco were anxious to please their master and had pushed themselves onwards. He was about to make his descent to Pont St. Pierre when he saw deep ruts which led down from the road obviously made recently by heavy carts. Intrigued, he stopped and dismounted, looking down into the river valley. From his viewpoint, he could see only the far bank and a flooded meadow, but he could *hear* animal sounds, dogs barking, what sounded like a bear's loud roar and some aggressive snorting, perhaps a wild boar. There were many horses neighing too and – was he hearing things? – a lion's roar. All the sounds were indistinct, mingled with the loud roar of the rushing waters below.

He quickly realised that the sounds were not random but had a pattern to them. He had been assured by Athina that he would be able to understand all animals in time and he had already developed a good understanding of Marron and Greco. Although he was too far away to make out the sounds clearly, he knew that they were talking to each other. He remounted Marron and gingerly made his way down the steep slope. He caught fleeting glances of what was happening below him, but it was not until he reached the shepherd's hut that he fully appreciated what he had heard. His incredulous eyes saw that most of the land, bar a small dry patch immediately below, was awash; the fast-flowing river was in flood on either side. He also saw gaily painted wagons neatly arranged on the small patch of remaining dry ground, but his gaze was drawn to what was occurring near to the far bank.

A huge boar was struggling through the water with a small dog, a little white terrier, clinging to its back, a thick rope clamped in its jaws. The strange companions reached the far shore just ahead of several horses and all the animals stood shaking themselves dry. He could make out a group of dark-furred bears seated on the ground beneath a large tree.

They appeared to be arguing. In the middle of the turbulent current stood a giant Pyrenean bear, the water almost covering his shoulders, guiding other animals across. The gendarme shook his head in disbelief, then took out his telescope to confirm what he had seen – yes it was a unicorn that the beast was helping. Other, equally unlikely animals stood on the bank of the river… and a huge floppy-eared dog. He had found Hugo Hound.

Moored in the calmer water was a makeshift ferry and Roland's eye traced the rope that the boar and his small companion had been pulling all the way back to the improvised vessel. There was another rope attached but this time it was looped around a tree some way up the hill, then round a second tree and back down to where the lions were standing. 'Good heavens' the officer thought aloud 'they're going to use *mechanics* to cross'. He looked at the river and saw then what his role must be. Quickly he rode down to join the great Hound. It was only when he got close to the bottom of the hill that he began to wonder if Athina's assurances that he would be treated as a friend were correct. Just how friendly were these three lions going to be for example? Realising that the time to ponder this had long gone he pressed on, while Marron tried valiantly not to betray his fear. Hugo glanced briefly at him then totally ignored the new arrival, returning to the task in hand. Roland could understand the Hound's barks. He was issuing instructions across the river: "Sangres, M. L'Ane says to walk round the tree over there to your left...your LEFT…yes, that's the one. Now walk back towards me until the rope is tight, yes that's fine; Ursian, can you harness up a couple of horses to that rope so that they can help Sangres? Good! Now, M. L'Ane, let's get the first of the wagons on board."

Roland was astonished when the great Hound stood on his hind legs as he harnessed up the Donkey – ah, this was M. L'Ane – using his front paws as easily as if they were human hands. Only when the wagon was on board and securely fastened (the Hound once more using his paws) did Hugo give his attention to the newcomer. Roland had dismounted and saluted him, unsure exactly what form of greeting would be appropriate in these circumstances.

"Good afternoon, I presume that you are Hugo Hound? I am Captain Roland Lebrun. I have been sent by Pellerin and Athina to assist you in any way I can."

Hugo wagged his tail excitedly and rubbed his huge head against the officer's thigh in greeting before throwing himself onto the ground, waving all four paws in the air excitedly. In an instant, the Hound was back on all four paws, looking, well, sheepish: "Sorry, old habits, you know. Thank you for coming; I need all the help I can get. We need to get those wagons and this lot" he waved a paw at the animals "as far away as quickly as possible."

"You're going to use this err ferry, right? So that the horses and that boar – Sangres Blacksnout isn't it? – will pull from that side and these lions here, they'll pull it back?" Hugo nodded, his face betraying a definite dog smile: "Yes, the lions volunteered to stay here – very unexpected that was, not like them at all." Roland saw that one of the lions had drawn a 'butcher's chart' of a unicorn in the mud. The leader was indicating desirable cuts to his followers who growled 'Oh yeah' each time he pointed to the chart.

Hugo introduced the gendarme to Messieurs Lucius, Fabius and Leonid first and then to M. L'Ane, the sad looking Donkey standing diffidently nearby: "We have no idea what his name is, and he's hardly said a word until today. However, we have now discovered how much he does know about ferries, river currents and mechanics."

"Very useful companion to have in the circumstances" agreed Roland. "I'll get on board the vessel. Once it hits that fast-flowing current it will need to be steered otherwise it might overturn or get swept away." The Donkey nodded sagely: "Yes indeed, they did have humans on the ferry at Monbezier although the river there was never as fast as this one. I think they spent most of the time chatting to the ladies rather than steering." He spoke in a slow, depressed tone, looking down: "Yes, that is a good idea. We were going to have to rely on pulling harder when the ferry hit the middle of the river. This will improve our chances a great deal, I believe. I do think though, M. Hugo –if you agree of course – that I should go back and forward on the ferry. I can call out to M. Sangres and M. Lucius how hard they should be pulling when we get to the faster current. I think the officer will be too busy to concentrate on that as well. However, I am but a humble beast of burden and I know…"

Hugo cut short the Donkey's rather tiresome self-deprecation. "Of course, of course. Capital idea M. L'Ane. I am sure that M. Roland will appreciate your help." Hugo looked meaningfully at the new arrival who nodded his agreement. "Right then, to work!"

The young officer walked to the bobbing 'vessel' and picked up one of two long poles lying, seemingly discarded, on the deck and resecured one in anticipation of a rough crossing. The poles were sturdy young tree trunks and seemed strong enough for the task he faced. They cast off and he poled the craft away from the land and across the flooded meadow. The shallow draught made this easy to achieve even with the weight of the wagon on board. The Donkey brayed out his instructions to Sangres and their speed picked up as the boar and his horse assistants took the strain.

Roland stayed at the back of the vessel digging the pole into the soft mud below. His vision was partially obscured by the wagon in the centre of the craft and he found that he was beginning to rely more and more on the Donkey's calls: "We're forty paces from the start of the fast water…thirty…twenty…ten. Sangres! Pull hard NOW. Lucius, more slack." Suddenly, they felt the impact of the torrent rushing upon the craft and pushing it downstream. Roland rammed his pole hard down into the riverbed, as hard as he could. Every time he pulled the pole up the craft would lurch farther downstream and the Donkey's commands became more urgent and strident: "Sangres, pull, pull harder. Lucius slacken off, no not enough. Sangres, big effort now. We're in the middle. NOW!" As they hit the middle of the current Roland braced himself, digging the pole into the river fiercely with all his strength. The vessel took a sudden violent lurch, tilting dangerously as the front rose from the water. The Donkey called to Sangres for a renewed effort and the craft inched slowly ahead towards the opposite shore. Roland dug in again then looked behind him. Standing there was an enormous bear, rivulets of water running over his thick dark fur. He was holding the second pole, mimicking Roland's every move. Heartened, the officer put all his might into steering the craft forwards until it left the strong current and reached the calm of the shallows. Donkey continued to shout instructions to Sangres and Lucius. "Ease off now Sangres, less slack Lucius" until he was satisfied that the ferry was near enough to firm ground that the wagon could be unloaded.

Roland courteously thanked M. L'Ane for his efforts and then looked behind him only to be soaked as Ursian deliberately shook himself dry without a word. The bear walked back into the waters again, wading out until it was deep enough then floating on his back as if he had not a care in the world.

The young officer noticed gendarme markings on the flank of one of the horses who came to manoeuvre the unloaded wagon but he said nothing. As soon as the wagon was safely ashore, Roland shouted to Hugo that he was ready to return. The Donkey trotted aboard once more and began to issue his orders to Lucius and Sangres, his loud harsh braying audible over a great distance.

Roland was a little put out by Ursian's behaviour. His help on the outward crossing had been invaluable but without the weight of the wagon on board the return journey would be much easier, and help would not be required. He set the pole in the water and steered for the opposite bank but was surprised by an icy cold spray of water as the huge bear climbed casually on board and seized the second pole, once again copying his every action. "A touch more to your left if you please M. Ursian" barked the Donkey. "We are aiming between those two trees directly ahead." Ursian merely grunted his assent: "Get ready, we are going to hit the current, Lucius, pull harder NOW. M. Lebrun, more to your left." This time when they hit the fastest flowing water they cut straight through it with only the slightest deviation from their course.

When they reached the shore, Hugo ran down to greet them, hugely excited, his thick tail wagging. "Ursian, this is Roland Lebrun. He is the help that we were promised. Captain Lebrun, if you have not been formally introduced, this is…sorry that *was* Ursian LeGrand." Ursian had turned abruptly and was loping up the hill, shaking his damp fur. He did not look back. "I apologise for him. Ursian doesn't like humankind very much. He has had a bad experience with them."

"Don't apologise Hugo. I know his story. Gilles Barbier told me. I fear we can only make one more crossing before we lose the light. Let's get one of the supply wagons over there." Hugo nodded his agreement: "I didn't want to send it across first in case the plan failed. Lucius, once the supplies are over there would you and the lads like to swim across for the evening meal then you can swim back here later?"

Lucius demurred: "Err, not really Hugo. How about you leave our food here for tonight - and our breakfast of course. We'll guard the other wagons for you. They'll be safe as'ouses with us. We lions are the Kings of Beasts aren't we lads?" The 'lads' agreed loudly. In the distance Ursian could clearly be heard chuckling to himself.

"That's uncommonly thoughtful of you Lucius, I suppose without having to swim back in the morning you will be fully rested and raring to go?"

"Exacterly" roared all three lions in unison at which a fully belly laugh could be clearly heard somewhere nearby

Hugo unloaded the meals for the lions and then Donkey helped Marron and Greco to pull the supply wagon onto the ferry and made it very secure. Hugo would make this crossing because he would distribute the evening meal. Just as the craft left the shore, Ursian ambled on causing a sharp dip at one corner. The Donkey once more took command. Hugo mused quietly: "Those lions are up to something. I just know it and I wish I knew what it was" but Ursian's only response was an almost inaudible chuckle before they all concentrated on the task in hand and steered the vessel through the rough water.

Roland watched as Hugo and Ursian fed the animals, fascinated by how organised everything appeared to be. When Athina had pleaded with him he wasn't quite sure what form his help might take. However, one thing was clear to him now, he would not be leading the animals. Hugo was most definitely in charge and the strange Donkey was every bit as competent a seaman as any on the frigates the gendarme had sailed on. The officer prepared his own evening meal and after he had eaten and attended to Marron and Greco's needs he was invited to join Hugo, Ursian and Sangres for their nightly discussions. Roland could sense the hostility emanating from the bear and felt he should try to clear the air: "Ursian Legrand, I know that you have suffered at the hands of humans, but I too am Paladin."

Ursian was clearly not impressed by this and instead of responding to Roland he addressed himself to Hugo: "He must think we are stupid. Of course, he's Paladin. How else could he understand us? Ask him to tell us what use he thinks he can be to us. Eugh, humans" he spat out the last words. Hugo looked at his companion and rolled his eyes in despair.

"I am a gendarme by profession" Roland continued, determined to make his point. "I was instructed by my commanding officer, General Destrier, to assist you. What connection there is between you and Destrier is beyond my knowledge, but it was Athina who asked for my assistance in the first place. I promised her that I would do everything in my power to help you.

Hugo, you know you are being hunted by Louis-Philippe de Garenne. I hope I can protect you. I am not alone, there are two other humans following behind who will also help. What limited time we have *we must use wisely*. If we all work *as a team* we should be clear of here by the day after tomorrow."

Ursian remained silent, hunched and exuding malevolence but Hugo agreed: "You're right. Pellerin said that we should cross this river and head for safety as soon as possible. Having a real human amongst us means that Ursian and I won't need to change shape so often. You've got to be happy about that at least, old friend?"

However, Ursian's expression did not change so Hugo continued unabashed: "Right then, as soon as the sun is up tomorrow we get started, agreed?" Satisfied, Hugo barked a final good night to Lucius and his lads across the river, telling them everyone was having an early night so that they could be ready the following morning. He listened for their reply but above the sound of the water the only sound that could be heard was loud snoring.

CHAPTER 51

Next day the crossings began after the lions had finally woken from their deep sleep. Although the meadows on both banks were slowly draining, the current was as treacherous as before and each crossing was fraught with danger. It was only Donkey's ability to judge the flow of the water that prevented catastrophe. He could spot tree trunks careering down the river and instruct his 'crew', both onboard and ashore when and how to take actions to avoid these hazards. By the end of the day only two wagons remained to be transported. Roland was well satisfied by the progress being made. If all went to plan, they would be clear of the river by midafternoon the following day whereas Louis-Philippe would have only just arrived at St. Pardoux.

It was the final crossing that caused the most problems. Hugo's plan had been that the lions would remain until everyone had crossed and then swim over once the ferry was safely at the other side. This was thwarted when Lucius insisted that they, as Kings of the Beasts should be carried across on the last ferry as a reward for all their hard work. "But Lucius" begged Hugo "we really do need you here. If we don't have you all controlling the rope at the back of the ferry it will spin out of control. Not even Ursian and M. Roland would be able to save it and the wagon and everyone on board, including you, would end up in the water." But Lucius shook his mane. The lions had to cross by ferry.

To Hugo's great surprise, Ursian intervened at this point: "I think the lions deserve a bit of a break, Hugo. They've worked hard over the last few days. There are plenty of horses over there. We can send two or three back over here. They're good swimmers. If you can stay here to deal with the harness, then they can swim back over with you?" Hugo agreed readily although he was a little confused. Usually when there was any argument with the lions Ursian settled it with a stern look. Now he was arguing in their favour, agreeing with Lucius whom he normally called a 'lazy furbag' or at best a pampered overgrown cat.

Three of the horses that Gilles Barbier had purchased happily agreed to swim back and be harnessed. They were proud to be asked to help. Hugo got them ready and instructed them in what they must do. Donkey and Roland then got the final wagon safely on board as the lions lined up at the water's edge to embark. Ursian sauntered down towards them and Lucius looked up at him and said quietly: "Thanks for that. You're a real mate. Not a word to anyone eh?"

"Not a word Lucius, they'll never hear from me that you lot are terrified of water. So, who is the King of the Beasts, would you say? Easy question – I shall give you a clue, the answer begins with a 'B'."

"Bears" mumbled the lion ungraciously.

"Sorry, didn't catch that" laughed Ursian. "BEARS" growled the lion.

"That's better, you agree, don't you?" Ursian glared at Fabius and Leonid who feebly raised their paw in assent, muttering 'yeah'. "Louder" roared Ursian so that those on either bank heard a sudden 'Yeah'. "Alright, now get on board." Ursian chuckled to himself, then caught sight of the human helper and glowering once more, he put his back into the task at hand although Roland noticed that every time Ursian took his pole from the water he managed to skillfully spray water over the lions.

As soon as the crossing was complete, Hugo unharnessed the horses and the four swam quickly across, negotiating the fast running waters without too much trouble. The officer waited for the

Hound to arrive "If we managed to get across using that thing as a ferry then I am sure our pursuer could do the same. I think it may be time to get rid of it." Hugo agreed and assured his human companion that he knew someone who would be only too happy to arrange that.

As Hound and man hitched up all the wagons and put the animals back into their cages, Ursian busied himself beaching the craft and then proceeded to smash the rickety vessel into two pieces, then four, then eight. Finally, he picked up each remaining piece with both of his huge front paws, spun his whole body around whilst standing on his hind legs and threw the remains as far into the strong current as possible.

Roland's spirits were further lifted when he caught a glimpse of three figures leading horses down to the shepherd's hut. He was pleased that although he was sure they had seen him, they concealed themselves quickly. No waving, no shouting. Obviously, they had taken to heart the need to be more discreet, especially after their behaviour at the Auberge des Etoiles!

Whereas Roland had ridden hard to catch up with the caravan, attracting attention along the way, Athina led the girls by a circuitous path making detours to avoid the little hamlets and villages. All the while they had not seen a living soul and the haruspex was satisfied that their presence was undetected. Thus, they only reached the river in time to see Ursian destroying the ferry. Kate watched anxiously as he flung the remains far into the river. The girls watched as Hugo Hound and the remaining horses swam confidently across and they could see Roland talking to Hugo who then barked at the bear. Hugo looked tiny compared to the great animal. Ursian then dragged the ferry ashore and started to smash it up. He threw the remains into the river and the caravan set off on its way, but Kate was agitated:

"Why did they do that? How shall we get across now?"

Athina nodded: "They need time. Louis-Philippe can travel much faster than them so anything to slow him down is most welcome. Your brother is still some distance away, but I would suggest that you prepare yourself for when he does arrive. The shepherd's hut is empty. No home comforts, girls – but it will keep you warm and dry and there is a fireplace where you can light a fire to cook. No beds either I am afraid, but the floor is dry. You'll be out of sight from the riverbank and hidden from the road. Light only a very small fire so that it won't be seen. If someone sees the smoke they will assume that the shepherd has come back. We will get you both across that river, don't worry. Just not yet."

Kate and Amélie had learned from Roland that an army marches on its stomach – in other words to keep well stocked up with supplies but found that they now had only enough for the remainder of that day. This included some wine, but they had wisely decided that after the episode in St. Pardoux the last thing that Amélie needed was wine, so when they sat down together for yet another meagre evening meal, this was not on the menu. Athina had flown off as usual when it was drawing dark and had returned some time before the girls woke up.

She had no news, although she hinted that she had been up to the High Valley:

"Now" said the owl haughtily, "I am going to take a rest, yes Amélie, even a haruspex needs some sleep. I suggest that you stock up on provisions as I think you may be stuck here for quite a few more days. I saw a notice up in the town that workmen are needed to repair the bridge, although work does not start until tomorrow. Hugo and the caravan have at least some time without being worried about their pursuers."

Kate had been very disappointed to see Roland disappearing into the distance when she was physically incapable of following him without a means to cross the river. She decided to go early into the nearest town, Pont St. Pierre, to collect some supplies and left Amélie on watch and Athina dozing in a tree, hidden by the leaves. She found it easier to sleep as an owl after spending so much of her time in that form.

Kate too saw the notice about the bridge rebuilding, a guaranteed five days' work was being offered and she was delighted. It meant that Louis-Philippe would be stuck on this side of the water for quite some time giving the animals a good head start. She was tempted to tear down the notice to prevent anyone from applying but realised that, at this time of year in a poor community, the news would already have gone out far and wide. She then glanced across the small square in the town centre towards the Town Hall and noticed about 20 men standing outside in groups, obviously hoping to be chosen for the work on offer. 'Oh well' she thought 'it will take probably another day at least to choose suitable workmen, putting the work back yet again'. She understood these things could not be rushed in her country.

She bought provisions from the tiny boulangerie/épicerie/bar in the little town; bread, a little wine, some dried meats and sausages, together with local cheeses, fruit and delicious local honey and made her way slowly back to their little encampment. At the hut Amélie was waiting and in the clear sunlight of midday they could now see the destruction which Ursian had wrought on the ferry. She had watched as he had smashed planks in two and wrenched wooden sleepers apart but now she truly appreciated the immense force that had been used.

The remaining broken pieces which had been thrown into the river were now tangled in a sunken tree, much closer to her side of the river which further demonstrated the powerful throwing ability of the animal. 'Thank goodness that he is on our side' she thought, a little concerned that the fiercesome giant was now Roland's travelling companion.

Nothing much happened that day and the few travellers that did arrive from time to time surveyed the scene and went off again, either in the direction from which they had come or off downstream attempting to find another crossing place. Some, with a look of puzzlement and a lot of head-scratching, would look at the shattered remains of the ferry but most shrugged their shoulders – broken bridges and defunct ferries were not an unknown occurrence on the angry river.

Around mid-afternoon on the day after they arrived, as the girls were dozing in the weak sunshine behind the little house, Pellerin arrived and settled in a tree whose branches overhung the doorway of the hut. Athina woke abruptly and went to speak with him, nodding in agreement as she listened to the great eagle's words. The great bird eventually bowed to the girls then swooped off, making a huge spiral and dropping steeply towards the river, circling and, with a noisy flap of his enormous wings, disappearing up into the sky. Athina returned with a frown on her face and they could see that she was concerned. Without any prompting, she explained: "Louis-Philippe should be here by nightfall. More worryingly, the *Loup Garou* which has been spotted is definitely Brochard. Pellerin says that he is now fully-grown and close to the height of his powers. He can travel by day *and* by night. Until now the eagles have kept track of him without any effort but last night instead of resting as usual, he just kept travelling. Pellerin is summoning more eagles from the High Valley and he has sent one of the Eastern clan of eagles to gather reinforcements, He has even asked the Eastern owls to lend a... wing This is serious. I will join in the search at dusk myself, so I am afraid that you will be on your own. I am trusting you both to deal with Kate's brother as best you can. This is the point at which your task will begin in earnest."

Athina could see the look of concern growing in Kate's eyes and continued: "Yes, Brochard is a very real problem for us all. He will make for the High Valley. It is their instinct. They know that their ancestors lived there and, despite being the worst kind of mutant, they believe that the High Valley should still be their home too. The Guard Bears should deal with him."

Kate interrupted: "You said 'should' not 'will'. What happens if they don't?"

Athina tried to be reassuring: "I know you fear for your young man's safety but Ursian has vowed that there will never be a repetition of the havoc wreaked by the Beast of Gévaudan. He knows more about those beings than any creature alive." Athina could see that the girl was unconvinced by this. "For your information, young lady, Lord Ursian is the head of the Clan that provide all the Guard Bears, they have always been Guardians of the High Valley, and he is the greatest Guard Bear of all. Do not assume that because something does not look like you, you are somehow superior."

Duly chastened, Kate bowed her head then turned to Amélie. She too was shocked that Brochard was now a fully-fledged *Loup Garou* and wanted to know how exactly one fought such a creature. Kate was reluctant to ask Athina for any further details but tried to convey a confidence she did not feel to her cousin. They would deal with Louis-Philippe when he arrived.

For the remaining hours of daylight without any other distractions, the girls watched the wild water of the river continue to rush down the valley but the low land at the water's edges gradually drained and there appeared now a muddy towpath some two or three metres wide where once only water had been. Then, just as the sun was setting low in the sky, Athina told them to make no sound or movement and they sat motionless as they waited anxiously: three horses were approaching. The hoof beats drew closer and they could hear Louis-Philippe's high-pitched nasal drawl as he berated André. He was ranting about a map and its inadequacies; a map André had seemingly purchased. With difficulty, the girls managed to repress the urge to giggle and gradually the sounds of the horses' hoofs receded towards the path which led to Pont St. Pierre.

As night finally fell, Athina left the girls but not before extracting a firm promise from them both that they would do nothing to put themselves in danger. They would simply watch over Kate's brother unless he posed a direct threat. "Remember, Kate" the owl said sternly "Roland will receive regular reports on your behaviour – from the eagles. Imagine how he will feel if he hears that you are putting yourself in danger? He will not be able to concentrate on the task in hand and that could mean serious consequences for us all."

CHAPTER 52

The journey from Neufchatel to St. Pardoux had taken almost three days instead of one day as predicted by Louis-Philippe. When they had finally reached the outskirts of the small town, the nobleman again insisted on André going ahead to "reconnoitre." On his return, Louis-Philippe again stressed the need for absolute secrecy. Innocently, the servant enquired if his master would be again using his false name 'Louis-Philippe Garenne' but apparently the young man now fancied using his mother's maiden name:

"I shall be Philippe, no, Louis Pompadour."

André groaned inwardly but smiled and congratulated his master on his inspired choice of name. Lodgings had been secured for himself at the *Auberge des Etoiles*, and for his master at the *Grand Hôtel d'Aquitania.* On their way into the town even Louis-Philippe remarked on the proliferation of Notices: 'No fires in the Town Square', 'No Eating in the Town Square',No Fairs', 'No Carnivals', 'No 'Menageries' (this last notice looking very new) and André's favourite 'No Travellers other than Gentlefolk or Persons on Official Business'Even unmarried couples were apparently forbidden from walking together without at least two chaperones. 'When I am Duc' thought the young man 'I'll get rid of that fool Lafitte-Dupont and replace him with someone like the mayor here, someone who knows how to keep order'.

In the evening, André found that he was the only guest at the auberge and after dining well with several glasses of local wine he began chatting with the proprietor. He gently coaxed from him that this was not a typical evening. It had been much busier the previous week.

"You get all types staying here. Last week I had had two young gentlewomen, sisters they were, proper ladies too. I couldn't believe my ears when I accidentally overhead that they had been at Waterloo! Didn't look old enough, they didn't."

At this André's interest was piqued: "That is interesting. I was there myself. I was in the army, an ADC to a general, sounds grand but to be honest I spent most of my time writing letters. What is interesting is that a couple of young *Vivandières.* helped my general to safety when he was wounded, and very brave they were. To my shame I cannot now remember their names." As André intended, the owner immediately went to find his register and began to look up the names of the young ladies who had been his guests.

"Yes, here it is. There was Jeanne; now she was very dark haired and then there was Simone, she was fairer and perhaps a little older. Their family name is Blanc. They were travelling with their governess, a Madame Dubois and a real governess she was indeed, if you know what I mean."

André feigned disappointment: "Oh, I don't recognise those names at all. It was rather a longshot anyway." He thought he had the answer but hid this with affability.

Slowly, over the course of the evening and several glasses of wine, André, without any prompting, heard about the annual turnover of the Inn, how much profit it made, who in the town was 'no better than she should be' and the goings on of the local schoolteacher. Why, mused André, was it always school masters and schoolmistresses who scandalised the locals? A more interesting snippet of gossip was that the local Gendarmerie Captain had taken quite a fancy to the darker of the Blanc sisters and from a further, more detailed description supplied by the innkeeper André was now sure that the 'Blanc' sisters were, in fact cousins of his acquaintance.

In his usual logical, thoughtful manner André tried to make sense of events: if it had been the girls, and he was fairly convinced it had been, then where was Roland? At the Gendarmerie barracks? Very possibly he would stay there, but surely, if he had been accompanying Catherine and Amélie he would have joined the other officer who had dined with them? The presence of this 'governess' also puzzled him; who was she? Then the name Dubois came back to him as he remembered that it had been a Madame Dubois who had been appointed governess to both girls after they had grown too old for the École Primaire in La Garenne.

They had been about ten years old then and this governess had remained with them until both girls were nearly eighteen. André had never actually met her because he had been travelling with the Duc to various wars for most of the time, but he recalled one letter from the many the Duc had received from home. Mlle. Catherine had added a polite recommendation that the education of herself and her cousin would benefit from the replacement of Madame Dubois as governess. Kate had been about thirteen at that time.

André remembered how the Duc had laughed heartily when he showed André that letter, praising his daughter's eloquence, grammar and even handwriting. The Duc had remarked that in fact her ability to write such a beautifully crafted letter was clear proof of Madame Dubois' skills as a teacher. The Duc had replied asking what benefits she expected from a different governess, perhaps more difficult lessons, or more Latin, to learn English or perhaps Ancient Greek history or advanced algebra? He had heard nothing further on the subject after that.

André, to satisfy his own curiosity, thought he might make some discreet enquiries at the local Gendarmerie but then reconsidered this course of action. Instead, he reached into his saddle bag and took out a small double-barreled pistol, which he cleaned thoroughly and having loaded it, he put into a pocket of his riding coat. He then took a beautifully tooled dagger from his saddle bag and put this in a specially made sheath inside his riding boot. Feeling well prepared, he murmured to himself: 'Yes my old friend, no matter what it takes' and he then retired for the night.

On the journey towards Pont St. Pierre the eagles were ever present; André caught sight of an old carriage, half concealed and abandoned near the road but made no comment. It struck him as perhaps significant, yet his master passed by without a second glance. By the time they were approaching the town, a full five days after leaving Neufchatel the sun was low in the sky. As they rode down the incline towards the town, Louis-Philippe took the opportunity to berate his servant over the inaccuracies of the map he himself had trusted so much. André, however, said nothing and when they reached the town they followed the old wooden signs indicating the 'Pont' to cross the river.

Of course, when they arrived at the point where once the stone bridge had been, there stood…nothing. André remembered having crossed the old bridge some years before but now there remained only the vestiges of the structure. A hand-made notice indicated that a temporary crossing was available further along the riverbank but before they went any further, André suggested they find accommodation for the night. His master summarily dismissed that idea:

"This is no time to be thinking of your creature comforts, man. We shall cross the river, and then and only then, think about making camp. Now fetch more supplies from the town. We have a lot of ground to make up due to your stupidity. We'll need plenty of food and get some good wine for once. I shall ride on ahead to this temporary crossing and wait there. Be quick" and without waiting for a response, the young nobleman rode off in the direction indicated by the crude sign.

The light was vanishing quickly at the river's edge when André caught up with Louis-Philippe once more. The young man waited on the bank where water lapped the muddy towpath. By lantern light they carefully skirted what appeared to be a lake until they saw a second sign pointing towards the river, showing a crude drawing of a boat without sails. Both men shone their lanterns in the direction indicated by this signpost but saw nothing; instead they heard sounds of a raging torrent. This finally dissuaded the young nobleman from venturing further. He was confident that they would cross the river the following morning, so they found a patch of dry grassland above the riverbank and Louis-Philippe ordered the long-suffering André to light a fire and set about preparing an acceptable meal.

Meanwhile, Kate and Amélie watched the glow of the fire below near the riverbank. Satisfied that nothing would happen that night they left their vigil to return to the shepherd's hut and lit their own fire. They even felt safe lighting one of their lanterns which allowed Kate to check and recheck her pistols. After they had eaten, Amélie could stand it no longer and had to ask - she could see that her cousin was hatching a plan.

"I am, err, waiting for the moon to rise so I can go down there and have a look around" Kate replied and even in the gloom she could sense Amélie's alarm.

Eventually her cousin could contain herself no longer: "Kate" she hissed, holding back the scream she wanted to utter "I am ashamed of you. You made a solemn promise to Athina but as soon as her back is turned, you are going to break it just like you always break your promises to my maman. I ask you, for once, to keep your word and don't do anything stupid! If the Guard Bears can keep a promise for hundreds of years, you can keep one for five minutes."

Kate was totally thrown by this unexpected and frankly out of character outburst. She was usually confident that her cousin would go along with any of her hare-brained schemes. Amélie had been her willing accomplice since their schooldays. She immediately set about soothing her cousin's obvious distress by explaining what she had in mind by 'having a look around'. Amélie remained unconvinced that "technically speaking" the plan didn't break Kate's promise. She had to remind Kate that not only had she promised Athina but Roland too. He had only allowed them to go on this journey *if they did as they were told.* "But Amélie" Kate retorted "I seem to remember that you treated that as a huge joke." The other girl could not resist giggling at this and reluctantly agreed that she would go along with the first part of Kate's plan but would see how that went before agreeing to the rest.

As the almost full moon rose in the sky the two girls cautiously made their way down towards the riverbank where Kate's brother and André had pitched camp. Amélie took with her a carbine and a pistol. Should Louis-Philippe emerge from his tent, she could warn Kate. Meanwhile her cousin crept cautiously towards the horses, tethered to a tree near the water. Athina had taught her the correct way to address horses to make them trust her and she was confident that they would make no sound to give her away. Slowly she untied the reins and still whispering gently, led the three horses off into the darkness.

When they were quite a distance along the towpath, Kate indicated to the animals that they should set off along the riverbank, assuring them of some good grazing in that direction. The horses nodded their heads silently and moved off, disappearing into the night.

After a brief wait to make sure that they had not been detected, the girls began to make their way back up the hill, the path lit in the darkness by the unexpected appearance of hundreds of tiny pinpricks of light in the grass – fireflies. Back at the hut they settled down for the night, having made sure that their own horses were tethered safely.

Next morning, they managed to brew a little coffee over the embers of their fire, careful not to allow any smoke to rise. They were able to watch unobserved from their vantage point and saw André, usually the first to stir, stretching as he went over to where the horses should have been tethered. Unhurriedly he looked around and then looked up sharply, his eyes seeming to connect with theirs and then he strolled towards his master's tent and shook the front flap violently; the girls could hear his voice clearly as he shouted: "The horses, the horses! They've gone Sir."

Louis-Philippe came out of his tent pulling on his breeches and surveyed the bank, shouting angrily at André for failing to tether the animals securely and once he had managed to struggle into his boots and donned a jacket, they both set off in search of their animals. From the hoof prints in the muddy earth beside the river they could see that the beasts had wandered downstream, but André was careful where he walked to obscure any other prints which might have been obvious.

Realising that the horses must be some distance away by now, with her brother and André in pursuit, Kate decided to put the second part of her plan into action. Amélie was rather more cautious but when she saw, using the old Duc's precious telescope how far the two men would have to go in pursuit of their animals, she felt it would be safe to accompany her cousin. Hastily they scrambled down the hill to the tents, Amélie taking up position behind a small rise with a good view of the riverbank stretching away so that she could act as lookout. When Kate arrived at her brother's tent she found exactly what she had been hoping for: the musket which he had had specially made at great expense. It was beautifully chased in silver on the barrel and it was his pride and joy.

She took this, along with a good supply of powder and ammunition, his small silver travelling clock, heavily engraved with the family crest and his initials too (she might sell it, she laughed to herself) and a rather evil looking, long bladed knife which he normally kept in a leather scabbard slung around his waist. Next, she emptied all her brother's fine shirts onto the ground right at the river's edge. Was it her fault if they floated away? Moving on to André's tent, she left alone his possessions but helped herself enthusiastically to the provisions he had stored in there, filling a leather valise with as much bread, cheese and dark cured ham as she could carry as well as wine. She made her way back towards Amélie, who was waiting, stiff with nerves and anxious to be off. There was still no sign of the two men although Amélie reported she could see a pair of eagles, some long way off still, which both girls knew could be a warning of Louis-Philippe's return. Kate presented the musket to her cousin who eyed it rather professionally and began to aim it at various objects, gauging the weight of the weapon and generally appearing rather too keen on having an opportunity to use it.

"Come on" muttered Kate "You will have plenty of time for that later" and carrying the bulging valise between them they climbed back up the hill to their vantage point. Staring downstream she could see the eagles high over the river as tiny dots in the distance. However, with the telescope she could make out the figures of her brother and André dejectedly making their way back to camp, leading the horses behind them.

"Kate?" asked Amélie laughing "what will happen if we get caught?"

Kate laughed too. "Well for a start we won't get caught and anyway, the horses weren't stolen, they 'liberated' themselves for a while. The musket, well that was bought with money set aside to maintain the Château. In my new position (well nearly) as Steward of the Eleanor Bequest it will be up to me to dispose of it. Oh, yes, and the nearest Gendarmerie is based at…guess where? St. Pardoux, I believe, dear cousin, you know the captain there?"

“Ah, I see” replied her cousin, with a tiny smirk “So, if all else fails, it will be up to me to ‘negotiate’ with Captain Belaudie on your behalf? Now how could I do that?”

At this, both girls collapsed in silent laughter, tears running down their cheeks, glad of this chance to release their tensions.

CHAPTER 53

Whilst Kate was preparing a meal of stolen bread and delicious fresh goats' cheese, to be washed down with fresh coffee, Amélie busied herself with making a thick muddy paste from topsoil and water which she used to smother the intricate silverwork on the musket. Kate looked quizzically at her cousin for an explanation, but Amélie simply said: "It's so bright and shiny. We might as well put up a sign saying we are here. Look, nothing will reflect on it now."

As a tired and deflated Louis-Philippe and his companion arrived back at their camp, from the opposite direction, came a small party of men, sitting on the back of a farm cart pulled by two oxen. The cart came to a halt close to the tents of the travellers and the men began to unload timbers, tools and long thick coils of rope onto the bank, singing and laughing amongst themselves. They were shocked to see the shattered remains of the makeshift ferry on the opposite side of the river. Louis-Philippe was also looking towards the wreckage of the ferry. In the confusion with the horses he had not realised that his plans had already been scuppered, the vessel was no more than a pile of firewood now. Leaving André to deal with the workmen, Kate's brother went back into his tent only to emerge a moment later screaming: "You thieves! Give me back my belongings, my clothes, my musket. Mark my words, you will be arrested. I will have you all executed."

One of the workmen stopped his task briefly to point out the pile of sodden, muddy clothes nearby, many of which were now floating slowly away. The white-faced nobleman was speechless while

André tried to gather up what clothes he could, spreading them on nearby bushes to dry. The distraught nobleman watched in despair as the white shapes disappeared for ever downstream and then began again his verbal assault on the laughing workmen. Eventually they had had enough and one of the men, a bearded giant in thick dusty trousers and a dark red woollen shirt took up his shovel and advanced menacingly on the red-faced Louis-Philippe. Fearing for his life, the frustrated young man retreated to his tent. Well, sulking *might* help.

Meanwhile, André tried to calm the situation by approaching the foreman of the gang of workers. The foreman said that he too had been in the Grande Armée, in the Sappers or Engineers' Corp which made him an ideal choice for bridge building. This enabled the two ex-soldiers to strike up an immediate rapport. The foreman explained that they were going to build a temporary bridge and then complete a more substantial, and hopefully, more resilient structure during the summer months when the river subsided sometimes to a mere trickle. The work would now be delayed as they had intended to use the ferry to transport the heavy timbers out into mid-stream where the broken pillars of the original bridge still rested on the riverbed. Now they would have to fetch even more wood to build a pontoon on which to transport these timbers. When everything was offloaded, the men sat on the ground to wait for the return of the cart with yet more supplies. Some then started work on a ramp that would connect from the riverbank to the first of the pillars, whilst several more started work on far more important structure: benches and a table for their lunch.

At exactly midday, which was announced by the bells of the church in Pont St. Pierre, all work ceased. The workmen sat down on the benches and prepared to have their lunch, which was wrapped in gaily coloured cloths and had been stored in large willow baskets in the shade of a tree. They immediately invited André to join them as they gathered that the two men now had no supplies. They ignored

Louis-Philippe, who remained sulking in his tent. The food was rustic and simple with bread, some cured meat, radishes and of course red wine, locally produced. Whilst they ate, André asked about the new structure to be built and whether something permanent could not be made from stone perhaps. The foreman shook his head:

"Happens every year…well for the last few years it has. There used to be a stone bridge in the town, but the blessed army blew that up to try and stop the English. Didn't do any good though. Wellington's lot just bypassed the town anyway and built a wooden bridge here. It was good enough for their needs but as soon as the river got full like this, it got washed away. We're a poor community.

We can't afford to rebuild in stone, but we will charge a toll for people to use this one. It gets washed away every time the river floods so then we rebuild it using the toll money, see. We'll never actually raise enough money to have the new bridge in the town anyway and the ferry, well the ferry is risky. The current here is much too strong most of the time. Also" and here he winked broadly at André "me and the other lads know we have guaranteed jobs here every year." Satisfied that he had supplied an unassailably sensible answer, the foreman poured them both more wine.

Occasionally, Louis-Philippe would risked poking his head out of his tent, looking longingly at the groaning table set for the workmen and at André drinking the copious if rough red wine but one day soon *when he was the Duc de Garenne* he would not have to beg food from these peasants. Sometimes being noble was hungry work.

Eventually the workmen got back to their tasks, sawing and carrying timbers back and forth with backslapping good humour. A small pontoon was established and floated out to the first stump in the river. Two of the younger workmen lashed together for safety climbed onto the pillar's broken summit and from the top they could lift some of the timbers from the ramp which had been built out from the bank. It was slow and sometimes dangerous work but after a day the first of the spans was in place.

His hunger now sated by the substantial lunch, André strolled back to the tents and his still-seething master. "Whilst you have been gorging your face, I have been sitting here starving, starving do you hear! How long are they going to take to build this wretched bridge?"

André, rather languidly – for the local wine was strong – replied: "Well, if all goes well, I believe it will take them 2/3 more days." At this his master erupted, his face contorted:

"And what are we supposed to eat in the meantime? These…these damned peasants stole all our food – no don't tell me it wasn't them. I know what these people are like."

André regarded Louis-Philippe almost pityingly: "Sir, I imagine that if we ride into Pont St. Pierre, we should be able to obtain more supplies."

Far from placating his master, this made the young man even more angry: "If that's the case, then why did you not ride there immediately this morning and buy food, you idiot? No, no you thought it best to let me starve while you consorted with those oafs, using your so-called military background to ingratiate yourself."

"But Sir" replied André mildly. "Did you yourself not tell me to leave all the thinking to you? I have been awaiting your ..." He got no further before his master roared at him:

"GET SOME FOOD" but André was in no mood for his master's ridiculous behaviour: "Thank you but I have already eaten. In fact I'm completely full."

"Go……goooo now" roared the young man, spittle flying from his mouth and André, having provoked his master sufficiently, calmly fetched his horse and the pack animal and rode very slowly in the direction of Pont St. Pierre.

From their position above the riverbank, Kate and Amélie watched this pantomime. They too had eaten well at lunch. Once André was out of sight of Louis-Philippe, he looked up into the sky searching for eagles. Whilst doing this he caught at the corner of his eye a glint, a reflection coming from high on the hill above. His attention was distracted from the flash of light when he saw not one but two pairs of eagles. One pair, as usual were high above Louis-Philippe's tent. The other pair were lazily circling directly above the spot where he had seen the reflection. His gaze was drawn to one of these eagles, which although far away, seemed much larger than all the rest. 'I'd like to see that bird close up. It must be a magnificent sight' he thought. The glint of light appeared once more, quite briefly, then he saw nothing more as he made his way into town.

He knew he would have plenty of time to ponder over this and the other events of the day because like all country towns, the shops would be closed until around four in the afternoon. Undoubtedly Louis-Philippe was not aware of this. The thought of his master trapped in his tent, hungry and forced to listen to the banter and laughter of common workmen brought a smile to his lips.

He was lucky and found a small café open and settled down with some coffee to wait. He knew for certain that the horses had been released deliberately because he had securely tethered them the night before. They were valuable animals yet the 'thief' was not interested in stealing them. Rather it seemed that their release was a distraction, but to what purpose? The food had been stolen from his tent but nothing else, for example the large amount of coin which he had brought with him for the journey. No, they had a specific target, a purpose, that musket. Everything else was done to disguise that, and of course to irritate the young nobleman.

'Well, that narrows down the suspects' he thought. 'Captain Lebrun? Unlikely; he might have wanted to disarm Louis-Philippe, but he would have stayed to arrest him surely. No, the sets of footprints André had seen in the mud beside the horses' hoof marks made perfect sense now. Small, dainty footprints which had disappeared at the start of the path leading upwards while those of the horses had continued by the riverside intermingled at times with some very strange paw prints and deep ruts. That left only two suspects: the "Blanc" sisters. He dismissed the thought that Roland might be with them. Anyone handpicked by General Destrier would not have let them give away their position so easily. 'If you were here Captain Lebrun then you're long gone and who ever took the musket did it to protect you. With that weapon, Louis-Philippe would have had an advantage over you; now he has only a single shot pistol'.

André let his mind wander as he collected the fresh provisions and started back towards the river. The eagles caught his eye once more. They constantly intrigued him. He recalled his fascination with the coat of arms of the House of Garenne when he had first arrived at the Château. The arms bore a representation of the Château itself with a bear and an owl in the two bottom corners. Above the Château were two eagles. He had asked the Duc what this meant: "It's believed that Eleanor herself designed it; legend has it that the Château represents her and all her successors but as for the rest well no-one really knows." André remarked that it appeared to him that the eagles were protecting the Château… protecting her successors perhaps?

"Yes, do you know I have never really thought of it like that, but I suppose that's as good an explanation as any."

Now there were a pair of eagles watching Louis-Philippe and a second pair protecting Eleanor's successor. He smiled to himself as he realised this. When he arrived back at the spot where he had first seen a flash of light he concentrated very hard and was sure he could see tiny movements. In direct line of sight of whoever was up there but unseen from the river camp, he stopped his horse on the track, turned to face the direction of the glinting reflection and doffed his hat ceremoniously, making an extravagant bow from the waist. He then rode on to face the wrath of his master.

Looking down, Amélie turned to her cousin: "Did you see that? What was that about?" Kate thought for a moment: "It must be André's way of telling us that he's spotted us. He wants us to be more careful. If he has seen us, then maybe Louis-Philippe could as well." At this Amélie shook her head vigorously: "No, I have not taken my eyes off him since André left and he has not once looked in this direction; he mostly stayed in the tent in fact. The only way he will know is if André tells him – do you think he might? Do you think that he knows it's us?"

Kate reassured her: "No, Amélie, André will say nothing. I trust him. He is sworn to protect me; I know just how smart he really is and before he died, papa told me the truth about him. Amongst the many services he performed for my father he was his spymaster. The best there ever was apparently." However, she heeded André's silent warning and placed the telescope out of sight. The two girls settled down once more to watch the riverbank. They saw André's return and from her brother's angry gesticulations, Kate could see he was far from happy. The workmen packed up and left in the late afternoon and as dusk finally became night they watched André light a fire. Having assured themselves that the men were seated at the rough table made by the workmen, their lantern illuminating a large plate of delicious looking food, the girls themselves left to do the same, washing their meal down some of her brother's fine wine.

Amélie did get some this this time, but not much. They went back to their watch as the moon rose and saw the two men seated at either end of the makeshift table, obviously not speaking at all.

"Are we planning another visit to their camp?" enquired Amélie sweetly.

"No, I think not. We can have a night off. It will take those workmen a few days to finish the bridge, so my brother is going nowhere fast. If we play too many tricks even he might get a bit suspicious. He obviously blames those workmen for what happened down there – we don't want to disabuse him now, do we?" As they laughed quietly there was a gentle flapping of wings nearby and Athina landed almost beside them, and in the blink of an eye, stood shimmering by the fire.

"I hear you two have been upsetting Louis-Philippe? Catherine, I believe I can safely say you are the first horse thief in the long and distinguished history of the House of Garenne. No, don't worry ladies, I think in the circumstances your forebears would be proud of you both." Kate smiled at this, both girls pleased that although Athina knew, she wasn't angry. Kate's first words naturally were: "How is Roland? Is he quite safe?"

"He's fine but they are travelling very slowly as you can imagine. The eagles spotted Brochard late this afternoon so at least we know where *he* is now. He is being tracked day and night and is still making for the High Valley. This is good news in a way for he cannot have detected Hugo's scent yet. Anyway, I will be seeing Roland tonight. Do you have any messages for him?"

Suddenly, the girl's eyes welled with tears she herself did not expect: "Please tell him I am thinking of him, all the time, and he must do nothing too dangerous."

"Of course, my dear." said Athina with unaccustomed gentleness "but well, leading a convoy of talking animals to a destination unknown to him could be considered rather dangerous." She smiled briefly before adding: "I was quite concerned when Aiguillin told me that he believes André Lacoste has seen you both here. That's why I came rather than staying with Hugo. I just wanted to make sure you were both safe and sound. Pellerin knows of this Lacoste and is certain of his loyalty to you.

The eagles assure me that he knows of their presence and regularly checks that they are in place. Your brother, Kate, is blissfully unaware of anything but his own discomfort. Obviously whatever Lacoste thinks, he has been keeping his own counsel."

"Athina, I am very touched by your concern for us. I swear we are in no danger. I know we can outsmart my brother and besides he is stuck down there for a couple of days at least. As for André, well my father trusted him literally with his life. Indeed, if it had not been for him and Lucien Lecaron, my father would have been left to die. I trust him totally. However, there are far more important matters than our wellbeing" and with this she hugged Athena with real feeling – although it was like grasping air – and Amélie kissed her cheek too. The witch stood for a moment in silence unused to such demonstrative behaviour, then slowly raised her arms above her head. The movement distracted the girls' eyes sufficiently for them to miss the moment of her transition and with a flutter of her beautiful wings, she flew off into the night sky, gaining height over the river beyond and headed off in the direction of the caravan, and the High Valley. When she had disappeared, Amélie remarked: "Do you know, cousin, if I did not know better, I might believe that strange creature cares about us."

Shortly afterwards, Amélie left the hut and went over to their vantage point just in time to see the lanterns in both tents below being extinguished. Satisfied, she returned to the hut and she and Kate settled down for the night.

CHAPTER 54

Despite Roland's efforts in getting the caravan across the river, and Ursian's growing respect for the human's determination, they were both still uncomfortable around each other and preferred to speak through Hugo. At least, the gendarme consoled himself, Ursian had at last stopped calling him "the human" although the bear still could not bring himself to address the officer by name.

The journey was very slow after crossing the river, sometimes less than a league a day, for the road was in poor condition and was becoming much steeper. It had been washed away in places by the heavy rains. Often the young officer would join Ursian and Sangres in helping to drag the wagons out of the deep ruts in the roadway, but still Ursian scarcely acknowledged his presence. The three lions, Lucius, Favius and Leonid helped too, trying to make up for their behaviour on the ferry. Occasionally they even thought it prudent to cower a little when Ursian was nearby – thus the balance of power was maintained, egos remained unbruised.

Although there had been no visits from the eagles, Athina kept them informed of events and they were aware that Louis-Philippe was currently stranded on the far bank of the river. Ursian spent what little spare time he had staring fixedly at the sky, observing distant specks in the distance and occasionally cocking an ear, then nodding sagely. Athina had also visited to warn them that a *Loup Garou,* confirmed as being Brochard, had been spotted and the eagles tracking him had temporarily lost him. Hugo looked startled at the mention of a *Loup Garou* but Ursian laid a paw comfortingly on his head: "I will explain all about these creatures tomorrow, best not to talk about them in the darkness." Better was the news, however, that it would probably take Louis-Philippe and André at least another few days to cross the River Adour. Having told them all this, Athina became quiet and thoughtful for a moment before speaking directly to Ursian: "I have to tell you, Lord Ursian, that I bring even more bad news for you.

We have had reports that the travelling fairground in which you were held captive for so many years…well I fear that your paths may soon cross. I must implore you, my friend, to put the needs of our travellers above your need for vengeance."

Ursian was visibly shaken by this news and the others could see his anger rising as he stood up slowly to his awesome full height, remaining on his enormous hind paws and let out a deep rumbling roar, displaying his terrifying gleaming teeth. He stood for a moment, his huge paws clenched and then sat down heavily upon a nearby log, clearly making a great effort to control his rage. For several minutes, he sat clenching and unclenching his huge paws, the sharp claws almost impaling his leathery palms as he growled to himself:

"Athina, I give you my solemn promise as a Bear that I shall do nothing to endanger the success of this mission by losing control. We have come too far to risk failing now, we are so close to home."

"Thank you, thank you my dear old friend" replied Athina "I know how difficult it must be for you to have made that promise, but you are amongst friends; allow Hugo and Roland here to guide you and I know they will provide you with wise counsel."

Satisfied that Ursian would remain calm, Athina turned her attention to other matters, asking after the health of the other travellers and then she made ready to leave. When he saw this, the Captain asked her if she would take a message to Kate for him. "Of course, but I must be getting forgetful in my old age. I have a message from her but probably it's the same message you wish me to take. She said that she is thinking of you all the time and not to do anything to endanger yourself. Now, wasn't that exactly what you wanted to say to her?" Roland could only nod. "I can read your mind my friend, just as I can with many other Paladins, and that includes Kate of course. I can sometimes even read the minds of human Poursuivants, but I prefer not to. I made the mistake of reading Amélie's mind in St. Pardoux when she met your friend and frankly, well her mother would be furious with her."

Athina laughed her strange owl-like laugh when she said this and then flew off into the night only to return a moment later: "By the way, young man, your future wife is now a very accomplished horse thief." She cackled once more and flew into the night.

Ursian sat in silence for a while and although Hugo knew that it was best to leave him alone when these black moods came upon him, the Hound together with Sangres and Mimi went to the great old animal and nuzzled his matted fur with their warm snouts in a gesture of understanding. Hugo left Ursian after a while and joined Roland to discuss the news which Athina had brought. The officer was still trying to puzzle out her parting shot about Kate but agreed with Hugo that it couldn't mean anything too serious as the bird had cackled with laughter when she said it. At least they had a good head start on their pursuers.

"Yes, true" said Roland "But once he is across the river it will take him less than a day to get to where we are now. He is on horseback and can travel faster than these lumbering wagons. Anyway, let's save that worry for another day. We still have other problems. How on earth do we protect ourselves if this Brochard attacks? I know nothing of werewolves except what I have read and what Gilles told me." Hugo shuddered at these words as he continued: "Tomorrow's biggest problem may be Ursian and his temper." Hugo nodded and then both were surprised to find that Ursian was standing behind them.

“If the problem was my temper, Lebrun” growled the huge animal, then I would have broken you in half for just saying that. You have just uttered the gravest possible insult to me; you have questioned a Bear Promise. A Guard Bear never breaks a promise.” Hugo was concerned that just as relations were improving between these two there would now be renewed animosity and he was aware that he was dependent on both if he was going to succeed.

“Ursian, my friend, Roland is not doubting your promise, nor am I, but he does share my concern that if you devote all your energies to controlling your temper – and you will undoubtedly succeed in this – then you may not be focusing fully on our task. To help you, we have both agreed to share some of your burden. Now sit down here with us and let us discuss tomorrow’s plans.”

After a few uncertain moments, Ursian joined the two and began to describe the route they must take the next day. He had claimed, back at Sanctuary Inn, that he knew south-western France like the back of his paw and this had proved to be true. The only problem was that Roland had difficulty reconciling distances with Ursian’s methods of measuring. He measured travelling time in ‘bear-days’ which was how much time a bear would take to travel a given distance. Eventually, by relating a ‘bear-day’ to the distances on his gendarmerie-issue map, the officer had made a very rough calculation that this was four times the distance that the caravan could travel on good roads in one day and these were anything but good roads.

Since they had left the river Roland had relied upon Ursian’s directions, but he was now beginning to approach vaguely familiar territory. He knew that the next town they would reach was called Oloron St. Marie and although the town was quite small it held a special importance for Roland. Three years previously, the defeated French army including himself had retreated over the Pyrenees, relentlessly pursued by the Spanish Irregulars and English forces. In the high narrow mountain passes ambushes and snipers had been a constant threat. It was only once the exhausted French troops had reached Oloron they had at last begun to feel safe.

The town was perched on both sides of a rocky gorge through which gushed a fast-flowing river. It had the only bridge across this torrent for miles around, which meant there would be no chance that the caravan could bypass it. For Ursian too this town had great significance: it was here, more than 10 years earlier that he had been sold to the fairground people. He feared it was more than likely that it would be in this town that he would meet them again. They usually visited twice a year.

Roland was thinking aloud. "We cannot avoid a confrontation if we are to pass that town while the Fair is still there. Times are hard, so when we do meet up, the fairground folk are likely to think we are in opposition to them and from what I remember of Oloron, there just isn't the room for two fairs at once. The streets are twisting and narrow and the square is very small.

Anyway, I remember it took our unit quite a while to negotiate our way through the town on foot – and as we have large wagons I can foresee problems, but we cannot wait until they leave. Soon Louis-Philippe will be on our trail."

"He's right, Hugo" Ursian nodded "I've seen many fights between those show folk and their competitors – that's how they'll see us. They have to make a living and they will fight to protect what they have – even if it does involve exploiting innocent animals."

"What should we do then? We can't stay here, and we can't go into the town because for one thing we are so outnumbered. Nor can we let anyone realise what we really are."

Roland remained silent for a while and then, raising his head with a smile he said: "I have the beginnings of an idea in my head, don't worry I need to think about it a little more but yes I think this could work." He must exploit the assets he had, his uniform and its authority! Hugo looked on sceptically but Athina had after all sent this human to help them and if he had an idea, well they would have to rely on him.

In the morning, he told Hugo and Ursian that he wanted the caravan to camp some distance from the outskirts of the town. He thought his scheme would work best early in the day when everyone was fresh. During the journey Ursian kept scanning the sky and would regularly tell Hugo what he understood of the eagles' movements above them. Only those birds immediately overhead were visible to Hugo and Roland but Ursian could see farther and he had seen a group of eagles some way off led by the legendary Pellerin himself. They were tracking the fairground on its way. He could even make out, on the farthest horizon, some of the young birds of the Eastern Clan – they must be following the *Loup Garou.*

By mid-afternoon the Captain, using his telescope, could make out Pellerin's clan, which were now circling high over what he calculated to be Oloron. He suggested to Hugo that this was as far as they should go that day. The road was becoming increasingly steep and the horses were sometimes struggling to pull the wagons and the animals in the wagons were struggling to remain upright!

They went through the routine for the evening; the horses with Unika and the Donkey were unhitched and allowed to graze quietly whilst Ursian took Lucius, Flavius and Leonid for a stroll. Meera climbed on to the top of one of the wagons to sleep in comfort and Sangres and Mimi went off foraging for berries and other available snacks (usually unsuccessfully now that the terrain was becoming more mountainous). After they had all eaten, Hugo allowed the animals to have some time together so that those who wanted to could chat and relax. This unfortunately rarely applied to the lions as the others were wary of chatting to these large fierce creatures, not just because they were aggressive but because they were also very sarcastic. One could never be sure whether their joking threats were jokes or threats.

Once all the other animals were safely taken care of or bedded down, Hugo, Ursian, Sangres and Roland, with Mimi lurking close by, sat down to discuss the next day's plans. Roland asked Ursian if he could tell him how many fairground people they could expect to encounter and how aggressive they were likely to be. "That's easy" growled the bear "if we appear they'll attack us with anything they can lay their hands on, staves, knives, axes, pitchforks, you name it and there'll be more than 30 of them. I've seen many fights between rival fairground folk and it's not a pretty sight. Ursian paused for a moment and from the expression on his face, Hugo and Roland could see that his temper boiled inside him. "Look", he growled "Let me loose in there tonight, by the time I'm finished the only ones left alive tomorrow will be women and children."

The officer shook his head: "No. There will be no killing. We will get by unscathed, trust me. Now this is what I propose. We just need everyone and especially the lions and all the bears to play their part."

Roland outlined his simple plan to Hugo and Ursian who both nodded in agreement, then Roland decided to go for a quiet stroll alone before turning in for the night. He was unaware that Ursian had followed him soundlessly. When they were out of Hugo's hearing, Ursian whispered "Lebrun, I can see a flaw." The gendarme was momentarily shocked and peered around him in the darkness to see the huge dark outline of the bear looming close to him.

"There is nothing to stop those folks following us and choosing their time to attack is there?"

"I agree with you Ursian, but I am hopeful that they won't. There is, if my memory serves me correctly, only one road in and out of the town. In terrain like this I can hold them off with my weaponry long enough for the caravan to get far away." Even in the darkness, he could see Ursian's vast head shaking from side to side: "No, it will be better that there are two of us. One against 30? Can't see that. I'll stay behind with you. I want revenge for ten years of humiliation."

Roland knew that he must handle this situation delicately: "No, Ursian, you made a solemn promise to guide Hugo and the animals to the High Valley. My task is to protect and assist. If we both die tomorrow where does that leave Hugo eh? Even if we have stopped the fairground folk, he is still in danger from Louis-Philippe and the Loup-Garou. You must stay with Hugo."

Wordlessly, Ursian lay one massive paw very gently on the human's shoulder and they walked back to the camp together.

CHAPTER 55

Roland awoke very early and retrieved his uniform from his pack together with his long musket and his carbine and filled them with a lethal mixture of ball and shot which would cause serious damage if fired. He also made sure that his pistols were loaded. In full military attire he took his coachman's clothes to Hugo who lay in the dust, licking his matted coat slowly. The soldier left the suit of clothes in the back of the wagon and proffered a musket to the dog. "Think you can use this?" he asked.

"Well at present I could have a problem." The dog looked down at his large paws "But I don't believe Lucien Lecaron would have a problem."

After everyone had eaten, the caravan moved slowly on with Hugo in the lead and Ursian in the middle of the procession. His wagon contained the snoring lions whilst Meera dozed on the roof. Those wagons without drivers followed each other, the horses guiding themselves without any difficulty. Roland rode towards the end of the caravan beside the stores wagon and donned a long thick cloak which covered his uniform whilst Mimi ran ahead acting as lookout (her favourite job). Sangres followed up in the rear, watching for anyone that might be following. Just as they came to the outskirts of Oloron, Mimi came running back barking wildly to Hugo that a rider was approaching. Hugo was still in his Hound form, having transformed only his paws to drive the wagon easily. He too wore a long cloak to hide his true shape. Hugo spotted the rider – it was a lad of about 12 years old, riding bareback and using a rope bridle on his pony which he controlled by digging his heels into the animal's flanks. As he caught sight of the moving caravan, he brought his mount to a sudden halt, turned, dug in his heels and sped off in the direction he had come. Roland rode up to Hugo and muttered: "Get ready" then rode back to Ursian to tell him that it was time.

"I won't let you down" muttered the great beast "***Roland***."

By the time the Captain had returned to Hugo's wagon, the Hound's transformation was complete - he was wearing Roland's coachman's outfit with his cloak over it. When they heard Ursian's loud growl that he was ready the caravan moved forward with Roland falling slightly behind as they got nearer.

Ursian was talking to Lucius and the other lions: "No killing lads. Remember, no killing."

Lucius shook his head, his mane flying all around: "No killing? what kind of bear are you?"

Ursian grew to his full height, overshadowing the lions "I am a *bear* who spent ten long years in captivity because every time I had a plan to escape the red mist descended before my eyes and thoughts of revenge took over. If I had thought a bit more and seethed a bit less…I might have escaped long before I did. Now, as I said, there will *be no killing*. Captain Roland has forbidden it." Lucius slowly nodded his head in agreement but could not resist a further enquiry: "Perhaps a little rampage then? Used to enjoy that we did" but a glance from Ursian and a frown was enough for Lucius to know that even the tiniest rampage was out of the question.

Oloron stood on either side of a deep gorge, high in the foothills of the Pyrenees. It was the gateway to the great mountain range beyond. The road had progressed steadily upwards from Pont St. Pierre until the whole of the town ahead became visible clinging to the sides of the gorge, the oldest part of Oloron rising behind crumbling defensive walls. There were two distinct levels: the ancient 'High Town' which staggered crazily upwards, appearing to be almost vertical with narrow cobbled streets winding towards the great ruined Château at its highest point. The old grey stone blocks were outlined against the green foothills of the mountains beyond. Near the ruin stood the tower of a Medieval church, the building itself lost in the jumble of narrow streets surrounding it. The 'High Town' was separated from the rest of Oloron by a deep ravine spanned by a very ornate bridge with a single narrow roadway. Most of the shops and inns were in the Low Town arranged around a tree-lined square where the market was held twice a week.

Roland noted that not much had changed here since his last visit, the wall still seemed to be in a state of disrepair and an air of neglect hung over the outskirts of the city. As they got closer to the narrow bridge a mob of angry shouting men appeared at the far end, pulling a cart laden with bales of straw. The men carried staves and cudgels and were gesticulating menacingly. They abandoned the cart in the middle of the bridge blocking the way forward. Hugo stopped his wagon about 20 paces from the angry mob. Just beside that wagon Roland sat quietly on his horse, waiting. He watched as two men detached themselves and walked towards him but instead of stopping, they passed him and strolled insolently along the line of wagons, inspecting their contents and occasionally running their staves along the bars. Roland did nothing, ostensibly just another traveller trying to enter the city. He rode casually forward until he was beside Hugo when the two men returned.

Ignoring Roland, the older of the two men, a large man with a dark ponytail which hung down the back of his grubby, brightly coloured shirt, addressed Hugo in a harsh voice in a French which was heavily accented by another language entirely: "You're not welcome here. This is our town. Turn around and go back to where you came from. But before you go, we'll relieve you of those mangy old lions, the bears and that horse rigged up like one of those unihorns."

Hugo turned to them and he spoke in his newly-found gruff human voice: “We’re not going back but we don’t want to interfere with your business either. We just want to pass through this town and be on our way. We are en route to Spain and have no need of trouble. However, I regret that I cannot part with any of my beasts, especially the lions as they are like friends to me. No amount of money could replace them.”

“Money? Money? You don’t get it, do you? We’re not buying these flea-ridden animals, we are taking them. Think of it that we are doing you a favour, you won’t have to feed them anymore” and so saying the leader turned to his cronies and shouted: “Come on lads, there’s only a few of ‘em that I can see, and it’ll be a good morning’s work for us. It’ll make up for the loss of that vicious old bear that escaped.”

Before anyone could move Roland rode forward to stand high on horseback facing the mob. He pulled his cloak aside to reveal the muzzle of his short-barreled carbine, pointing at the chest of the leader. Addressing the mob in general he said in a clear, forceful voice: “Strictly speaking, there are more of us than you think!”

Still not understanding what Lebrun was doing, the leader of the mob said harshly: “Get out of here, Monsieur, this is none of your business. Go on, get on your way.”

Roland chose this moment to very slowly throw back his cloak revealing his smart inform. “Wrong again, Sir. This is very much my business!”

At the sight of his uniform, the mob fell back a step, almost as one for not only was the carbine trained upon them, but they saw that in addition, in his belt, the gendarme officer had a brace of pistols too. For additional effect Roland unbuckled the leather scabbard attached to his saddle to withdraw a vicious looking sabre. Hugo then pulled aside his cloak, revealing a musket seemingly casually held across his lap but in fact pointing straight at the head of the older man who, when he moved slightly to one side, found that the musket barrel followed him without any obvious movement from Hugo.

The mob stood taking all this in and Roland decided to press home the advantage of surprise and rode forward, causing them to retreat several steps. He then spoke: “I am Captain Roland Lebrun of the Gendarmerie Nationale, attached to the personal staff of General Georges Destrier, the commander of the Gendarmerie. The only way you will steal from this gentleman” and he nodded towards Hugo “is by killing me first. He and his friends are under my personal protection. Now, before you even think of acting I ask you to think long and hard. True at present there are more of you than there are of us, but you would do well to remember that my squadron is but a short distance behind us. Did you, when you awoke this morning know the date on which you were born? Of course you did - but how many of you also knew the date on which you will die? Continue as you are doing and that could well be today. Think how your wives and children will feel if you never return and bring down the wrath of the gendarmerie on them too. Even if you succeed today General Destrier is known for his vengeful nature.

You cannot hide…your friends will betray you eventually through bribery or fear. You will never sleep peacefully again.”

The ragged crowd of fairground folk became still as they considered this speech, some muttering to each other. Roland’s words had been delivered slowly both for effect and to give Ursian time to carry out his part of the plan, but any lingering indecision was banished when they spotted an enormous man with teeth suspiciously reminiscent of a wild animal advance towards them accompanied by three lions off their leashes. As they came level with Roland, Ursian growled “SIT” and the lions obediently sat, growling gently. Not far behind, the Fighting Bears sat on their haunches emitting low warlike snarls, glad to be able to exhibit their natural aggression to good effect.

"This man here, your leader is he? He said he would take these 'mangy' lions. Now's his chance." Roland grinned and as he said this, all three big cats sprang up and roared ferociously at the men standing before them. The plan had been for Ursian to instruct their actions, but they had heard the mob's leader refer to them as "mangy" – a grave error of judgement. They opened their huge mouths wide enough to swallow those nearest to them and the crowd felt hot fetid breath upon them. At Ursian's urging, but reluctantly, they crouched once more waiting for his next command: "Prepare to attack." This was enough.

The remaining mob members fled yelling, falling over each other in their haste and clambering back over their cart. Several were trampled in the rush to escape. Within moments, the bridge was empty save for the cart which Ursian seized in his huge paws and threw over the parapet into the river some 50 feet below. Tumbling and turning, it smashed to splinters against the rocks scattering hay bales and loose straw in its wake.

Lucius and his pride swaggered unbidden back to their wagon where they lay down, lazily basking in the admiration of their fellow travellers whilst the Fighting Bears returned in formation to their cage, still muttering but content. The caravan set off through the town but encountering almost no-one. In the main square they passed by the travelling fair, but strangely, no-one was tending the stalls and booths.

Roland motioned Marron to stop in the square and sat, still holding his carbine, whilst Hugo led the caravan towards the south and out of the city. As soon as the last wagon had passed, the gendarme left his post and rode after them, waiting on a small rise above the town where he could clearly see whether anyone had followed.

Only when the last wagon was out of sight did he follow, keeping a watchful eye on the road behind them. After an hour, he was satisfied that the plan had worked. The fairground rowdies posed no further threat. He spurred Marron on to catch up with the last wagon of the caravan Roland immediately announced that he intended to ride on ahead of the convoy and return later in the day. Hugo was disappointed because he had grown used to the gendarme's comforting presence and now felt rather alone. However, by mid-afternoon Roland was spotted riding towards them once more and he resumed his task of guard, riding alongside the last wagon.

At their regular meeting that evening, Ursian called for silence, then rose and began to address the group, using Roland's full name and rank properly for the first time:

"Captain Roland Lebrun, I hereby apologise. I, Ursian le Grand, was wrong and allowed my hatred of humankind to prevent me seeing you clearly. Without you I might easily have let Hugo down and endangered my companions. I freely admit this. From now on, whatever you wish of me, I am your servant…Sir" and with this he made a deep and surprisingly graceful bow.

"No, no Ursian" replied his new friend, "I am in your debt. If you had not arrived with the lions, then I think that there might have been some bloodshed back there. Only *you* prevented that." Ursian acknowledged this praise and nodded his thanks: "Gracious words, Captain Lebrun, but I know that I am forever in your debt and I will never fail you."

Delighted that his two friends were no longer at odds, Hugo asked the gendarme where he had gone that afternoon. "Just having a look at the lie of the land, Hugo." replied Roland. "I was trying to use the time we have at our disposal because I fear that we have only a little of it left and the road becomes far more difficult as we make our ascent."

"Maybe less time than we had hoped." grunted Ursian "We are getting close to the Gates to the Valley, but there were more and more eagles flying above us today and just look at all the owls up there."

Hugo and the Captain looked up but couldn't see a thing other than stars. "The *Loup Garou* must be close to the Gates You must have seen the other eagles?" He looked at the Gendarme who shook his head. "Both pairs who were patrolling the riverbank were on the move today. It can only mean that our pursuers have crossed the river – and your friends too. It's a rare honour indeed to have Aiguillin himself watching over *them.* A *Loup Garou* on the loose and he is escorting ladies instead…hm, only Athina could have arranged that! You are a very lucky young man." Ursian chuckled to himself.

Suppressing an almost overwhelming desire to ask his new-found friend exactly what he meant by this, Roland's sense of duty took over: "Ursian, are there any villages between here and the Gates?"

"Not really, well a couple of hamlets but most humankind around here are farmers or shepherds who live further up the mountain. The locals keep themselves to themselves; they used to be a friendly bunch but then came the *Loup Garou* that escaped our clutches. It caused havoc up here so whenever strangers show up now the locals lock their shutters and bolt their doors."

"Well for once that is good news. We've tried as much as possible to keep a good distance between ourselves and that Renegade. Now I think we need to change our tactics, Ursian. We can't risk a fight with both the *Loup Garou* and Louis-Philippe at the same time. We need to eliminate one threat. I think that'll be easier if we jettison the wagons."

Ursian was nodding his great furry head in agreement. "You are right my friend. We can manage without the wagons now. We are close to our goal and so the pretence is no longer necessary. As for the Renegade nobleman, I can eliminate him." Ursian nonchalantly examined his extended claws.

"Sorry Ursian but I would prefer to deal with him in my own way." Ursian's expression fell and he turned his glum face to his new friend, shrugging his shoulders, baffled once again by humankind. After they had agreed on their course of action, they settled for the night, looking forward to an early start and the next day's events with both expectation and trepidation.

The animals were now allowed freedom to walk about, so long as they kept up with the group, liberated from their travelling homes to graze and sniff at will. Only the smaller animals had a problem with this and they were often carried by either Ursian, Sangres or on the backs of the horses. Since crossing the river at Pont St. Pierre, the majority of the animals had been cooped up for most of each day and now revelled in their new-found freedom. Sangres and Mimi, along with Meera, were assigned to keep the stragglers moving.

For the time being, a few horses pulled the now empty wagons at the rear, making much better progress with the vehicles unencumbered by the weight of their occupants over the uneven track. Roland had a plan for these wagons too. Meanwhile, Ursian kept an eye on the eagles, which he said had now flown beyond Oloron.

Soon they passed through a narrow gorge, its rugged grey rock walls towering above the travellers. A fast-flowing river ran along the base of the gorge with many small torrents which splashed down over the dark grey stones. The uneven pathway lay beside the fastflowing river and the travellers were forced to keep close together to pass through the gorges, the wheels of the empty wagons sometimes balancing precariously on the edges of the roadway. At the head of the gorge, Roland called a halt. Although the river still flowed on beside them, the gorge had widened out onto a pasture on either side, which rose upwards to the foothills which surrounded them. He dismounted and walked over to Ursian: "I think this is an ideal spot, don't you?"

Ursian gave a wide grin and went towards the back of the procession, encouraging the stragglers and keeping an eye out for any animals who had fallen too far behind. Last to arrive were the slower, grazing animals. Ursian uncoupled the horses from the wagons and whispered in the lead animal's ear, telling it to lead its companions towards Roland at the head of the gorge. The few remaining supplies were secured in leather bags and strapped onto the horse, Donkey and a very reluctant Unika. The horses clip-clopped off, glad at last to be free whilst Ursian set about pushing the heavy wagons backwards once more, shoving each into the other until they formed an impenetrable barrier at the narrowest part of the rocky chasm. Whilst the animals watched in amazement he began to smash each wagon into planks then shards, wrenching the bars from their side and pulling off the huge painted wheels as easily as plucking a berry from a bush.

When Ursian had reduced their travelling homes to shattered timber, he carefully piled the broken wood across the pathway blocking it completely. He took a gaily painted HUGO'S AMAZING TRAVELLING MENAGERIE sign which had been left untouched and placed it upon the top of the highest pile. He surveyed his handiwork for a moment and then made his way back rubbing his paws together in satisfaction and gave the closest thing to a smirk.

All the happy animals were now roaming freely in open pasture to graze and feel grass under their feet once more. The lions, however, whom Ursian had appointed Hugo's personal guard, remained behind. They would not let the special Hound out of their sight. Hugo and Roland were in deep conversation and the floppy ears of the Hound danced as he nodded his head vigorously at what he was being told: "You're sure that he will come this way?" Hugo pointed his muzzle towards a slope rising from the meadow.

Roland nodded confidently "Yes, I rode on ahead to this point yesterday and now the road is completely blocked he can come no other way. Ursian and I will climb to the top of the gorge there and from that point we can see right back to Oloron in one direction, almost to our destination in the other. We cannot afford to be surprised but of course we also have the eagles to help us. Come Ursian, let us take up our position."

Before the officer and his giant companion set off, the bear had a few words with Lucius so that he fully understood what was expected of him – and the consequences, should Ursian catch him and his pals slacking – or sleeping! However, Lucius had a question of his own. "I know you're the King of the Beasts, Sir, but me and the lads have been set a very important task, haven't we?" Ursian nodded "Well, don't you think we should have a title too – perhaps Kings of the Jungle? At this the fur on Meera's thick neck stood on end, as she listened intently. "But you don't even live in a jungle! If anyone is entitled to be called that it has to be a tiger."

Lucius looked as crestfallen as a lion can look but Ursian whispered in Meera's ear then turned to Lucius and announced: "Of course, from now on the lions will be forever known as Kings of the Jungle." Satisfied with this, and allowing himself a smirk at Meera, Lucius returned to Favius and Leonid. "Lads, we are now officially Kings of the Jungle" he said. Favius, sitting on his haunches, rather like a very large cat, put one of his front paws in the air saying: "Well, that means we are the Three Kings, right?" Lucius gave this some thought and replied: "Well, how about one king and two princes, eh?" and swaggered off, his two henchlions muttering behind him. Meera however knew that she was Queen of the Jungle!

CHAPTER 56

Roland and Ursian made their way upwards and carefully climbing to the promontory which formed the end of the gorge. There was some vegetation, small shrubs and gorse bushes and even a few straggly stunted pine trees which seemed to grow out of the bare rock itself. Looking down they could see the remains of the wagons and in the distance two riders were approaching from the direction of Oloron, monitored above by a pair of high-flying eagles. A second pair of birds followed much farther away. They must also be shadowing someone – it had to be Kate and Amélie. Through his telescope he finally got a glimpse of the pair, riding slowly, cautiously keeping a good distance between themselves and the two male riders approaching the gorge. Roland could see that both girls rode rather awkwardly, holding the reins in one hand and he guessed that the other handheld one of their weapons. Both wore heavy riding cloaks with the hoods almost obscuring their features, but he could still easily distinguish his Kate who rode taller in the saddle than her cousin. Ursian looked up: “Friends of yours? Are they of the Lady Eleanor’s family perhaps?”

Surprised by Ursian’s words Roland nodded: “Well, yes…but how...?”

“Oh, my eyes are far better than your magic looking glass my friend. Even from this distance the family resemblance is very striking. Of course, I did hear Pellerin’s Clan talking of how one of the Garenne girls had defied Athina, not once but twice. The last time that happened, well it was the lady Eleanor herself.” Ursian permitted himself a small chuckle, which sounded more like a happy growl, just at the thought of anyone, animal or human, standing up to Athina. Then he asked: “Now, should we warn Hugo?”

Roland nodded seriously and Ursian went as close to the edge of the huge cliff as he dared. He could see the distant figures of the waiting animals far below. He reared up onto his hind legs and began to beat his deep barrel-shaped chest with his dark padded paws, the sound carrying far down into the valley. He ceased only when Hugo raised his head in acknowledgement and watched as the Hound went around to each of the waiting animals barking his instructions. Slowly, all the animals came down from the pasture, those farthest away running to join their companions. They took what cover they could in the surrounding undergrowth, Sangres and Mimi chivvying them into position with enthusiasm. Man and bear watched the animals gradually begin to blend into the surrounding countryside until all that was visible were two Fighting Bears, propped against a tree, one of whom was casually rubbing his thickly furred back against the tree trunk, scratching distractedly. Hugo and his phalanx of bodyguards were climbing to a spot previously agreed with Roland, above and behind the other animals. However, Lucius and his henchlions were not being very helpful in climbing the slope. Lucius insisted that he must walk in front of Hugo, forgetful that a Hound's nose is extremely sensitive. Hugo would have infinitely preferred not to be downwind of the lion! The remaining lions flanked the Hound and all three moved in precise military formation: "Is this really necessary?" asked the frustrated Hound.

"Ursian told us not to move one footstep away from you, at all times. Now we don't want to upset Ursian do we lads?" Hugo thought to himself, 'no you don't, do you? In case Ursian tells the other animals about you being scaredy-cats, afraid of a little water?'

Having observed that the animals were in place and that Hugo and his 'minders' were making their awkward progress to the agreed spot, Ursian went back along the ledge and hid himself in some rather prickly gorse which he used to great effect to scratch his thickly furred rump. Roland, who had been watching the ecstatic bear, turned his attention back to Louis-Philippe and André who were now entering the narrowest part of the gorge. He watched as they halted abruptly when confronted by the debris of the wagons with the sign "HUGO"S AMAZING TRAVELLING MENAGERIE" perched on top of the splintered planks.

The two men had very different reactions to the scene. Louis-Philippe had been in a good mood since they had stayed the night in Oloron and heard tales of a lone gendarme facing down an angry mob whilst protecting a strange menagerie. Now here was proof that he had been right all along, He had tracked down not only his special Hound but was also on the brink of eliminating that cursed gendarme.

Even the word "Hugo" had had an almost terrifying effect on the young man. Now, ignoring the obvious, that the way forward was well and truly blocked, he gloated over his prowess as a detective. André, on the other hand had other concerns. He had been puzzled as to what such an experienced, presumably well-regarded officer was doing escorting a menagerie; this man had travelled almost half the length of France only allowing his pursuers to see what *he* wanted them to see! Now here he was and almost advertising his presence.

They regarded the debris blocking their way, the massive pile of timbers topped by a brightly coloured sign; on one side, the grey glistening rock of the gorge rose high and sheer, on the other between the road and the wall of the gorge was a fast-flowing torrent, swirling around large boulders, its steep banks impossible to climb. Only André appreciated how precarious was their current position. If there was to be an ambush, this would be the perfect place. 'We are sitting ducks in this narrow gorge' he thought. He looked up at the sky above and then behind them. The birds he thought must be shadowing Amélie and Kate were getting closer. Then he noticed that in addition to the eagles shadowing himself and his master, another pair of the majestic birds were now ahead of them. 'Heaven help you, Louis-Philippe, you don't know what you are meddling in' he thought but said nothing. Instead he said: "Sir, we do seem to have an extremely large obstacle in our way. I know you will give me your guidance."

As André suspected, Louis-Philippe had no idea what to do next. He did what he did best, tried to turn the question back on André: "Lacoste, you must have learned something from the years you spent in the Grande Armée - beyond polishing my father's boots. What would your beloved Napoleon have done?"

'He wouldn't have got us into this mess and such easy pickings too' thought the exasperated André but he replied: "Well he would have used cannon fire to blast away the obstruction, Sir, but as that's not really an option, he would probably have retreated whilst researching a better solution."

"**Retreat**?" Louis-Philippe spat out the word, his good humour rapidly evaporating. "Ha, that's the difference between that upstart and a real General who would never contemplate retreating. A man who would choose death before dishonour."

Clearly Louis-Philippe was back in his imaginary role as General, with André as his foot soldier. André inwardly shuddered and thought that this might be true but, in his experience, such 'real' generals mostly chose the death of their men, not themselves. Too angry to speak, André stood in silence while Louis-Philippe dismounted to study the debris and the treacherous river before him, clearly at a loss as to how to proceed but also trying to understand how the obstacle had got there.

Meanwhile, André looked up once more at the skies and saw that now their eagle escort had joined up with those ahead and behind and the six enormous birds of prey were flying in great circles over the gorge, sometimes out of sight for a moment but always coming back to their original positions. So, he thought, the girls are very close by now. He assumed that Captain Lebrun was somehow responsible for the wreckage of the wagons, so he too must be nearby - perhaps just ahead. Of one thing he was certain, if it was Lebrun then the man had no intention of killing Louis-Philippe because being trapped in this gorge would have given him ample opportunity to do just that.

Louis-Philippe eventually announced: “I have solved our problem! We will not *retreat*, Lacoste, we will retrace our steps back down the gorge until the sides become less steep and make our way by climbing up and going around.” He looked triumphantly at his companion, but André was too busy thinking of Kate and Amélie because if Louis-Philippe doubled back now he would soon discover them. To avoid this, he shouted at the top of his voice: “Excellent idea Sir, yes let us retrace our steps.” The sound echoed down the steep gorge and he knew that his voice had carried well when we saw two eagles peel off from the group above them and fly back down the ravine.. Louis-Philippe gave André a sideways glance – was he being mocked? - and turned his horse around. The two men set off the way they had come, André leading and trying to travel as slowly as possible.

When they reached a place where the solid rock face gave way to a slightly gentler slope – although still very steep for a horse – Louis-Philippe dismounted and studied the climb. He pronounced it possible and leading his mount he began falteringly to climb up the side of the slope. André too dismounted and saw that on the other side of the path there was what appeared to be a cave with bushes growing at its opening; he doffed his hat towards this opening behind his master’s back and then followed up the slope.

Alerted by André’s loud proclamation, Kate and Amélie had gone quickly back the way they had come until they saw an eagle flying in front of them indicating a large, deep cave, partially concealed by bushes and undergrowth. Persuaded by Kate who spoke to them softly, the horses obediently went in, even though it was dark and smelled of damp and bear. They promised her that they would make no sound and then the girls went forward to keep watch. Amélie brought with her a carbine which she laid on top of a boulder. She also had two pistols and placed them in easy reach. While they waited, Kate drew one of her own pistols and cocked that, the loud click echoing in the dank cave. She looked across at her cousin and saw that the happy carefree Amélie she knew and loved had vanished, and instead there was an Amélie she had seen only once before, grim faced, determined and unafraid. This was the girl she had been with at Waterloo, surrounded by the dead and dying but determined to carry on nursing and tending to them no matter the revulsion she felt at what she had seen.

As Louis-Philippe came into view, Amélie slowly moved the carbine to have a clear shot at him. He dismounted and looked around. Kate was watching him closely but snatching a glance at Amélie saw that her finger was tight on the trigger of the gun. Louis-Philippe called to André and started to lead his horse up the slope away from the cave. With relief, she saw that Amélie's finger on the trigger had relaxed. When André came into view, he glanced briefly in the direction of the cave as he dismounted, then followed Louis-Philippe up the rocky incline – hesitating briefly to bow in their direction!

"What now?" asked Amélie.

"We follow but on foot and at a very safe distance. I think we can leave the horses in the cave. Somehow I don't think we will be too long."

When the two men had disappeared, the girls collected up their travelling arsenal and strapped the weapons to their backs. Kate explained quietly to their horses what was happening and promised some good grazing as soon as they came back to collect them. The girls then set off following the path taken by Kate's brother. They proceeded cautiously up the sloping gorge side, picking their way among the small boulders and taking cover in thick clumps of scrubby bushes intent on remaining hidden from sight and making as little noise as possible. Kate whispered to Amélie: "What would you have done if Louis-Philippe had spotted us, cousin?"

A moment later Amélie replied almost too calmly: "I would have killed him. Uncle Philippe told me when he taught me how to use a gun that if I took a shot at any animal, I had to kill it, never leave it injured or in pain. He also told me that I must never consider firing upon a fellow human being unless there were compelling reasons to do so, and if there were, then I must shoot to kill. I truly believe that your father would have approved of my actions if I was trying to protect you and moreover, did not Maman instruct me to look after you – as you must look after me." Kate looked at Amélie, considering what she had just said, and wondered then if she really knew her cousin. "I don't think Maman would want you to become Amélie the Assassin" she quipped back, still unsure of her feelings about all this.

"No Kate. An assassin would have killed him there and then. I had a clear shot. I think I showed enormous restraint." 'Hm' thought Kate, I am seeing a whole new side to my cousin'.

After a steep climb, the rocky path flattened out onto a plateau which ran the length of gorge far below. Kate and Amélie eventually reached this and caught sight of Louis-Philippe and André some distance ahead, now out in the open. In one of the few thickets on the plateau, the girls waited, their dull and now very dusty travelling clothes blending in perfectly with their surroundings.

From his position, Roland had seen the two men reach the plateau and quietly started to make his way forwards toward them, using the scrubby bracken as cover. Louis-Philippe was so focused on the view below that he saw nothing, but André looked up towards the ever-present eagle escort, now gathering above them, and thought 'I believe that the trap is being sprung'. Louis-Philippe meanwhile looked over the edge of the precipice towards a distant meadow. Exultantly he cried out "Lacoste – look it's the dog, its Hugo Hound! I have found him." André approached the spot where Louis-Philippe was leaning over the edge and saw a miniature group of animals one of whom was a handsome hunting dog. Clearly his master had seen only what he wanted to. "Oh yes, Sir, I can see a dog - but I fear you may not have noticed that he is accompanied by three very large lions and, if I am not mistaken, there are also some bears nearby. Sir, you have a single pistol. I am no expert on wild animals but somehow I suspect they may not be entirely friendly."

Louis-Philippe laughed in a slightly crazed way. "Exactly Lacoste, for once you've hit the nail firmly upon the head – so you will go down there and find out just how unfriendly they are. The only choice for you is whether I kill you here and now and throw your body to those lions to distract them, or you go down there, divert their attention and allow me to retrieve *my* Hound." The young man's laughter was becoming more and more maniacal. Elation and terror had gripped him in equal measure.

"Lacoste, it was always my intention to kill you. *You* poisoned my father against me, I know. However, it will be so much more sporting to see you take your chances with those lions; it will be as though we were back in Roman times…" Louis-Philippe's face was suffused with the inner glow of his vivid imagination. "Now get down there, and..." Suddenly the nobleman stopped as he felt the shock of cold hard steel pressed to his neck. His head was abruptly yanked backwards by a tug on his hair and he heard a voice he had last heard in La Garenne.

"I am very sorry. The games have been cancelled and the lions will not be killing anyone today."

Despite his very real predicament, Louis-Philippe was full of bravado: "Lacoste, we have an unexpected visitor! I would like you to provide him with a very warm welcome, the warmest you can devise." André smiled in Roland's direction: "of course. I believe I can provide the warmest of welcomes."

Louis-Philippe snarled: "Get on with it then man."

"Captain Lebrun" continued André "Delighted to meet you once more. M. Louis-Philippe has asked me to *welcome you warmly…."* but André was interrupted at this point: "For heaven's sake you idiot, shoot him, shoot him!"

André smiled disarmingly: "Sir are you asking me to shoot Captain Lebrun? Surely not!"

By now Louis-Philippe was very agitated indeed, for the knife was pressing into his throat: "Oh God, shut up, shut up. Just **kill him**."

"*Sir,* with respect, you have often pointed out that my military experience was limited to polishing your father's boots so you must know that I do not carry a pistol. Anyway, I don't think Mlle. Catherine would be very pleased. She has indicated to me that she holds the Captain here in great affection."

Louis-Philippe's face reddened with apoplexy and a vein in his temple throbbed dangerously as Roland turned to André, smiling warmly: "Indeed yes! I have now proposed marriage to her and she has graciously accepted. With the full approval of Madame Giscard."

As André began to offer his heartfelt congratulations at this news, Roland slightly relaxed his grip on Louis-Philippe, who screamed: "Don't be ridiculous! When my sister marries, it will be to someone of MY choosing. That silly little chit of a girl seriously thinks she is going to marry a…policeman?" His predicament was overshadowed by his angry disbelief...until Roland wrenched his head back even farther whilst applying pressure to the small of his back with a firm knee. André meanwhile decided to turn the screw just a little more: "I am sure your father would have approved. General Destrier had already written to him to praise the Captain in glowing terms. Your aunt, Mlle. Catherine's legal guardian, has authority to approve the match. You may not remember but Mlle. Catherine's birthday is very soon. When she reaches her majority, she will assume the title of head of the House of Garenne. Will not that be a proud day for the Garenne family? Of course, then she will be free to marry whomsoever she chooses."

The whole thing was too much for Louis-Philippe. Captured by his enemy, his *servant* breaking this news to him…his servant's **insolence…** He began to struggle furiously and unsuccessfully to free himself from the gendarme's grip and despite the pain he was in, he screamed: "She will never take from me what is rightfully mine. How that she-witch ever got around my father after she became a common camp follower, a cheap doxy, amazes me."

CHAPTER 57

Roland was just about to apply perhaps fatal pressure to his prisoner to silence him when they all heard Kate's voice: "Well, brother dear, I did it by admitting what I had done. By the way this cheap doxy has a pistol pointed at your head, and it's the one that Papa was always worried about – you know, the one with the extra light trigger which is prone to go off all by itself. Oh, and I am not alone. Cousin Amélie is just dying to find out how accurate her new weapon is. Do you know, we found it down by the river a few days ago? Now wasn't that careless of someone?"

Louis-Philippe sagged and fell silent, it was all more than he could bear. The Captain took the opportunity to propel him to a nearby tree where he forced him to sit down, tied his hands and tethered him to the tree trunk. He then tied the young man's ankles together. All the while the nobleman said nothing at all. When he was satisfied that his adversary was immobilised, Roland could at last turn to Kate whom he embraced as he told her how much he had missed her. At last they separated, and she went to greet André, who became quite embarrassed when she threw her arms around his neck. As he was extricating himself André said: "Mlle. Catherine, may I congratulate you on your betrothal. However, you must never allow yourself to display affection so openly towards a servant." Kate replied indignantly: "André, you are not and have never been a servant; you were my father's confidante and trusted advisor, his best friend in battle and you are Trustee of the Eleanor Bequest. Those are not the positions of a 'servant'. Anyway, on the day I marry, I want you to stand in place of my Papa. I am sure that is what he would have wanted, so no more of this 'servant' rubbish;

you are my friend and always will be – oh and I insist that you wear your Insignia at my wedding."

Meanwhile, Amélie had retrieved Louis-Philippe's pistol which, after a quick examination, she added to her growing stockpile. Roland slipped his arm around Kate's waist both as a display of affection but also to annoy her brother. As the group waited, very slowly Ursian shambled into view. Roland announced to the awestruck group: "Let me introduce to you to my good friend Ursian LeGrand."

"Your friend? Nothing would surprise me, Captain Lebrun" replied André but in fact he was extremely shaken when Ursian stood up on his stocky hind legs and walked over towards them.

On Louis-Philippe's face there was a look of pure terror. Kate and Amélie weren't exactly sure of the correct greeting for such a mighty beast, so they made graceful curtseys to him whilst André, seeing that everyone seemed extremely at ease with this fearsome animal made an elegant bow. Their awe was compounded when Ursian made an equally elegant bow to each of them as Roland introduced them by name. Catching sight of Louis-Philippe cowering on the ground, Ursian walked towards the shivering wreck, sniffing the air theatrically.

"Hm, Renegade, definitely Renegade" spat Ursian distastefully and raised a huge paw with the claws extended. He swept them close to the terrified nobleman's face. To everyone's amusement, Louis-Philippe promptly fainted. Satisfied, Ursian went to the edge of the slope and gave a mighty roar, beating on his chest to attract Hugo's attention. Hugo began to bark excitedly, and the sound reverberated across the pasture bringing more and more hidden animals out from their cover. Roland led the girls and André over to watch this amazing sight. There was no need for him to point out Hugo as they had all known the Hound when he lived in the kennels at the Château. However, Hugo was now fully grown, and his sheer size amazed them. The gendarme pointed out Lucius, Favius and Leonid, still sticking annoyingly close to Hugo, as instructed, mirroring his every step. The Fighting Bears, relieved of their duties, were already busy collecting stones for a new game! Closest to Hugo stood Mimi with Sangres, Monsieur Donkey and Meera the enormous tiger. The girls and André marvelled at how the animals seemed to be co-existing quite happily together, meat eaters, grazers and natural foes alike but their astonishment was complete when the beautiful white Unika galloped towards Hugo. "Captain, some things can still surprise me" said André, laughing.

The gendarme announced that he was going down to feed the lions, explaining that they were on extra rations as they, in their new positions as bodyguards, would be missing their sleep. Meanwhile, he asked Kate and Amélie to go and collect their horses which he assumed they had left tethered below the plateau. Kate gave him a quizzical look: "Do you really love me?" she asked. Without a moment's hesitation, he replied: "Of course I do. I am surprised that you even need to ask."

"Well" said Kate "every time we meet up you find a reason to leave me, you dumped me in Paris so you could sail off to some tropical isle, you left me behind in La Garenne to chase after the Lost Patrol, you abandoned me on the road from St. Pardoux to help some animals cross the river....and now you want to go and feed some hungry lions. Honestly, your excuses get weaker and weaker." she laughed "Not this time, I am coming with you." Roland was about to argue but Ursian interrupted: "I can assist Mademoiselle Amélie to collect the horses and I will clear the roadway of the obstruction on the way back. Don't need it now. Mademoiselle Catherine, could you ask Mlle. Amélie if she is agreeable?"

Kate hesitated, not quite sure how to phrase such a question, or indeed how her cousin might react. Then she smiled sweetly: "Amélie, dearest, instead of both of us going to collect the horses and bringing them back, M. Ursian here has kindly volunteered to accompany you and he will clear the roadway so it will be much easier for you to return, while I can go to feed the lions." Amélie looked at her cousin in disbelief. The first time she had seen this giant was at the river's edge where he had demonstrated his considerable strength. She had guessed he was responsible for the debris left in the gorge – single-handedly. However, now she looked at Ursian she realised that she wasn't afraid at all. As with Gilles Barbier, she sensed that nothing bad could happen whilst he was around and, surprising herself, she happily consented. Ursian bowed to Kate and then lowered himself slightly, putting one of his furry arms almost flat upon the ground. Amélie understood the gesture and seated herself gently on this 'arm' whereupon the bear scooped her up. Amélie immediately reached one of her arms around his thick prickly neck to help her balance. It was at this moment that Louis-Philippe began to recover from his dead faint, just in time to see his cousin grasped in the arms of a giant bear as she rested her head against his broad, thickly furred chest and waved delightedly at Kate. He swooned once again.

CHAPTER 58

André had witnessed this spectacle with bemusement, not quite sure whether he should believe his own eyes but what was one more in a series of events which he could not understand? Perhaps now he had met up with Roland again, the officer would provide a rational – or at least less fantastical - explanation of all this but as he saw Amélie and Ursian set off, he seriously wondered if there could ever be such an explanation.

Roland went to revive the prone nobleman once more by slapping him across the face, none too gently. He pulled him up by grasping the front of his jacket and dragged the sagging form up the trunk of the tree. When Louis-Philippe was swaying on his feet, Roland freed the young nobleman's hands but left his ankles tethered. He then dragged the young man across the rough ground, holding him by his coat and threw him unceremoniously across the saddle of his mount, tying both hands to one stirrup and his tethered feet to the other. Louis-Philippe protested loudly as this was done until Kate whispered in his ear: "We are all going down now brother, to feed the lions. Roland – remember, my future husband? – well, he has assured me that the lions are quite gentle, except when they are disturbed by any loud noise. I suggest therefore, dear brother, in your own interests that you remain very, very, quiet. Of course, it's up to you." Kate left him to think and began to load all the weapons onto André's horse after which they set off down from the plateau and towards Hugo and the waiting animals.

When they had descended as far as the beginning of the broad pasture, Hugo persuaded Lucius at last that Kate and André were friends, humans he had known in his hometown, and that he should go and greet them, but Lucius firmly but courteously refused to leave his charge unaccompanied. Ursian might still hear that the lions had been slacking. So, Hugo with his tail wagging furiously, flanked by his three large if slightly moth-eaten bodyguards, approached the newcomers. Hugo introduced the lions first to Kate and then to André, with Kate translating his barks and whines for André's benefit. For a moment he paused to wonder how she knew what the Hound was saying but by then nothing seemed impossible. Hugo suddenly noticed Louis-Philippe and he made his way to look up into the red, upside down face of his enemy, Lucius close by his side. When his face was almost touching that of the young nobleman, Hugo let out a long, low growl, baring his teeth. The lions were very surprised as Hugo had never ever demonstrated even a hint of aggression all the time they had been travelling together. Lucius asked gently: "Who is this, Hugo?"

Hugo explained that this was the man who wanted to capture him and was responsible for the death of his beloved master. When the lions heard this what could they do? In turn, they got as close as they could to Louis-Philippe's horrified, sweating face and roared ferociously, their glistening teeth almost touching his cheek and their hot breath – which was none too pleasant - wafting over him. Roland intervened at this point and agreed with Hugo that perhaps it might be best to keep the lions away from the nobleman.

Hugo had to extract a solemn promise from Lucius, as leader, that the lions would not hurt Louis-Philippe – yet.

Lucius, who loved to have the last word did however make one proviso: "Yeah, of course Hugo, we promise, but well it is only a lion promise." At this Roland moved the horse with its human burden to the far side of the pasture, having collected some handcuffs from Greco's saddlebag. Helped by André, he pulled Louis-Philippe down from the horse's back and tethered him once more to a tree trunk, this time with handcuffs holding his hands behind him. The lions watched but did not stir from Hugo's side.

Satisfied with his handiwork, Roland led Kate and André over to where Donkey was grazing quietly and took out some slabs of dried meat wrapped in oiled cloth from the gentle old animal's paniers. Lucius insisted that each lion should be fed in turn so that two would always be in position, guarding Hugo – but of course as leader it was only fair that he should be first. Just as each had eaten their fill and were returning to their positions, Ursian and Amélie appeared at the end of the gorge, Amélie riding her own horse and leading the other two with Ursian strolling along beside her. Even though she was some distance away, the grin on her face was evident. As they came into the pasture, Ursian noticed Louis-Philippe tethered to the distant tree and made a slight detour so that he passed close to the captive.

Ursian stood before the terrified man, rose to his full height and let out a blood-curdling deep growl which exhibited his large yellowing incisors. Having made his point, Ursian then went over to Hugo and the lions who were delighted by his return. Their guard duty was suspended for the time being: they could sleeeep.

Kate was quietly relieved at the return of her cousin. She had been certain that Amélie would be safe with Ursian but what if something had gone wrong? What would Aunt Marianne have to say when she found out (as she surely would from Athina) that Kate had left her only daughter alone with a giant Pyrenean bear? Amélie told her excitedly of the journey back to the horses, and then after they had collected the mounts, Ursian's incredible strength in clearing the roadway once more: "The pile was so high and wide that I thought it would take days to clear but he just picked up huge chunks at a time and threw them into the river.

I've never seen anything like it. What he did to the ferry? – well, that was nothing compared to today. He's really gentle too; I know he understands what I say but I do wish I had your skills and I could understand what he is saying too."

Kate and Amélie had picked up some supplies at Oloron and between those and what André had brought, there was enough for at least a couple of days. The gendarme was especially relieved to see fresh(ish) bread and devoured what Kate laid out for lunch. Amélie amused herself aiming the 'liberated' musket at Louis-Philippe who wasn't too sure whether she was joking or not. Nor was Kate. After they had eaten, Amélie took some food over to the nobleman and fed him, piece by piece. Initially, he refused to eat anything and turned his head aside but when he saw Amélie start to eat it herself, he ate greedily while Amélie spoke gently to him: "Now cousin we are going to play a little game. I am going to place this lovely green apple…on your head. You're in no danger; my aim is *almost* 100% accurate, especially with my new musket." Louis-Philippe blanched and shivered so violently that the apple immediately fell to the ground: "Get away from me, you are mad, mad" he cried but Amélie merely smiled sweetly and whispered in his ear: "You see that enormous *bear* over there with Kate? He is called Ursian. He doesn't like you. He does, on the other hand, like me. As for the lions – they don't like you either. Alternatively, that huge boar, that's Sangres that is. He, well he hates huntsmen, all huntsmen…do we understand each other, cousin? Now, stay very, very still whilst I fetch the musket."

This time he tried very hard to remain motionless but at the last moment, his attention was drawn to the arrival of a huge golden eagle which swooped out of the sky and landed on the pasture close to Kate and André. The very slight movement of his head caused the apple to slide slowly down into his lap. His last conscious moment was filled with the sound of the click as the trigger was pulled. "Bother" cried Amélie, "I completely forgot to load it."

When Amélie rejoined André he asked her if she knew what was going on. The beautiful eagle was standing on the ground at the centre of the group comprising Kate, Ursian, Roland and Hugo, who were all listening avidly to what was being said.

Amélie sought immediately to reassure him: “That magnificent bird is Pellerin and he’s very important. Even Athina the owl curtseys to him. That’s of course when she is looking like a witch. She hates that word by the way. Insists we call her *haruspex.* She has been with us since before Montbezier where we met the Barbiers – oh, they’re bears you know. Anyway, Pellerin commands all the eagles even those from the East who are helping to find this Werewolf.” Seeing André’s confused expression, she explained: “You remember Sergeant Brochard, the one who was commanding the Lost Patrol? Well he’s a *Loup Garou* now! Yes, I know that sounds mad. It might be best if my cousin explains to you. She can understand what the animals are saying, and I can’t, yet.”

André frowned at Amélie. “Thank you, Mlle. Amélie, that all makes, err no sense at all actually. I can’t imagine what your mother will say about all this.”

“It’s fine, really, André. Maman knows what we are doing. Athina explained everything to her when she told her about Kate and Roland.”

“Yes but, err… didn’t you just say that Athina is an owl? Or a witch? Would she by any chance be somehow connected to a person known as Madame Dubois? A lady who, it seems, recently stayed with her two charges at St. Pardoux?”

“Yes, André, the very same, but how did you know?”

“I have never met the lady, or owl, or witch, but I did hear talk in St. Pardoux that two young ladies, accompanied by a certain Madame Dubois had stayed there. Yes, I heard quite a bit about their stay.”

Amélie coloured, remembering Captain Belaudie. “Ahem, yes. So, Louis-Philippe knew we had been there. I suppose that is how he got onto our trail?” but André shook his head and explained that his master had stayed in a far grander establishment than he himself and almost certainly had had no inkling of the girls’ stay. He also told her that he was sure that Louis-Philippe had never suspected that a musket had been trained on him most the time they had spent by the river. André laughed: “A fine general he would have made.”

“Fantasising again was he? When we were young, we would play at soldiers, but in truth he was never just a soldier, he would always a brigadier or something.” André was about to respond but their attention was diverted by the sight of another fabulous golden eagle which was circling above them. It landed close to Pellerin and bowed its regal head in turn to the whole group. André looked at Amélie, raising his eyebrows: “Another of your friends?” he queried, smiling. “No, although I am sure he is friendly, he’ll be working for Pellerin, I assume.” André studied the two eagles. He had been fascinated by these birds throughout the journey. Now here, right in front of his eyes were two of these magnificent creatures in deep conversation with his young friends.

When the eagles had finished their business, they flapped their huge wings in unison and took flight but then, to André’s even greater astonishment, they flew in his direction, hovering a few feet above him. They bowed their great heads towards him before flying up and into the sky, soon becoming invisible to the naked eye.

CHAPTER 59

Ursian remained in deep conversation with Hugo, Roland and Kate. The bear was doing most of the talking, accompanied by much gesticulating. He was drawing lines on the ground with a broken branch to illustrate what he said. When he had finished, he strolled over to Lucius and spoke at length with the lion whilst the gendarme went to inspect all the weapons they had, changing over from lead to steel shot, both for his own and for the girls' guns. He loaded Amélie's newly acquired musket with the ammunition Kate had taken from her brother's tent. Kate returned to André and Amélie, who by now were anxious to know what had been going on. Kate was clearly hesitant about saying anything in front of André, but he spoke first: "It's alright, Mlle. Catherine, I have just heard Amélie's "explanation." I think I can truly say that there is now – and I may be repeating myself - nothing you can say to surprise me anymore."

Kate took a single deep breath before she began: "Well the first eagle was called Pellerin. He has just told us that the *Loup Garou* is very close to the Gates of the High Valley, our destination.

Ursian, who knows all about these creatures, says that it will try to gain entry under cover of darkness but will certainly fail; only a Guard Bear can open the Gates" said Kate as though everyone knew this to be a fact. "But, if for any reason, Brochard –that's our Brochard, the sergeant from La Garenne. He's a Werewolf now…"

Yes, yes, Mlle. so I've heard but please go on" interrupted André.

"Well, if he does escape the Guard Bears, well we have to stop him. He could endanger Hugo and if he got out of this valley again he could do untold harm, just like the Beast of Gévaudan." André's face changed at the mention of this terrifying creature, but he simply nodded. "Mlle. Catherine, may I know the name of the second eagle?" Kate smiled: "Of course, André, that was Aiguillin, he's Pellerin's son.

He came to tell us that he's spotted some patrolling Customs Officers coming this way. Roland is hopeful that he can persuade them to take my brother into custody whilst we finish what we set out to do." André asked no more questions – 'Sometimes ignorance is bliss' he thought to himself.

Roland rejoined them and distributed the arsenal, warning Amélie: "They are all now loaded with steel shot so no more pranks eh? I want to get Louis-Philippe back alive to stand trial."

"Sorry but I was just paying him back for that horrible wine merchant he was trying to marry me off to; now I still want revenge for that weak-chinned lawyer, you remember?" She looked at Kate "the one that couldn't eat without dribbling…" but Kate interrupted her cousin: "I am sure that Roland will be fascinated later to hear of all the inappropriate suitors my brother has tried to foist on you and me too, but this is neither the time nor place." Becoming very business-like she turned to Roland: "Should we not get started? We still have some way to go." He nodded his agreement whilst Amélie continued mumbling softly to herself, refusing to be put off "or that old school friend who kept falling off his chair, oh yes and the cousin on his mother's side, with the enormous…"

"Amélie" barked Roland, quite sharply "Can you get your things together and be ready to leave?"

Shaken out of her reverie, she did as Roland asked as he turned to speak to André: "M. Lacoste, time is short, and I know Kate has informed you that we are close to a patrol of Douaniers. I am hopeful that they will take Louis-Philippe with them and relieve us of the responsibility. It is, of course, your choice whether you accompany them. I believe they are returning to Oloron. From there you could return to La Garenne. If you choose to remain with us, then I must warn you that there is great danger ahead."

André was nodding his head: "Sir, Roland, I thank you for giving me the opportunity to leave, truly I do but…" he turned to look at Kate "I too have unfinished business here. I made certain promises to your dear father: I would try to protect your half-brother from his own actions. Now I believe that is no longer possible, but this does not absolve me from the promise I made regarding you. I will come with you and try to help. If there is, as you describe it 'great danger ahead' I would appreciate the loan of a pistol and please, you must call me André."

Kate nodded briefly at her cousin who reluctantly parted with the pistol she had 'borrowed' from Louis-Philippe. Roland was preparing to offer André some assistance in the use of this weapon when he saw the man slip his hand into his coat and bring out a small pistol. André looked the young man straight in the eye: "I can promise you that this little beauty is accurate and absolutely lethal at up to ten paces – but I imagine you are not expecting our fight to be at such close quarters?" Roland watched impressed as the other man took the pistol from Amélie, examined it very professionally, weighing it in his palm to gauge the balance and pronounced it satisfactory. He stuck the weapon in his belt, obviously very much accustomed to doing so.

CHAPTER 60

Hugo and Ursian once again marshalled all the animals except Marron and Greco safely out of sight in the undergrowth. Roland had decided that he had a better chance of persuading the approaching Customs Patrol to take custody of his prisoner if he appeared alone, so he asked Kate, Amélie and André to remain out of sight too. Louis-Philippe's mount had needed little persuasion to join the rest of the animals. Roland waited alone with his prisoner. However, before André and the girls concealed themselves, Amélie could not resist whispering softly in Louis-Philippe's ear "Another apple, cousin?"

Watching from their hiding place, they saw the patrol of Customs men riding slowly into the meadow. Four bedraggled prisoners stumbled along behind the men on horseback, each one linked to the next using leather belts at their waists. Roland greeted the patrol with a formal salute. After exchanging pleasantries and local news for a few moments, Roland showed their commander his warrants from General Destrier. Even this far from Paris and in a different branch of government service the mere mention of Destrier's name had an electrifying effect. Roland had correctly guessed that at least some of the Customs men would be ex-army so he announced that he had found one of the killers of Colonel Lucien Lecaron. The colonel's death had been widely reported but only that it had been in a hunting accident. Seeing this fop, trussed up in front of them got the reaction Roland was hoping for. Nothing would be too much trouble. His request that they take his prisoner with them whilst he searched for the 'accomplice' was greeted with great enthusiasm. He asked their senior officer to witness his formal charging of the prisoner:

"Louis-Philippe de Garenne, I hereby arrest you for the willful murder of M. Lucien Lecaron, Chevalier of the Legion d'Honneur, former Colonel of the Twenty-Seventh Cavalry Regiment. You are hereby committed to the custody of these Douaniers to be kept at their garrison at." he looked at the officer questioningly "Oloron Sir" the man replied, and Roland continued: "to be held there for my return whereupon you will be taken to Perigueux to stand trial."

During this recital, Louis-Philippe remained silent and subdued but as the reality of his situation finally dawned on him, that he, a nobleman might be executed, some of his former arrogance returned: "How dare you believe that you have any authority over me, the rightful Duc de Garenne" he spat, but in his determination to assert his authority his tongue spoke before he could hold it - he made a fatal error: "That…that peasant was on MY land. He had stolen MY Hound and I had every right to shoot him. Since when was killing peasants a crime? The monarchy is restored, we aristocrats are back in control at last. Release me immediately." He seemed strangely unaware that he had just condemned himself in his determination to assert his authority. The men gasped in astonishment; even Roland had not expected so forthright a confession.

To prevent more of the young man's ravings, or any mention of Roland's companions he applied a makeshift gag, whilst Louis-Philippe protested with muffled grunts, his cheeks bright red with anger. He listened powerlessly when the officer once more addressed Roland: "Are you absolutely sure you need to take him all the way to Perigueux? Accidents often happen on these treacherous mountain passes."

"Much as I might like an accident to happen, Monsieur, I am afraid that knowing Georges Destrier as I do" Roland exaggerated "I am sure that he would prefer a trial to an accident, but I do thank you for your err…suggestion."

Satisfied that his captive was in the safe hands of men who understood his crime only too well, Roland roped Louis-Philippe to the last of the prisoners on foot but even this unfortunate looked none too pleased at having the nobleman as his travelling companion. Watching from their hiding place, Kate and Amélie saw Louis-Philippe being almost dragged along at the rear of the prisoners. They had all overhead his outburst about Lucien's murder and were shocked.

Once the Customs Officer with his men and his reluctant prisoners had disappeared on their way towards Oloron, the strange convoy set off once more with Ursian leading and Hugo proceeding amid his phalanx of guard lions. The humans brought up the rear. Roland rode alongside Kate, with André and Amélie behind them.

After an hour or so, Ursian led the convoy along a narrow well-trodden path overland into another valley, its sides becoming much steeper and narrower to form a gorge. In fact, it was so narrow at times that there was only enough room for a single horse to pass through, the rider able to touch the rock face on either side. Roland and Kate recognised the contours of the land from Ursian's descriptions and were impressed by the accuracy and detail he had provided, especially as it had been over ten years since he had last seen it.

When they reached wide green pastureland once more they could easily make out where the trail was heading and using his trusty telescope, Roland could see in the distance, flying high in the sky, several moving specks which he assumed were the eagles, those tracking the Beast. He guessed that far below the great birds lay the Gates they sought although he could see nothing but the sheer sides of high mountains in front of them. Slowly they began to lose the light and Ursian selected a spot on the edge of a lush green field. He suggested that they stop here and make camp. The humans helped this time in distributing the last of the provisions and Ursian formally introduced Kate to the rest of the animals. He insisted on calling her "the Lady

Catherine de Garenne" to which she would respond each time "Please, just call me Kate."

After all the animals had been fed, Hugo with his lion escort and Ursian stayed with the humans for their own evening meal. which was washed down with the remains of Louis-Philippe's personal wine. Kate and Roland provided a running translation for André and Amélie as Ursian explained that he wanted two on guard duty always in the unlikely event that Brochard decided to retreat in their direction overnight. Ursian said he would take the first watch along with Hugo but Kate and Amélie insisted that they should do their fair share, so they took the second watch. This suited the bear perfectly for he wanted Sangres on his best form for what might happen the next day. Meanwhile, Lucius went to talk to Ursian:

"So, this is the reward we get for looking after Hugo? First rubbish food and we're not good enough to take a turn on watch?" but before Ursian could reply Hugo intervened: "But Lucius it is because you have protected me so well that Ursian is rewarding you. You can sleep now without interruption after your long, arduous day my friend. Then, if the alarm is given I am sure you will be wholly refreshed and of course will be the first ones to spring into action."

As Lucius swaggered off to explain to his companions how well thought of they were, Hugo looked at the others and rolled his big brown dog eyes upwards: "Cats! I will never understand them" and his long ears flapped from side to side as he shook his head.

Everyone was under instructions that if the news came that Brochard was close by, they had to tell Ursian then protect Hugo. Even after his watch was over, Ursian continued to pad around the camp taking deep sniffs of the night air and mumbling to himself.

Roland joined Kate and Amélie towards the end of their watch. He was curious to know more about André who would be joining him shortly to take the last watch of the night. He spoke quietly not wishing to disturb Amélie's concentration; she was gazing intently out into the darkness like a seasoned sentry expecting an imminent attack.

"Kate, André intrigues me" whispered Roland. "I like him, but..." He was surprised by the sharpness of Kate's tone: "Why, what is that you don't like?" she demanded.

"Nothing, nothing at all Kate. It's just I would like to know a little more about him. For example, this morning I heard you asking him to wear his 'insignia' at our wedding? I overhead Pellerin tell Ursian that André should be treated as a 'true Paladin and friend even if he is humankind'. I have learned the hard way that no-one tells Ursian what to do and that he is no friend of humankind, yet he meekly accepts this eagle's instruction - and what about those eagles bowing?"

"Do you not think him worthy of such honour, Roland? I can tell you that if papa was still alive he would have been delighted to witness such a scene. You have seen only the subservient side of dear André, Estate Manager, servant. I know all about the real André. Papa's troops were never ever ambushed in Spain. Now why do you think that might be?"

"Good intelligence, I suspect" replied her fiancé. "I was a very junior officer in that campaign and I just assumed that those above me knew what they were doing – only way really."

"Well yes, you're probably right but in papa's case he used a skilled spymaster: André. It was he that met with the agents in enemy territory and kept the troops safe from any surprise attacks, even the very junior officers."

Roland tried to say something, but Kate was now in full flow, her voice rising: "Papa confided to me that André had tried to refuse the Legion d'Honneur. Only when Napoleon himself ordered that he accept it did André agree. The Emperor said that if André refused a second time it would be taken as a personal affront. Some day you might like to ask him to show you the citation although I doubt that he will – he keeps the Sash and Insignia with it in a locked box. You probably know that both Papa and Lucien Lecaron were both Chevaliers of the Legion; what you don't know is that André is a Commandeur! Now do you still feel qualified to ask questions about him?"

Roland could only hope that Kate would be half as fierce in his defence and looked extremely sheepish when he was at last able to speak: "I am sorry. I admit I was completely taken in by his behaviour with your brother."

"I understand your feelings of course. He is so good at diverting attention that its easy not to see the real man. I did ask him once about his time in Spain but he will not discuss it. I think there may be a personal tragedy involved. The English didn't take kindly to spies, did they? All I know is that papa called him the bravest man he had ever met. I too am sorry dearest, that I got so angry with you, but it made my blood boil sometimes to see how my brother treated him."

When the two men took the last watch together, André was keen to discover Roland's part in Louis-Philippe's ill-fated journey. Roland admitted he knew the strange drayman who had supplied André and Louis-Philippe with misleading directions and confirmed that the eagles were watching Kate's brother all the time. It had been Ursian that destroyed the ferry over the Adour and he admitted that, for whatever reason, he could speak to the animals, as could Kate. he was still a little reticent about offering too much information, but this was partly because he still felt somewhat reluctant after years of military training to admit that they were doing all this because some talking bears and an owl had pleaded with them! Still less did he want to bring up the shape changing so he was glad of the interruption when Lucius, roused from his deep sleep stalked over and sat with them: “It’s not fair you know. Bears sleep for months on end and he has the nerve to call me lazy.” Obviously, this had been praying on his mind for having delivered this observation Lucius swaggered off back to his pride, his long-tufted tail swinging from side to side. André asked what the lion had said, and Roland explained that it was friendly rivalry between the lions and the bears: “They seem to delight in scoring points off each other.” But André was not to be put off now he had Roland to himself. “Now, tell me just what an officer of the Gendarmerie is doing halfway up a mountain, leading a strange assortment of animals?”

The young officer laughed uncomfortably: “Actually André I am accompanying them not leading them. Hugo Hound is leading them and that’s a very long story” but beyond that, he would not be drawn. It would be time enough for explanations when and if they reached the High Valley safely.

CHAPTER 61

As the first signs of dawn appeared over the mountains they heard the distinctive flap of wings heralding the arrival of an owl. Even before the snowy bird had landed, Ursian was alongside Roland ready and waiting. She spread her wings and took a moment to compose herself before bowing her head towards Ursian: "I regret that I bring bad news. A battle has been raging all night at the Gates." The bird hesitated: "I am so sorry to tell you that your son has been gravely injured; your brother Hernursian once again badly underestimated the power of the *Loup Garou* and got trapped. Fitzursian rescued him but sustained serious injuries - the Beast has torn his flesh viciously. You know how serious such wounds from a *Loup Garou* can be. Nevertheless, your son fought bravely on all through the night and managed to keep the Beast at bay, but he has lost much blood and grows ever weaker." Ursian showed no emotion: "My son would never give up. As for my brother, he will be banished! It was his fault that the Beast of Gévaudan escaped and now this. Tell me, who can replace Fitzursian?"

Athina replied quietly: "It should have been your grandson but your daughter Ursianina insisted…"

"I would expect nothing less from her" interrupted Ursian gruffly "but tell my grandson, Oursovi that he must fight alongside her although he is still young."

The haruspex nodded her understanding but reminded Ursian of just how young his grandson still was and that he had much to learn. She felt it would be better for Ursian's brother to fight alongside Ursianina because of his experience. At this, the great animal shook his huge head angrily: "Hernursian, is no longer my brother. His name will be expunged from all the Rolls. He will banish himself TODAY. Oursovi must fight. It was what he was born to do. Tell him to make me proud." Athina knew any argument was pointless with an angry bear, so she flew off back in the direction of the Gates, leaving Ursian sitting in deep thought.

Roland moved towards him and sat down, attempting to put his small human arm around Ursian's huge shoulders in consolation. Kate came upon them a while later, with Ursian's eyes fixed on the distance, imagining the scene at the Gates. When Roland caught sight of her he asked her very quietly to fetch Hugo who came immediately, for once without his 'bodyguards'. Roland told the Hound what had happened, and Hugo decided that he must now take control.

"Ursian, my dear friend, you have done enough. You have escorted us since the beginning and we are now very close to the High Valley. You have more than discharged your promise. Go now and help your daughter, she needs you."

The bear rose onto his hind legs and stood for a moment, dwarfing his companions. Hugo thought that he was going to become angry, but the wondrous animal remained calm: "Hugo I appreciate your concerns and I know that you mean only the best, but I made a Bear Promise, a solemn vow that I would get everyone to the High Valley and a bear…"

"Never breaks a promise" intoned Hugo and Roland together. Kate saw that her fiancé and the Hound were not going to be able to convince their friend to go on ahead, so she decided to take matters into her own hands: "Ursian, I believe that you know my family well?" Ursian grunted his agreement. "I am sure that the Lady Eleanor would have relieved you of your promise; so now I am pleading with you. Leave us and assist your daughter. Please cousin

Ursian. Roland will guide us. Athina sent us to help so now you must go to your family. Their need is greater than ours at this moment."

Ursian raised his paw to stop Kate: "No, neither I nor my family could live with the shame if I do what you propose. I will have broken a Promise and Ursianina will have failed as a Guard Bear by accepting help, even from her father. She will have shamed the wonderful efforts of her brother too. No, it cannot be done, I am sorry."

Kate was not used to being thwarted and part of her wanted to shake Ursian and shout at him, but Hugo seemed to read her mind: "Bears will tell you that they only work by instinct, but a Promise is the one thing that overrides those instincts, so to ask him to break a Promise goes to the root of his being, Mlle. Catherine."

"Hugo is right and anyway you need me with you. I have fought these 'beasts' before" added Ursian and in truth he needed to say nothing further. None of the others had even a clue about how to combat a *Loup Garou.* Roland resumed his watch with Ursian by his side, but he was puzzled. Surely if Werewolves were unable to pass through the Gates, then what was to stop the Guard Bears closing the gates and waiting until the evil renegade just gave up? He was unaware that his thoughts were voiced aloud until Ursian slowly shook his enormous muzzle, "It's not that simple. If we didn't bother to fight them, believe me, they would never give up trying. It is in their bad blood as it is in ours to want to go to the High Valley; it is no longer their sanctuary place, but their ancestry drags them back as powerfully as our own. They might retreat into the world again to cause havoc as the Beast of Gévaudan did, but they would inevitably return. There would never be any safety or any peace if, every time the Gates were opened, the guards faced an assault by these evil souls. Believe me it is better this way. We must prevail, even if…." Ursian could not finish his sentence and it was obvious his thoughts had gone at that moment to his daughter.

Hugo summoned all the animals, telling them that they were to move on and that everyone had to move quickly – there must be no stragglers today. Amélie and André waited anxiously to hear Ursian's news from Kate and Roland.

All the animals were ready to leave and becoming a little restless, their whinnying and growling becoming louder in the silent valley. Ursian took his place at the head of the column, followed by Lucius, then Hugo and the other two lions. Meera and Mimi, an unlikely alliance were at the rear with the humans helping them keep the stragglers in order. Although the animals were excited about their destination, they were easily distracted by fresh grazing or the sound of a bird nearby.

Donkey was at the very back of the procession and was easily able to keep up the pace set by Ursian. His lack of speed was compensated by his sure-footedness over the very rough terrain. Kate, who was riding closest to him tried to engage him in conversation without much success. Since his efforts at the river he had relapsed into his normal silent morose plodding, replying with only a 'Yes' or a 'No' to all questions asked of him. She decided it was high time she asked Donkey if he had a name:

"Donkey, I do feel very rude addressing you simply as 'Donkey', but I am sorry I do not know your name. You do have one, don't you?" She was rather taken aback when instead of his usual gentle response, the Donkey snapped:

"Of course, I do, but no one seems to be clever enough to work it out. I did think that your young man would have done so but obviously he wasn't interested in a mere pack animal. We beasts of burden are always being overlooked." The last thing Kate had expected was a churlish and self-pitying response. As Donkey again fell silent, she leaned across to Roland and muttered: "Did you not say that Donkey could work out, just by looking at the river currents when the animals had to pull the hardest? That he seemed to have an almost mathematical ability to calculate such things?"

Roland confirmed that this was indeed true and after some thought Kate turned once more to the sullen animal: “Your name, it’s not Archimedes, is it?”

Donkey’s long sad face was transformed, and he brayed joyously for once: “Of course it is! At last someone I can converse with on my level.”

Kate was delighted with herself for having figured this out but was rather less happy when her fiancé joked: “My future wife is the intellectual equal of a Donkey” – a singularly double-edged compliment. He only just managed to miss the edge of his beloved’s hand as she attempted to ‘wipe’ the grin from his face.

By mid-morning they knew that they must be getting very close to the entrance to the High Valley. They had been climbing steadily higher, following narrow pathways known to Ursian to avoid the most difficult of the rocky climbs.

They were amazed by the sheer number of eagles searching the sky ahead of them and Ursian led them forward into yet another narrow gorge whose rugged walls shut out the sunlight. At the end, the pathway spiraled upwards steeply, and the terrain was even more stony and barren, with just straggly gorse and stunted bushes along the way. They could not see their destination but the air was colder, their breath puffing out before them in the morning air. Quite suddenly, the path fell away steeply and led into a very deep and wide natural amphitheatre, with boulder-strewn sides and an oasis of greenery and small trees at its centre. The sides rose all around the bowl-shaped depression save for on the far side which seemed, at least on first sight, to be a sheer cliff face. Roland was the last to reach the edge of the amphitheatre and traced the path towards the central ‘stage’ which was perhaps 300 paces away. His eyes scanned this area until he caught sight of three figures. Ursian pointed out his grandson Oursovi ‘a growing lad’ (according to his grandfather) and Ursianina, Ursian’s daughter. These were both magnificent animals, the sun glinting sharply off the large metal studs which adorned their surprisingly well-made leather armour. The third creature was or had been Brochard.

CHAPTER 62

For Louis Philippe de Garenne this was the greatest humiliation he had suffered in his life, a prisoner being dragged behind four stinking peasants, not even civilised enough to speak French. They were conversing in something akin to Oc, the Southern regional language. Some of the residents of La Garenne spoke in that tongue but not the sort of people that he would ever bother to converse with. He had however picked up a smattering of the language over time and now he began to pick up some of the words they were using. They came from the Spanish side of the nearby border and had been caught stealing sheep. The two youngest men, boys really, were scared at the thought of the guillotine which they were convinced was to be their fate, but the oldest man told them not to worry: he had a plan.

The straggling group had followed the road to Oloron passing through the gorge which had earlier been completely blocked. Louis-Philippe glanced quickly towards the river. Wooden debris lay all around, but his eyes were drawn towards a rock on the other side of the gorge. On the top of this rock rested a sign which read "Hugo's Am zing Mena..." The sight of this only served to depress him further. Worse was to come. Instead of continuing to Oloron, the patrol turned off the main road and followed a rough track back up into the mountains. It was then he recalled what the officer in charge had said to Lebrun about the frequency of "accidents" especially in the high mountain passes. He panicked as he remembered Lebrun's reply. Even though the gendarme had said that General Destrier would prefer a trial to an accident, that hardly constituted a direct order, did it? Lebrun had even thanked the officer in charge for the suggestion. Louis-Philippe knew for certain Destrier would have no such qualms – that man wanted him dead. Louis-Philippe had detested his father's old friend and he knew the feeling was reciprocated. His half-sister and their stupid cousin might call him "Uncle Georges" but he knew better. General Destrier was a traitor, a damned Republican, how could the king, the rightful ruler of France allows such a man to remain alive, never mind in office. Louis-Philippe's mind returned to his principal concern, himself.

He was convinced that he was being led to his death, he just knew it. Why? Because of his accursed half-sister; Lebrun must have agreed to an 'accident'. With him out of the way, Kate would get control of a fortune.

He forgot in his mania that she would soon be Steward of the Bequest and convinced himself that this fortune was obviously the only reason anyone would be interested in her, she was after all not much more than a common camp follower. 'They've planned it all. Oh, how could I have been so blind' he raged in his mind. However, the young man had not realised that he had spoken aloud until a sound close to his ear brought him back to his senses: "Ah, there's none so blind as those that will not see" said the voice of the old thief in front of him.

The Customs Men made camp for the night and released the prisoners from their bonds but hobbled their ankles. Their hands remained free, so they could eat the poor fare offered to them, even less now that there was an extra mouth to feed. Louis-Philippe's discomfiture was increased when the oldest smuggler dragged himself over to the nobleman's side: "I overheard t'was you who killed that Lecaron" he said in heavily accented French. The young man froze, remaining silent with terror. "He may have been a hero in France but not over there" the man nodded towards the Spanish side of the mountains. "My elder brother and I joined the irregulars and fought against the French. Gave them a right good hiding most of the time until one night…Lecaron's men set upon us, they did. They took no prisoners and I was lucky to escape with my life; my brother were'nt so lucky. He got killed - so you're among friends here." The older man spat noisily near Louis-Philippe who could not prevent himself leaning back to avoid the man's noxious garlic laden breath. It was with great relief that he saw the customs men had come into the clearing to secure the prisoners for the night.

He was dragged along the ground and his hands were tied together around a tree. He protested loudly at this indignity and received a cuff around the ear for his troubles. Silent now, he watched as the old man who had spoken to him was dragged across the ground and secured to his companions with a chain. The douanier who did this bent down, his face close to that of the oldest prisoner.

It seemed for just a moment that he was whispering in the other man's ear. Then the guard stood and walked briskly away, back to his companions around the fire.

Louis-Philippe was intrigued but too exhausted to care that much and swiftly fell into an uncomfortable sleep. He was woken by a soft voice in his ear. His mind registered that this was the voice of the old thief, both from the heavily accented French but more the powerful stench. The nobleman felt the cold steel of a flat bladed knife being pressed upon his neck as the man muttered: "Don't make a sound, I am going to loosen your wrists. We're off now. The alarm will be raised when the guard changes which won't be long. That'll be your opportunity! They'll be so busy looking for us…. you can get away. Good luck to you although it strikes me that I have but postponed your destiny. If you dare to try and follow us I shall kill you with my bare hands!"

The stench receded gradually into the darkness, but Louis-Philippe could still imagine the knife against his neck. As the feeling began to fade he heard a faint noise in the darkness and saw that one of the Douaniers was lying near where the smugglers had been chained. Silently the men had slipped away. Slowly the man began to stir and called to his companions. Louis-Philippe listened as he told his officer that he had been making sure that the prisoners were secure when he had tripped (or been tripped). He had fallen heavily, striking his head on a small rock. As evidence of this he pointed to a mark on his forehead. That was the last thing he remembered until now. The officer shone his lantern directly into the man's face and satisfied by the man's explanation, began a cursory search of the area around the camp. This only confirmed that the four prisoners had disappeared.

"I don't know how far they will have got but we have to find them, men. You, Henri stay and guard our new prisoner. You may have to answer to me about the four that got away; if *he* gets away you will be answering to General Destrier."

Hastily, the patrol rode off, leaving Henri seated on the ground rubbing the bump on his head. Louis-Philippe applied his mind to how he too might now escape. He had slowly wriggled his hands free from the bindings which had been almost cut through, but his ankles were still bound. He was certain this "Henri" was the one he had seen earlier with 'old garlic breath'. He must have taken a bribe. Initially Louis-Philippe thought he could probably offer a far greater bribe to the man but soon realised he had nothing to offer about his person, no valuables, no money, nothing and he understood an IOU would be of no use whatsoever. He sat wracking his brains and gradually a plan came to him. He slipped his right hand from behind the tree and felt around by his side until he found what he wanted. Then he quickly put his arm back into its place once more.

Henri looked very surprised when Louis-Philippe addressed him: "So, Henri is it? I saw you, you know. I saw you whispering with the old prisoner." Even in the darkness he sensed the man was panicking at these words: "Don't worry though, I shan't say a word. Your secret is safe with me. In fact, I can make your night's work even more profitable. I have something in my pocket that's worth a great deal. You know I am a wealthy man. Just free my arm for a moment and I shall get it. It's all yours, you shall be rich, rich beyond your wildest dreams. I just need a small favour."

"What?" cried Henri "Please, please I cannot do this. Destrier would come after me and my family. He is a powerful man. I couldn't do it. Never!" Then his tone changed: "but of course I shall help myself to whatever is in your pocket and there's nothing you can do about it. Where you're going you won't need money." The Douanier was feeling brave in front of the tethered man and smiled in the darkness. Louis-Phillipe braced himself as the guard bent over to examine his pocket and then quickly, with his freed left hand he grabbed Henri by the throat, holding the man tightly whilst with his right hand he picked up the sharp-edged rock he had found and brought it down hard on the man's skull several times. He continued to strike the man's head with the rock long after the luckless Henri had slumped motionless across the nobleman's legs. Louis-Philippe pushed the body away in disgust and swiftly untied his feet. He touched the body with his boot to confirm that the man was indeed dead and gingerly investigated the man's tunic to get a pistol which he put into his waistband. A single remaining horse was tied to a tree nearby, but Louis-Philippe was somewhat dismayed to find it had no saddle. He did not have time to fashion a bridle now – he must get away.

It had been a very long time since he had ridden bareback and it took him several attempts to get astride the horse and position himself comfortably. On this rock-strewn terrain, it was going to be a lot more difficult than in the stable yard where he had first learned to ride. Even now, after all that had happened, the fact that both his sister and his cousin had been more adept at riding riled him. He headed back down the trail he had been forced to walk up earlier. As he rode, his train of thought was disturbed by the sound of several loud gunshots in the distance echoing far above him. Until now he had not thought about the consequences of killing a douanier, only of regaining his freedom. What would happen when the others returned and found the body? They would certainly try to track him down. At this thought a shiver passed through his body. He recalled the old man's words before he left: had he 'postponed his destiny'? Did the old man see him restored to his rightful place – or a prisoner once more, or worse still, facing *Madame la Guillotine*, back in use but now for criminals?

Nervously he fingered his neck, feeling the prickle of a blade there and then dug his heels into the flanks of the horse but instead of making his way down the valley he rode upwards towards the mountains in pursuit of that strange convoy of animals and humans. He was drawn by a force he did not understand. The further he forced the horse on into the mountains the more he felt almost drawn forward to his destination – even though he did not know what that was. An almost magnetic attraction. Some part of his mind focused on freedom, Spain, anywhere far away from here but most of his mind focused on his half-sister and revenge. He had by now firmly established her as author of all his misfortunes and he was so distracted by his anger that he completely failed to notice the place where his quarry had left the roadway. It was therefore some time before he realised that the force that had been drawing him towards the mountains was weakening as he rode; he had lost the trail. Retracing his steps, he felt that pull becoming strong once more as he studied the road for signs. Retracing his steps, he found the churned-up path that the travellers had taken and followed their trail. His speed was restricted through the narrower gorges but where the land opened into broad green fields and meadows he pushed the horse on to a gallop. By the time he reached the place where the caravan had made camp the previous night he could see clearly many hoof prints; the trail was hot.

CHAPTER 63

Roland and the others stood together in shocked silence. The drama playing out below in the amphitheatre was as surreal as it was breathtaking. Brochard, now hideously transformed into a grotesque parody of wolf and man, climbed the steep side of the basin, scrabbling into the undergrowth on the far edge of the natural depression which apparently ended at the sheer cliff face. The two huge bears watched as the creature licked his many wounds. Ursian noticed that the beast was paying special attention to his right foreleg and went to talk with Sangres and Mimi for a moment. Watching the action below the bear announced: "It won't be long now; he'll make one final attempt at the Gates. After that, well he'll either be dead or he will give up for *the moment. Be* ready – despite his injuries, as soon as he picks up the scent of Hugo his hatred will reinvigorate him, even if for only a short time, and he will then be a truly formidable opponent. Don't underestimate him. Everyone knows what they must do?"

Kate, Roland and Amélie had already spotted some rocks behind which to take cover. André had taken up a position beside Hugo where he could, he hoped, intercept the Beast if it got through the waiting cordon of animals which Ursian had organised lying in wait beyond the rim of the bowl-shaped depression.

Meanwhile, Roland had selected a precariously high pile of rocks where he felt he would have a good shot down onto the centre of the clearing. Amélie was insistent that she had to conceal herself behind the pile of rocks immediately to Roland's right and so, while Kate took up her own position nearby, Amélie readied her not so small arsenal of weapons. With a musket clutched in her hand, she selected her best vantage point for a clear shot and then began to arrange her other weapons beside her balancing them on the rocks – the Gendarmerie-issue musket, the carbine (to which she enthusiastically attached the bayonet), and then her pistols.

She stood up into the position where her first musket shot would be taken then carefully reached out to her right, making sure she could reach all the other weapons.

She repeated this action but this time with her eyes closed, like an automaton. As Roland and Kate watched, fascinated, she repeated her actions, again taking each weapon in turn to the firing position and then closing her eyes once more and doing the same thing. After numerous attempts at each weapon, she opened her eyes finally and smiled in satisfaction.

The young officer looked at Kate, raising his eyebrows; she explained: "It's her party piece. She memorises exactly where each gun is so that as soon as she has fired one, she can reach easily for the next and has no need to look away from her target. Papa taught us both to do it almost as soon as we could lift a gun; he thought of us two as the sons he would have wished for, I think. Aunt Marianne, however, she really disapproves." Her fiancé raised his eyes and shook his head in disbelief, wondering just what sort of family gatherings there had been.

He took out his telescope and surveyed the clearing to study the *Loup Garou* in more detail. The Beast was almost exactly as Gilles Barbier had described. Standing at its full height, it was more than 2 metres high, its upper body covered in stiff, reddish brown fur which was thickly matted. The skin on the lower part of the Beast's body was noticeably scaly, reminding Roland of pictures of the creature 'armadillo' he had once seen in a book. Along the length of its crooked back stood a thick brush- like line of hair and the head was that of a wolf but with an elongated and malformed jaw and the addition of two pointed tusks, one on either side of the ugly muzzle. Saliva hung in sparkling rivulets from the creature's open jaw. It had enormous paws, elongated and knobby. Even at this distance, the long, pointed claws on each of them could clearly be seen.

Roland saw the two Guard Bears readying themselves for battle once more. Oursovi was standing on his hind legs, beating his thickly furred chest. Although Ursian had referred to him as a 'growing lad' at this moment the gendarme thought he was almost the size of Ursian himself. Ursianina was also in the clearing, walking on her four paws towards an area on the lower slopes of the bowl's side where thick bushes grew in a tangle, with large boulders strewn amongst them. It was here that Brochard waited. Ursianina walked around the clumps of thorny bushes slowly, head down, but emitting a terrifying growl as she walked.

After three circuits, she stopped directly in front of Brochard and raised her large body up onto her hind legs. She raised one huge paw above her head, as if waving, growling angrily. Roland and Kate listened intently to the noise and were able to 'know' what she said: 'I am Ursianina, Scion of the Clan of the Guard Bears, daughter of Ursian LeGrand, he who slew the Beast of Gévaudan. My Clan has guarded the Gates for as long as they have existed. No one comes here uninvited or has ever breached the Gates to Elysium and neither shall you. Come forward and fight."

These words reminded Roland of the challenge of medieval knights and he realised that of course some of those knights may well have had common ancestry with Ursianina. She fell back onto all fours shaking her enormous head and growling as if daring the Beast to come forward then she turned away from his hiding place disdainfully and walked slowly to the centre of the clearing. The Beast must have thought he had some chance of surprising her. As the humans watched in horror, it made a frantic charge in her wake but before it could strike, Ursian's daughter, with surprisingly balletic grace, spun back to face him, her huge jaws open as she began to rise to her full height. At the same moment, the young Oursovi who had waited for this opportunity, ran forward on all fours to block the Beast's retreat. He too then stood on his hind legs. The Beast was caught between the two giant animals and Ursianina continued to advance slowly, her jaws working. Brochard must have known now that he could not escape by returning to his hiding place, nor had he regained enough strength to take on a Guard Bear, let alone two.

Glancing around anxiously, he spotted the path which led towards the rim of the depression and back down to the Low Valley and knew that it might be his only way of escaping. He was unaware that an unpleasant surprise awaited him there. Summoning all his energy he feinted to the side of the Guard Bear's mighty arm and attempted to break away from her, but she was agile for such a large creature and as he ran past, she managed to land two heavy blows with her paws, one across the creature's head, making it spin, the second delivered with claws fully extended. This blow ripped through his right foreleg, already badly damaged.

He faltered briefly and almost fell but summoning the very last of his strength he staggered upwards towards the rim of the bowl, setting his sights on the path to freedom which lay ahead. Oursovi was all for following him but his aunt stopped him: "We have done our duty tho' I would have preferred to kill him. Our obligation is to guard the Gates and we must never neglect that. Anyway, I sense that your grandfather is close by. He will deal with the Beast from now on." Oursovi had been only a cub when his grandfather had left the High Valley and he was excited at the prospect of the return of the legendary chieftain who had nominated him, above all the others to guard today. The two huge animals now retreated towards the cliff face to wait.

Brochard was in pain and climbing became increasingly difficult but as he loped on he sniffed at the air. Many new scents assaulted his efficient snout but one, one special one, was familiar to him. His mind was clouded by powerful, strange thoughts, thoughts of a previous existence, of a threat, a dog, a Hound called Hugo. His Hound by rights…the cause of his pain and suffering…he relived the time he had spent rebuilding his shape into the hideous malformed creature he had become. He hated it. He knew that he could never possess Hugo as he had once hoped, but if he could not, then no-one would. Such was the angry turmoil he felt inside him that he almost forgot to concentrate his powers on healing his wounds, his mind clouded by the power of hatred. He must focus now on this and stopped on the steep path to inspect the recent wounds inflicted by Ursianina. He used his waning power as forcefully as he could to make the worst of the pain subside and the Beast rose once more and began his slow journey, his natural caution blunted by what had happened to him. His gait was crooked as he limped badly on his right side.

At last as he began to feel a little of his strength returning a sudden shot rang out and this time his right foreleg collapsed under him. Roland glanced at Amélie who was even now discarding her cousin's much-prized musket in favour of her own service-issue one. He looked at Kate and whispered: "Your father taught her well – her shooting does them both credit."

Ursian spoke to the waiting animals, especially the lions, to ensure that they were ready then he grunted to Hugo: "Your best Hound howl my friend, if you please." Hugo obliged happily, letting out a long, resonating and plaintiff howl that filled the valley below and rose eerily into the air. The Beast looked up from his position crouched on the path, his sensitive snout pointing straight towards Hugo. The pain in his leg was excruciating and almost all-consuming but Brochard immediately knew, he recognised the sound and smell of that…that Hound. Intent on killing him, the Beast channelled all his thoughts and energies into that task, momentarily forgetting the pain of the latest wound. As he staggered dangerously up the path towards his nemesis he came within normal musket range and three more shots rang out. Two shots entered the injured right foreleg of the Beast, further weakening him; with the third Amélie had aimed for the left foreleg. Although all three shots had hit their target after only a few moments the Beast seemed to recover. It started its uneven charge towards Hugo once more and the three humans were readying their carbines for another shot when all at once Sangres burst from the undergrowth beside the path, Mimi clinging grimly to the thick fur on his back. They could only watch as the old boar hit the Beast with his mighty head, his broken tusk boring into its right shoulder and he managed to push the Beast to the ground. Tiny Mimi then launched herself ferociously from Sangres' back sinking her sharp pointed little teeth into the Beast's neck, shaking her little head back and forth as the Beast roared in pain and anger.

The boar pawed the ground and launched himself once again charging into the side of his quarry then retreated, readying himself for another onslaught. Sangres charged as fast as he could and leapt up, powered by his strong back legs to bury his fearsome tusks once more into the side of the Beast, this time injuring it grievously. Sangres now backed away, exhausted by his efforts. At that moment Hugo howled again wildly, distracting Brochard from his pain. The *Loup Garou* had only one thought now, through all the pain and exhaustion...killing Hugo Hound.

The disorientated Beast suddenly swerved towards Kate, Roland and Amélie who had to hold their fire for fear of hitting Mimi, still grimly hanging onto the beast's bloody neck, like a tiny wriggling collar. The Beast drew close to the waiting guns, close enough for the humans to feel the heat of the thing's fetid breath, see his drooling jaws; at last a clear shot was possible.

All the shots found their mark and Amélie then also used all her pistols, dropping each in turn and reaching for the next mechanically. All her shots found their target. The Beast felt the burning hot impact of the shots but still it ran forward, impelled by hatred and anger. It no longer had the mental strength to repair itself; its remaining strength was focused on Hugo's piercing howls and the enemies he saw before him. Not until the last moment did he notice Ursian standing with the cordon of animals at the top of the path. The Beast careered onwards and made one final feint to avoid both guns and animals, but he was too weak. Ursian pulled himself up to his full height, raised one of his enormous paws and swatted the Beast as if it was a fly. The *Loup Garou* fell to the ground, panting for a moment but again, miraculously, managed to pull itself up, snarling viciously at the growling big cats. Sensing victory, the cats began to inflict increasingly powerful bites and scratches on the failing Beast. Ursian had trained them well - better ten small injuries to weaken than one single attack.

As Brochard tried vainly to rally his strength, he was able to throw the flailing Mimi from his matted neck, her small form flying through the air and landing heavily on a sharp rock where she lay motionless. Now he could see what had been clinging to his neck he recognised Hugo's little companion, the little terrier who had led him into that dark forest, now it was she who was ultimately responsible for all that had happened to him. The power of hatred was such that it rallied his waning strength momentarily, oblivious to the bites and scratches of the big cats, he threw himself upon the unconscious Mimi, intent on wreaking his revenge.

Amélie stood transfixed with horror but then realised what she must do and grabbed her carbine, its glittering bayonet fixed and ready. She leapt from her hiding place and ran at Brochard, closely followed by Roland and Kate clutching their pistols. Ursian too saw what the Beast was about to do and ran towards it just as Amélie threw herself at the swaying bloody figure, plunging the bayonet with all her strength deep into the creature's neck. Meanwhile, Ursian reached out to slash at the Beast's back but his extended claws clutched at emptiness…a blood curdling scream split the air and echoed amongst the rocks. The sound rose in intensity, piercing and painful to the animals' sensitive ears. Then, slowly, the dreadful sound became fainter and fainter as though it was rising into the sky…and then…an eerie silence. No trace of the beast remained.

CHAPTER 64

Louis-Philippe had heard Ursianina's growls, the deepest and loudest sounds he had ever heard during his years of hunting. He had dismounted or rather had slid awkwardly off the back of his mount and made his way up on foot until he could see what was happening. He successfully managed to avoid being seen because the focus of attention was elsewhere. He was just in time to witness Brochard's final vain assault. He had never believed in *Loup Garou* but here, before his eyes, was such a creature. He watched as it tried to make its way out of the 'arena'. An old saying came to his mind 'the enemy of my enemy is my friend'. 'This is my opportunity' he thought 'two of the biggest bears I have ever seen have so far failed to kill the Beast. What chance do my sister and her stupid cousin stand? He'll crush 'em underfoot. Only a true hunter will be able to slay that creature'. Then he heard the plaintive howl of his own Hugo Hound. At last the gods were on his side. He had been brought to this place for a reason. 'The Beast will dispatch my enemies and I shall capture Hugo.'

He took his stolen pistol from his waistband and trying to remain out of sight he observed the ferocious creature. He heard shots ring out and saw an old boar repeatedly charging at the Beast, but the creature, amazingly, shrugged off its many injuries. Distracted by the *Loup Garou*, he failed to notice Sangres, now crouched in the undergrowth trying to regain his breath. The old boar, however, did not fail to notice the young nobleman. Years of trying to protect his clan from hunters had taught him to be very wary and something about this human triggered a memory deep inside him. With his remaining strength Sangres charged once more, driving a sharp dirty tusk into the thigh of the human. He shook his huge head vigorously from side to side until eventually he tossed the screaming man aside like a rag doll. "Revenge" thought the animal "is sweet."

Louis-Philippe landed badly, his leg crumpling beneath him. He lay panting trying to assess his situation. He knew instinctively that the awful cry had signalled the end of the Beast – and with it the end of his hopes. He saw the pistol lying on the ground near him and knew he had only one shot, but he would make that count. Even though he might die in the attempt, he would have the comfort of knowing his sister would never steal his inheritance.

Amélie lay flat upon the ground where a moment before she and the Beast had been locked together. Before her stood her carbine, its bayonet skewered deeply into the earth as testament to the strength she had exerted in its use. Roland was about to offer his assistance to her when they heard the voice of André: "GET DOWN! Everyone!" Instinctively Roland and Kate threw themselves face down upon the ground beside Amélie but when Kate raised her head slightly she saw not the Beast reincarnated but the staggering figure of her brother, blood streaming from a wide gash in his thigh, weaving towards her, clutching a pistol which was aimed directly at her head. Unable to move, she felt rather than saw a shot whoosh above her head and watched as her brother crumpled to the ground and lay motionless.

Roland helped Amélie to her feet and they went over to Kate who was sitting on the ground staring at the hunched body of her brother. The girls hugged each other, the shocking events of the day and what they had done now beginning to have an effect on them. Roland looked across to where André stood, a pistol still smoking in his hand, tears coursing down his stricken face. He came towards Kate and bowed stiffly: "Forgive me Mlle, it was the only course left to me. I had to do it." She rose slowly and put her arms around the man, kissing him on both cheeks: “I know, André, I know. Thank you.”

Ursian picked up the tiny form of Mimi gently and cradled the little terrier in his arms. She wasn’t moving and he laid her down once more on the ground where Hugo nuzzled her comfortingly. Sangres, nursing a sore head sat down beside Mimi, murmuring some rather harsh-sounding boar grunts but she remained still, her inquisitive dark eyes now closed and her chest motionless; it was useless. Mimi’s last attack upon the Beast had meant the end of his miserable life, but also hers. Lucius, Favius and Leonid came to nudge her gently with their long noses and Lucius spoke with great gravity: “She fought like a lion, didn’t she lads?” His lion companions, licking their claws, sat on their haunches and each raised a huge padded paw in salute. Amélie and Kate sobbed quietly and Hugo released one single desolate howl of sorrow.

Roland went to inspect the body of Louis-Philippe. The shot had been straight to his heart. He retrieved the dead man’s pistol. Roland knew Louis-Philippe could only have acquired it in one way – making his escape. Kate, Amélie and Ursian soon joined him and Kate looked down at her brother’s dead body impassively: “We must bury him here. The journey back to La Garenne is too long and moreover I could not allow him to be buried near to my father, nor to the man he murdered. It would dishonour their memories.” Her words were cold and without emotion. “Roland, André, I have no knowledge of such matters. At Waterloo, there was no time for any ceremony. The bodies were piled high and then put into trenches…” the memory of this clearly still haunted her mind.

Ursian stepped forward: “I once saw a humankind ‘funeral’, although I did not understand it. This place is in sight of the Gates of the High Valley however and no Renegade should be buried here, but there is a place further back along the road which would be appropriate. I will gladly assist if you will allow me?”

The slow procession set off, Ursian carrying the body of Louis-Philippe in his great arms. The four humans walked behind Ursian with Hugo trotting faithfully alongside. Sangres had been left behind in charge of the menagerie. Lucius, forever truculent, had thought about arguing this decision. He felt he should have been in charge but having been awake for more than five hours preferred to take a well-earned a nap.

The little group reached the spot that Ursian had chosen. As if she knew what had happened, Athina was already there, dressed this time in a sombre grey robe. She hugged both Kate and Amélie in turn as Ursian lay the body down and began to scoop huge pawfuls of earth, then rocks from the ground until he had fashioned a grave large enough for a man. Ursian gently laid the body in the hole and Roland, who had attended many, far too many, funerals of friends and comrades recited the words of the military service. The bear was ready to scoop huge pawfuls of earth into the grave when Kate stepped forward indicating that she would like to say a few words.

Roland looked at his fiancée marvelling at how well she appeared to be coping with these shocking events. She was shaking a little and her voice faltered as she began to speak: "It was my father's wish that we" she looked at her cousin 'learn the language of England." Amélie winced at the memories. "Our governess made us read the works of a William Shakespeare. One of his plays was entitled Julius Caesar and I recall that after Caesar is assassinated, his friend Mark Antony gives his eulogy. I hope that I can now remember the words correctly: he said: 'the evil that men do lives after them, the good is oft interred with their bones.' Roland was watching Kate, but his eyes strayed to Athina who was positively glowing with pride. "Well, I wish that the opposite may happen now. My brother died an evil man and it is my hope that it is this evil, which is now interred with his bones, rather than the good. One day I truly hope that Amélie and I will be able to remember the good times we once had with him when we were children, long before this…terrible madness afflicted him."

She stopped speaking and looked down at his pale face, tears slowly seeping from her eyes. "I hope that whatever tormented you so, my brother, has left you forever." She picked up a handful of earth and bowed to scatter it upon her brother's face. Roland did likewise then remembering Kate's words about the 'evil being interred' took the pistol which Louis-Philippe had obviously stolen and threw this into the grave. Amélie and André scattered a little earth too and finally Athina took a piece of heather and threw this in as well. The haruspex hugged Kate and wiped away her tears, then Roland took over and held Kate tightly whilst Ursian finished filling the grave. It would remain unmarked. Taking note of the surroundings in his mind for the inevitable report he must one day make to Destrier, Roland led the little group back up the mountain.

They rejoined the other animals at the spot where the Beast had been so successfully defeated. Ursian rummaged on the ground and eventually retrieved a piece of steel shot which he sniffed with his huge nostrils. Satisfied that he had found what he was looking for he walked back to the group of human onlookers who were somewhat confused.

"Mlle. Catherine, could you please translate for me?" Ursian asked courteously and began a rather formal speech: "We are all most grateful to the humans for your efforts on our behalf in dealing with that infernal Beast; our thanks go especially to Mlle. Amélie who forever more will be known by our kind as "Amélie the Vanquisher" Her name shall live on in legend in the High Valley for what she has done today. Could you please ask her if I may retain this for a little while? I will return it to her." Ursian held up the battered steel ball and bowed low in front of Amélie, who had listened with interest but without any understanding to the bear's growls. Ursian went on then to thank Sangres formally but the boar's rheumy eyes returned often to the still form of his friend, Mimi. Meanwhile, Kate relayed Ursian's words to her cousin who immediately nodded her assent, puzzled but agreeable.

CHAPTER 65

The natural amphitheatre where the battle had taken place was now peaceful. The two huge bears who had been engaged in the battle were nowhere to be seen. At the far side, the rock face seemed as impenetrable as ever. Then Ursian called out loudly: "Open the Gates" and, as if by magic, two enormous, armour clad bears materialised seemingly out of the rock itself. Roland immediately knew that these two magnificent animals were the Guard Bears Oursovi and Ursianina whom he had seen in action earlier. He recalled that just before Louis-Philippe had been captured, Ursian had been close by but the young nobleman had not noticed him. He marvelled that these animals, gigantic by normal standards, seemed to be able to merge into their surroundings.

The cliff face now appeared to be shifting silently, almost melting away, to reveal a gigantic pair of iron gates, studded and finely wrought with long spikes at the top. An elaborate lock was attached to their centre. As the gates opened inwards, they revealed a high stone archway and the path which had previously ended in the amphitheater could now be seen to extend far into the distance. They were looking at the High Valley, Elysium itself. As the space between the two white cliff faces grew, the onlookers could see that the path rose and fell between green meadows carpeted with wildflowers. There stood tall pine trees and beyond them was a solid wall of dark green, a forest. Figures could be seen moving in the meadows, too far away to make out in any detail but many were four-legged. It was becoming late afternoon in the 'real' world but beyond the gates of the High Valley the sun still shone brightly. Dark waves of birds swept across the intense blue sky in formations and everyone at once felt an indefinable sense of tranquility, despite all that had happened during the day. Kate saw that the Valley was surrounded by dark purplish mountains, some very high with a white cap on their peak and something glittered at their foot, a wide river fed by many powerful waterfalls. There was, they realised, an unnatural silence beyond the cliffs; they felt they were being watched yet saw nothing nearby, at least at first.

"Hugo, Ursian I believe it is time to say goodbye" said Roland, with a great sadness in his voice. He went to ruffle the thick fur around Hugo's neck then proffered his hand to the great bear. "I promised that I would see you safely to the High Valley. We humans will wait here now until the last of the animals passes through the Gates and then my promise is fulfilled, my friend."

Before Ursian could even take the extended hand, Athina was beside him glaring fiercely: "And so where do you think you are going, Roland Lebrun?"

"I must return to La Garenne, Madame Athina. We humans cannot enter the High Valley so..."

"Why not?" enquired the haruspex sharply.

"Well, you told us that we couldn't" Kate joined in, trying to shield Roland from Athina's anger.

"Rubbish Catherine, I told you that no Paladin of humankind had ever returned to the High Valley not that they could not return. Surely you must wish to visit the land of your ancestors? Before you try to start an argument just for the sake of it..." she drew breath "André Lacoste has also been invited by Pellerin himself to join us as an honoured guest."

To ward off further debate, Roland intervened for by now he knew how much Kate enjoyed a good argument, especially with Athina. "Madame Athina, we would be delighted to join you in the High

Valley; we would love to see the land of our ancestors." Kate nodded meekly in agreement and so the procession set off on the last few steps of its strange journey.

News of events beyond the Gates had reached all the inhabitants of the Valley and as the unlikely procession passed through the wide opening in the cliff face – its sides shimmering slightly – more and more creatures could be seen coming from the farthest pastures. At the forefront of the welcome party stood the Guard Bears, easily distinguishable from the other bears by their sheer size and by the simple but effective leather armour which they wore, their huge chests covered by strips of woven hide studded with thick metal bosses.

Standing just behind the Guard Bears were many cubs, all born after Ursian had left the Valley so many years before, jostling rowdily and tumbling on the grass in their excitement. Since birth they had been told about the great Ursian, his past exploits and now, here he was, in the flesh. The cubs had been forbidden to go beyond the line marked by the Gates but paid no attention to that and one after another, they spilled out from between the cliffs into the amphitheatre beyond only to be chased back by an increasingly frustrated Oursovi. Ursianina, as the senior Guard Bear, looked on nonchalantly whilst her nephew sought to stem the flow of small furry forms as best he could.

Oursovi might have fought a *Loup Garou*, indeed the youngest Guard Bear ever to have done so, but he was no match for determined, excited cubs. Eventually, Ursian decided that enough was enough and called to Ursianina to let the cubs venture beyond the gates…just this once.

As each animal entered the High Valley, Ursian stood by introducing them to his waiting wife and family. Representatives of all the animal Clans had come down to the Gates to wait, looking for any one of the newcomers who might be related to them. When introductions were over, the newcomers were quickly absorbed into the throng greeting their newfound 'families'.

The tightknit group of Fighting Bears loudly greeted their cousins and immediately set up an impromptu game with them, amid much shouting and the occasional growl!

Last through the Gates were the humans who were to stay with Ursian in his cave, Amélie carrying the still form of little Mimi wrapped in a silk shawl she had retrieved from her saddlebag. Ursian explained at length the part that these humankinds had played in the defeat of the Beast, praising Amélie especially, using the 'bear' form of Amélie, *Ursalie*. Ursian had explained that URS or OURS was the Guard Bears' clan name and the end of the name denoted the individual animal. It was considered the height of bad manners to use only the individual bear's name. Now Amélie was an honorary Guard Bear, they had bestowed the name ALIE upon her, Amélie being difficult for a Bear to pronounce.

Before Ursian took the humans to his home he said they must first put Mimi to rest. As he said this, his face was grim and pained. He called his brother Guard Bears to help him prepare a suitable burial place for such a heroine, very near to his cave. In a few moments it seemed they had scooped out enough rich loam to create a shallow trench and Amélie insisted that the little dog remain wrapped in her fine shawl. Hugo, Sangres, Ursian and the humans stood with heads bowed as the tiny bundle was laid in the ground and Hugo was unable to hold back a chilling Hound howl as the earth closed over his dear friend. Ursian gently patted Hugo's head: "Don't worry, my friend, she will always be remembered here for her bravery.". Finally, they left the spot, all except Sangres who remained standing beside the shallow grave for some time.

All the bears including the cubs, who had by now been rounded up, bowed in turn to each humankind. The cubs seemed fascinated by Amélie and would not leave her side until Ursian told them to give her some room to move. The very strange group made the short journey on foot to the cave where they would all stay. Traditionally, the Guard Bears occupied the caves nearest the Gates.

As they moved off through the lush green pastures, they stopped now and then to admire the view and just breathe the air which almost crackled with joy and contentment around them. Behind them they heard a grinding and creaking sound, loud but not threatening. Glancing back, they saw that the Gates were once more closing on the outside world and where before there had been a rift in the huge cliffs, once again there was a solid wall of vine-hung rock.

Ursian and Ursetta, his wife, showed the humans to their quarters which were a series of dry, warm side chambers cut into the end of a small tunnel detached from the main cave. Bedding had been provided: clean straw and fern branches covered a paillasse of woven twigs. The humans discovered that this was surprisingly comfortable. After they had explored this part of the cave, Ursian took them on a full tour of the great cave complex, introducing them to each member of his Clan, a long and laborious process for them all, considering the number of relatives and the fact that all the names, to their ears, sounded confusingly similar.

Each member of the Clan bowed to them, but most particularly to the newly christened Ursalie, who by now was being followed by a growing number of playful cubs. Amélie was clearly enjoying her newly exalted status. She joked to Kate that 'of course, I will expect this kind of homage from you but as you are family, one curtsey a day will suffice.' In response, Kate leaned over and whispered something quietly in Amélie's ear which made both girls blush: "Catherine de Garenne, I am shocked, I didn't think you knew language like that! What would Maman say" laughed Amélie. Roland overhead and was most amused by their banter, pleased too that the dreadful events of that day appeared to have left few scars on the young ladies.

Their mood became more serious when they reached the part of the cave where Athina was tending to the injured Fitzursian. Athina was cleaning the wound with moss soaked in a clear but very pungent liquid, she then applied a thick grey paste to the exposed flesh of the wound. The foreleg was dislocated but not broken, she explained. It had taken the full force of the Beast's fury when he had gone to his uncle's rescue. She enlisted his father's help to put the limb back in place. The injured beast remained silent as Athina explained how this would be done and then the Ursian took the limb and pulled very hard, letting it fall gently into place. Fitzursian nodded weakly as Athina explained that the wounds were clean and would heal over time, but he would have to walk on his hind legs, keeping any weight off his foreleg.

Amélie watched, fascinated: "It would be better if she put the arm in a sling" she said quietly.

"Yes, it would but as you may have noticed, bears don't have much call for fabric" replied Athina, scathingly.

"Sorry, just thinking aloud. I was only trying to help…" Kate intervened at this point to save her cousin's embarrassment by telling them both she had an idea. She disappeared back into the depths of the cave and returned with a tight bundle of silk which she handed, rather sheepishly to Amélie. The bundle contained a very fine petticoat. Without comment, Amélie studied the damaged limb trying to gauge how much fabric would be needed to make a good sling before reaching down into her riding boot and removing a large knife. She cut the pretty garment into wide strips. Kate blushed at this display of her undergarments before Roland, who tactfully looked elsewhere.

With Athina's help Amélie quickly formed and applied a makeshift support. On the way back to their quarters, Amélie could not resist having a jibe at Kate:" Well that was a surprise! Rather more exotic than our normal traveling clothes." Kate looked away as she muttered that Aunt Marianne had always told them both to be prepared for every eventuality – well indeed Kate had, and she had been right; the petticoat had at last been useful. Amélie smiled thinking to herself that had her Maman been present, she would have described this as a 'Kate's truth'. Both girls remained silent for a while but Amélie, emboldened by her exploits, could not allow Kate to slip off the hook so easily and had to ask: "So what else was in your saddlebag? What other essentials? A ball gown suitable for a wedding perhaps?"

"Don't be ridiculous, Amélie" replied Kate huffily – then had to laugh out loud.

CHAPTER 66

The new arrivals both human and animal quickly settled into their new surroundings. Even Unika discovered another unicorn, a stallion called Unicarus. Although delighted to find one of her species, she was also slightly miffed that she was no longer unique. Sangres was overjoyed to discover that not only was he welcomed into a tribe of wild boar but treated with the enormous respect deserved by one who had not only helped the caravan to reach safety but for his part in killing a *Loup Garou*, a task previously only performed by a Guard Bear. Since he had run from the forest to protect his old tribe he had sometimes felt rather lonely and isolated, even amongst his friends in the caravan and he felt keenly the loss of little Mimi. Now he had a new 'family' and his position as a patriarch was assured. He did spend time often at Ursian's cave where he was a welcome guest. It was rumoured in fact that Ursian would sometimes ask for his advice. A *bear* asking a boar for advice? Unheard of.

Hugo was adopted by a pack of chasse Hounds and he relished the freedom which he had, relieved of all responsibilities and happy to be what he really was a young, carefree Hound, sniffing and foraging in the nearby forests. The other Hounds did notice a change in him, however, after he had received a visit from Ursian, Athina and Pellerin. A permanent frown seemed to have developed on his already wrinkled brow. Clearly something was troubling him. Roland felt he must ask the Hound why he seemed so sad.

"I don't know; it's just that I have never been so content but it appears I am needed to help rescue those in other Sanctuary Inns. I know it is my duty, they need me but…"

Rather surprisingly, Lucius was the first of the ‘returnees’ as they became known, to master shape changing, followed quickly by Meera. His favourite trick – of course – very quickly earned him censure from Ursian. The lion could transform himself into a beautiful white stallion and he would trot daintily towards Unika and Unicarus, attract their attention by pawing on the ground and would then execute a perfect front-leg bow in front of the two unicorns. When he had their complete attention, he would change very quickly back into his lion form and let out a great roar. “Gets em every time” he chuckled to Favius and Leonid. Meanwhile, Meera amused herself by changing from an Indian tiger into a white Siberian tiger and admiring herself in one of the many lakes. She also perfected the trick of moving her stripes around her body, changing their position and colour at a frightening rate. Lucius moaned that this gave him a headache which merely made her do it even more, and with greater speed. Eventually Lucius was forced to make her the offer she had been waiting for: he would surrender his title of King of the Jungle; she could take that too if she would just PLEASE stop.

Favius and Leonid discovered (after some trial and error) that they too could change shape but not without a few initial setbacks. Leonid’s first effort found him changed not into a fearsome giant but a frog, which Favius promptly pretended to step on. Only Ursian’s swift intervention saved Leonid from becoming a very flat frog. Archimedes joined the horse clan and steadfastly refused to even try and change his shape, but he did become a frequent visitor to the cave where he too was treated as an ‘honorary’ bear; he would seek out Kate to have what he called ‘real conversation’. He was a true intellectual snob. “If I have heard one horse tell me that the grass is greener on the other side of the valley, I have heard it a hundred times. Of course it is. That’s where the river is, it’s obvious, but you just can’t use reason with them.” He complained frequently for his total lack of humour far outweighed what he had acquired in intellect.

Whilst the animals settled themselves in their new home and began to practice their new skills, the humans were also trying to adapt to all that they discovered in this High Valley paradise. André was the least well prepared for all that he saw. Until he had left La Garenne, his life had been governed by the knowledge that eventually there was a logical, rational explanation for everything. Now he was in a world where this no longer applied. He was in a world where he had learned creatures could become different creatures. Athina spent a lot of time in her human form translating Pellerin's explanations of the behaviour of the eagles in which André was very interested.

He would take himself off into the hills and spend hours just watching these magnificent birds but since everything Pellerin and the other eagles told him had to be translated for him, he still felt rather left out.

Amélie found herself being bowed to at every opportunity. Ursian would spend hours in his human form with her explaining the different bear sounds and slowly she began to understand simple words and tried them out on some of the others. She gradually began to string together some simple phrases but unfortunately, she was not as good at this new form of communication as she liked to imagine. Ursian returned to his family cave one day to find his relatives convulsed with laughter, some rolling in the dust of the cave clutching their fat furry stomachs with mirth. He roared in mock anger at the Clan who were showing such discourtesy to an honoured guest. The young cubs slunk away, chastened then Ursian asked her to repeat what she had said so that he might correct her.

Unfortunately, when she repeated her phrase he too failed to contain his laughter and collapsed guffawing in front of the humiliated Amélie, tears streaming down his big face. Unamused for once, she stalked out of the cave to metaphorically lick her wounds. That evening when she was alone with Kate she asked her cousin cautiously: "Kate, you understand the bear tongue, what is wrong with this phrase?" Amélie repeated her phrase very seriously and Kate really tried hard to keep a serious expression on her face – she failed, convulsed like the others in hysterical giggling but refused to explain. Even though occasionally a cub would develop a fit of giggles when Amélie spoke to them, no-one ever told her what awful thing she might have said.

Despite these setbacks, she was a very determined young woman and persisted with until she found that she could speak an intelligible, if rudimentary, form of bear and could understand much more. Ursian was very keen that his family should be able to read and write human words. He knew that if they were, like him, to venture out into the outside world they would need these skills even if they had to keep them hidden from humankind.

Amélie undertook the task of teaching the younger animals, sitting before the group like a stern schoolmistress. The bears would transform their chubby paws into something resembling a human hand, able to hold pieces of chalk.

Clumsily at first, they copied the letters of the human alphabet which she wrote on a piece of polished rock face in front of them. To begin with, the lessons were chaotic; even Amélie was no match for their sense of fun and playfulness and misunderstandings were plentiful. However, when Ursian stepped in to help translate, things quietened down. The young bears particularly liked the part of their lessons where they could redecorate their cave walls with clay coated paw drawings of bison and woolly mammoths and other weird animals that their parents had described to them.

Ursian had told Roland that sunrise across the High Valley was always spectacular so on the first morning of their stay, he and his fiancée had risen early and left the cave to observe it. They had not been disappointed. They watched, transfixed, as the sheer sides of the mountains slowly became suffused with a soft pink glow which intensified to a deep mauve and red as the sun rose slowly in the sky. Ursian joined them and he sat contentedly soaking in a sight he had not seen in the past ten winters. As the display came to an end the bear turned casually to Roland: "It's a good thing for both of us that Athina made me promise not to hurt you." He started to chuckle "If I had killed you I would have had to banish myself for killing a fellow Oursi". He obviously found this highly amusing and slapped his thigh quite forcefully, then more gently slapped Roland's back. Neither of his companions appeared to be sharing his sense of humour.

"I studied the earliest Rolls last night and Athina was right – alongside my great, great grandpapa Pristinian, is written the name of his brother Fractus – that was his 'old' name. He was one of the Oursi who decided to take human form and adopted the name Hugh of Lebruin. Fractus left the High Valley with the legendary Roland and fought alongside him at Roncesvalles. Of course, he was a Paladin and you are a direct descendant.

All those Paladin who followed Roland took the name Lebruin to remind them of their connection to the bears of High Valley. Over time this became shortened to Lebrun. So, you are both my cousins – if a little distant. In fact, you are almost as close to me as old Gilles! I must add your name to the Rolls." Ursian was muttering to himself now "Hm, should it be after Fractus or between the Lady Catherine and young Ursalie?"

Whilst the bear was stroking his nuzzle and contemplating this problem Kate asked: "Cousin Ursian, is that 'Lady Catherine' me?"

"Of course, all the members of the House of Garenne are inscribed in the Rolls. I must tell you that I struck out your brother's name last night." His face was a blank mask for just a moment, then he continued brightly: "Now, was that not an excellent sunrise? I expect you'll want to explore the High Valley whilst you are here?"

Both nodded enthusiastically and Ursian pointed towards a mountain in the far distance: “Always stay this side of that river, see just at the foot of the mountains? Once you are on the slopes beyond it you are in danger. That is called First Mountain. Each Clan emerged from one of its caves (we call them Gates) and when our time in this world is over it is to the Gates that we must return. There is no coming back from First Mountain”. Ursian’s mood lightened once more when he issued another warning: “Oh, and never venture into the Cave of the Northern Bears after dusk. You’ll be safe enough, but you may feel a little, err, uncomfortable. They start drinking in earnest after dark. Oh yes, and never, ever, ever accept a challenge from the Fighting Bears to a game of stones – most of their games last beyond a human lifespan.”

CHAPTER 67

Ursian left them, still chuckling to himself but Kate was perplexed: "I don't understand some of this. We are all *cousins*? What does that mean? M. Lafitte-Dupont has had me study every single Steward of the House of Garenne since the beginning and there is definitely no mention of a Lebrun or a Lebruin. Those studies have covered hundreds of years, right back to Guillaume and Eleanor - there seem to be few facts about either of them. It is as if they appeared out of thin air. But *of course*, that could be the explanation. Athina would know; *she* was around then so I shall go and ask her!" Roland nodded but cautioned her once more about Athina's extreme reaction to the name 'Eleanor'.

Undaunted, Kate sought out the haruspex who was sitting outside Ursian's cave, combing out her long silvery hair. "I wonder if you could help me?" she asked with great politeness and not a little trepidation. "Cousin Ursian tells me that I belong to his Clan, the Oursi, but none of my ancestors bore the name Lebrun or Lebruin. I only ask because when I become Steward of the Bequest I have to ensure that I have all the facts. I don't want to miss something if M. Lafitte-Dupont's records are incomplete…or…" her voice trailed off as she studied Athina's face for clues.

"Catherine, I know you well enough to know when you are not telling the complete truth, but I think that you may have been trying to protect my feelings…you know very well that all the Bequest's records have been kept meticulously. What you really want to know relates to Guillaume and …his wife". Kate looked sheepishly at the ground and nodded.

. “I ask you to be patient with me. There is something long neglected which needs my attention. Pellerin is right, now is the time. When this thing is over I will explain, truly I will.” Athina looked troubled as she squeezed Kate’s hand and then abruptly changed the subject. “Of course, you have Oursi ancestry - part of you must have known that. Ursian is a distant cousin, did you not wonder why you automatically addressed Ursian as Cousin Ursian?

This is a greeting only used between senior Guard Bears. Amélie too is related to the bears, you know.” Athina laughed as they watched the young lady in question rolling on the grass outside the cave, under a pile of squabbling cubs.

Roland and Kate frequently rode off down into the Valley taking picnic lunches of fresh bread (made by Kate under the watchful eye of Ursetta) with delicious ewe’s milk cheese of which Ursian’s wife was exceptionally proud. The recipe had been handed down from her Grandmother, Oursi Iratti, and was now being produced by humankind in the Low Valley too. Athina seemed to be far more relaxed about them being unchaperoned than she had been in the outside world although Aiguillin would fly over them several times every day and there were always eagles patrolling near the river.

Ever since they had been reunited at the Sanctuary Inn, Kate and Roland had spent little time on their own and now they took the opportunity to find out more about each other. They also began to start thinking of their future together. Roland had regretfully decided that to be able to support his future wife in the manner to which (he assumed) she was accustomed he would have to leave the Gendarmerie for more lucrative employment. He could not imagine Kate being happy as an officer’s wife, likely to be posted to another town at a moment’s notice. His father and Roland’s uncle had built up a successful wine business in Paris which his uncle now ran alone. He wanted his own son, together with Roland to take over the reins and Roland felt that this could be his future.

However, Kate was less than happy at the thought of moving to Paris, leaving her beloved La Garenne. She explained that she did not have 'a manner to which she was accustomed'. She received a comfortable quarterly allowance which was controlled by her aunt for now. Most of this she saved to finance her 'little excursions'. Growing up, she had received a small amount of pocket money, but the dreaded Mme. Dubois had insisted that she had to earn it, doing chores including scrubbing the kitchen floor and in the late summer helping with the harvest on the neighbouring farms. Jokingly she asked if a life of servitude was what Roland had in mind for her, but finally she was forced to explain that her life was already mapped out as Steward of the Bequest. Now it was time to explain the truth of her responsibilities.

Roland was considerably shaken as she detailed the full extent of the wealth available in the Bequest, and its obligations. Roland already knew that the venom spouted by the late Louis-Philippe had been far more than sibling rivalry, but Kate assured him that her half-brother had had no real inkling of the size of the Bequest. What she told him made Roland realise that her life could well have been in danger every day if Louis-Philippe had lived. Kate dismissed his concerns. "I was never in any danger from my half-brother, well at least until recently. André had sworn to my father to protect me, which of course he has done."

The days gradually became longer, the light leaving the Valley later and later. The snow was melting from the peaks of the highest mountains far beyond the Valley - they both knew that the time had come to return to La Garenne. They spoke first to Athina who asked them to postpone their departure for a few more days as the next day there was to be a meeting of the Grand Council, only the fifth to have ever been held and Ursian was to be appointed as the Premier Bear, not just Chieftain of the Guard Bears but also as President of the Grand Council of Elysium. All these were honours which had been bestowed upon him during his enforced absence from the Valley.

Although he had been made aware of these since his return, with characteristic modesty he had not mentioned them to Kate or Roland although Hugo knew but had been sworn to secrecy.

Early the next morning the cave of Ursian's Clan was a hive of activity. Ursetta, Ursian's large happy wife was organising food for everyone, including the humans. Ursianina supervised the younger bears who were all assembled at the back of the cave where a clear waterfall ran into a crystalline pool. Each would wash under the falls and shake themselves dry then present themselves to Ursianina; she would either let them pass or take them by their scruff and throw them back into the pool.

Once all had eaten breakfast, a magnificent spread of berries and fruits, home-made bread and honey, Ursetta and Ursianina busied themselves getting everyone ready and eventually Ursian led his entire Clan and his guests out of the cave in procession. Ursian led the group proudly with his wife and his daughter at his side and young Oursovi just behind them, his chest bursting with pride at being seen with his distinguished grandfather. Next came Fitzursian, now recovered sufficiently from his injuries followed by Amélie, André, Roland and Kate. Sangres walked beside Archimedes, both 'Honorary Bears'. Then came the rest of Ursian's bear Clan, the smaller cubs trying to run ahead and keep close to Amélie. From two large caves on the other side of the valley emerged the other bear Clans and from further up the valley could be heard, and then seen, the lions, with Lucius prominent amongst them, a herd of elephants, horses walking in twos, a small band of assorted tigers and leopards happily dwelling together. There was an especially large contingent of wild boars too. Meanwhile, flocks of birds flew overhead, the huge eagles leading them and even the owls, rarely seen in daylight, flew low above the heads of their animal companions.

Bringing up the rear of the vast group of animals came the Hounds, yapping and barking with delight and led by the proud

Hugo Hound. They all made their way down the Valley until Ursian stopped in a grassy meadow dotted with yellow and white flowers. There were several natural green knolls in the meadow forming perfect platforms and Ursian's clan occupied one of these. Ursetta motioned to Kate, Amélie, Roland and André to sit on some boulders in the meadow, with Sangres and Archimedes close by. As each Clan arrived, the leader would join Ursian and their members would occupy one of the knolls. Hugo, Lucius, Favius and Leonid together with Meera and all the horses, including Marron and Greco, took their places beside the humans. Pellerin and Athina landed beside Ursian in the centre of the meadow. Last to arrive were Unika and Unicarus who took up a position behind a group of horses but Ursian called Unika to join the others at the front, which she did, but ensuring she kept her distance from Lucius.

Ursian then rose and growled greetings to everyone assembled. He thanked all the animals for their part in getting the caravan to safety. As each animal was mentioned all the Clans would cheer or stamp and even Lucius and the lions managed to cheer Unika. This they did in the traditional manner, standing on their hind legs and waving their huge paws in the air shouting: "Yeah" whilst vigorously fist-bumping each other!

Ursian called then for silence as he approached the end of his long list of names, with only Hugo, Sangres, Lucius and the humans unmentioned. He turned his back on the gathering and indicated towards one of the large mountains which surrounded the Valley. The humans could now see that, seemingly carved into the rocks were what looked like monuments to various animals. There were the shapes of several bears, an eagle, and an owl, a lion and another bear that looked like Ursian. The rest of the mountain side appeared to be covered in a shimmering veil of mist, a low silken cloud which hid whatever lay beyond.

Once he had everyone's attention and all the whickering, whinnying and barking had finally subsided he began: "Today, the Grand Council honours our newest legends" and with a great sweep of his arm the mist covering the mountainside cleared to reveal detailed carvings of Hugo Hound, Sangres with Mimi perched on his back, Archimedes and Lucius. This was greeted with tumultuous and prolonged cheering, whooping, hooting, barking and stamping. Roland translated for the benefit of André and Amélie.

Ursian once again managed to restore order and addressed the humans standing together: "I am afraid that our skills do not extend to carving human features but nevertheless you will always be remembered by us as true legends just as the bravery of Mimi the Terrier will live on in the stories of the bears and their descendants. We hereby honour her memory. Now, I have some mementos which I hope you will accept as a token of our gratitude. André Lacoste" Ursian's voice echoed around the Valley. "You were a loyal companion to our Cousin, Duc Philippe de Garenne and although the promise that you made was indeed onerous, you fulfilled your duties in the manner of a bear."

Roland translated but also explained that this was perhaps the highest compliment Ursian could give as he translated. Ursian waited a moment, seeming almost emotional then continued: "You saved the life of our Cousin Catherine de Garenne." He stopped, bent down and picked something from the grass then walked towards André, who could feel the ground vibrate as the great animal approached. To his surprise, Ursian bowed low in front of him proffering a gift whilst Pellerin and two of his clan flew close to him, hovering somewhat precariously, bowing their great heads. He took the object from the paw of the bear who returned to his place giving André an opportunity to inspect his gift: this was a heavy, solid rectangle of black granite fashioned into a writing stand with an intricate inkwell and two neatly made holes for quill pens each made from an eagle feather. The quills were each inlaid with white gold engraved into which, in minute detail, were runic symbols very like those which he had seen in Ursian's cave. The inkstand itself bore a white gold inscription upon it; a phrase written in old French. André was still able to translate this though: it said, "No matter what it takes."

Ursian then addressed himself to Roland: "My Cousin, my true friend, I apologise before this gathering for my behaviour to you. You helped us when we were in dire need of help, you protected us, and you helped kill the *Loup Garou*. You truly deserve the name Lebruin. After the great Roland fell at Roncesvalles, my great great grandfather found Roland's Oliphant." Ursian bent to retrieve a strange white ivory hunting horn, trimmed with intricate gold piercing. He walked towards the Captain proffering it with both paws: "I believe it should have a fitting home in La Garenne." Roland was stunned by his gift, not only a magnificent piece of art but a real heirloom from a time he had only read of in books.

Turning then to Kate: "Lady Catherine, my dear Cousin, we are honoured that a descendant of Lady Eleanor has come to our Valley. Your family has never hesitated to help us, and you have followed in that tradition. It gives us all great pleasure to know that the families of Lebruin and Garenne are now to be united once more and I look forward to attending your wedding celebrations, assuming you have a place for a slightly overweight 'drayman's assistant!'" She smiled at this as the bear continued: "One of my ancestors made a small gift which he had intended to give to the Lady Eleanor on her marriage, but it seemed inappropriate after, well, the tragedy that occurred."

Once again Ursian bent and retrieved something lying at his feet. It was an ornate box made of polished sheets of agate, which he offered to Kate. Within it she saw, lying on some fine silken fabric, a narrow circlet of gleaming white gold with a raised central portion. Into this was set a magnificent sapphire flanked by two smaller stones. Ursian removed the circlet from the case and placed it very gently upon Kate's head saying: "It is going home at last."

Kate was too overwhelmed by the moment to respond. Lost for words she stood and threw her arms around Ursian, clinging to his fur as her feet left the ground. The moment was brief as she realised that her reaction might be seen as inappropriate but instead the assembled crowd began to bellow and stomp on the grass with their huge feet. Ursian disentangled himself, clearly moved, and made his way back to the Council Members. Kate was adjusting her new headpiece to make it secure when she was touched by a slim hand, that of the haruspex Athina, who whispered: "It suits you my dear. It would please me greatly if you would wear it on the day you marry." Before the girl could react Athina was again perched beside Pellerin, an owl once more.

Then came perhaps the most emotional moment of the day: Ursian turned back to the human group and singling out Amélie with his eyes then pronounced only one word: "Ursalie!" before his voice was drowned out by the noises from the young bears who whooped, grunted and beat their chests, followed by the rest of the other Clans. He waited for them to calm down, but the din continued until the young girl stood up and put a finger slowly to her lips. At this – and much to her own surprise – all the animals fell silent. "Ursalie the Vanquisher" roared Ursian as he raised his paw to maintain the silence. "My Clan it was who composed the ode in honour of Roland of Roncesvalles and the other fallen Paladins. It is still being recited today. In French that poem is known as the Chanson de Roland. Today, my brothers and sisters, I am asking all the Clans to do the same in your honour. I hope it lasts for as long in memory. My Clan's younger members have already composed the first verse."

Ten of the oldest cubs came forward and stood facing Amélie who was blushing furiously by now. One by one they started their recitation under the beady eye of Ursetta and Fitzursian She stood transfixed during this recital, understanding barely one word of it. Once the last one had finished, the throng started whooping and stamping. Order was eventually restored and Ursian addressed Amélie: "When we are finished our writing, you will return to hear it in its entirety but in the meantime, we have fashioned a small memento to show our appreciation for your bravery. He brought a small box and indicated that she should open it. She did so to reveal a pendant on a long shining chain, both made of the same white gold as Kate's circlet. The pendant had small sapphires surrounding a highly polished but battered musket ball. Ursian leaned forward and placed the thin chain around her neck. Unable to contain herself any longer, she threw her arms around his thick fur neck, hanging on as her tiny feet left the floor but slowly slipping back to the ground. The moment came that the animals and the humans had been waiting for as Ursian announced: "Now, Cousins, brothers and sisters, let the feast begin."

Ursetta joined her husband as they both led the way to where long tables groaning with every conceivable type of food had been laid out. The food catered for all the guests, even the humans - a small party of bears had been sent to obtain humankind delicacies the previous day. Ursian himself and Fitzursian got behind a makeshift bar and started dispensing from barrels marked "Great Bear Ale' filling tankards for the humans and small bowls for the dogs, larger ones for the boars and buckets for the elephants. The lions fortunately were forbidden to drink in case they 'accidentally' ate the unicorns. They were known to be an ugly bunch when drinking. They growled resentfully but then began to join in the festivities when they saw the tables covered with food. For once, the Fighting Bears and their entire Clan had abandoned their endless games of stones, with its inevitable arguments and were there in force.

The humans examined the gifts which Ursian had bestowed on them. Kate was particularly interested in André's inkstand and more particularly in the meaning of the words inscribed upon it:

“André, you have never fully explained what you promised my father but now it has been fulfilled, perhaps you can? These words, they are something to do with it, aren’t they?”

André nodded slowly: “You will recall that your father’s instructions were that, as Steward you must set aside all personal feelings. Do only what is right?” Kate nodded solemnly.

“I have already been tested in this regard and it is not as easy as it sounds” she said seriously.

“Your father was tested by his oath to the very end of his life, Mlle. Catherine. He knew that the right thing to do was to appoint you his successor, but his personal feelings almost prevented him.” André paused: “He never doubted that despite your youth you would be a worthy Steward, but he feared that by nominating you, he would put your life in danger…”

“Indeed, from my own step-brother” said Kate flatly.

“That is true, Mlle. Catherine and he was proved correct. I helped your father do what was right by promising him that I would protect you…”

“No matter what it takes?” smiled Kate, but she already knew the answer to her question.

“Yes, Mlle., those were your father’s dying words to me.” André’s voice broke as he said this, and Kate took his arm and hugged him close to her: “Thank you, thank you, dearest André.”

The party lasted all day and long into the evening, some staying until the early hours of the next day. However, Kate, Roland and André, unable to eat or drink a mouthful more, left in the early evening and returned to the cave leaving Amélie, who definitely should not have been drinking, last seen trying to teach Lucius to dance on his hind legs. In the morning, she was discovered lying in a corner of the cave, snuggled in a group of cubs who were keeping her warm. She clutched her pendant as she slept. Her mama might not have approved of such louche behaviour.

CHAPTER 68

The following day, Kate and Roland left their cave and wandered down into the Valley; they could hear sounds of some festivities continuing with raucous and tuneless attempts at singing far away in the direction of one of the other Clan caves, the one that Ursian disdainfully referred to as 'the Northern Bears' an obviously less well thought of part of the Clan of the Fighting Bears.

Ursian came to walk with them: "Hope you don't mind if I join you?" Both nodded their assent but wondered if Ursian had a special reason – which became clear when they came across Athina, in her haruspex form standing beside a handsome middle-aged man with long greying dark hair, thin elegant hands and rich, elaborate clothing which was of another time, although not one which they could identify. It seemed that this meeting had been planned and after the usual courtesies, Athina introduced.... Pellerin. Neither of them had ever really thought of him having a human form or who he was, nor of his relationship to Athina. Ursian positioned himself upon his sizeable posterior on the ground in front of Roland and Kate.

"I know you will be leaving us and I will sorely miss having you here – not a sentiment I thought I would ever express about any of humankind. The Grand Council has asked me to enquire about your future plans once you are wed."

Slightly taken-aback, Kate replied: "Well, we have talked somewhat about that but have come to no decisions yet. All we know is that Roland will be leaving the Gendarmerie. I am certain Uncle Georges will understand."

"Of course he will. However, I cannot imagine this young man putting his feet up by the fireside in the Château all day long and you Mlle. Catherine, seem to have developed a taste for adventure yourself." The bird-turned-man spoke in a deep melodious voice, very slightly accented. He had almost a lilt in his speech.

Ursian nodded his great head in agreement: "Absolutely, you have already helped us get the *first* of our Poursuivants home, and Pellerin was correct. We did indeed need human assistance. The Council has therefore agreed with me that we should…err…ask once more for your help in getting all the other Sanctuary Inns emptied then we will be able to issue a general Call to Sanctuary. You can help us fulfil our Promise."

Both Athina and Pellerin fixed the human couple with beseeching eyes and waited.

"We will help you, won't we Roland?" She stopped and looked at him and he took up where she had left off: "This is something I know we can do, but preferably next time without any *Loup Garou.*"

Pellerin nodded gravely: "Thank you both. I wish you well and every happiness together". He bowed gracefully to Athina who smiled warmly at him. The next moment, he was once again a magnificent eagle, and with one powerful flap of his huge wings, the beautiful bird rose up high in the sky leaving Athina with the young couple. Kate, who was always willing to score some points off the haruspex asked her: "You tried your very hardest to prevent me following Roland, but you seem now intent on making our lives a series of 'adventures'. Do tell me why this sudden change?"

"I am sworn to protect the heirs of Eleanor. I was worried that you could have endangered yourself by doing something reckless, but I know now that you wouldn't do that" and to ensure that she had finally got the last word for once, she transformed herself hastily into a snowy owl to join Pellerin.

Roland laughed to himself, but Kate was frowning. Her eyes narrowed to slits as she mumbled: "Next time, Athina Dubois, next time." Her fiancé looked at her quizzically: "I thought we had agreed there would be no more arguments with Athina, so there won't be a next time will there?"

"Nonsense" barked Kate "I only promised I would watch my words concerning Eleanor, but anything else…oh, alright I will try."

Next day, a motley collection of people and animals made its way down the valley. Roland and Kate led the way followed by André and Amélie and the packhorses laden with bags. Kate had decided that her brother's horse should remain in the High Valley, she wanted as few reminders of him as possible when she returned home. Behind them came Ursian and Hugo, Sangres and Archimedes and the entirety of Ursian's family.

Athina soon joined them, dressed in her long robes and seated on a small white pony, together with Lucius, Favius and Leonid leading a large pride of lions. Some elephants lumbered across the hillside, then more horses, Unika and her new mate, Unicarus came, and above flew Pellerin with the entire eagle Clan moving in gentle circles. As they approached the hilltop at the head of the High Valley, they saw before them the Low Valley through the wide archway, the great Gates already open in readiness for their departure. The procession passed slowly through the gates and stopped to make their numerous farewells to each other. Fitzursian came to the two girls and clasped each one in his huge arms, while Archimedes whickered and brayed quietly –his way of saying goodbye.

Final farewells and promises to return made, the humans finally set off on their long return journey taking with them many gifts and even more blessings from their friends in the High Valley. They made a slow and blissfully uneventful journey down through Oloron once more – no townsfolk spoke to Roland nor dared look at his companions when they stopped to buy provisions – and ultimately reached Pont St. Pierre and its newly built bridge. The bridge was being reinforced while the flooding had receded, and the water had calmed to a gentle flow. The workmen were very pleased to see André once again and invited the travellers to join them for lunch. Kate and André went off to buy additional supplies for their journey and to share with the companionable group of workmen and travellers who sat at the makeshift tables near the river's edge. They all enjoyed an excellent feast – with wine of course – then bade farewell to the jolly group, by that time jollier by quite a few litres of the local red wine.

Once the little procession had left the river, they journeyed on towards St. Pardoux, retracing their steps and made their final camp about three hours' ride away from the small town, looking forward to the next day when they would arrive by lunchtime and at last get a cooked meal and sleep in a real bed. They had all grown accustomed to sleeping either on the ground, wrapped in their blankets or at best the twig pallets used by the bears, but nothing could replace the comfort of a goose-down mattress for weary bones.

After they had attacked their cold food voraciously, Athina announced that she had 'business' to attend to and after transforming herself hidden in a nearby coppice, as her owl self she disappeared into the night sky.

"Emergency coven meeting?" joked Amélie as she watched the white shape disappear in the gloom.

"I heard that, Amélie Giscard" came the faint reply – all but André laughed, even Amélie, who realised that in fact she had not only heard the hooting sounds but understood them. Up until then she had only mastered some 'bear' and a little 'horse', and she was delighted. They spent a comfortable night as by now the weather was warmer and the hours of darkness remained warm. At daybreak, they broke camp although Athina had not returned, which was not unusual. Her movements were unpredictable as always. They led Athina's pony with them and rode steadily until Roland reined in Marron and told the others to stop. He listened intently for a while and then whispered: "I think we had better take cover. I can hear horses approaching fast. No idea what business they might have with us but just in case. Better be safe than sorry after what we have been through."

They led their horses around to the back of a ruined house just off the road where Roland took his carbine and crouched behind the empty window at the front of the old building, waiting. The girls did likewise, and they waited in silence. Before long the sound of horses' hooves became louder and, much to everyone's relief, a troop of gendarmes came into view. Roland stood and went outside so that he was completely visible. He left his carbine behind the wall of the house and walked down on to the roadway to greet the men. The patrol came to an abrupt halt and the officer, a captain, gave a very formal and correct bow of greeting to him, followed by a salute. Roland returned it although his uniform was almost unrecognisable, tattered and stained with mud as it was. The other captain was immaculate, and his insignia indicated that he was attached to headquarters in Paris.

Roland immediately recognised him. It was Destrier's ADC whom he had met briefly in the General's office.

"Captain Lebrun? I am Captain Fauchard, we meet again. General Destrier presents his compliments to you and your friends and extends his invitation to lunch in Saint Pardoux, where accommodation awaits you all." Roland signalled to the others and leading the horses they emerged from the ruins. Riding along, he wondered aloud how General Destrier had managed to time his arrival at an obscure town so far away from Paris to coincide with their own arrival: "By the same means as he knew of our betrothal, a little bird told him" answered Kate, laughing.

As they rode into the main square, Fauchard turned to Roland: "You will all be staying in the Hôtel d'Aquitania, lunch will be served at 12.30 but the General has requested *your* arrival at noon." They stopped outside the Hôtel and when they had dismounted Roland took the opportunity to retrieve the weaponry provided by Belaudie although Amélie was very reluctant to part with 'her' carbine until Kate agreed that Louis-Philippe's fine silver-etched weapon was now definitely Amélie's. The horses were entrusted to the groom and a porter collected the baggage, somewhat surprised by the weight of the girls' bags and the presence of a very fine gun barrel protruding from one of them. Roland told them he would be back shortly and followed Fauchard over to the barracks where he had been assured that a clean uniform and a hot bath awaited him.

The girls followed the porter into the main foyer of the hôtel and were only a little surprised to see Athina waiting to greet them; they were by now used to her turning up unexpectedly but were astonished to see that she dressed today in a fashionable morning gown, her long hair braided and wound into a bun. She was also accompanied by Amélie's mother, Marianne! Both girls ran towards her and threw their arms around her in delight. However, they were not accorded the warm welcome they had been expecting. Madame Giscard pushed them both away from her firmly whilst she stood back looking them up and down with a very critical eye. "I have never been so ashamed in my life. I looked out of my window a few moments ago to see some gendarmes escorting two ruffians, obviously brigands, possibly even highwaymen very soiled by their travels and misadventures and now under arrest. But no. To my horror, I realised that it was the two young ladies to whom I have devoted my life! I bring you up as ladies but instead you look like common vagabonds. How you imagine you can enter this establishment in such a condition is beyond me."

Without another word, she grabbed each girl tightly by the arm propelling them up the staircase with Athina gliding before them.

At the top of the stairs Marianne opened a pair of ornate double doors into a large bedchamber where a huge iron bath stood, half-filled with steaming water. "That, in case you have forgotten, is a bath. I have brought with me some more appropriate attire for young ladies." She pointed to the large bed where two outfits each were laid out, elegant dresses which the girls would normally wear for formal occasions. "Lunch will be served in precisely one hour. I know it will be difficult for you to appear semi-presentable in that time but please do not be late."

Marianne stormed out of the bedroom, accompanied by Athina, leaving both girls bemused and rather embarrassed but Madame Giscard's face was wreathed in smiles as she hugged Athina. "You see! It can be done; I always told you that you needed to be much firmer with her."

In the bedroom, Kate looked at herself in a mirror for the first time in many weeks and then she looked across at Amélie. Both of their faces had smears of mud from the road and their riding boots and clothes once black were now in various shades of brown and grey where mud and dust had coated the fabric, each stain representing the type of countryside they had passed through. "You know, sometimes I really do not see why your mother makes such a fuss" but Amélie had picked up one of the dresses which lay on the bed: "I am so glad Mama brought this one. It brings back such happy memories for me. I wore it when I stuck a hatpin in M. Despierre's posterior."

"Ha! Did he even notice?" laughed Kate.

"Only when it went in far enough to draw blood" sniggered Amélie

CHAPTER 69

Roland Lebrun had a spring in his step as he crossed the square despite the weight of his heavy sack of weapons. He knew that one chapter in life was ending and soon he and his fiancée would be embarking on their new life together.

Even the prospect of meeting and lunching with Destrier didn't dent his feeling of wellbeing, in fact he was pleased that he could tell the General face to face that he would be leaving the service of the Gendarmerie, rather than writing a letter. However, something in the back of his mind told him that Destrier already knew. This was the man who had congratulated him on his non-existent report regarding the Lost Patrol and on his betrothal. The General knew things that he shouldn't. Destrier was rumoured to have an extensive network of spies but …well it didn't make sense…then, looking up he saw about a dozen eagles some soaring in the sky, two perched high on a nearby rooftop staring down at him. He nodded to himself at this sight.

On the notice board outside the barracks there was a solitary grubby sheet of paper:

"All Ordinances and Edicts previously made by me are hereby revoked. Claude Duclos, Mayor of Saint Pardoux."

The notice was dated the previous day. Pushing open the double doors of the building Roland saw, to his amusement, that the corporal at the desk immediately stood to attention and saluted him – things were very different from his last visit here.

Roland handed over the cache of weapons and the corporal accounted for their return in a vast ledger, asking him to sign against each entry. Deferentially, he then ushered Roland into Belaudie's office. The place was a complete shamble: on the floor were piles of files with hand-written notes on top of them, obviously hastily scribbled.

Two bulging valises were alongside the unsteady piles. On the back of the door hung two uniforms, one neatly pressed, the other not so neat. From a third peg hung an impressive greatcoat and hat. Propped up at the side of the overburdened desk were a musket and a sabre and on the desk itself lay two pistols, partially hidden by the scattered papers. Belaudie himself sat in the single chair, behind the desk looking very glum. He looked up but only nodded briefly at his friend – not quite the welcome Roland had been expecting. Eyeing the pair of valises, Roland enquired: "Going somewhere then?" in an attempt to lighten his friend's mood.

"Prison I expect, although with luck I shall only be dismissed from the service" growled Belaudie. "I've been relieved of my command here. I've been instructed to brief my successor on everything this afternoon. He's Destrier's ADC so I am terrified he'll find something wrong." He indicated the overflowing files scattered on the floor "then I am off, tomorrow, to heaven knows where."

Roland looked shocked: "the last time I was here you seemed to be getting to grips with everything. What on earth has happened?" Belaudie looked up, glad of the opportunity to unburden himself but hesitated: "My friend, you must be at the Hôtel d'Aquitania at precisely twelve noon looking more like an officer and less like a Corsican bandit, in the words of your friend Destrier. There on the door, that's a clean, pressed uniform for you. Please, please don't be late – I seem to be in enough trouble as it is. Oh, yes, I was also instructed to tell you that you will be meeting someone very important. I can't imagine who would be more important than the General though."

"Jacques, look, I promise you that I will not be late but if I am, it certainly won't be your responsibility. Now tell me, please, what's been going on."

Belaudie sat back in his chair, still far from comfortable: "Well we had a signal from Paris last week – they always seem to coincide with your visits, my friend. Anyway, I was instructed to book all five rooms at the d'Aquitania for last night and tonight, no matter who was already staying there. I also had to arrange a formal lunch for seven people, which I duly did – much to the Hôtelier's delight. Well, Destrier arrived last evening and took up residence but from what I heard, only two of the rooms were occupied.

I heard that from his men who were billeted at our barracks. At eight this morning he stormed in here and carried out a full inspection, which seemed to go well enough. He even congratulated me on my arrest of the mayor for breaking one of his own laws and making him rescind all his other silly laws too. Then he inspected the armoury – I was dreading that, but he scarcely mentioned the missing weapons or why you had requisitioned so many. I swear he even chuckled when he saw how much ammunition you had taken. He seemed to know all about whatever you were doing and assured me all the weapons, minus most of the "special" ammunition would be returned today. By the way you were five minutes later than he predicted." Belaudie laughed mirthlessly at this.

"Well, it certainly seems that you have passed muster" said Roland, hoping to cheer up his friend.

Belaudie nodded: "That's what I thought but then he sat down in my chair and started asking me questions. He was alone at first and then I was really taken aback. I told you about those two young ladies and their governess? Well she joined us! I have absolutely no idea why she was with the General. She sat down and he says: "I believe you know Madame Dubois? She is one of my closest *confidantes*." Then they questioned me about my career to date, the time I had spent with you in Spain, our relationship…then Madame

Dubois leaned over and whispered something to him. That's when it got really awkward. He asked if I had ever been betrothed and I said no. Then he asked: 'so what about the girl in Salamanca, Senorita Consuela Dimaria'? Heaven only knows how he knew about that." Roland couldn't prevent himself laughing at this.

"It's not funny, Lebrun, my career obviously hangs in the balance and they're asking me about my love life?"

"Sorry, Jacques, but I do remember you running through the streets, hotly pursued by her four brothers!"

"Still not funny. I still wake up in a cold sweat over that sometimes; being trapped by the British was a lot less scary. I explained it had been a misunderstanding but then the whole conversation got even stranger.

I could have sworn someone was behind me, but I was too nervous to look and meanwhile Dubois's eyes were boring into me as I explained what had really happened in Spain. The senorita's family had mistakenly believed I was offering marriage – that was all her idea! Anyway, I blustered a lot but his next question sent me into a panic."

"What did he ask?" Roland was fascinated now.

"He wanted to know if I made a habit of getting young ladies intoxicated, and if I did, what were my intentions? To be honest, with those eyes boring into my very soul and the General's angry face in front of me I can't remember what I replied, could have been anything. The governess just stood and left the room, didn't say a word. The atmosphere lightened a bit when she left though, even the feeling that someone was behind me vanished. Then just as I began to relax, just a little, Destrier dropped his bombshell – no explanation – I was relieved of my command with immediate effect. I know you know more about all this than you are telling me. You work for Destrier, the old crone is his confidante and she was here the last time you were. She's no governess, that's for sure, so these two girls, they're in league with Destrier as well? You're all in this-whatever this is - aren't you? You told me never to mention that those girls had been to Waterloo, why? Not that I ever have. I really thought that 'Jeanne' liked me; although that's probably not even her real name, is it? Both were having a huge joke at my expense. I know I'm in a mess, even if I don't understand why, but the last thing I need is your help." Jacques was gabbling, his words gushing in an angry torrent. He was obviously angry, bewildered and even a bit hurt that his old comrade was a part of this.

"Jacques, Jacques, honestly, you are completely wrong. The girls certainly don't work for Destrier, but they do know him, they are his god-daughters I swear."

"Ha, now even you are laughing at me. Just make yourself respectable, would you and leave me in peace" Belaudie growled.

Roland stood up, took the pressed uniform and turned once more to plead with his friend: "Look, Jacques…" but got no further for Belaudie refused to look up but instead indicated the door and muttered: "Just go, will you."

At precisely five minutes before noon, clean-shaven and immaculately dressed in a fresh uniform, Roland looked every inch an officer except for his now very long dark hair, which he had bound into a neat queue. He strode into the Hôtel d'Aquitania past two sentries who snapped to attention and fell in beside him as escort towards the Hôtel dining room where another was stationed. Roland was rather surprised by this 'guard of honour' but waited whilst the third knocked at the closed double doors and without waiting for a response, opened them. He showed the Captain into a large, well lit room where Destrier stood waiting, standing beside a small table on which rested a shabby, battered briefcase.

The younger man stood at attention, saluted and formally greeted his commanding officer: "General Destrier, Sir" barking out the words as if on a parade ground. Destrier didn't return the salute, however. Unexpectedly he smiled in response: "Oh stop man! I often considered employing a double just to take care of all the saluting I must do. I absolutely hate all that and my name is Georges. The girls have always called me 'uncle Georges' although I am not exactly part of the family. The Destriers have always been close to the House of Garenne though since…well since the beginning really." He did not elaborate on this but continued: "Now, I hear that you want to leave my service? I shall be very sad to see you go. You are the sort of senior officer we need but I am certain our paths are destined to cross frequently in the future. However, before you are finally discharged, you must file reports on events to date."

Roland blanched. How could he tell anyone what he had experienced? The General reached into the battered briefcase by his side and silently handed Roland a sheaf of papers, three report folders, neatly assembled. "This one is about the Lost Patrol; this one deals with the demise of young Louis-Philippe and the third accounts for the death of Lucien Lecaron and the disappearance of Raoul Lecaron."

Astonished Roland slowly leafed through the reports, beginning with the account of the Lost Patrol:

"This is the Report of Captain Roland Lebrun, Investigating Officer, Paris the 20th day of March 1818. I solemnly swear as follows….

Roland read through "his" report which explained how Brochard had bullied his men into following him in his quest to retrieve a valuable animal which he intended to steal and sell for personal gain. ('True' he thought); that Brochard had been killed in a brawl ('one way of putting it') and the so-called Lost Patrol had left for the New World to avoid trial and imprisonment ('Well, true. ***A*** New World anyway').

He was still reading when Destrier interrupted him: “I thought mention of the ‘New World’ was quite appropriate. We sold off the Louisiana Territories in the Americas, so we can’t search for them there can we?” Roland smiled and read the rest of the document cursorily before signing it at the places indicated. He next opened the folder dealing with the untimely death of Louis-Philippe de Garenne who had, apparently, been killed in a hunting accident in the Pyrenees (‘true’ thought Roland), where the young nobleman had got too close to a wild boar and had been badly gored (again true). His subsequent death had been witnessed by no less a personage than M. André Lacoste, a Trustee of the Eleanor Bequest and a Commander of the Legion of Honour (once again factually correct). He had been buried where he fell. Once more Roland wordlessly signed the document and then turned his attention to the final document where he read that a fresh investigation into the death of Lucien Lecaron had uncovered serious flaws in the original investigation overseen by Captain Vincent Falaise, still based at the barracks in La Garenne.

The cause of death was due to a single pistol shot fired at close quarters and was most certainly a deliberate act. However rigorous enquiries have failed to uncover the identity of the assailant. There is no connection between the death of the victim and the disappearance of his brother, Raoul Lecaron. Sightings of this man around Monbezier had been confirmed by a M. Barbier, respected member of the local community who subsequently swore that a man answering Raoul’s description had fallen into the Dordogne River and was believed to have been drowned, although no body had been recovered. ‘It was true, no body was ever found, nor could be’ thought Roland.

Roland hesitated briefly before signing this third report, not sure if he could do it but Destrier noticed and tried to set his mind at rest. “We at least owe this to Marie Lecaron, man. A renegade from the House of Garenne – soon to be your home Roland, took the life of her fiancé. She endured a terrible life with his brother and whatever you think of her, she deserves better. This allows the mayor to declare Raoul officially dead, so she will be free to marry again if she wishes and inherit the Lecaron farm. You hesitate perhaps but think of those reports of yours from Corsica, all those stolen sheep? Really? How many hungry families did they feed…those reports had me wondering…"

Roland picked up the pen once more and signed. Destrier then took all three reports and put them back in the briefcase. Case closed.

CHAPTER 70

"Now, young man, tell me what you know about Captain Belaudie. He's a friend of yours, I believe?"

"Well *I think* we are still friends, have been since we started our training together. I would still trust him with my life, indeed in Spain I often did. He's intelligent, courageous, and as honest as the day is long. He's rather unhappy with me at present, however. Feels I may have been responsible for whatever is about to happen to him."

"Ah" said Destrier without further comment: "No skeletons in his cupboard then?" he raised his bushy grey eyebrows in question.

"None at all" replied Roland firmly.

"Glad to hear it. I have formed an excellent opinion of him myself. He is a real prospect for the service and Madame Athina likes him too – now that is unusual – although she did give him a hard time this morning. In fact, if I didn't know her better I would say she had almost a soft spot for him. Oh, one final question if I may, do you think we can rely upon his discretion in *all* circumstances?" Roland nodded "Absolutely."

"Excellent! The posting I have in mind for him will require absolute discretion."

"Well he's certainly worried about his future, err Georges. Could I please give him some comfort and assure him he is not facing imminent execution?" Roland laughed. Destrier chuckled in response: "Oh, I do like to keep you young men on your toes…but perhaps…"

Just at that very moment there was a tap on the dining room door. Athina entered, accompanied by André and another elegant lady. The anxious guard announced each of the new arrivals, introducing André as 'Commander of the Legion of Honour, M. André Lacoste' at which he blushed furiously. As for Madame Athina, she was introduced only as 'the Lady Athina'.

The third lady was apparently Madame Marianne Giscard. ('Ah, thought Roland, Amélie's mother, no doubt). Roland was quite taken aback when his formerly relaxed companion snapped to attention in front of André. The General saluted him and spoke formally: "Commander, it is a great honour and a privilege to finally meet you."

How Roland wished Kate could have witnessed this scene, knowing how intensely proud she was of her father's friend. General Destrier introduced Roland to Madame Giscard as aunt and guardian of his fiancée: "Ah the rather elusive Captain Lebrun? I trust you are going to remain with us long enough to have lunch?"

Roland could not fathom out whether this was said in jest or not and his face betrayed his confusion. He was put at ease when she smiled saying "It's alright. I know that Georges must carry the blame for your sudden disappearances. It cannot be easy having him as your commanding officer. I have heard a great deal about you from Madame Athina but now I would like to hear from you about how you met my young ladies after Waterloo. They only feed me the snippets of information they think I need to hear. Even Athina, my oldest friend and Pellerin too seem to have glossed over some details. Just how bad were things when you met them?"

Roland had no choice but to begin his account but was mightily relieved when there was another knock on the dining room door which burst open this time. Before the flustered guard managed to utter a word, Kate and Amélie rushed in and ran to General

Destrier, both crying 'Uncles Georges' in unison. They almost bowled over the rather stout officer as they both embraced him.

Eventually, a blushing Destrier managed to extricate himself and could continue his interrupted conversation with André and Athina, leaving the two girls to join Roland and Marianne. Both curtseyed to her and Kate asked: "Dearest aunt, do we now have your approval?"

Madame Giscard made a great show of looking them both up and down frowning, but she was unable to hold her stern expression and broke into a warm smile as she embraced them in turn. Looking then at Amélie, she studied the white gold pendant around her daughter's neck: "I want to hear all about this, *Ursalie*?" but before Amélie could speak, Kate anxiously begged her aunt to spare her a moment.

"Roland, you have something to ask my aunt, haven't you?"

Her aunt raised her hand to silence the gendarme before he could begin: "I know exactly what you would like to ask and although I did indicate to Athina that your match had my approval, I am very much afraid…that now…" but she was unable to finish before Kate exploded:

"Aunt Marianne, how could you? I am in love with Roland. I am begging you to give your agreement to our marriage. Please. Please."

Her aunt rolled her eyes dramatically at the young officer, raising them skywards. "IF I may continue, what I was about to say before I was so very rudely interrupted. was that my niece no longer needs my permission. Today is her birthday and so she has reached her majority. I am no longer her guardian – and if I may so, that is somewhat of a relief!"

Kate, who had begun to work herself into a furious state, now looked completely non-plussed. "No, I can't believe it. I had completely lost track of the days. Of course, today is my birthday. However, Maman we would still like your blessing. It would mean so much to me…err to us, just to hear you say that you approve." Marianne put an arm around each of them, holding them tightly: "Of course I do. Welcome to our family." At a signal given by Destrier to an unnoticed waiter, crystal flutes were distributed to the assembled company containing the best champagne available locally and then Destrier proposed a toast: "To Kate on her birthday, to Kate and Roland on their betrothal and welcome back safely."

Over a superb lunch, Amélie and Kate gave a spirited account of the battle with Brochard and their time in the High Valley, only interrupting their tale when servers arrived with each new course. Marianne seemed horrified by all that she was hearing but the girls sensed she had already heard all about it. Slowly the meal drew to a close but not before Roland repeated his earlier request to visit Jacques Belaudie. Immediately Amélie stated her intention of accompanying him and was quite taken aback by Kate's sharp retort: "Amélie Giscard, a lady always waits for a gentleman to make the first advance. You demean yourself by pursing a man you barely know, especially at a barracks." This outburst effectively silenced all those around the table, each of whom looked at Kate open-mouthed with amazement. Even Roland looked stunned as he stuttered: "Really Kate?"

Gradually, Kate's colour deepened as she stuttered: "That, well that was different, entirely. There's no comparison." She tossed her head defiantly but could not hide the blushes that betrayed her embarrassment. Amélie's face fell further as Marianne began: "For once, I totally agree with Catherine and under normal circumstances such lack of decorum could not be allowed. However," here she smiled archly at Kate "life for you two girls has been anything but normal since you both embarked on your latest adventure. Kate has set a precedent and it would be unfair of me not to allow you the same freedom."

Kate gasped but stayed silent at a look from her aunt. “Therefore, you may accompany Roland although I do think it appropriate that your cousin chaperones you, after all she has a far greater knowledge of the inner sanctum of a barracks!” Despite the shocked looks of everyone at the table, she continued: “Now, wear your cloaks, it’s will be chilly later.” The matter was closed.

Amélie excitedly took her leave of everyone at the table but before Kate could accompany her cousin and Roland, Kate’s aunt asked to speak to her privately for a moment: “Athina, Georges and I err, well we think this young man would be entirely suitable for Amélie, so I ask you not to err, interfere. Do you understand my dear?”

Kate now completely chastened nodded her assent: “I am so sorry, dearest aunt, I am just making myself look foolish today,” Marianne’s silence spoke volumes. As the girls left the dining room, Marianne joined Athina, smiling: “Well I would never have thought I would hear her say the words ‘I’m sorry’ without the threat of punishment. That’s a first I must say.”

The girls walked across the square, Kate arm in arm with her fiancé. Roland warned Amélie that Jacques Belaudie was unhappy with him and it seemed, the whole world. It might be better if he went into the building alone to explain to his friend that Destrier was not going to have him shot at dawn and that Amélie was definitely not a duplicitous spy. The officer strode on ahead through the heavy doors of the barracks asking the duty corporal whether the Captain was in his office. As he had half-expected, the corporal replied: “Yes, he is sir, but he left instructions that…” but he barged his way through and hammered on the door. Without waiting for any response, he pushed it open and confronted his colleague who was still busy sorting through his voluminous files. The file open on the desk bore the name “Claude Duclos, Mayor.” Very surprised and quite cross Belaudie looked up at the intrusion: “I left strict instructions not to be disturbed…especially by you.”

"Well, that really wasn't the welcome I was expecting as the bearer of glad tidings" interrupted Roland, before Jacques could continue. "I take it you're not in the least interested in General Destrier's glowing opinion of you, nor that there is a very pretty young lady not fifty paces from here who is very anxious to be reacquainted with you. Perhaps I should just go…Can't keep two pretty young ladies waiting, can I?"

Roland turned on his heel and reached for the doorknob, but Belaudie exclaimed: "No, wait, wait a minute, what did you say? "Roland grinned at him and with studied casualness began "Well, you know I was having lunch with General Destrier, err *Georges,* today. Very good food in the Hôtel by the way, most impressed. Anyway, over brandies he let slip that he thought you were rather…" Jacques' impatience was palpable as Roland deliberately pondered: "What were his exact words? Ah yes, he said you're an excellent prospect; he likes you very much and even Madame Dubois was most impressed with you. By the way, might be best not to refer to his closest adviser as 'an old crone' eh? Just call her Madame Dubois in future. Now must be off."

"Wait, wait, I can't take all this in" Belaudie stood anxiously, his hand outstretched to Roland: "What did you say about a young lady, is it Jeanne? Does she really want to see me?"

Roland's face remained impassive: "I am sorry my friend, there is no-one called Jeanne waiting outside."

He grinned broadly. "I wanted to introduce you to Mademoiselle Amélie Giscard who *is* waiting to see you.

You were quite right, 'Jeanne Blanc' never existed.

But you have my solemn word that Mlle. Giscard never meant to make fun of you. Oh, there's one condition you must observe – never, ever ask her what she has been up to since she left here. Sorry, I really can't explain this, but it is very important." Belaudie nodded his agreement instantly. He was only interested in the future at that moment. "Now come with me, Jacques. The ladies will be getting cold outside." Roland put an arm around his friend's shoulder and led him outside into the square, past the astonished corporal.

Amélie and Kate had stayed in the square, apparently admiring the architecture but watching the barrack gates. Whilst they stood together Kate apologised for her earlier behaviour explaining that she had – as was not unusual – spoken without thinking. To take their minds off events, Kate regaled her cousin with her plans for her wedding – at length - until they saw the two officers approaching. Roland formally introduced them both to Jacques Belaudie: "This is Mlle. Amélie Giscard, niece of the late Duc de Garenne and this is my fiancée, Mlle. Catherine de Garenne, the Duc's daughter."

Introductions over, Roland was very surprised when Kate suggested that Amélie and Jacques might like to take some coffee at the *Auberge des Etoiles*, the place where they had first met. She and Roland would take a stroll and join them later. Amélie lost no time in seizing her opportunity and took Jacques' arm familiarly as they crossed the square to the inn. Her laughter was soon heard echoing towards Kate and Roland: "That was very liberal of you my dear" said Roland "I thought you would insist on chaperoning them like a mother hen after that impressive outburst at the Hôtel ."

Kate, still embarrassed, told him that her aunt had specifically asked her to allow Amélie some freedom, but she also had another reason: "We too can take some time to be together, walk together and do what other engaged couples do, no shape-changing dogs or talking Donkeys, or indeed Athina watching…"

"No irascible talking bears either. Just the two of us, two perfectly ordinary people taking a stroll. Well, in fact not that ordinary, as we have recently discovered and despite the half dozen eagles watching our every move." laughed Roland, pointing upwards at the birds perched high on the buildings. Kate laughed too: "I am going to have to speak to Pellerin about this, I don't want us being spied upon…especially on our honeymoon." Even Roland was shocked this time.

Eventually they rejoined Amélie and Jacques who were deep in conversation. He was promising that he would write as soon as he knew where he was being posted; she in turn promised that she would prevail upon her 'uncle Georges' to allow him leave of absence to visit her. They barely noticed that Roland and Kate were there.

Next morning, after a hearty breakfast, they all assembled in the courtyard. Athina, Marianne, André, Amélie and General Destrier were to travel in Destrier's coach. Amélie, however, changed her mind at the last minute when Jacques Belaudie rode into the yard leading a packhorse with two valises slung across it. Roland asked if he was joining them and Jacques explained his orders were to report to General Destrier promptly at 9.00 a.m. to accompany him on the journey up country to La Garenne, *his new posting*. Of course, as soon as a delighted Amélie heard this she began to rummage in her own valise for riding clothes and boots and insisted on rushing back to the Hôtel to change. Mounted eventually on her own horse, she rode proudly beside Jacques.

For the sake of her mama and appearances she even agreed to wear a riding skirt instead of breeches. They set off, led by six members of Destrier's personal guard, Kate and Roland, followed by Amélie and Jacques and finally the coach, with the packhorses tethered to it. Bringing up the rear came a further six of the General's personal guard. All the while eagles flew above them, wheeling and soaring effortlessly.

It was a far cry from their outward journey. With the need for secrecy gone, they stayed at comfortable inns along the way, eating good food and drinking wine.

Belaudie joined the group for meals and even began to relax in the company of Athina (or "Madame Dubois") and as for Destrier - although protocol demanded that he address the General as "Sir" or "General", the old man called him Jacques. He bore in mind Roland's final words to him and tempting as it was to ask, he never broached the subject of Amélie's adventures. In fact, he had almost forgotten until the party reached the outskirts of Monbezier and Destrier told him he would have to dine with his own men that night because one of the General's trusted advisors would be joining him that evening when matters of a private and urgent nature would be discussed. In good time, the General assured him, he would gain a greater understanding of these matters but in the meantime, he must be patient.

Despite the feelings which Belaudie knew he had for Amélie, he feared now that he might never really know her. Both girls were very open and friendly to him even though on first meeting, he had thought Kate rather standoffish. However, their openness and youth seemed at odds with all that had clearly gone before or their participation in a meeting with one of Destrier's trusted agents. His mind focused on the beautiful pendant which Amélie now always wore. He often noticed her clutch the necklace almost like a talisman. He was certain that the centrepiece was a highly polished musket ball, misshapen from contact with its target. Was this a part of the 'special ammunition' which had not been returned? He thought about Roland's relationship with the General who treated him more as a beloved nephew than a subordinate. Would he too, in time, become a confidante of his own Inspector-General? Ah well, time would tell. At least his fortunes were changing for the better.

That evening at dinner in the Grand Hôtel de Paris, the "trusted adviser" joined Destrier and his friends. For the occasion, Gilles Barbier was wearing his 'Sunday best' suit, obviously made for him when he was a much slimmer figure, perhaps a hundred years earlier. Gilles was in a jovial mood, anxious to hear about the encounter with Brochard and eager to have news of the High Valley and his friends there.

He already knew that Ursian had left the Valley, this time in the guise of a dog, an extremely large dog, accompanied by Hugo Hound. That meant that Gilles and 'the missus' would soon be going home which made him smile even more. André had recognised Gilles from their previous encounter and already knew that he was in league with Roland in sending Louis-Philippe off on his wild goose chase but looked somewhat confused when Gilles described Ursian as his Cousin.

"It's simple, André" explained Roland: "Gilles too is a bear, one of the Clan of the Guard Bears." Despite his resolution to avoid Giant Bear ale, André took a great swig from his tankard at this information; after all, it would rude indeed not to partake of the work of such a great brew master. Gilles bade them farewell and was last seen driving off into the night on his beer cart, chatting amiably to his horses.

The two girls, Athina and Marianne were sharing a room. After Gilles' departure, Amélie seemed unnaturally quiet and withdrawn so her mother asked her gently what was troubling her and was surprised that Amélie replied with tears in her eyes: "Although I missed Jacques this evening I now realise that he can never be totally in my life. There is a part of me that I can only talk about with others like me, other who know what I know. A large part of my life must remain hidden from him. When we were talking to Gilles this evening I became fully aware of that, but I cannot stand the thought of losing him now…" tears fell from her eyes unchecked as her mother hugged her: "Amélie, Amélie, your friendship with

Jacques has only just begun. He is of humankind; you are a Paladin. I too am a Paladin and I knew this from an early age – yet I still fell in love with your father, he was humankind. If you feel that you still want to be betrothed to this young man, and of course if he feels the same, then I promise you Athina will help you. She always has, you know. Jacques will accept you for who you are, just as your father accepted me. Now, dry your eyes."

The next morning the party left Monbezier and made their way downhill towards the ferry crossing. Those who remembered looked towards the dark forest where the Sanctuary Inn was hidden and reflected upon what might have been had they never entered it.

Kate was lost in her own reverie as she stared at the forest when Athina, who was in the carriage, leant across and whispered: "don't worry, this was always your destiny" and of course, if anyone knew that, she did.

The ferryman saw the party coming down the slope to the riverside and seeing the gendarmes, resigned himself yet again to lost income but his face lit up when he recognised Captain Lebrun. He graciously welcomed them aboard, the coach with the ladies travelling first and then in two more crossings, the rest of the group including Destrier who wanted to 'stretch his legs' with a couple of gendarmes acting as escort.

Roland took the opportunity to ask the General something which been puzzling him: "Of all the officers in the service, why did you pick me to investigate the matter of the Lost Patrol?"

"As you must by now realise, I know quite a bit about Paladins and the like. Athina was pretty certain that you had Paladin blood. Aiguillin, he's Pellerin's son, told her that you were the only one to help those brave girls to escape from Waterloo. Everyone else was too busy saving their own skins but not you. She will never admit it but that impressed her mightily, the mark of a true Paladin and coupled with your name she, well, put two and two together. Of course, by the time she spoke to me I had dispatched you to Réunion, for your own safety.

Athina wanted to know more about you so I very quickly arranged for your posting to Corsica where the eagles could keep watch over you. It was then that I began to really read your reports; you were finding criminals that had eluded whole companies of gendarmes in the past and I thought she might be right. So, when I needed someone to investigate the goings on in La Garenne, you were the obvious choice. If you weren't a Paladin, I could put my hand on my heart and honestly say that the matter had been fully investigated by one of my best officers – and if you were, then you would discover the truth anyway. About yourself that is. I knew by then what had happened to the Patrol but thank heavens you spotted Brochard was missing. That, my boy, is why I chose you. Oh, yes and Athina insisted that I make it up to Kate for sending you so far away and stranding her in Paris, broken-hearted.

I think she may even have been trying to play Cupid. Don't tell her I said that eh? Kate will never know how devoted Athina is to her." The ferry bumped against the far bank and Destrier resumed his place on the coach.

CHAPTER 71

For the rest of that day and the following one they retraced their steps back to the Inn at St. Antoine where they would stay overnight before reaching La Garenne. One of Destrier's officers had ridden ahead to arrange yet another feast but after the meal Kate and Roland excused themselves to find a quiet corner near the log fire. The wooden bench was large enough for two, but she contrived to sit very close to him, with her eyes closed, seemingly oblivious to the arrival of Athina.

"Could you spare me a moment of your time?" the haruspex enquired softly. The girl sat bolt upright, hastily disentangling herself from her fiancé and sat down primly on the opposite bench, looking much like a naughty schoolgirl. Athina rarely asked so politely for Kate's attention but now she was smiling: "I promised that I would tell you all about Eleanor when I judged the time to be right. Tomorrow you will be home, and your lives will never be the same again, so I think that now is the appropriate time." Roland started to rise but Athina motioned to him to remain seated. "This concerns you as well as Kate." This was a rarity; Athina had only ever addressed Kate as 'Catherine'.

"Kate is about to take on great responsibilities and will need your support. These matters concern my family too and as you are soon to be a part of that, young man, you should hear what I have to tell you." Athina saw the look of surprise on both young faces. "Yes, you heard me correctly, my family…our family." Athina was now bathed in the same warm shimmering glow as she had been when she had spoken back in Sanctuary Inn but this time, it did not feel as if she was shielding her emotions. She seemed genuinely at ease. Kate, almost without thinking, tried to stop her from continuing:

"No, please Madame, I have seen how much pain it causes you when Eleanor's name is mentioned. I would rather not know than cause you any more sorrow. I do not *need* to know more."

"That is so very understanding of you, my dear, but believe me I no longer feel any pain. I can speak of Eleanor now only with pride; there is no more sorrow. We are finally reconciled.

This should have happened a long time ago. I should have listened to Pellerin…" her voice dropped for a moment: "I once told you I used to visit my friends at the Court of Charlemagne. I did not go alone. Pellerin always accompanied me for Charlemagne often sought his wise counsel. We would adopt human form although I always suspected that the great Emperor knew the truth. We had always been close, but it was on one of our visits to the Court that we realised it was more than friendship. We were in love." She paused and looked down. For a mere second Roland saw not a mysterious haruspex but a young vulnerable woman. 'Ursian was right! There is a strong resemblance' he thought.

"We are still in love; we had two beautiful children, twins, the very first births of our kind in the High Valley. We were of different Clans and in that other terrible place our offspring would have had the choice of which Clan they must join. In the High Valley we had made our own choice of form and we felt we should allow our children to do the same. Aiguillin, he never hesitated, he was born to be an eagle, just like his father. Even today he rarely leaves Pellerin's side. Eleanor, well she was always more difficult."

Roland and Kate exchanged dumbfounded glances on hearing this.

"One day" continued Athina, seeming not to notice her listeners' expressions "she would want to be an eagle, the next an owl, she never could make her mind up. So, she remained without an adopted form. She wasn't the only one like that back then. Not all who had journeyed with us had settled on their permanent forms. One of these was a young member of the Clan of the Chief Elder, an Oursi. His family had suffered more than most in the Wastelands. He had lost both his parents and been taken in by one of Ursian's great forebears. His name was Guillaume. He and Eleanor became friends, happy to remain without form together. It was only when the Grand Council issued the Edict to help the Pilgrims that Guillaume finally decided on his form: he would be humankind.

I advised him not to do so but he was adamant. He was going to devote his life to helping the unfortunate out in your world. After all that had happened to him it was indeed a selfless decision.

I feared the worst however and pleaded with my daughter not to follow suit but to no avail. She had made up her mind. She defied me."

Kate recalled the phrase Athina had used back in the Sanctuary Inn: 'even some very close to me'. She instinctively reached out and touched the pale hand of the haruspex as she continued, a noticeable catch in her voice "Despite all my efforts they left the High Valley together and journeyed north towards a place called La Garenne. Your birthplace was not as quiet then as it is now. It was an important gathering place for Pilgrims, but they were being attacked and robbed daily and in dire need of protection.

The Master of the Order of Knights Templar had heard of this and dispatched a company. When they arrived, they fortified a hill overlooking the town to serve as their base. Guillaume considered enlisting, but the Order at that time forbad their members to be married. Instead he raised and trained a company of local men to fight alongside the Knights. When news of their exploits reached the ears of the Master of the Order he recommended Guillaume and his men to the King, Louis IX, who conferred the title upon him, Comte de Rouen. As you well know, the Order became very powerful, very rich, too rich for the King's liking in fact. It was Pellerin who heard that the King had decided to have the Knights declared heretics, enemies of both the State and the religion of the

King. When Pellerin warned the Master, he told his men immediately and many joined other Orders, like the Hospitalers. However, some just slipped away, never to be seen again. Guillaume was very concerned. He had married his Eleanor according to the humankind tradition but just a week later he received a summons from the Master asking for his help in a "delicate matter".

The story has become a legend. Guillaume met with the Master, now a very old man and then set out to return to La Garenne with only a small band of Knights but they were ambushed by the King's men near Monbezier. Guillaume fought a rearguard action to enable his companions to escape. A few days later the surviving knights reached Eleanor's home bringing with them the awful news and a baggage train. She already knew that her husband had perished. Her brother Aiguillin had witnessed his death and flew to her with the news.

The remaining Knights did have their revenge, they fell upon the King's men near Monbezier then disappeared forever. They left behind them not only their legend but that baggage train together with a letter from the Master of the Templars addressed to Eleanor. In this letter she was asked to 'do the good I should have done'.

Aiguillin came and found me, broke the news, and of course I went to her immediately to console her and to persuade her to come back with me to the High Valley where she, a young widow, would be safe. Again, she defied me. She was determined now to remain at La Garenne. She told me she had been inspired in her grief by the words of the Master of the Templars. She had discovered that the baggage train was filled with unimaginable humankind riches! She would use those riches to 'do the good' for which they had been intended. While I was with her she drew up the terms of her Bequest. Good would be achieved not only during her lifetime but beyond and for as long as the line she and Guillaume had established remained." Athina sighed heavily, unable to continue for a moment. "She had discovered that she was to have a child."

Everyone remained silent, waiting. "Well, of course I knew what would happen. Her line would grow more human with the passing of each generation and I also knew that riches corrupt the human spirit just as rust corrodes the strongest of metals. She might do good, but her successors might not. She should abandon this nonsense and return with me to safety. Of course, she called me a hypocrite for wanting to protect her whilst knowing that others were making sacrifices. We both became angry and words were said that well, might have been better unsaid. We parted on bad terms… I, I never saw her again in this world."

Roland glanced at her expecting to see some outward change, but she remained serene, yet it seemed to him that a light had suddenly been extinguished. However, tears were welling up in his fiancée's eyes. Gently Athina wiped them away with a delicate hand embroidered handkerchief.

"My anger lasted for a long time, a very long time. Her father and her brother were frequent visitors and would bring me news of her progress

She had set in motion the construction of the Château and raised a company of men at arms who provided patrols to protect the Pilgrims in the absence of the Templars. They would also tell me how my grandson – she called him Hugo - was growing. Both were anxious that I resolve the argument, but this just made me angrier; surely they could see that Eleanor had to accept that she was in the wrong and beg my forgiveness? I was angry even with my beloved Pellerin, how could he be so obstinate? Truly, I do not know whether my anger was a result of her defiance or my own sorrow. I knew that if she didn't return to Elysium then she would be lost to my world before her time, like all humankind and so it was. One day, Pellerin returned to tell me that she had left the humankind world, but it had been her last wish that I help him and her brother guide and protect her heirs so that they would fulfil the terms of her Bequest.

I am ashamed to say that I was torn between agreeing and hoping that one of her successors would prove me right after all. Over the centuries the Stewards have proved that in fact she was right and I was so wrong. I am sure the estimable M. Lafitte-Dupont has provided considerable proof?"

Kate nodded, recalling the long hours she had pored over ancient documents in the Mairie.

"I still find it difficult to say this, but I could not admit that she had been right – my pride would not let me. Even after all that time it rankled that my child had known better than me. Roland, I am afraid Kate has inherited the stubbornness of our family. She is as stubborn as my own dear Eleanor, and perhaps myself." There was no rancour in her voice and she was actually smiling indulgently.

"So…" she continued more briskly "until recently and despite Pellerin's best efforts, nothing changed. Not that long ago I came across another willful young lady who defied my wishes when I knew that she would only be a hindrance and would be better off staying at home. Again, I was proved wrong and I have apologised and rightly so. I didn't need Pellerin to point out that if I could apologise to my many times great granddaughter then I should swallow my pride and make my peace with my own daughter." Athina ceased speaking and sat back, a contented glow seeming to emanate from her whole being as she continued: "and at long last we are reconciled."

The haruspex sat back, exhausted by her long speech and by the revelations it had contained. "So now you know the full story. I would like to thank you, my dear, for your part in it." She leant over and kissed Kate on both cheeks. "I will leave you to resume whatever you were doing" she whispered archly then positively glided across the room to join the others.

The young couple sat lost in thought. They could hear the chatter from across the dining room and the noise from the bar next door, but nothing truly registered with them. Kate took note of her living ancestor's advice and slowly sank back with her head on her fiancé's shoulder. It was Roland who spoke first: "I know how André feels. Just when you think that there was nothing more that could surprise you, something else comes along. I had no idea what she was going to tell us about your ancestor Eleanor. That she was her daughter though…I never expected that!" Kate shook her head:

"Ever since Athina came back to check that Amélie and I were safe and well after we had, err, liberated some of my brother's possessions, I suspected that there might just be some link between us; it was as though she truly cared about us. It makes sense now; she was looking after members of her family just like any grandparent would."

"Well I was completely wrong! I suspected that there was something between you and her, but I thought she might have been your old governess, Madame Dubois in some sort of a disguise. I noticed that there were times when she seemed immensely proud of you, like a headmistress seeing one of her pupils do well."

"Hmm" snorted Kate "Nonsense! Madame Dubois was an absolute tyrant. She hated me with a passion and I hated her. There is no possible way that she would have been proud of anything I did.

I promise you that if that old crone walked into this room right now there would be a blazing row. We argued every day sometimes twice or three times a day for as long as I can remember. She was so stubborn. Athina's different. I know we've had our disagreements, but she is rather sweet really. I can't imagine anyone having an argument with her."

Roland kept his own counsel and stroked Kate's hair and she closed her eyes so she did not see him smile and roll his eyes. Luckily, the noise from the bar drowned out the faint chuckle that wafted from across the dining room.

Next morning, they all rose bright and early, eager to get going. Almost as soon as they left St. Antoine, Kate became even more animated than usual. She pointed out to Roland all the little farms on the way, told him who the farmers were, the names of their children, showed him where she and Amélie had learned to swim, the trees they had climbed and the caves they had used to hide in. She was very much back in the countryside that she loved. The sight of the gendarmes was enough to cause most residents to scurry indoors, but when they caught sight of Kate they would relax and wave. She always returned their waves and smiles, clearly in her element and obviously very popular with those who lived around La Garenne.

They stopped briefly outside the Manoir where Marianne Giscard and Amélie lived, and Kate explained that when her father had been away this was where she had been raised ever since she was a baby. Roland looked through the iron gates at the house itself. The fine house was built in a grand style, very beautifully proportioned with a white gravel driveway leading up to the steps of the building. Nearby, however, was another much older, ruined but still substantial building. Roland guessed this might have been built many hundreds of years before the present Manoir. Kate looked around, making sure she could not be overhead.

"I am going to ask André to get that renovated; Amélie and Jacques will need somewhere of their own when they are married, don't you think?" she whispered.

"Papa built this newer Manoir for Maman Marianne and Uncle Charles when they married so I think we should do the same for Amélie."

Roland smiled: “You are of course assuming they want to get married, aren’t you?” Kate looked at him as if he was speaking a foreign tongue: “Of course they will” and made it clear from her expression that this would be the final word on the subject.

CHAPTER 72

When at last they reached the outskirts of the town of La Garenne, Belaudie left Amélie with whom he had been riding and took his place at the head of the procession. Kate and Roland followed with Amélie and André just ahead of the coach.

Roland reined in Marron a little leaving his fiancée to ride alone behind the guard of gendarmes, like a medieval princess, before she slowed and insisted that he ride by her side.

As the procession travelled farther into the centre of the market town they passed the covered marketplace, the Town Hall on one side and the gendarmerie on the other. People came forward on all sides to see what was happening and François, the mayor's assistant, ran out to see Mlle. Catherine. He also recognised Captain Lebrun from his earlier visit and walked briskly into the office of M. Lafitte-Dupont to let him know that the Garennes were back. The little man peered over his spectacles and said that he would most certainly be visiting the Château in his capacity as Notary. Falaise eventually deigned to come out of the barracks, about to give those shouting in the square a piece of his mind as he had been trying to nap but looked horrified when he saw the patrol passing by, escorting a fine coach emblazoned with the coat of arms of the Gendarmerie Nationale, the motto picked out in bright gold lettering.

Worse still, that Captain who had given him so much trouble earlier asking so many impertinent questions of himself and of his friend was riding alongside the late Duc's daughter, the one Louis-Philippe had referred to as 'that trollop'. Since they had all left La Garenne, Falaise had heard nothing from his great friend but assumed – he now saw incorrectly – that Louis-Philippe had dealt with the meddlesome gendarme. He had not of course been informed of the General's earlier visit to Madame Giscard mainly because no one liked him enough to gossip with him.

On the General's visit the previous week, he had driven straight to Madame Giscard's home without stopping at the barracks, so seeing the carriage now, with Lebrun and all these new gendarmes and his friend's half-sister, well it was all a bit of a shock to poor Falaise. He rushed back into the barracks, frantically tidying, hastily hiding the accounts ledger. He knew that Brochard had been less than honest, but Falaise was inclined always to leave such tiresome matters to someone else anyway. He had no idea about such trivialities. Now the number of bills and receipts spilling out of the drawer where the accounts books were kept told him just how wrong he had been - on the spur of the moment he snatched up all the loose papers and flung them into the stove to burn.

Seized by panic, he hastened to the stables, grabbed the first mount that was ready and rode off for the rest of that day. He had not seen his friend Louis-Philippe but perhaps he had been riding in state in that fine coach. "That's his style" he thought to himself but then why was his friend's haughty half-sister at the centre of the procession and to judge from the huge smile on her face, enjoying the attention?

At least, he consoled himself, if Louis-Philippe had returned then some fine days of hunting would soon follow. What he could not make sense of was the smartly dressed gendarme patrol escorting the carriage. He recognised the coat of arms emblazoned on the door of the coach, it came from Paris, and he remembered that Lebrun had been from Paris too. Ever the optimist, he wondered if they were his new command? A lot better turned out than the last rabble, he thought. He knew that eventually he must go back and hearing the church bells tolling six o'clock in the distance, but confident that no-one would disturb him after that time, he rode slowly back to the barracks.

At the Château, André, Kate and Marianne had quickly got everyone settled. Kate insisted that the gendarmes who had escorted them should stay in the guest quarters which she hoped would be more comfortable than the barracks. Once everyone had been allocated their rooms, an evening meal was organised. For so many people to eat at the same time (again Kate insisted the troopers should dine with them) the poor housekeeper and stable hand had rushed down into La Garenne to ask for volunteers. Many had volunteered, some out of a desire to help, most to find out what was going on!

Kate then embarked on a tour of the Château with her fiancé, who was staggered to find out just how big it was. From a distance, it did look very impressive but wandering the empty corridors of the upper floors Roland often found it difficult to gauge his whereabouts. Many of the rooms were completely empty of course for the work of restoration would take many years, but Kate made her way around with practiced ease, from cellars to battlements. As they came towards the end of the tour she pointed out a room at the end of a corridor but did not open the door. "That is my bed chamber for now but soon it will be our nursery." In her excitement she ignored her own indelicacy but Roland himself blushed.

"Now, over here" she indicated double doors at the head of the staircase "this was the suite of rooms used by my father and mother, and now they will be ours." She opened the grand doors and led the young Captain inside. This room was colossal, dominated by a huge four-poster bed. He looked around in awe: "There's enough space in here for an orchestra."

"Well I think that might be a bit grand but if you did want to be serenaded by a string quartet then I am sure that can be arranged" and she laughed as she closed the door. Somewhat footsore, they both returned to the great hall to join the others.

General Destrier had changed his clothes and was now resplendent in his full-dress uniform, braid and medals gleaming in the firelight, his heavily engraved sword resting against his leg, every inch the General: "Catherine, I would like to borrow Roland if I may, to accompany me on my inspection of the local barracks. I can assure you that this will be his last official duty, but I believe it may be something he will enjoy – especially since Falaise won't be expecting it. Tomorrow, his life will be his own – and yours of course" he laughed.

The two men walked towards the guest quarters and Destrier invited Captain Belaudie to accompany them on an inspection tour of what would be his new command. They rode down the hill to the square and, watched surreptitiously by the local townsfolk, across to the barracks to find that the gates were locked. Destrier was unamused and was about to pound on the door but was persuaded that they should retire to the local café where they could keep watch. As the bell tolled six o'clock they strolled into the bar and the owner recognised the Captain immediately but was slightly overawed by the two men with him, especially the General in full military magnificence. They seated themselves at a table near the window where they could observe the square. The bar owner quickly came over:

"I am delighted, Captain, to see you again and of course your companions. Some red wine perhaps? And for you gentlemen?" Jacques Belaudie ordered a wine but Destrier grunted: "Did I not just hear the clock strike six? Three glasses of cognac, if you please." Destrier fixed his companions with a steely look: "So where do you think he is? As we passed through the town square earlier, I did see someone open and close the gates so just where has that idiot gone?"

Roland agreed and confirmed that he had spotted Captain Falaise at the gates. The General harrumphed at this but was more interested when Roland admitted that certain 'skills' acquired whilst living in Corsica meant they would not need a key to the locked barracks. The general gave a loud guffaw and told Jacques:

"Oh, you'll have an easy time of it while you are here, he's a skilled burglar, his wife-to-be is an accomplished horse thief and young Amélie is an excellent shot, I'm told. If there's a crime you can just arrest the three of them" and this seemed to amuse him heartily. Before Jacques could respond a movement caught Roland's eye:

"Look, that's Falaise riding towards the stables now. I think it's time for you to meet him, don't you?" The three men walked unhurriedly across the square out of sight of the main gate of the barracks so that when Falaise re-appeared from the stable block they remained unobserved until he put his hand into his pocket to retrieve his keys. Roland grabbed his wrist: "Ah Captain, Inspector General Georges Destrier is very eager to make your acquaintance. He doesn't like to be kept waiting." Roland took the keys from his limp hand and opened the heavy door pushing the forlorn man ahead of him. Destrier and Belaudie followed and they found lanterns and lit them.

Destrier took the chair behind the desk: "Captain Falaise, I believe you already know Captain Roland Lebrun. This gentleman is Captain Jacques Belaudie. He is your successor, in charge of the garrison of La Garenne.

Now, the way I see it your situation is as follows. You have three choices: you may resign from the Gendarmerie Nationale but be warned we will go through in the minutest detail every bill, every receipt, every payment that has been made since you arrived here, was it five years ago? You will then repay every single sou that cannot be accounted for. Your accounts are of course up to date?" Falaise blanched: "or, you may decide not to resign, in which case I will bring you before a Military Court. You will be found guilty of gross incompetence and dereliction of duty. You never did investigate properly the death of Colonel Lucien Lecaron at the hand of your friend, did you?" Falaise spluttered when he heard this, protesting wordlessly as the General continued: "You will be sentenced to a minimum of ten years hard labour." Falaise stood white faced and literally trembling; he was in urgent need of a chair now. The General continued, very calmly: "There is of course a third option: you will immediately be relieved of command here and you will accept a posting overseas, to a destination of my choosing." Roland noticed a wry smile on the face of the General. "You will not return to France during my lifetime. Now what is it to be?"

Falaise did not hesitate. He doubted whether Brochard's ledgers would stand up to any scrutiny and of course all the recent bills were now just smouldering ashes. He would be ruined. He had suspected - but never questioned - Louis-Philippe's likely involvement in the death of Lecaron but now he was being offered what he saw as a lifeline. "I have always quite fancied a life in the colonies, Sir, and I thank you for the opportunity to redeem myself." Destrier smiled a sinisterly: "What a wise choice if I may say so. Your friend Louis-Philippe confessed in front of witnesses to the murder of Colonel Lecaron. I dearly wanted to see him stand trial but sadly he escaped from custody and, err, met with a fatal accident." Falaise's face went ashen grey, and this time he sat down heavily. His friend was dead, but he at least had survived with a new career. Somewhere warm, he hoped!

The following morning, Kate, Marianne and André were in the old Duc's study when Rene knocked on the door to inform them that M. Lafitte-Dupont had arrived. Madame Giscard motioned to Kate that she should now sit at her father's desk whilst Mr. Lafitte-Dupont bustled in, bid good morning to everyone and took his customary place at the small table beside the main desk. Marianne and André sat facing the young girl. Her aunt spoke first:

"Before we commence, there are a number of matters which we must address in your capacity as mayor."

The lawyer dipped his pen into the nearby inkwell and held it poised to write.

"I must report the unfortunate demise of my nephew, M. Louis-Philippe de Garenne."

The little man raised his eyebrows but remained otherwise impassive. "He was involved in a hunting accident in the Pyrenees and was buried where he fell." At this, the Mayor murmured "My deepest condolences" to Kate then continued to write, his head down.

"There are two further fatalities of which you should be aware Monsieur. Sergeant Brochard of the local gendarmerie was fatally injured in a brawl at about the same time as my nephew died and it is believed that M. Raoul Lecaron drowned in the River Dordogne close to the town of Monbezier. General Destrier of the Gendarmerie Nationale has kindly provided written reports of these incidents for your records." She handed a sheaf of papers to the mayor, who nodded silently.

"Captain, or more correctly *former* Captain Roland Lebrun will provide you later with details of the present whereabouts of the remainder of so-called 'lost patrol'. It is my fervent hope that this series of unfortunate incidents which have lately befallen La Garenne and its inhabitants is now at an end." At this, M. Lafitte-Dupont nodded his head gravely and put down his pen, leaving the unopened reports for later.

"Now on to happier news, Mr. Mayor" Marianne continued, smiling: "I am delighted to inform you of the betrothal of my niece, Catherine de Garenne to Monsieur Roland Lebrun. They wish to marry very soon, and I thought perhaps this coming Saturday was as good a day as any? Will you kindly conduct the ceremony for them? I would be most grateful if you could arrange for the whole town to be invited to the celebrations after the wedding, which will be held in the grounds of the Château."

The lawyer beamed broadly and Marianne waited while he busied himself with collating his papers making further copious notes, then continued: “To business now: in our absence, a messenger from King Louis XVIII arrived at the Château and brought these.” She handed two sealed envelopes to Kate, both addressed to her brother Louis-Philippe. “I would like you to open these in the presence of the Mayor, Catherine. I already know the contents of one since, as Trustee I have already received a copy. The other is a mystery to me too.”

The girl looked intently at the two envelopes, both with the elaborate *fleur-de-lys* royal seal with “Louis of France” impressed into the wax. Slowly she opened the first envelope, taking out the stiff vellum letter and scanning it quickly.

“I have been instructed by his most Gracious Majesty King Louis XVIII to advise you that he will confirm you, Louis-Philippe de Garenne, in the title of Duc de Garenne, a noble title and one of the oldest in our Kingdom. He has asked me to advise you that at present, for reasons of state which he is sure you will understand, the title does not confer its former privileges. In time His Most Gracious Majesty is confident that he will be able to restore all the rights and privileges enjoyed by your predecessors.”

Signed

For his Gracious Majesty King Louis XVIII

Armand du Plessis, Duc du Richelieu

She carefully folded the letter and replaced it in the envelope which she then handed to André. “Please place this with my brother’s effects. I think it is time to put his affairs in order” she said rather formally.

She broke the seal on the second letter, again scanning its contents very quickly:

"I have been instructed by his Most Gracious Majesty, King Louis XVIII that he has received and given the most careful consideration to your request that the terms of the ancient Eleanor Bequest be set aside, and all the assets currently held by the Bequest should be transferred to you, Duc Louis-Philippe de Garenne.

"His Most Gracious Majesty in Council has studied the various judgements, decisions and variations made by his august predecessors and considers some of these to be incorrect. However, he is forced to agree with the decision of his most illustrious predecessor, King Louis XIV who stated:

"The Eleanor Bequest was drawn up many centuries ago and, in my view adequately expresses the intention of its creator, the Lady Eleanor de Garenne with regard to the future disposition of the fortune."

This Bequest is the second oldest institution in France, second of course only to the Monarchy itself. To question the legitimacy of the Bequest is tantamount to questioning the legitimacy of this glorious monarchy and as such cannot be countenanced.

Accordingly, your request is denied."

Signed

For his Gracious Majesty King Louis XVIII

Armand du Plessis, Duc du Richelieu

Expressionless, Kate passed the single page to the Notary, who peered at it anxiously through his pince-nez, and read it in silence. He placed it carefully into one of the many thick files balanced on his desk and looked once more at his notes, made some hasty amendments before speaking:

"Firstly, may I welcome you all back to La Garenne from your recent travels. May I take this opportunity to offer my congratulations on your betrothal Mlle. Catherine. I will of course be honoured to officiate at your marriage." He hesitated and glanced down at his notes before taking a deep breath: "Err, on a point of err protocol, you Mlle. will be entitled to apply for the title of Duchesse de Garenne …" he looked up and caught Catherine's expression of horror before continuing nervously: "Of course Mlle. I am not suggesting that you make such an application, merely pointing out that the option is, err, available, to you." His hands were now shaking as he once more consulted his notes and spoke: "I was aware that the late Louis-Philippe de Garenne had raised a challenge to the terms of the Eleanor Bequest and, as expected, it has failed. It is therefore my duty as Notary to the Eleanor Bequest to confirm that, subject to the usual caveat, I have satisfied myself that Mlle. Catherine de Garenne is the true Steward of the Bequest for as long as she lives."

The fussy little lawyer got up slowly from his chair and made an awkward bow despite the size of his paunch which meant that his bow was more a bending of the neck. Kate lifted her hand demanding: "A moment, please. What is the *usual caveat*?"

Lafitte-Dupont coughed discreetly, knowing he must answer but reluctant to do so. Eventually he indicated a small bound parchment which he handed to her. "I think you will find all the information there, Mlle. de Garenne; it has been a duty carried out by all the Stewards – oh and you have to return your father's ring, too." Lafitte-Dupont fumbled in his waistcoat pocket and handed to Kate the ring her father had always worn on the smallest finger of his right hand. Puzzled, she took the ring wondering how the lawyer had obtained it. She had thought Louis-Philippe would have taken possession of it. To whom must she return it? She turned it over lovingly in her hand looking at the insignia. The ring bore the crest of the Garenne family and the initials “PdG.” Marianne rose to place her arms comfortingly around her niece, whispering: “Come, it is now time, come with me.” Intrigued but not alarmed by their mysterious behaviour, Kate followed her aunt.

CHAPTER 73

Kate was led out of the main doors of the Château ceremoniously and down into the courtyard, with André and Lafitte-Dupont following, in silence. They went around to the rear of the building where there was a large outcrop of rock, part of the plateau of rock on which the Château had been constructed. Here was the imposing tomb constructed where her father had been interred, alongside the Mausoleum of her mother. Here too lay Lucien Lecaron, his tomb a simpler affair, but well-tended.

They passed all the other elaborate tombs constructed over the graves of her ancestors until they were standing before a tomb hewn hundreds of years ago from the living rock. She had been told in childhood that here lay the remains of Eleanor de Garenne. She saw that Athina had arrived and alongside her waited Roland, Destrier and Amélie who stood watching as the little mayor knocked on the heavy wooden door to this ancient tomb twice and handed Kate a lantern, motioning her inside. He gave no explanation and she caught sight of Roland's face, slightly ashen and concerned. She herself was more than a little afraid. 'He knocked' she thought, 'Why?'

Tentatively she edged forward, breathing dust and dead air. She held the lantern in front of her, clutching in her other hand the forgotten parchment given to her by the mayor and her father's ring. After a few moments she came to another door which swung open silently and as if in a daze, Kate walked forward. As soon as she passed through the old iron door it creaked shut on its ancient hinges.

Kate somehow expected this part of the tomb, where the sarcophagus must lie, to be cold, damp and unpleasant but she was surprised to find that it felt quite warm and more like a bedchamber than a tomb. She sensed rather than saw that the room was vast and very high and she tried to accustom herself to this gloomy, ill-lit space, waiting for whatever must come. Her hand on the lantern shook making the weak light waver around the walls of the room. Suddenly, iron flambeaux on the walls of the chamber spouted flames, casting shadows all around and flickering brightly. By their light she now saw, in the centre of the chamber a hand-hewn block of stone some 6 feet long by 4 feet wide, on which lay an ornately carved sarcophagus with wreathes of lilies and woodland flowers chiselled into its sides. On its lid was carved an inscription written in very ancient French around which ivy lay entwined. The lid also bore a marble tablet. Kate put down her lantern since the torches now filled the chamber with a bright, comforting light and she was able to see quite clearly – clearly enough to read at last the parchment she had been clutching and which, in the excitement, she had quite forgotten.

As she began to undo the tapes which held the parchment sheets together she quite clearly heard a voice close to her: "Don't be afraid, please place the ring on the marble tablet before you and then read the document." Too terrified to disobey, or even look round, Kate gently placed the ring on the top of the sarcophagus and with numb fingers she struggled to open the parchment sheets, afraid lest she drop them and be forced to search for them or have to look behind her. She heard the voice once more:

"Catherine, please do not fear me. Calm yourself and take your time. I have all the time in your world." Kate knew then who was speaking; there was something reassuring about the voice and telling herself to be brave, she unrolled the parchment and began to read aloud, in a firm if slightly breathless voice:

"I am the Lady Catherine Marie Eleanor Mortaigne de Garenne.

I am the daughter of the late Steward of the Eleanor Bequest, Duc Philippe de Garenne and I proclaim that I am his nominated successor. I pledge that I shall fulfil my duties as a Steward of the said Bequest from this moment until the time of my death and at the appropriate time, I shall nominate a worthy successor."

Kate took another deep breath as she refolded the parchment, careful not to let any pieces of the flaky paper escape her hands. She was unsure what she should do next but was certain the disembodied voice she had been hearing would tell her.

"That was very nicely said, my dear. I hear you have already achieved great things, so your father chose well. Now, your ring is ready and waiting for you. Please put it on." The girl looked around her uncertain of what the voice meant but when she looked at the marble tablet where her father's ring had lain, she saw in its place a much smaller, more delicate circlet of living gold from which sparks of fire still leapt. As the fiery halo subsided she read on the cartouche of the delicate ring the initials "CdeG." Cautiously she put out a hand towards it. It was already cool to the touch and she placed it upon the ring finger of her right hand, feeling overawed.

"And now, one more thing, if you please Catherine. If you could kindly turn just a little this way so that I can see you more clearly?" Kate turned, very slowly, towards the voice fearful suddenly of what she might see – there was no-one visible, but she sensed a warmth as she heard: "Yes Guillaume was correct. You do look like me, but it was such a very very long time ago…I am told that you are to be married? Please tell me about this young man." The voice was becoming gradually weaker with each word. She felt she had to keep this presence here, with her, and she began to speak quickly: "His name is Roland Lebrun and he too is a Paladin. He is very brave and" the voice interrupted her:

Of course he is brave, Catherine. The Lebruns have always been brave. My Guillaume was a Lebrun and three Lebrun brothers fought alongside him, such brave men, but so long…ago" and then the voice gained a little strength once more: "I have a small wedding gift for you both. Please accept it. I wish you both all the happiness you may know in your world."

Kate looked away for a moment to allow her eyes, which were fogging with tears, to clear and caught sight once more of the place where the ring had lain. There now lay a small leather pouch which she picked up. "We thank you" she said.

"No, thank you for coming my dear. Many would have been afraid – as you may appreciate I get few…visitors although I always enjoyed my conversations with your dear father and now at last my mother has forgiven me and I her, so she too will visit me. I regret, Catherine that for me this has been...a…very…long day but I would always welcome a visit my……dear." As the last words were spoken, the torches around the walls of the chamber began to dim very slightly, and then more noticeably.

She knew that her audience was finally over so by the light of her lantern Kate returned to the large iron door to the outer chamber. This opened for her and as she left the vast chamber she heard a sigh of pleasure, then the door closed behind her. She stayed in the outer chamber to allow her eyes to adjust once more and then walked through the second door into the sunshine of the 'real' world. The door shut behind her with a hollow thud but her eyes were still adjusting to the glare when, to her amazement, she saw her aunt, the person who had raised her from a baby, curtsey deeply. André and the Mayor were bowing low and all three intoned "My Lady Catherine." Even Athina and Destrier curtsied and bowed. Worse was to follow: her closest friend Amélie tried to follow her mother's example! Meanwhile Roland, unsure of what was happening, was torn between trying to bow like the others and rush forward to hold his love, who was visibly shaken.

"Oh, for pity's sake everyone, stop this now" cried Kate "I am not the Lady Catherine; I am Kate. I always was, and I always will be."

Destrier turned to Athina: "It's almost like having her back in this world" he whispered, "that same look, the smile even the mannerisms…"

"Yes, oh yes Pellerin, and the same temper, the same stubbornness… ah" sighed Athina, smiling fondly at the General.

Later when the betrothed couple were alone Kate asked Roland whether he had thought about getting her a wedding ring. At this he began to blush and stammer, but she just laughed then:

"Well, luckily for you a very old lady indeed has been your saviour" and she opened the leather pouch to reveal not one but two finely wrought rings; both bore the inscription "**CdG:RLB**" on the outside. On the inner rim of the smaller, more delicate ring there was another tiny inscription. Kate held the ring close to her eye to read it. Two sets of initials were interwoven there: **EdG:GLB**. Her ancestor had given them not only a ring for Roland to wear but had surrendered to them also her own ring given to her by Guillaume all those centuries ago.

♥♥♥♥♥♥♥

Meanwhile, in the town of La Garenne itself the locals were interested to see that not only had Hugo Hound returned but he had brought with him an even bigger, shaggy but rather vicious looking friend! The two dogs walked through the centre of the town and climbed the cobbled street which led to the Château above, trotting alongside a brewers' dray cart driven by a large figure wrapped in a cloak. The cart was laden heavily with barrels labelled "Giant Bear Special Celebration Ale".